"I'm so sorry, Captain," Phlox was saying in tones that dripped with grief. "He's gone."

A pause. Then Phlox spoke again: "Computer, record that death occurred at nineteen-hundred and thirty-three hours, fourteen February, 2155."

Feeling unaccountably calmed by the knowledge that the deed had finally been done, Trip opened his eyes. He looked up again at his reflection, which looked bizarre and funhouse-distorted in the curved, too-close metal ceiling of the chamber. He could see that the Denobulan physician had certainly managed to make him look gruesome, in spite of the haste with which he'd had to work. A large, livid burn snaked down his neck, and a profusion of other wounds and smudges covered both his flesh and his torn uniform.

So this is what it's like to be dead, he thought, really trying on the idea for the first time. *Funny. Doesn't hurt quite as much as I thought it would.*

— STAR TREK —
ENTERPRISE®

THE GOOD
THAT MEN DO

MICHAEL A. MARTIN
& ANDY MANGELS

Based on *Star Trek*®
created by Gene Roddenberry
and
Star Trek: Enterprise
created by Rick Berman & Brannon Braga

POCKET BOOKS
New York   London   Toronto   Sydney

An *Original* Publication of POCKET BOOKS

 POCKET BOOKS, a division of Simon & Schuster Inc.
1230 Avenue of the Americas, New York, NY 10020

ISBN-13: 978-0-7434-4001-1
ISBN-10: 0-7434-4001-3

This Pocket Books paperback edition March 2007

10 9 8 7 6 5 4 3 2 1

Cover art by Dennis Godfrey

Manufactured in the United States of America

For information regarding special discounts for bulk purchases, please contact Simon & Schuster Special Sales at 1-800-456-6798 or business@simonandschuster.com.

For Don Hood, who has shared my life
for almost twelve years,
and who often lives up to the phrase
"the good that men do."

—A.M.

For my wife, Jenny Martin, for understanding
and patience above and beyond the call;
for James Martin and William Martin,
whose treks are just beginning;
and for Army First Lieutenant Ehren Watada,
a man of wisdom, conviction, and courage who
has brilliantly exemplified Sun Tzu's dictum,
"He will win who knows when to fight
and when not to fight."

—M.A.M.

HISTORIAN'S NOTE

The main events in this book take place early in 2155, just after the crew of the *Enterprise* stops the xenophobic group Terra Prime from destroying Starfleet Command ("Demons" and "Terra Prime").

"People sleep peaceably in their beds at night only because rough men stand ready to do violence on their behalf."

—George Orwell (1903–1950)

"He that would live in peace and at ease must not speak all he knows or all he sees."

—Benjamin Franklin (1706–1790)

"All war is deception."

—Sun Tzu (5th century B.C.)

"The future is up for grabs. It belongs to any and all who will take the risk."

—Robert Anton Wilson (1932–)

"The evil that men do lives after them;
The good is oft interrèd with their bones."

—William Shakespeare (1564–1616)

PROLOGUE

**The early twenty-fifth century
Terrebonne Parish, Louisiana**

ALTHOUGH LIGHT-YEARS SEPARATED HIM from his home-world, the cool rain falling through the moss-covered trees reminded Nog of Ferenginar. The smell was different here, of course; the Louisiana swamps were redolent with decay and rot, and the lukewarm rain—falling at not quite a *glebbening* level yet, but close—added a dampness that made the humid air almost palpably pungent.

Nog stepped wide to avoid a greasy-looking puddle, and almost immediately regretted it as a sharp twinge went up his hyperextended left leg. Making sure the pack he carried slung over his shoulder was secure, he crouched down onto his right knee, his fingers deftly massaging the pained left leg.

It seemed strange to him that the newer leg, regrown from his own tissues years ago to replace the biosynthetic limb he'd needed because of an injury suffered during the Dominion War, should always be the one that gave him trouble. Of course, a few of his other joints suffered aches and pains as well—it was all just part of the process of getting older—but his new left leg should have felt better, not worse, than either his natural limbs or the now-discarded biosynthetic one. His doctors had examined him several times in recent years, but they could never find anything inherently wrong with the new leg, and always ended up telling him that he probably just favored it differently than the bionic part he'd spent so many years getting used to, thus creating unfamiliar stressor points on his left side.

Nog stood, peering up the path before him and thinking about his friend. *Why did he choose to make his home so far off the beaten track?* He imagined young Jennifer probably didn't relish playing in the yard—*if he even has a yard*—since hew-mons generally seemed to have an aversion to muck and dampness.

Another dozen meters, and as he rounded a bend in the pathway, he saw the two-story house directly ahead. Soft light was visible through several round-topped windows, and a wisp of smoke curled out of a chimney on the home's southernmost wall, drifting lazily up through the damp twilight air. The fact that a fire was burning and lights were on gave Nog hope; he wanted to surprise his old friend, and hadn't contacted him to let him know he was coming.

The murky pathway ended at the edge of a small expanse of open, well-tended lawn, and Nog stepped onto a cobblestone walkway that meandered through the green on its way toward the home's front door. He wondered idly if Jake had helped create the walkway.

Nog stood in front of the door, his hand raised and poised to knock. He noticed that Jake didn't appear to have any other kind of signaling device mounted on or near the door, and wondered when his old friend had become such a Luddite. No com panel, no security device . . . it was so different from what Nog was used to.

He rapped his knuckles loudly against the door four times, then took a step back. He heard something—or someone—stirring inside, then heard indistinct muttering. The sound made his heart leap; although he couldn't make out what was being said, it was the speaker that mattered, not the speech.

The door cracked open several centimeters, and light spilled out from inside, momentarily silhouetting the tall, dark-skinned man who stood there peering out.

"Greetings, old man," Nog said, remembering what Benjamin Sisko used to call Dax. It seemed somehow appropriate now, here, as he saw his friend's eyes widen in delighted surprise.

"Nog!" Jake Sisko's voice cracked slightly as he shouted his friend's name, and then he opened the door wide, holding his arms out.

Nog stepped forward, opening his own arms and clasping them around Jake's torso. It was only after he had hugged his friend for several seconds that he remembered that he was soaking wet. He pulled back, looking up at Jake.

"I wasn't sure you'd want to see me," Nog said.

Jake's expression changed instantly—was it bemusement registering there?—and he good-naturedly whacked the Ferengi on his shoulder with the palm of his hand. "Right. Whatever. Bygones, Nog."

Turning, he gestured inside. "Let's get you out of the rain and into my warm, dry den. Then you can tell me what brought you out to my hideaway in the middle of hurricane season!"

Nog stepped inside, purposely keeping the grin on his face. He wondered if the problem he was bringing Jake would constitute a stronger storm than the weather outside.

Jake Sisko pulled the cork from the top of the bottle with as much élan as he could muster, given the way his fingers were cramping up these days. He poured two glasses of the dark liquid and set the bottle down as Nog reached for one of the deep, round wineglasses.

"Twenty-three seventy-six? That was an . . . interesting year," Jake said, looking at the date on the bottle.

Nog had chosen an Italian wine, a rich pinot noir that smelled enticingly of fruit and oaken casks.

"Not as interesting as twenty-three seventy-seven," Nog said, grinning. "But I know how much you hew-mons like the older vintage beverages." He hoisted his glass toward Jake.

Jake raised his glass as well, regarding the dark liquid inside thoughtfully and giving it a gentle swirl. "You've certainly come a long way since the old root beer days back on the station."

Nog snickered. "We live and we learn, Jake." He paused to swirl the contents of his own glass. "To an old friendship."

Jake clinked his glass against Nog's. "Not *so* old," he said, smiling. He took a sip, eyeing the Ferengi over the rim of his glass. His friend still looked barely a week older than his teens.

"Well, not so old for *you*," Jake finally added, smiling. "I swear, you Ferengi don't ever seem to age."

Nog grinned back, his sharp, pointed teeth gleaming. "Oh, I've had a few nips and tucks over the years, Jake," he said, running his right hand over his right lobe. "Don't want my lobes to get too droopy. Hard to get an-other wife if I look like a melting candle."

"Haven't you had *enough* wives?" Jake asked. "I think I've lost of track of how many times you've been married. Three? Four?" He caught himself before mentioning that he hadn't been invited to several of the weddings.

Nog pondered for a moment, then grinned sheep-ishly. "I guess it depends on whether you count Diressa as a separate wife both times I married her." He gestured toward the rest of the spacious house. "Speaking of which, where's Korena?"

"She's on Bajor," Jake said. "The weather's better there, and I wanted some time by myself to write. I've got half a dozen novels started, but nothing seems to be grabbing me and shaking itself out of my brain." It was a bad metaphor, and one Jake never would have used with anyone who didn't know better; a problem writers faced since the days of ink and papyrus was that non-writers thought the creative process came to them like a visiting muse, depositing a manuscript on their desk as simply as a replicated cup of *raktajino*.

"I read your latest about six months ago," Nog said, settling back onto a replicated nineteenth-century chair. Its tall back, padded with a rich red velvet, towered over the diminutive Ferengi's head, making him look like a child. "It was quite entertaining. I wasn't able to figure out who the killer was before you revealed it . . . or *them*, actually."

"Well, that's part of the fun of writing a mystery set in the era before scanning technology," Jake replied. "The detectives have to work a bit harder to figure out their cases." He took another sip of his wine. "Rena was also very happy with that particular book."

"She was surprised by the ending, too?" Nog asked.

"No. She's happy that it got optioned. They're supposed to be making a holoprogram out of it. On Mars."

"Ah-ha, *profit!*" Nog raised his glass in a mock toast. "I always knew that girl had a bit of Ferengi in her."

Jake grimaced slightly, mocking his friend right back. "She couldn't care less about the profit. She just likes seeing my credits and telling people about her famous-but-reclusive husband. Besides which, holo-authors are *so* much more respectable and important than book authors these days. Didn't you know that?"

Nog rolled his eyes. "Not that old song again. I think you've had more than your share of fame."

"More than I ever wanted," Jake said, nodding.

There was a flash of movement to the side, and Nog

flinched as a fat ball of gray and brown fur jumped up on the arm of the chair, and then collapsed heavily onto his lap.

"Ah, cue the cat. Odo has decided to join us," Jake said.

Nog's eyes widened sharply. "Odo? You mean—"

Jake almost choked on the sip of wine he had taken. He swallowed loudly and wiped his hand over his mouth. "Not Odo-Odo. *Cat*-Odo." He laughed. "What, did you think I've been keeping the station's old security chief around here as a pet all these years?"

Nog shrugged, staring peculiarly at the cat, which padded around on his lap, kneading its claws in and out against the thankfully tough fabric of his uniform pants. "I don't know. Stranger things *have* happened to us."

Jake raised an eyebrow. "Not *that* strange." He leaned across the table, making sure his elbows didn't topple either the wine bottle or the glasses, and scooped the chubby cat off Nog's lap. "Here, I'll take the constable off your hands."

Nog took a sip from his glass, and then fidgeted for a moment. "Actually, I don't want to make it sound like I had to have a *reason* to visit you, but something just came up and I thought of you."

"So, what is it?" Jake leaned forward slightly. Odo jumped off his lap and scampered away, undoubtedly heading toward his food dish.

Nog pulled a small isolinear chip out of a pocket in his tunic. The firelight glinted off it, making it appear as though it had a firefly trapped within its slender, emerald-colored confines.

"I discovered this when I was researching twenty-second-century warp mechanics," Nog said. "I was digging around in some of the newly declassified files."

Jake raised an eyebrow. "Declassified files? From where? By who? And when?"

Jake peered at the chip, as if trying to divine its secrets just by studying its translucent surface. "The *when* is part of what makes this complicated. It concerns events we've been *told* happened in 2161. But the *real* events actually occurred years earlier, in 2155. And I can't tell whether the *where* and *who* are related solely to Section 31, or whether this apparently deliberate cover-up was something sanctioned by those in charge during the earliest days of the Federation."

"All the answers aren't in the declassified information?" Jake was intrigued, especially with the mention of Section 31. It hadn't been so long ago that the secretive organization—a shadowy spy bureau as old as Starfleet—had finally been exposed and, Jake hoped, rooted out once and for all.

"I *hope* they are," Nog said, interrupting Jake's train of thought. "But as soon as I started to get into it, I thought 'I know *one* hew-mon who would not only find this fascinating, but also might be able to write a bestselling book about it.' So, here I am."

Jake chuckled. "I see. Well, that certainly *sounds* intriguing. But do you really think this is important enough that people will care, two hundred years after all the facts and fictions have become part of dusty history?"

Nog looked surprised again, and then his features took on a conspiratorial, almost sinister, cast. "Jake, from what I've seen, this story involves hew-mons, Andorians, Vulcans, Denobulans, and Romulans. It has kidnapping, assassination, slavery, death, resurrection, and cover-ups. And it may just change *everything* we know—or everything that we've been told—about the founding of the Federation itself."

Jake found himself grinning widely. It had been a long time since he and Nog had played detectives in the shadowy corridors of Deep Space 9, trying to solve the mystery behind some strange occurrence or other that they were naively certain would stump even the formidable deductive abilities of Constable Odo. And now, he felt the same surge of boyhood adrenaline rush into his system.

He held out his hand for the chip.

"So, let's get to it."

ONE

Day Five, Month of Tasmeen
Unroth III, Romulan space

DOCTOR EHREHIN I'RAMNAU TR'AVRAK stood before the research complex's vast panoramic window, listening to the control center's background wash of electronic chirps, beeps, and drones as he looked out over the remote firing site where the prototype would shortly thrum to life. For the past several days, every console in the cramped control center had shown reassuring shades of orange, with hardly a hint of the green hues that Romulans tended to associate with blood and danger. The only green the elderly scientist had seen since his arrival here more than ten of this world's lengthy rotations ago was that of the carpet of forest that spread from the base of the gently rolling hillside beyond and below the control facility's perimeter walls, all the way to Unroth III's flat, eerily close horizon.

Unlike most of his research staff, Doctor Ehrehin was unwilling to keep his gaze perpetually averted from the sea of greenery that lay beyond the control room windows. But he also refused to allow the forest's alarming hues to unnerve him, concentrating instead on the soothing, ruddy light of the planet's primary star, which hugged the forest canopy as it made its preternaturally slow descent toward evening. Despite the low angle of the diffraction-bloated sun, several long *dierha* remained before the wilderness outside would become fully enshrouded in darkness.

"It is time, Doctor," said Cunaehr, Ehrehin's most valued research assistant. "Are you ready to begin the test?"

His gaze still lingering on the forest that sprawled beyond the window, Ehrehin offered Cunaehr a dry, humorless chuckle. *A better question would be, Is the* prototype *finally ready to begin the test?* he thought, leaving the query unspoken lest he draw the unfavorable attention of the malevolent cosmic force that sometimes caused field tests to go awry in new and unexpected ways.

"I have my instructions, Cunaehr," Ehrehin replied, keeping his reedy voice pitched only barely above the room's background noises. "The admiralty is watching from orbit, and they have *ordered* me to be ready by now. And so we are. Please prepare to initiate the test on my signal."

"Immediately, Doctor," Cunaehr said. Ehrehin knew without turning that his assistant was hastening back to his own console.

Ehrehin considered the bird-of-prey that now circled this remote planet, and wondered whether or not the admiralty truly expected today's test to succeed. Then he banished the thought, refusing to allow the military's obvious reticence about posting any of their people on the surface to threaten his composure. In fact, the notion that a prototype field test could make the admiralty look unnecessarily fearful had quite the opposite effect on him, buoying his spirits and increasing his confidence.

Steadying himself against the neutronium-reinforced concrete wall into which the window was set, Ehrehin turned to face his associates, all of whom were busy either running or monitoring several semicircular rows of consoles. Despite his recurrent misgivings about the military-enforced pace of his team's research, he realized that he was waging a losing battle against the triumphant grin that was already beginning to spread across his lined, weathered face.

Standing beside his console, Cunaehr ran his fingers through his perpetually tousled, jet-black hair in yet another vain attempt to tame it. He cleared his throat loudly, quickly capturing the attention of the science outpost's thirteen other research personnel. All of the project's staffers now stood alert at their stations, the staccato rhythm of their professional conversations momentarily halted, their usually busy hands now stilled above their consoles, their eyes turned toward Doctor Ehrehin in silent anticipation of his words.

"Thank you, my friends, for all the labor and sacrifice you have given this effort so far in order to realize our collective dream," Ehrehin said, raising his thin voice slightly. "The time has arrived for us to make history. Now we shall light the torch that soon will bring near the farthest reaches of the heavens. At last we will achieve *avaihh lli vastam*.

"The warp-seven stardrive." *And there can be no margin for error this time*, he added silently, wondering yet again whether the Romulan Star Empire's military was right to worry that Coridan Prime—or perhaps even one of the other recently Terran-aligned worlds—had already equaled or even surpassed the painstaking work of Ehrehin's team.

Cunaehr began slowly applauding, and the rest of the staff immediately joined in until the hand claps escalated into a torrent. Ehrehin's smile broadened as he held up a single wizened hand to call for silence.

"Shall we?" he said once the room had quieted.

At Cunaehr's deliberate gesture, the team members resumed their vigilant poses behind their respective consoles, leaving Ehrehin with little to do other than to watch and wait as orders were exchanged and relayed, and a countdown began, reinforced by an emotionless synthetic voice generated by one of the computers. No one appeared to be breathing for the duration. Ehrehin suppressed a tremor in his left hand as the machine crisply pronounced the numerals that represented the last five *ewa* in the countdown sequence.

"*Rhi*.

"*Mne*.

"*Sei*.

"*Kre*.

"*Hwi*."

A low rumble came a moment after the computer reached "*Lliu*." Ehrehin rather likened it to thunder, except that he felt it deep in his bones rather than hearing it directly, as he did the crisp, businesslike voices that were ringing out across the small control center.

"Power output rising along predicted curves," Cunaehr said. "Holding steady."

The man behind Cunaehr nodded, adding, "Power output consistent with a velocity of warp three."

"Confirmed," chimed a woman's voice from a nearby console. Others made noises of agreement. Ehrehin heard several jubilant shouts as the first dilated moments passed and everyone in the room appeared to resume their regular breathing patterns. The monitors continued showing orange and amber as the subaural rumbling continued and intensified.

Cunaehr smiled elatedly in Ehrehin's direction. "Warp three already from a standing start."

But Ehrehin felt that a victory celebration might be a bit premature. "Gradually reduce the containment field diameter, Cunaehr, and reinforce it. Increase the power yield incrementally."

"Warp four," Cunaehr said after relaying Ehrehin's orders, his eyes riveted to his monitor. "Five. Six."

"Continue until we reach maximum yield," Ehrehin said, grinning in spite of his caution. It was working. Warp seven really was within reach.

"Fluctuation," said the technician seated immediately

behind Cunaehr. The sharp note of alarm in the young woman's voice was unmistakable.

"Compensate," Ehrehin said automatically.

"Warp six point five," Cunaehr said.

"Containment instability," another tech reported.

"Reinforce!" Cunaehr barked before Ehrehin could interject.

The room was suddenly awash in green as the hue of the banks of monitors and gauges changed in unison, accompanied by numerous horrified gasps and pointed exclamations from across the length and breadth of the room. Ehrehin's attention was drawn back to the window, through which he watched the preternatural orange light that was washing across the horizon. The distant rumbling gradually became audible, not quite drowned out by the rising clamor of alarm klaxons. But Ehrehin found *this* orange light anything but reassuring.

THOOM.

Chaos. A hard jolt made the floor jump. A bank of unanchored instruments leaned forward and tipped over with a resounding crash. Someone cried out in pain. A ceiling beam collapsed directly on top of a man and a woman, spraying emerald blood across the floor and showering the rear wall as several others struggled toward the now partially blocked exit. The overhead lighting flickered and failed. A frantic voice boomed over one of the room's com speakers, saying something about beaming to the safety of an orbiting bird-of-prey before it was too late.

Cunaehr had somehow moved to Ehrehin's immediate right, and was shouting into his ear. "Doctor! We have to evacuate immediately!"

No wonder the military didn't want to post any of their people down here, Ehrehin thought bitterly as he watched a trio of bleeding, injured technicians vanish in a blaze of amber light as the bird-of-prey's transporter seized them.

An earsplitting crack barely preceded the fall of another beam. This one narrowly missed Ehrehin, brushing just past his right arm as it neatly stove in Cunaehr's skull. Outside the window, Ehrehin could see the fires of Erebus consuming the forest as they swept hungrily from the test apparatus toward the control complex. The control room shook, twisted, and began to tear itself apart. The air stank of coppery blood and ozone.

Ehrehin noticed that the room was already nearly empty, and hoped that whoever hadn't died here already would make it to safety. Then his skin began to tingle; he knew that he was either being transported up to the orbiting bird-of-prey, or was about to discover what it felt like to be vaporized, along with the wreckage of the control complex.

Considering the way the admiralty sometimes dealt with failure, he wasn't at all certain which fate was the preferable one.

TWO

Friday, January 24, 2155
The Presidio, San Francisco

CAPTAIN JONATHAN ARCHER smiled broadly as he looked over his shoulder and up into the rapt faces of four of his most valued officers. Ensigns Hoshi Sato and Travis Mayweather, Lieutenant Malcolm Reed, and Doctor Phlox, *Enterprise*'s chief medical officer, stood on the steps just behind and above Archer on the broad spiral staircase that overlooked the wide meeting room. Here representatives of Earth, Vulcan, Tellar, Andoria, and Coridan were beginning to take their seats around a series of large, curving tables arranged in a broad semicircle. They were in turn surrounded by assorted VIPs from Starfleet, Earth's various governmental ministries, and numerous allied and neutral worlds, as well as a fair number of headset-wearing media people.

Among the ranks of the journalists, Archer spied a slender, youthful woman with straight brown hair whom he recognized immediately as Gannet Brooks, Ensign Mayweather's former girlfriend. A quick backward glance confirmed that the young helmsman had also picked her out of the crowd. Mayweather didn't appear exactly thrilled by the possibility of bumping into her again so soon after the revelation that her journalistic credentials were merely a cover for her Starfleet Intelligence work during the recent Terra Prime crisis. Archer was disappointed, though not surprised, to note that Starfleet Intelligence had apparently seen fit to place one of its agents in the midst of today's proceedings. Fortunately, Hoshi's most recent translator modifications had made the diplomats' networked communications devices far more eavesdropping-proof than ever; Ms. Brooks would find that her work was cut out for her today.

Archer turned his attention back to the ring of observers, which suffused the air with a low gabble of anticipatory murmurs. Thanks to the broad circular skylight built into the chamber's high, vaulted ceiling, the room was bathed in an early afternoon light that saturated the sections of the room not illuminated by ceiling-mounted fixtures.

An odd feeling of déjà vu seized Archer at the scene now unfolding below him and his crew. He turned to Phlox and spoke quietly. "Didn't we just do this two days ago?"

Phlox smiled sagely and pitched his voice as low as Archer's. "I'm sure I don't need to remind you, Captain, that the Terra Prime attacks have strained relations between many of the founding members of the Coalition of Planets."

Archer returned the doctor's good-humored smile with a rueful grin of his own. "You're right, Phlox. Some things aren't forgotten very easily." *Or forgiven,* he added silently. Terra Prime, whose avowed purpose was to evict every alien from Earth and move into the galaxy pursuing a doctrine of humanocentric force rather than interspecies cooperation, certainly deserved to be forgotten, and belonged in the dustbin of history. But Archer knew in his heart that the misbegotten terror group *had* to be remembered, in order to avoid a repetition of its shortsightedness and violence.

It was forgiveness that Earth and her allies had to seek, rather than forgetfulness. Earth needed remembrance, not amnesia.

Archer had seen Terra Prime's agenda up close, had lost a member of his crew to its fanatical "Earth first for Earth's people" agenda, and had nearly asphyxiated on Mars while apprehending the radical movement's founder, John Frederick Paxton. Staring such naked hatred and xenophobia directly in the face had been one of the most harrowing experiences of Archer's Starfleet career. And he knew full well that his friend Phlox had been on the receiving end of xenophobia himself, during the crew's shore leave on Earth immediately after the resolution of the Xindi crisis that had gripped the entire planet for almost a year.

"I imagine that each of the Coalition envoys feels an urgent need to reinforce everything they already agree on as they start negotiating some of the Coalition Compact's stickier points," Phlox continued. "It's quite a testament to the goodwill of all the parties involved. Not to take anything away from the persuasive power of the speech you gave in front of the delegates the last time we stood in this room, of course."

"I never claimed that public speaking was my strong suit," Archer said. "I'm sure you've noticed that the Terra Prime incident frightened the Rigelian government into withdrawing from the Coalition, regardless of everything I said to try to stop it. And the Rigelians weren't the only ones, Phlox."

Phlox shrugged. "There would have been still more withdrawals had you not spoken, Captain. And the ones that *did* opt to leave will be back one day, you mark my words."

"Maybe. Maybe not. I just hope I didn't make things worse by shooting my mouth off."

Phlox offered a sniffing chuckle that was clearly meant to dismiss Archer's doubts as absurd. "Far from it, Captain. From what I've observed, your words did indeed inspire the remaining delegates to work even harder to prevent this new Coalition from self-destructing before it can truly begin. In fact, you might be the main reason why these people are gathered here today instead of warping back homeward to explain their withdrawals to their respective governments."

Archer was rapidly growing uncomfortable with the drift of this conversation, and his forehead and cheeks had begun to feel entirely too warm. He waved his hand as though expecting Phlox's overly effusive praise to scatter like smoke. "Your job is safe, Phlox. You really don't have to keep sucking up to me like this."

But the Denobulan physician was undeterred. "You'll recall that it was Ambassador Soval who began the rather resounding round of applause that followed your remarks. I'm certain you've noticed by now that he isn't very easily impressed."

Archer nodded, his gaze lighting briefly on silver-haired Admiral Sam Gardner, who was standing in the forefront of the crowd of onlookers beside the stern-faced Admiral Gregory Black and the ramrod-straight, crew-cut MACO commander, General George Casey. Archer recalled that nearly four years earlier, Soval hadn't been bashful about recommending that Admiral Forrest pass him over for the assignment of commanding *Enterprise* in favor of Gardner, who then had yet to exchange his captain's bars for an admiral's desk. Until only about half a year ago, Soval had rarely missed an opportunity to remind Archer that he continually looked askance at both his captaincy and his judgment.

"I've got to admit," Archer said, "Soval can be tough, even as Vulcans go."

Phlox's smile briefly widened to preternatural size before returning to typical human proportions. "Precisely, Captain."

"So the delegates need to emphasize and reinforce all their points of agreement in the wake of the Terra Prime attack," Archer said. "That makes sense. What *doesn't* make sense to me is doing it in front of a live audience. They must have already had a closed-door meeting to nail down the substance of whatever they're planning to announce today."

"No doubt, Captain," Phlox said. "But the general public suffered a great deal of psychological trauma at the hands of Terra Prime. And although the terrorists' actual casualty count was thankfully low, the incident partially reopened some of the profound wounds inflicted by the Xindi nearly two years ago."

"People don't easily forget seven million deaths," Archer said, his mood darkening with the onslaught of bitter memories. Archer suspected that forgiveness for what the Xindi did would probably come only after there was no one left alive on Earth capable of remembering firsthand the horror of March 22, 2153. *That's a wound for future generations to heal,* he thought, pining momentarily for a utopian future he knew he'd never glimpse himself. *All the more reason why the Coalition of Planets has to succeed.*

Phlox continued, "Like any demagogue, Paxton played to your people's basest fears by reminding them of their vulnerabilities. Therefore the public needs reassurance most of all. And what better way to reassure the public than with what Commander Tucker might refer to as a 'dog and pony show'?"

Archer felt a wistful twinge at Phlox's mention of his oldest friend. He wished Trip could be at his side for this historic occasion—and that the Terra Prime affair hadn't made it necessary for both Trip and T'Pol to be away now on bereavement leave. He couldn't think of anything worse than what the two of them were facing now. Fortunately, Earth's Prime Minister Samuels was calling the day's proceedings to order, forcing Archer to set aside the woes of his absent friends and colleagues.

The crowd of onlookers quickly quieted as Samuels made his way to the press podium set in the center of the open torus formed by the conference tables. Archer wondered how many people besides himself were aware that Samuels had once belonged to the Terra Prime organization. Archer wondered what would happen should that fact ever become common knowledge. Would it tear the delicate new Coalition apart? Or would it be regarded as something positive, a sign that people can always change for the better?

Archer sincerely hoped for the latter.

Samuels, a ginger-haired, genial-looking man of middle age and medium height, flashed a broad smile at the audience as the journalists' vid units zeroed in on him. A slender, palm-sized rectangular electronic translation device—one of the units that Hoshi had recently upgraded specifically for use by all of the Coalition delegates and their support staffs—was conspicuously visible on the lapel of the prime minister's smartly tailored navy blue jacket.

"We've gathered here again, in the same chamber where we began our initial discussions months ago, to demonstrate that recent events have made the governments of five worlds more determined than ever to forge a peaceful interstellar community. Allow me to introduce Ambassador Anlenthoris ch'Vhendreni of Andoria; Ambassador Lekev of Coridan; Ambassador Gora bim Gral of Tellar; Ambassador Soval, Ambassador L'Nel, and Ambassador Solkar of Vulcan; and Interior Minister Haroun al-Rashid of Earth."

Samuels paused briefly after each name, giving the diplomats sufficient time to rise from their seats and offer respectful nods or bows to the onlookers and journalists. Minister al-Rashid was a picture of quiet competence in a black suit that emphasized his dark, intelligent eyes. The Vulcans were resplendent in their dusky, bejeweled formal robes, each of them a study in dignity and poise, while the Andorian and Tellarite envoys, each flanked by a pair of junior functionaries, struck a much more martial impression in ornate formal dress based on the military attire of their respective worlds.

Coridanite Ambassador Lekev wore a much simpler, formfitting suit, dominated by his people's traditional diplomatic mask. Lekev's face was covered in a metallic material shaped into the stark features of a humanoid skull, while overlapping bands of chitinous, lobster-colored fabric wrapped his cranium, giving him a faintly crustacean appearance. Unmasked, Coridanites were visually distinguishable from humans only by their prominent nasal ridges and raised forehead striations. When masked, however, they appeared even more alien than either the dour, blue-skinned Andorians or the hirsute, porcine, and often obstreperous Tellarites.

Archer suppressed an ironic grin when he saw that Ambassador Gral of Tellar and Ambassador Anlenthoris ch'Vhendreni of Andoria—the latter being better known simply as Thoris—both appeared far more ill at ease in the presence of the masked Coridanite than they were with each other. *This is going to be a long journey*, Archer reminded himself. *Maybe the only way it can get started is with baby steps.*

"Let me begin by publicly announcing the resolution of a major negotiating impasse," Samuels continued, his enthusiasm escalating audibly as he played to the press. "The governments of Tellar and Coridan have at last reached an accord over the controversial issue of trade sanctions against the Orion Syndicate . . ."

Once Samuels finally concluded his nearly ninety-minute presentation, Archer understood that Doctor Phlox had been absolutely right about the necessity for

Samuels' "dog and pony show." After all of the principal delegates had taken their respective turns at the lectern, public faith in the coming Coalition Compact—Samuels had renewed his pledge to have the document's final draft ready for its official signing within six weeks—had to be on the rise, especially if the reaction of Archer's own crew was any indication. The captain had noticed that all of his people had stood enthralled throughout the proceedings, including Malcolm, who rarely took the words of political figures at face value and sometimes tended to fidget when not kept intensely focused on some urgent tactics-related shipboard task or other. Archer could see clearly that all of his people were overwhelmed by the historical significance of this day.

The Coalition of Planets was transforming from dream to reality, right before everyone's eyes. In a matter of mere weeks, the nascent alliance treaty already known across the sector and beyond as the Coalition Compact would become interstellar law, binding five sovereign worlds together inextricably in common, peaceful purpose.

Admiral Forrest would have loved to see this. Archer couldn't help recalling his late superior officer, the man who had sponsored his captaincy and had defended it from the beginning, through rough and smooth times. Forrest had died more than six months ago in a terror attack carried out by an aggressive and xenophobic Vulcan official named V'Las, a man cut from the same cloth as Terra Prime's John Frederick Paxton.

Leaning toward Hoshi, who stood between Phlox and Reed and Mayweather, Archer said, "So how does it feel to be an up-close eyewitness to history, Hoshi?"

She replied quietly after a lengthy and uncharacteristically tongue-tied pause. "It's kind of embarrassing for a linguist to have to admit this, sir, but I don't think I quite have the right words for it."

"I know exactly how you feel," Archer replied with a chuckle. Gesturing toward the new translator unit that hung from the lanyard encircling his collar, he added. "But thanks to you, all the delegates *did* have the right words."

Archer watched the assembled diplomats as they stood around the open circle formed by the conference tables, accepting congratulations and handshakes—or respectful gestures, in the case of the standoffish Vulcans, whose touch-telepathic abilities made them understandably disinclined to allow physical contact—from the Starfleet brass, Earth government officials, and other assorted notables. And it all took place before the all-seeing electronic eyes of the media, who were even now spreading the day's words and images throughout the sector and beyond.

In spite of his hopes for the future, Archer couldn't help but wonder how many other outlying civilizations would take the news being made here today as a reason to become as paranoid as the Xindi had been.

Now *who's being paranoid?* Archer thought, trying to force himself to relax.

Malcolm leaned down to speak *sotto voce* into Archer's ear. "Is it just me, or was Ambassador Lekev going out of his way to point out every small nit in the fine print?"

Archer had harbored similar unvoiced thoughts during the presentation, though he wondered if he hadn't been singling Lekev out for unusual scrutiny because of the decidedly inhuman aspect presented by the ambassador's mask.

"Maybe we've all got to learn to look past masks, Malcolm," Archer said, eager to give the Coridanites the benefit of the doubt.

"Maybe learning to get along with other species is a beginner's art," Travis added.

Archer feared that Mayweather might well be right about that. But before he could think of a suitably upbeat reply, his communicator beeped, its tone indicating an incoming signal from *Enterprise*. He pulled the small device from his pocket and flipped its metal grid open with a practiced flick of his wrist.

"Archer here. Go ahead, *Enterprise*."

"O'Neill, sir," said Lieutenant Donna "D.O." O'Neill, her no-nonsense tones rendered slightly metallic by the communicator's tiny speaker. She paused, apparently to stifle a sudden cough, before continuing. *"Enterprise will be ready to break orbit and get under way for Vulcan within the hour, per your orders."*

Vulcan. There Archer would finally be reunited with Trip and T'Pol—and would no doubt see the grief still lingering on both their faces, T'Pol's tight Vulcan emotional control notwithstanding. Once again, Archer wished that Trip and T'Pol were here instead of there, focusing on the future and hope rather than on the past and despair.

"Acknowledged, D.O.," Archer said. "Shuttlepod One will dock with *Enterprise* in about forty-five minutes. Then I'll want best speed to Vulcan. Archer out."

And let's hope while we're gone that nothing spooks these delegates the way Terra Prime did, he thought as he flipped the communicator grid closed.

THREE

Thursday, January 30, 2155
Vulcan's Forge

THE HARSH, DRY WIND stung his exposed skin. Commander Charles "Trip" Tucker III was glad that it was twilight, even if the area was still quite hot. He didn't know how the Vulcans withstood the heat, given all their layered heavy garments. For the occasion, he had asked for a set of ceremonial robes; it seemed fitting, even if he was soaked in sweat underneath them.

The Vulcan who had helped clothe him had also given him a matching swath of fabric intended to allow him to surreptitiously cover the neurotherapeutic sling with which Phlox had outfitted him; the weapons-burst he had taken to the shoulder while fighting Terra Prime on Mars the previous week had caused some residual, though thankfully reversible, nerve damage to his left arm. He'd be wearing the sling for another week, at least.

T'Pol was somewhere inside the mostly rebuilt T'Karath Sanctuary. He assumed that she was making whatever preparations needed to be made. He hadn't attended many Vulcan funerals, and hadn't particularly had the time—or the desire—to read up on them during the few days it had taken the speedy Coridanite diplomatic vessel to ferry them here.

"Commander Tucker?" The voice was even and crisp. He knew it belonged to a Vulcan before he even turned around. He was not surprised to recognize the shorter woman, even if her shaggy brown hair had now been swept up under a tall cap.

"Minister T'Pau," he replied, bowing slightly toward her. He supposed that she must have just returned from the recent round of Coalition negotiations on Earth.

"I hope everything has been comfortable for you, under the circumstances," she said, nodding courteously. "Our workers have been laboring night and day to turn this desolation once again into a sanctuary."

"I've been most comfortable, ma'am," Trip said. "Your workers have done a great job over the past six months." He had only seen in holograms what the original T'Karath Sanctuary had looked like. As was the case with many Vulcan religious and philosophical refuges, it had been designed and built to be a part of the low desert hills, rather than something separate from the inhospitable natural world that surrounded it.

"T'Karath was once a significant part of our history," T'Pau said, stepping forward and looking out over the rocky canyon that sloped away from the sanctuary proper. Trip admired the neat rows of hardy, ground-level plants that adorned the canyon's ruddy, rock-strewn sands. He'd overheard one of the workers refer to these newly planted leafy succulents as *kylin'the*, which were supposed to possess healing properties. The sight of life returning and persisting so stubbornly in such a hostile place made Trip feel something that strongly resembled hope.

"A history that stretches back to the time of Surak," T'Pau continued. "The sanctuary was mostly destroyed during a . . . long-past conflict among our people. More recently, my Syrrannite sect used it as a refuge, until the High Command made the decision to wipe us out. Much of what remained from the past was destroyed by the aerial bombardment."

"It's good that you're rebuilding, then," Trip said. "It'll stand as a monument for your people for the future."

T'Pau turned and regarded him with one eyebrow raised. "For now at least." She pursed her lips, and turned back to the expansive view in front of them. "Vulcan's future is unknown. Hundreds of years from now, this sanctuary may well be forgotten once again."

"I hope not," Trip said.

"Is that the reason you are interring her here?" T'Pau asked. "So that she will be memorialized in a place you think will hold importance in our future?"

Trip was momentarily appalled by the question. *Every time I think the next Vulcan can't be any ruder than the last one, I get proved wrong,* he thought.

Before he could respond, he saw T'Pol step out of the entrance behind them. She was dressed in elaborate royal blue robes not unlike those he wore himself, though she didn't look at all uncomfortable in them. Around her neck she wore the IDIC symbol her mother had sent to her shortly before her death.

"No, Minister, that is not the reason we are interring Elizabeth here," T'Pol said. "We do not choose to do this out of some attempt to publicly memorialize our . . . daughter. We do this because my mother is buried here as well. She would have appreciated knowing her grand-daughter."

T'Pau nodded. "Even if only for a short time. That is logical." She paused for a moment, and then added a question. "Do you think she would have accepted the child, given its . . . mixed parentage?"

Trip realized that his face was betraying his emotions—annoyance at the moment—and willed his features into a calmer countenance. He knew that T'Pau had been close friends with T'Les, the mother of T'Pol. They had even been at the sanctuary here together when

T'Pol and Captain Archer had arrived. Shortly afterward, Archer—who was carrying within him the *katra* of Surak—had found the long-lost *Kir'Shara*, an artifact that contained the writings of Surak. The discovery was almost simultaneous with the bombing of T'Karath, during which T'Les had been killed.

In the aftermath of the destruction, T'Pau, Archer, and T'Pol had delivered the *Kir'Shara* to the Vulcan High Command, just in time to stop the traitorous Administrator V'Las from launching the people of Vulcan into an ill-advised war against the Andorians. Shortly thereafter, the High Command was dissolved, and a reformation of Vulcan government began. T'Pau had been made a minister, and since that time had led the movement to spread and adopt the philosophies and teachings of Surak on a planetary scale.

So if she was an ally of T'Les, and she and her society both got some real benefit out of what Archer and T'Pol did here, then why is T'Pau acting this way? Trip didn't dare ask the woman, and didn't really need to. He had dealt with enough Vulcans to know that their suppression of emotions made them seem uncaring and unkind much of the time.

T'Pol answered the minister before Trip could. "My mother was a highly respected faculty member at the Vulcan Science Academy. If for no other reason than this, she would have found the first offspring ever to be produced by a Vulcan and a human to be fascinating. That Elizabeth was the product of her own daughter's genetic material would—I have no doubt—have encouraged her to accept the child."

Before T'Pau could say something else that might make the tension even more unbearable, Trip held his right hand up. "Minister, if it's all the same to you, we'd like to begin the ceremony for Elizabeth now."

T'Pau nodded, almost imperceptibly. "Certainly. The

priests have prepared the chamber for you. They have only to deliver the vessel containing the child." She turned to walk away. "I will make certain that all work ceases until you are finished, so as not to disturb the proceedings," she said over her shoulder.

"Thank you," T'Pol said, her voice flat, and quieter than normal. She turned to look at Trip, her dark eyes wide.

He hesitated for only a moment before reaching out and pulling her into a hug with his uninjured right arm. He felt her frame stiffen against him before relaxing almost imperceptibly.

He knew the tension was not just because of the pending funeral service. It was more personal even than that. Their relationship had all but dissolved last fall—even after T'Pol's divorce from her husband Koss, whom she'd been forced to marry in order to get her mother reinstated at the Academy—then seemingly rekindled almost two months ago.

The discovery just last week that, six months earlier, Terra Prime scientists had created a binary clone child, using stolen DNA from Trip and T'Pol, had hit them both like a tsunami. The radical Terra Prime isolationists had hoped to use the Vulcan-human hybrid as a way to show humans what would happen should they ally themselves with alien races. And although the terrorists were defeated on Mars, the one good result of their plans—the cloned child, which T'Pol had named Elizabeth to honor Trip's late sister—did not survive long.

Doctor Phlox had explained that Elizabeth had died because of flaws in the cloning procedures used to create her, but that didn't make the loss any easier on the girl's "parents."

During the few days since Elizabeth's death, Trip and T'Pol had tried to comfort each other, but something seemed fundamentally broken now. Even when Phlox had related his subsequent discovery that whatever incompatibilities might exist between human and Vulcan DNA wouldn't prevent Trip and T'Pol from reproducing together in the future, the news had seemed depressing rather than hopeful.

Now, Trip felt T'Pol push away from him, away from his embrace, away from the safety of his arms, away from his emotions. She did not look up at him, but turned quickly.

"We should go," he heard her say, but all the strength was gone from her voice. She may not have been crying outwardly—her face displayed no emotion—but Trip had never heard her *sound* so . . . crushed.

As T'Pol walked away, he couldn't help but wonder if *this* was really the moment when their relationship finally ended.

The torchlight flickered over the chamber walls of the room chosen to commemorate T'Les. Each of the Syrrannites who had fallen at the sanctuary was interred in a different chamber, with each commemorated by a small monument to mark his or her sacrifice.

T'Pol had initially been surprised at the presence of the monuments, since it seemed an extravagant, almost emotional response to death, mandated by T'Pau. But the minister had reminded her that symbols helped to focus memories, and focused memories were more easily controlled and brought to heel with the stern rigors of logic. While she couldn't argue with the statement, T'Pol still perceived a certain sentimentality attached to the various obelisks, spires, and markers.

As she attempted to meditate, kneeling on the floor opposite Commander Tucker, T'Pol recalled one of the last conversations she had had with her mother, elsewhere in this very sanctuary. They had argued about the Syrrannites, whom T'Pol had opposed. They had quarreled over the aims of Surak's teachings, the efficacy of the leadership of the High Command, and the overly forceful manner in which T'Pau had tried to retrieve Surak's *katra* from Captain Archer. "I shouldn't have come here looking for you, and I don't want anything more to do with you," T'Pol had told her. Minutes later, when the High Command attacked, her mother had been mortally wounded.

T'Pol was holding her when she died, shortly after T'Les had admitted that she had joined the Syrrannites' cause to help her daughter learn to control her emotions. "I have always been so proud of you," T'Les had said, just moments before drawing her last breath.

Much had changed for T'Pol since then, at least concerning her understanding of Vulcan philosophies. Although she had always steadfastly refused to believe in the existence of the *katra*, the experiences that Captain Archer shared—with what he felt was the living spirit of Surak dwelling inside him—were difficult to dismiss. Something had led Archer to the *Kir'Shara*, and had given him the knowledge required to activate it, thereby revealing the true, undiluted teachings of Surak. Whether that was actually Surak's *katra* was something she still debated even now, but even if it was solely some kind of trace memory engram of a man thousands of years gone, it was proof that Surak had lived on past his death, at least in some limited fashion.

And if he had—or if his *katra* had—then it was not hard to imagine the *katra*s of others surviving somehow still, beyond the physical bounds of living flesh.

Meditating here, in front of the sepulchers that contained the remains of her mother and of her own daughter, T'Pol felt herself clinging to the hope that neither of them was truly gone. That perhaps their *katra*s *did* exist, perhaps embedded in the very stone, sand, and soil of this hallowed place.

Of course, she also had to admit to herself that her

hope was undeniably born of emotion. Her mother had often admonished her for having so little control over her emotions, and while she didn't agree with that assessment, in the nearly one-year period since she had conquered her addiction to trellium—the substance that allowed her to free herself from the grip of logic and emotional constraint—she had known that her ability to control her emotions was now clearly, perhaps irrevocably, damaged.

There were times when she blamed this damage for her continued feelings for Charles Tucker, and yet she knew that even that explanation was disingenuous. Love, while commonly thought of as an emotion, was certainly possible for even the most logical and restrained of Vulcans. Partners loved each other, family members loved each other . . . it wasn't the love itself that was the issue, it was the emotions that accompanied it. Joy, sadness, ambivalence, anger, fear, comfort—all of these had come to her, and had sometimes threatened to overwhelm her, during the times she'd shared with Trip.

Even now, as she looked over to him, kneeling on the stone floor, his head bowed in prayer, tears streaming down his dusty cheeks, T'Pol felt herself torn. She wanted to go to him. She wanted to comfort him and seek his comfort in turn, but she also wanted to reject him, to gird herself against weakness and vulnerability.

She knew that their love was undeniable. Just as she knew it was untenable.

Unbidden, she felt a sharp laugh escape her throat from deep within her. It was a laugh born not of mirth, but rather spawned by something very akin to despair. It seemed to echo inside the chamber for an uncomfortable eternity, though she supposed it had probably remained in the air only long enough to cause Trip to open his eyes and look at her.

In that moment, she was lost. T'Pol squeezed her eyes tightly, willing away the tears that welled up in them. She clenched her teeth as her lips trembled. She felt the IDIC symbol that hung from the chain around her neck—the centuries-old symbol, delivered to her by her ex-husband, but given to her by her mother. The metal and stone in the symbol were cold in her hand. Cold and dead. As was her mother. And her child.

No. *Their* child was dead.

In the short time she had known Elizabeth, she was astonished at the instinctual bond she'd shared with the tiny creature. The girl had laughed and cooed several times, but mostly she had just stared at T'Pol and Trip with those dark, round eyes, a sense of nearly complete serenity radiating from the core of her being. Even while in the throes of her terminal fever and sickness, if T'Pol and Trip were both present, Elizabeth had barely cried. It was as if she suppressed only the *negative* emotions, allowing only the positive ones to come through.

Was that happiness and calm related to the synthesis of her parents' Vulcan and human DNA, or had it been a function of her individual personality? The answer to that question would never be known.

T'Pol felt herself trembling, could hear a keening sound she knew was coming from within her. The waves of loss rolled through her mind, washing over every emotional barrier she possessed.

She felt a hand on her shoulder, and opened her eyes. Through the blur of unshed tears, she saw Trip in front of her, tears streaming down his own face. This was a recently familiar sight; he had cried in her quarters last week, and then again several times during the Coridanite ship's flight from Earth to Vulcan. But this time, she was crying with him.

Every part of her wanted him to enfold her in his arms, wanted him to protect her from her own feelings.

But he was more emotional than she was. She knew that the more she was with him, the more she would lose control of herself, of the carefully constructed mental barriers she had erected, of the intense passions they kept at bay.

She was broken inside, and she knew that both now and in the future, Trip would only keep the fractures open.

Their child was dead.

And she knew that their feelings for each other must, by necessity, *by logic*, die as well.

And yet, through her tears, she saw her own arms reaching out for him, saw him moving toward her, felt the comfort of his embrace, the strength within him.

For a long time, they held each other and cried, for all the losses of their past, their present, and, perhaps, of their future.

FOUR

Day Eleven, Month of Tasmeen
Dartha City, Romulus

THE HEAVY TIMBER DOOR suddenly banged open to admit a pair of hulking, ill-tempered Reman soldiers into the dank gloom of the cell. Valdore i'Kaleh tr'Irrhaimehn felt his stomach rumble in anticipation of yet another of the imperial dungeon's meager and infrequent meals—until he noticed that the guards were carrying neither food nor drink.

"Thank Erebus," Valdore said, seated on the edge of the rude stone cot where he had slept for the past several weeks. "Waiting down here for my appointment with the executioner had begun to grow tedious."

Neither of the spectral white faces confronting Valdore betrayed any sign of amusement. Of course, Remans weren't known for their keen sense of humor. "Come with us," the guard on the right growled as his silent counterpart bared his fangs, manhandled Valdore to his feet, and affixed a set of stout manacles upon his wrists. Valdore looked up from his shackled wrists and noticed that both Remans stood a full head taller than he did.

"Let's not make this take any longer than it has to, my brothers-in-arms," Valdore said. Being executed was by far preferable to slowly rotting away or starving in such a godsforsaken place as this.

As his armed escorts marched him through the convoluted stone *drabbik* warren of the cell block, Valdore closed his eyes, walking blindly as he listened to the echoing clatter of the uniformed Remans' boots, which utterly drowned out his own rag-wrapped footfalls. Concentrating on the sounds, he tried to imagine exchanging his tattered, ill-fitting green prison attire for a standard military uniform, but couldn't quite get his mind around the idea. The realization threatened to overwhelm him with despair. *Has confinement so diminished me that I can no longer even visualize what I once was?*

Valdore had lost track of the exact number of weeks that had passed since the start of his confinement, no doubt partly because of the windowless cell to which the First Consul had banished him. Being spared a return to those cramped confines was a blessing, no matter the reason; the prospect of his own imminent death gave the disgraced Romulan admiral only a sense of relief.

Next came a growing hollow pang of disappointment as the guards conducted him up from the intricate maze of subsurface catacombs into the vast, cathedral-like spaces of the Hall of State. Valdore knew by then that his disgrace was not destined to end in so tidy and merciful a fashion as he had allowed himself to hope.

Unless First Consul T'Leikha had lately taken up the practice of dispatching her political prisoners in the midst of the finery of her richly appointed audience chamber.

Valdore said nothing as he was marched roughly toward the silver-haired, aquiline-faced woman who was seated in an attentive, almost vigilant pose on the raised dais before which he and the guards had come to a halt. Still bound in wrist shackles and flanked by the armed Remans, Valdore was made to stand perhaps a dozen long paces away from the First Consul.

Somewhat closer to the First Consul, and guarded closely by another pair of raptor-eyed Reman soldiers, stood a second prisoner. Valdore blinked for several moments before he realized that he recognized him, despite the man's thinning white hair, averted gaze, and defeated, stoop-shouldered posture.

Senator Vrax? Valdore thought, not willing to tempt fate by speaking aloud unbidden in the presence of the First Consul. *I, too, am only a prisoner now,* he reminded himself.

"*Jolan'tru,* Admiral," said First Consul T'Leikha.

A bitter laugh escaped Valdore's lips in spite of himself. "I am no longer an admiral, First Consul. Perhaps you read of it in the newsfeeds."

T'Leikha chuckled, her smile gleaming like a burnished Honor Blade. "I have decided to correct that injustice, Valdore. As has a majority of my colleagues in the Senate, several of whom have the ear of the Praetor, just as I do. It seems, Admiral, that the Romulan Star Empire once again urgently needs your service."

The First Consul appeared content to wait silently for his reaction. Valdore said nothing, hoping that he wasn't revealing just how nonplussed he was by this dramatic change of fortune. Remus had circled the Motherworld several times since he and Vrax had been removed from their respective posts and imprisoned as punishment for their discovery and defeat by the Earther-allies against whom they had been working in secret. Neither the Senate nor the First Consul were known to reverse such precipitous decisions lightly. All Valdore understood with any certainty was that circumstances must have changed greatly since he and Vrax had been incarcerated. *Something has gone terribly wrong,* he thought, glancing at Vrax and wondering just how much his erstwhile colleague knew.

Valdore nodded in the direction of the broken former senator. "And what is to become of *him*?"

"Your restoration to the admiralty cannot come without a price, Valdore," T'Leikha said, as though lecturing an obtuse servant who lacked a grasp of the intuitively obvious. "Someone still must take the blame for the calamity that befell your prototype drone ships. The Senate will back my recommendation that he be executed for betraying the Praetor's military secrets."

Despite her unconcealed contempt for the miserable wreck of a man who slouched before her with downcast eyes, Valdore could feel only pity for his old colleague. Whatever Vrax's failures—whatever disagreements they'd had in the past—Valdore knew that Vrax deserved better than this.

Valdore turned away from Vrax so that he could meet the First Consul's sharp gaze directly. "His dishonor can be no worse than my own. *I* was responsible for losing the prototype drone warships to the Earthers and their allies. Vrax merely supported my own misguided efforts."

The First Consul leaned forward and regarded Valdore again in silence. Then she smiled. "You are no less noble for your lengthy ordeal in our dungeons, Valdore. And no less brave."

Valdore returned her smile coolly. "I have very little left to lose, First Consul. And therefore very little left to fear."

He paused to look back toward the broken man, pausing for a dark instant to rejoice that confinement had not treated him nearly so brutally as it had Vrax. The sight of his old friend brought unbidden wistful memories that spanned many decades. "Vrax and I served together in the Senate long ago, First Consul. Until I was expelled . . . for posing an imprudent question."

T'Leikha nodded. "I am aware of your record, Valdore. You and Vrax were friends—at least until you questioned the wisdom of the Romulan Star Empire's doctrine of unlimited expansion."

"And I doubtless would have been executed for it, had

Vrax not intervened directly on my behalf. He persuaded First Consul Aratenik to help him convince the Praetor to spare my life."

"So?" T'Leikha asked. Her eyes narrowed, as though they functioned as a gauge showing precisely how much patience remained behind them.

"So the Senate would no doubt listen to *your* recommendation for clemency as well," Valdore said, looking T'Leikha squarely in the eye. "As would the Praetor himself."

Her brow had begun to furrow in incompletely restrained fury. "You forget your place, Valdore. Your family is not so powerful as you seem to think."

Valdore met the continued onslaught of her gaze without flinching. "If members of my family were influential enough to free me from imprisonment, they certainly would have done so long before now. Therefore I must assume that *you* have brought me here, First Consul—and that you did so because you *need* me. Otherwise you would not have seen fit to *change* my 'place.'" He gestured toward Vrax without breaking eye contact with T'Leikha. "So, given my evident importance to you, I *respectfully* request that you spare this man's life. The Romulan Star Empire may one day have need of him again, just as has proved to be the case with me."

T'Leikha paused to digest this, then nodded toward Vrax's guards, who swiftly began conducting the slope-shouldered prisoner away. For a fleeting moment before the former senator exited the chamber, Vrax's gaze locked with Valdore's.

Valdore glimpsed both anger and despair in his old friend's once roc-sharp eyes. He realized then that if his request for clemency was to succeed, he had very likely done his old friend no favors. *Sometimes you either end up in charge,* Valdore thought, *or else you end up executed. There doesn't seem to be much middle ground.*

But he couldn't concern himself with that now. His stomach rumbled hollowly, and noisily enough to make him wonder whether his Reman guards might be startled by the sound.

Again turning his attention fully upon First Consul T'Leikha, Valdore said, "I require a meal, a bath, a clean uniform, and communications with my family. And then I want a briefing about *everything* that has happened while I have been . . . away."

T'Leikha nodded. "All of that has been prepared. You will have until tomorrow morning to prepare a coherent strategic plan for presentation to the Empire's Military Tribunes, and to the Praetor himself." She grinned like a predator anticipating a kill. "Welcome back, Admiral Valdore."

After taking a swift meal and an equally swift shower, and then properly attiring himself in a uniform tunic that now felt disconcertingly loose across his chest, Valdore took a seat at a triangular table in a small conference room located deep in the bowels of the Hall of State. Here he endured a briefing that was anything but brief. The uniformed centurion who was conducting it— a young man named Terix—was copiously thorough, so much so that Valdore could not help but feel overwhelmed by all that had occurred since his confinement had begun.

But he knew he hadn't the time to dwell on that, for there was far too much to do. Nor did he wish to consider overmuch the mortal danger he was in, since the Praetor's own intelligence service was no doubt watching him closely for any sign of disloyalty, now that he once again had access to so much highly sensitive imperial military data.

He concentrated instead on the renewed sense of overarching purpose that once again consumed him.

The Empire's adversaries had moved forward considerably in their plans during Valdore's detention. Earth and its allies were now close to formalizing a mutual defense pact that might be better described as a permanent confederation. Five highly advanced, starfaring worlds capable of interposing themselves between the Romulan Star Empire and its necessity-driven ambitions for expansion could soon present a unified military front to the outworlds of the Empire's ever-broadening— and ever more diffuse—frontier. And that hostile front might even succeed in beating back the Empire's massed forces, given the reliable new intelligence reports indicating that Coridan Prime now apparently possessed *avaihh lli vastam*—warp-seven-capable vessels—at least in prototype form.

They could very well strangle us within our own territory, Valdore thought with increasing agitation as he listened to Terix and reviewed the many classified text files, flat and holographic pictures, and graphs that the centurion had provided. *If the Coridanites should share this technology with the rest of the worlds in this so-called Coalition of Planets before our Empire can bring its own countermeasures online . . .*

Valdore did not want to pursue the thought to its conclusion, though he couldn't stop himself from visualizing the national banners of Earth or Vulcan or Coridan fluttering in the Apnex Sea's cool breezes over all of the ancient domes and arches of Dartha's venerable Government Quarter, including the stately vastness of the Romulan Senate itself. Even without the Coridanites' warp-seven-capable technology, the Coridan system's abundant dilithium reserves would not only greatly strengthen Earth and its Coalition of Planets, but they might also benefit the uncouth creatures of the Klingon Empire, longtime adversaries whose own expansionist tendencies rivaled those of Romulus itself.

Putting aside his apocalyptic speculations for the moment, Valdore leaned toward Terix and interrupted him. "Centurion, what is the current status of our own high-warp research projects?"

Still standing between Valdore's table and the wall screen that currently carried a map of the Coalition of Planets' projected boundaries along the Romulan frontier, the young briefer scowled down at his boots for a moment. He was clearly about to convey some bad news, and was just as clearly worried about being held personally responsible for it.

After being prompted with a curt monosyllable, Terix said, "The first full-up test of the new stardrive was undertaken earlier today, Admiral, on Unroth III."

"*And?*" Valdore asked in a low growl, making an intentional display of impatience; he hated verbal tiptoeing of this sort.

"We received official word about the results about four *dierha* ago. The prototype failed, explosively. The resulting energy discharge completely destroyed the prototype and the research complex, and blew off a good portion of Unroth III's atmosphere."

Unroth III. Valdore recognized the designation as belonging to a remote frontier world, far from the Empire's better-traveled military and commercial corridors.

"Survivors?" Valdore asked.

The centurion appeared relieved that he now had somewhat better news to impart. "Fortunately, Doctor Ehrehin and several key members of his research team were safely evacuated just before the conflagration escaped the containment measures."

Valdore nodded, thankful for whatever good news he could find. After all, the Unroth disaster could have been far, far worse. "What are the prospects for getting the project back on track?"

A subtle expression of fright crossed Terix's forehead

once again. "A new prototype is several *khaidoa* away, Admiral. Even if the new stardrive had passed all its tests and were to go into mass production tomorrow, Coridan would still be far ahead of us. So far, only the internal political dissension that now divides the Coridanites has prevented Coridan Prime from sharing its warp technology with Earth, or any of the other Coalition worlds."

Now Valdore understood both the suddenness and the urgency that had motivated both the Praetor and the First Consul in their decision to free him and restore his military commission.

They saw him as the Empire's deliverance.

It was therefore Valdore's mission either to expedite the work of Ehrehin and the Empire's other premier warp engineers, or to buy them whatever time they might need to gain the technological upper hand. Using whatever means might prove necessary.

Valdore stared at the brown-and-blue world that now filled the screen that dominated the wall before which Terix stood. Coridan Prime itself was clearly the key to this business, because of its technology and its vast dilithium resources—both of which had to be denied to the worlds of the still-forming Coalition of Planets. *The central world of the Coridan system must be the primary target for any attack*, he thought. *Regardless of Earth's political role in the alliance.*

But he also knew that a conventional military campaign against Coridan could generate many undesirable and unintentional consequences for the Empire. Coridan was home to some three billion people, whose wealthy, resource-rich society would doubtless be roused to considerable wrath should Valdore initiate a direct attack that could be traced back to Romulus.

Therefore the only solution to the problem was to launch a wholly *unconventional* campaign.

"Show me the most recent reports from Chief Technologist Nijil's office," Valdore said. "How far has he progressed on his warship-cloaking research since my . . . sabbatical from duty began?"

The bleak look on Terix's face grew even bleaker. "Unfortunately, this new stealth technology remains adequate to conceal only small devices, such as mines or probes. It could be decades before it will become practical to use it to conceal an entire ship. I fear that the setback we suffered as a result of the loss of the original prototype cloaked bird-of-prey nearly three *fvheisn* ago may well have ensured that."

Valdore scowled at the bleak memory of the explosion that had vaporized the experimental cloaked bird-of-prey *Praetor Pontilus* after its extremely power-intensive stealth system had caused a catastrophic antimatter containment failure. But he understood all too well that such losses, however tragic they might be, were necessary for the protection of the Empire.

"What about telepresence drones, then?" Valdore asked, barely suppressing a wince as he mentioned the project that had nearly brought his career—and his life—to an ignominious conclusion.

The centurion brightened. Switching the image on the screen to a schematic diagram of a modified *T'Liss*-class bird-of-prey, he said, "I am pleased to report that Doctor Nijil's section *has* made significant progress in this area, Admiral. The telepresence systems used in the earlier prototypes have been rebuilt and greatly refined. In fact, several new drone ships now stand ready for combat duty, except . . ." The younger man's voice trailed off, and his earlier expression of discomfiture returned.

"Let me guess. Nijil has no telepathic Aenar pilots in his care at the moment."

Terix nodded unhappily. "We currently have no telepaths rated to fly these ships, Admiral."

Why am I not surprised? Valdore thought. He had seen for himself how reticent Nijil had been about pushing his lone Aenar pilot past the point of brain damage or death, even when such extremes were demonstrably necessary for the success of the mission. Nijil was an obsessive, committed tinkerer when it came to the inanimate metals and ceramics and electronics that made up his hardware creations. But he was frequently far too soft for his own good—and for the good of the Empire—when it came to making harsh but necessary demands of the living, breathing "wetware" that sometimes had to be sacrificed to the cause of either science or warfare.

Valdore wondered if he could manage another Romulan slave raid against Andoria's Aenar subspecies without drawing undue attention to the Romulan Star Empire—and without precipitating a concerted counterattack by several Coalition worlds before he felt confident that the Romulan military was ready to handle it.

Of course, such situations are tailor-made for intermediaries, he thought. He already knew whom he intended to contact about obtaining—discreetly—all the Aenar pilots he might need. With a career military man's crisp economy of verbiage, he instructed Terix to contact the particular man he had in mind and to report back to him the moment he succeeded in raising him via a secure subspace com channel.

Dismissed, Centurion Terix placed his right fist over his left lung, his elbow over his heart in a textbook-perfect salute. He turned smartly and exited the room, leaving Valdore alone with his thoughts, and with the *dathe'anofv-sen*—the Honor Blade—that hung at his side. He drew it from its scabbard and considered its deadly brilliance as he balanced the fine weapon in the palms of both hands. He hoped that the actions he was about to undertake wouldn't force him to feed the blade's hungry, gleaming edge with his own life's blood, though he knew he wouldn't shirk from such a duty should honor demand it of him.

Finally satisfied that he now had at least an inkling of the strategy and tactics he would have to outline for the Praetor and his tribunes tomorrow morning, Valdore finally felt sufficient confidence to contact the only other people in the universe whose approbation meant more to him than that of either his military or civilian superiors.

Sweeping the stacks of papers and data slates to one side of the table, he activated the communications terminal before him and waited for the images of his wife and children to appear on the screen.

FIVE

Monday, February 3, 2155
Andoria

HRAVISHRAN TH'ZOARHI STOOD QUIETLY in the frigid breeze that moved continuously through the dimly lit, ice-encrusted cavern. He closed his eyes and exhaled, sending plumes of vapor curling upward over his head. Having been raised in some of Andoria's coldest climes, he found the chill wind stimulating and life-affirming, evocative of the simpler, happier days of his childhood. A time long before life's inexorable and unforgiving circumstances had seen him take up arms to defend his people. Or had forced him to bury his beloved bondmate Talas, whose murder at the hands of a treacherous Tellarite diplomat—*that* zhavey-*less swine Naarg*, he thought—remained an open wound even now, months after the fact.

A time, he thought, his frost-caked antennae turning downward, *when I was still just plain Shran.*

But he found it difficult to extract any real, substantive joy from the raw, visceral sensation of cold air that flowed all about his body. For one thing, the tingling in his incompletely healed left antenna—it was still not quite three-quarters regrown after Jonathan Archer had cut it off in a ritual *Ushaan-Tor* battle—was a constant irritant, as were the headaches and feelings of vertigo the damaged sensory organ still caused on occasion. And despite the small crowd of quietly joyous people that now surrounded him—warm, welcoming folk who hadn't hesitated to take him in after the Andorian military had summarily cashiered him for losing his command, the *Kumari*, to a Romulan sneak attack—he felt isolated, alone. However sightless the Aenar standing all around him might be, there was just enough tenebrous, microbe-generated light in the spacious chamber to spotlight Shran's uniqueness here; Shran was the only blue-skinned mainline Andorian in the entire underground city of the Aenar.

Aside from their obviously unusual pigmentation—all of the perhaps five thousand Aenar who still dwelled beneath Andoria's northern wastes were albinos—there was little to distinguish these people from their cerulean-hued cousins, at least visually. And like their far more common blue Andorian, the Aenar could not reproduce without the participation of four distinct sexes: *shen, thaan, chan,* and *zhen.* Also like Andorians, the Aenar possessed frost-white hair and prominent cranial antennae that not only provided EM-band sensory input but also swayed and danced in response to their emotions.

Watching the slow, stately approach of the *shelthreth* party, Shran considered the emotions that most distinguished Aenar from Andorian, perhaps even more than did the albino people's unique and formidable telepathic abilities. For the Aenar were as gentle and pacifistic as Shran's folk were passionate and contentious. Despite their diminishing numbers, an augury of imminent extinction in Shran's estimation, the Aenar seemed to have made their peace with a hostile universe in a way that Shran had never managed to do, and probably never would. He often envied them their upbeat outlook and their gentle serenity.

But he also sometimes quietly raged at them for their entrenched belief in passivity.

Yet he couldn't help but wonder just now if either

Andorian or Aenar was destined to survive without the other.

Without any conscious volition he could recall, Shran had begun the morning by mentally composing a poem about what was to occur on this day. Or perhaps it would one day become a song, with lyrics set to dirge-like music, inspired by Shran's own losses as much as by Jhamel's poorly suppressed grief for her brother Gareb, whose death had closely coincided with that of Talas. However it came out in the end, he already knew with certainty that if he ever managed to see it to completion it would be a sad, morose thing indeed.

And why not? he thought. After all, he was about to bid farewell to a woman with whom he once, if only very briefly, had hoped he might build a future, a *shelthreth* bondgroup, and perhaps children. They might even have created a future together that would bridge the vast gulf that separated two very disparate Andorian peoples.

Jhamel.

In spite of all the mental discipline he had learned to marshal during the many months he had dwelled among the Aenar, he now found that he was utterly unable to keep a rising sense of desolate melancholy at bay. He supposed that it must have set up a keening wail that was telepathically audible to everyone else in the room, despite the ingrained aversion of Jhamel's people to intruding upon the thoughts of others without first securing their express permission.

Get hold of yourself, Shran thought as he watched the crowd part to admit the *shelthreth* procession, in which Jhamel was radiant in her snow-white gown, despite the semidarkness. *Just wish her well. She deserves all the happiness you can imagine, and more.*

"Thank you for that, Shran," Jhamel said, stopping only a few long paces away from Shran, her mind speaking gently and sweetly, and apparently only to him. It

was a silent sound, like the memory of delicate, crystalline bells. *"And may you find such happiness as well."*

A second telepathic voice intruded then, and Shran immediately realized that this one was being mentally broadcast to everyone gathered in the room.

It was clear to Shran that the originator of this thought-stream was the white-robed woman who stood facing Jhamel and the other three members of her *shelthreth* party; Shran recognized her at once as Lissan, one of the Aenar people's most respected leaders.

"My dear friends," Lissan said wordlessly to the dozens of blind, silent, and eagerly attentive Aenar telepaths who stood around the *shelthreth* party in a broad ring, their collective breath rising toward the cavern ceiling in delicately curling pillars of ivory-hued vapor. *"We have gathered to witness the joining of these four kindred souls in the bonds of* shelthreth, *the honored, sacred estate established in earliest antiquity by Uzaveh the Infinite, the omniscient and omnipotent creator of the world. As Uzaveh instituted the Great Joining that brought together the wisdom of Charaleas, the strength of Zheusal, the love of Shanchen, and the passion of Thirizaz to form the First Kin, so, too, do we sanctify today the* shelthreth *of these four."*

Shran allowed a small smile to cross his lips as he recognized the ancient names, familiar to him from the bedtime tales and devotions of his youth. He found it gratifying to discover that the similarities between the Aenar and Andorian peoples seemed to extend even to the ancient myths that made up the very underpinnings of their respective cultures.

Shran suddenly noticed that Lissan had lapsed into telepathic silence, her pause filled by a soundless, psionic murmur of approval that rolled across the dozens of onlookers like a wave. Shran assumed that the sheer positive intensity of these sentiments had ensured that his own decidedly nontelepathic brain could receive them.

Lissan motioned to one of the two Aenar males of the *shelthreth* group, a young man whose white ceremonial attire was not unlike that of Jhamel. He stepped forward, his milky, sightless eyes fixed directly ahead, his expression frozen in ancient ceremonial solemnity. He was of the same sex as Shran—a *thaan*—and appeared to be about Jhamel's age, approximately fifteen years Shran's junior.

"*Anitheras th'Lenthar,*" Lissan said, "*will you become Whole, entering the blessed state of* shelthreth *with your entire heart and soul?*"

The young man, whom Shran knew better as Theras, telepathically recited words steeped in age-old ritual as he took a step toward Lissan. "*I will, without reservation or hesitation.*"

"*Onalishenar ch'Sorichas,*" Lissan continued, addressing the other young male of the quartet with the same query. Shenar responded in the same manner that Theras had; he gently took Theras's hand, his blind face refulgent with a look of almost religious ecstasy.

"*Lahvishri sh'Ralaavazh,*" Lissan continued, asking the ancient *shelthreth* question yet again. Vishri, the stolid young woman who stood beside the taller, more slender figure of Jhamel, stepped forward, recited the ritual words in turn, and joined hands with Shenar.

"*Thirijhamel zh'Dhaven,*" Lissan said, prompting Jhamel to step toward her three bondmates and telepathically recite the time-honored words. He hoped that the spirit of her brother Gareb was somewhere near, perceiving the proceedings by whatever means the Aenar departed might have at their disposal.

Even in the cavern's low illumination, Shran found Jhamel's innocent beauty gently awe-inspiring, and more than a little humbling. At that moment, he pitied the entire Aenar race for being unable to see her in quite the same way he did.

Get a good look at her, Shran, he told himself, while carefully schooling his mind to keep a low enough profile so as not to be casually overheard, least of all by Jhamel herself. *You won't be seeing much of her anymore.* He tried to memorize every contour of her face, despite the strange, distorting shadows created by the cavern's dim lighting.

Very soon, memory would be all he had of Jhamel. His small civilian transport vessel, the only real property he possessed now that he no longer drew an Imperial Guard salary, was already waiting for him, prepped and ready and tucked away in a convenient hollow in the ice and snow that lay outside this very cavern. Once he had said his farewells to Jhamel and her bondmates, he would be gone, seeking his fortune in the sometimes unsavory world of freelance interstellar commerce.

Shran watched in wistful silence as his beloved took the hands of Vishri and Theras, closing the tight circle of four. The *shelthreth* now complete, she projected her thoughts, quoting scripture that Shran attributed to an early liturgical codex of the Temple of Uzaveh.

" '*When you are Whole, as I am Whole,' Uzaveh said, 'then shall you return to my presence and assume your place at my side.' *"

Lissan extended her arms above her head as though supplicating great Uzaveh Itself. "*My friends, you are Whole. I now pronounce your* shelthreth *complete in the sight of the law, the people, and the Throne of Life of Uzav—*"

As Lissan inexplicably paused, a ripple of confusion passed through the crowd, like a collective thought being broadcast on some channel Shran was unable to access. But the interruption and the oddly tense body postures of so many people were more than enough to alert Shran that something was terribly wrong.

Shran heard a buzzing hum, and it took a moment for him to realize that he was hearing it with his ears rather than within the interior spaces of his mind. The sound seemed bizarre here, out of place, but his months-long stay among the placid Aenar hadn't so blunted his military instincts that he'd fail to recognize it.

Transporter beam, he thought as the sound of a materialization sequence ceased but for the confusing echoes it continued to cast across the length and breadth of the voluminous ice cavern. Concentrating hard to avoid being overwhelmed by the alarmed telepathic gabble swiftly rising around him, he turned quickly in a circle, seeking to locate the intruders.

A brilliant energy-weapon discharge, as blue as heartblood, lanced the air nearby, betraying the location of at least one of the intruders. Acting on instinct, Shran dived to the icy ground to lower his profile as a target, seeking cover even as he reached into his heavy jacket in search of his sidearm.

Two more blasts sliced the chill air, filling it with the tang of ozone as he realized that he was unarmed. He felt utterly naked. *This is the* last *time I follow rules written by pacifists*, he thought with a pungent curse, not wishing to dwell on what usually happened to pacifists whenever they encountered unscrupulous aggressors.

Jhamel!

"Shran!" She was crying out in panic inside his mind.

He rose to a crouch, searching for the *shelthreth* party, but without any immediate success thanks to the confusion all around him. He struggled to ignore the collective terror that filled his mind, as well as the numerous inadvertent jostles and kicks that the fleeing crowd was inflicting on him.

Shran was soon relieved to find Jhamel not far from where she had originally stood, despite the sea of swiftly moving, agitated bodies that prevented him from reaching her quickly. Jhamel clung to the hands of two of her bondmates, Shenar and Vishri, both of whom seemed utterly paralyzed with terror. Shran noted that Theras had apparently vanished, and wondered if he had simply fled the side of his *shelthreth* partners. Lissan had remained beside them, standing proudly, apparently trying to quell her people's fears and direct an orderly exit of the cavern.

Before Shran could make his way through the panicked crowd toward Jhamel, a blast caught Lissan squarely in the chest, causing her to crumple to the ice like a rag doll. A hulking, rifle-wielding form, bundled tightly in thermal gear, abruptly came into view and tossed a small metallic object onto Lissan's insensate form.

She abruptly disappeared in a shower of ruddy sparkles.

The combined flashes of weapons and other transporter beams soon raised the light level across the cavern enough to enable Shran to see the partially exposed faces of the nearest attackers quite clearly. He recognized their distinctive jade-green skin immediately.

There could be no mistaking their identity.

Orion slavers.

It was impossible at the moment to tell exactly how many intruders had entered the cavern, and Shran knew that discovering that bit of data was of overwhelming importance. But he also knew that obtaining a usable weapon was at least as vital at the moment.

More beams flashed in rapid succession. More Aenar bodies went down, then vanished in columns of light. Shran moved quickly, counting the assailants, calculating angles of fire and approach. *There are eight of them,* he thought as he circled behind one of the intruders, careful to crouch below a row of hoarfrosted stalagmites as he moved. *No, nine.*

Fighting off a feeling of vertiginous nausea brought

on by his injured antenna, Shran leaped at his selected target, a ponderous giant who stood more than a head higher than the tallest Andorian soldier he had seen in all his time among the battle-toughened troops of the Imperial Guard. He slammed hard into the alien's thickly muscled back, wrapping his arms around his neck before the other man could react.

I suppose they weren't expecting a welcome like this from a bunch of pacifists, Shran thought, grinning savagely. His slightly asymmetrical antennae lashed back and forth like angry serpents as he applied every iota of his strength to the task of squeezing the burly slaver's throat.

But the Orion was hugely strong, his broad back and neck reminding Shran of ancient Andoria's powerful cavalry mounts. While still holding his rifle by the strap, the Orion was trying to grab Shran's arms, obviously in an attempt to throw the Andorian over his head. Shran knew that if his opponent managed that, the fight would be settled immediately in the Orion's favor by the greenskin's rifle.

Absurdly, Shran thought of something the Terran pinkskin Jonathan Archer had said to him once during an unguarded moment in the captain's personal mess: "It's not the size of the dog in the fight, Shran," Archer had said while scratching the neck of his peculiar Earth pet. "It's the size of the fight in the dog."

The Orion turned in a circle, roaring like a wounded beast. Shran hung on, screaming out in a ululating Andorian battle cry. His nails sank into green flesh like pitons being driven hard into the unyielding ice of the northern wastes. Over the Orion's shoulder he caught a brief glimpse of Jhamel, her face frozen in a rictus of horror as people fell to the slavers and continued to vanish all around her.

Shran tightened his grip, screamed another battle cry,

and lowered his face to the Orion's jugular. He sank his teeth into the sweaty, verdant flesh with a predator's ferocity. Hot, dark ichor splattered him in steaming fire-hose pulses. The Orion crashed to his knees, pulling Shran down just as energy beams lanced over both of their heads.

Then Shran was standing over the giant's already cooling corpse, rifle in hand, steam from the slaver's bloodied, slain form rising all around him. Ushaan-Tor *combat without the blades,* he thought with grim humor.

Shran's military training took over, and he found cover quickly, ducking behind an icy pillar. He began firing, guided to his targets by their muzzle flashes. Four Orions fell in fairly short order, and the remaining slavers seemed to be increasingly confused and panicked. Shran wasn't certain just how many Aenar the slavers had succeeded in beaming away, but he could see that many had made it to the exits, thanks to his efforts.

Was Jhamel among them?

But there was nothing he could do to answer that question at the moment. All he could do was continue moving to new cover, finding his targets, and firing. *Zhavey-less bastards!* he thought as yet another slaver's body crashed hard onto the ice before sledding roughly down a frost-slicked incline and into one of the cavern walls.

Shran was beginning to notice that his targets were growing as scarce as the Aenar, almost all of whom had by now either fled or been captured. He caught another glimpse of Jhamel, who had bravely stayed behind, apparently intent on helping every last Aenar get to safety. Beside her was Theras, who evidently hadn't fled or been captured after all.

Shran grinned and resumed his continuous search for new targets, trying to cover Jhamel's efforts. *Maybe I'll drive them all off before they can do any more—*

Something abruptly slammed into Shran then, spinning him as though he were a small moon that had been dealt a glancing blow by a passing asteroid. His feet slipped out from under him, in spite of the heavy, studded treads built into his cold-weather boots. The entire left side of his body was suddenly numb and paralyzed, which prevented him from stopping himself as he slid down a slope on the icy cavern floor.

Must have been hit, he thought, feeling woozy as his slide continued unchecked. More energy discharges stitched the ice all around him, filling the air with superheated steam and the tortured creaks of breaking ice and grinding stone. He was keenly aware that *he* was now a target, no doubt of the highest priority.

The maw of a large, dark crevasse—perhaps opened up only moments earlier by the firefight's relentless volleys, maybe even by one of Shran's own blasts—yawned hungrily before him. He flailed with his good right arm to arrest his tumbling, sliding descent, but succeeded only in entangling himself awkwardly in the strap of the Orion rifle he'd been holding when he'd fallen.

The accelerating sensation of sliding abruptly ceased, replaced by the gut-churningly familiar vertigo that accompanied orbital freefall in ships not equipped with artificial gravity. His nervous system charged with survival-instinct panic, Shran realized that he was falling feet-first into the crevasse, tumbling toward the fathomless, unilluminated spaces below.

His right arm lashed upward as he dropped, and the sensation of weight returned with a suddenness that slammed his jaw shut and probably loosened a few of his teeth. He looked up and saw in the gloom surrounding him that his rifle strap had snagged on a stony, ice-covered outcropping. Awkwardly restricted to the use of his right arm and leg, he gripped the strap hard and struggled to pull himself back up over the crumbling lip of the crevasse.

Inching upward, his head cleared the ice-crusted verge, giving him a reverse view back up the path of his unplanned and haphazard descent. He caught sight of Jhamel, still calmly assisting what Shran hoped were the last few Aenar stragglers in escaping the predations of the Orions. Near her was Theras, who seemed every bit as paralyzed by fear as Jhamel was composed and self-possessed.

Until she crumpled to the ice in a strobe-flash of light, struck in the back by an Orion energy-weapon discharge. Theras hurried out of sight—fleeing!—even as a pair of the slavers converged on Jhamel's motionless form and tagged it with a communications beacon that enabled them to have her beamed away.

"No!" Shran cried, pulling himself, one-handed and one-legged, up onto the creaking, groaning ledge. Fueled by rage and adrenaline, he dragged himself slowly toward the two slavers, one of whom very calmly raised his weapon, changed its setting, and took careful aim in Shran's direction.

He didn't bother looking away as he braced himself for the brutal heat of the beam he expected to take him down to final oblivion.

Then the surface directly beneath Shran cracked sharply and gave way, spilling him back into the crevasse while sparing him from the Orion's weapon. An energy beam lashed out over his head, missing him by a wide margin, not that it mattered now. Time dilated as he plunged into the frigid darkness below.

A rough, sharp shock followed, and oblivion came.

The tingling and pain that commingled along the left side of his body, coupled with the biting cold of the surface on which he suddenly found himself sprawled prone, convinced Shran that he wasn't quite dead—at least not yet. He wasn't certain how long he had been unconscious, but the return of sensation to the part of his body that had been clipped by the Orion weapon told him that enough time had passed for his nervous system to begin returning to normal after the fierce stunning it had received during the firefight.

Jhamel!

He beat back his fear. *Think, Shran, think.* The Orions had her now, along with Uzaveh-only-knew how many others. They could already have been under way at high warp for hours now, and might be anywhere in the sector, or maybe even farther away than that.

And that zhavey-*less coward Theras ran instead of standing up to defend her.*

His rage rekindled, Shran struggled into a sitting position and tried to haul himself to his feet. Nothing seemed broken, but he was frustrated by his inability to get his studded boots underneath him as his knees and elbows ineffectually sought purchase on the glassy ice on which he lay. He sighed in frustration, his breath curling upward like coolant leaking from an overheating warp core.

I have to get back to surface. Back to the ship. Find their trail before it grows as cold as this cavern.

After making another failed attempt to stand, he noticed that the darkness was beginning to give way to a diffuse, amber light. His antennae twitched, responding to what felt like someone's physical presence, which he'd somehow not noticed before now. The ice shifted behind him, and Shran craned his neck toward the sudden cracking sound.

Something grasped him firmly by the shoulders, and a disembodied voice inside his head shouted, *"Move!"*

A flurry of hot hailstones came down around him, scorching his jacket and trousers wherever they touched him. One of the thumb-sized, glowing objects landed momentarily on the back of his right hand, and he flipped it away onto the ice with a strangled cry of agony.

Ice borers, Shran thought, watching the slow rain of the tiny creatures, which was illuminated very faintly by the energy of their own heat-generating bodies. He recalled how he'd once been badly burned by the very same type of subterranean grubs during his youth. Ice borers provided the people of Andoria with a great deal of usable heat, but they also posed a serious hazard to anyone unfortunate enough to be directly beneath them when they chose to make a vertical downward passage through a mass of ice.

The patter of the small, incendiary bodies quickly slowed and stopped, leaving only a shotgun scattering of faintly glowing holes in the floor and ceiling of the cavern as the light levels quickly receded to stygian darkness.

That darkness concealed the identity of whoever had just dragged Shran to safety. *"Are you injured, Commander Shran?"*

"It's just plain Shran now. And I've been in far worse shape than this." Shran cradled his burned hand before him as his rescuer attempted to help him get up on his feet.

"Thank Uzaveh I managed to find you."

Well, at least I know he's not one of the Orions, Shran thought. He leaned against his benefactor as he experimented with putting his full weight on both of his feet simultaneously.

"Who are you?" Shran wanted to know.

"It's me," said the voice inside his head. *"Theras."*

Shran found it difficult to rein in the contempt that surged through his soul at that moment. His instinct was to push the coward as far away from him as possible, but he restrained himself, not eager to risk taking another awkward tumble into the icy darkness.

"Theras. I thought you had run away."

"*I ran to find* you."

"Stop speaking inside my mind, Theras," Shran said, his words as sharp as fléchettes. Only Jhamel had his leave to take such intimate liberties.

"I apologize for the intrusion," Theras said, his voice sounding hoarse as though from long periods of disuse.

"I'm not the one you owe an apology to, Theras. Jhamel was captured because you decided to run instead of staying to help her."

Theras's voice took on a pleading tone that Shran found quite hard to distinguish from whining. "Shenar and Vishri were taken as well. I didn't know what to do. I only knew that I had to make sure that *you* escaped and survived."

"*Me?*"

"You, Commander. So that someone could take some sort of action to recover my bondmates."

A low growl was slowly building deep within Shran's chest. "*That's* how you justify abandoning Jhamel?"

"What could I have done against the attackers? What could *any* of us have done?" Theras paused, as though allowing Shran time to assimilate the pain that was clearly audible behind his words. "You know that we Aenar are all committed pacifists, Commander."

Pacifists.

As much as he admired Jhamel's commitment to peace, Shran doubted that he would ever fully succeed in getting his mind around the concept of pacifism. Sometimes the choice was between fighting and dying. Otherwise scum like the Orions would inherit the universe.

But now was not the time to stage a philosophical debate, or to dwell on blame. Jhamel had been captured, or worse. The best-case scenario was that she was being sped away from Andoria at multiples of the speed of light at this very moment.

"All right," Shran said. "I *will* take action, starting now. First, I need to alert the Defense Force about what's happened here, just in case the Orions covered their tracks thoroughly enough to completely avoid detection on their way to and from Andoria's surface. Maybe the military can track down the slavers before they find buyers for their latest . . . acquisitions."

Shran closed his eyes, pained and enraged at the thought of his sweet, trusting Jhamel being condemned to the cruel uses of slavery at the hands of uncouth outworlders, the way her late brother had been.

"I pray that that this can be done," Theras said.

Shran took a tentative step forward, realizing that he would be as blind as the Aenar until they found their way out of the crevasse.

"Pray all you want," Shran said, clenching his right fist and ignoring the flaring pain of the burn on the back of his hand. "*After* you help me find my way back to my ship."

"What if the slavers have found your ship?"

Shran paused for a moment before replying. "Then *I'll* pray, Theras."

SIX

Sunday, February 9, 2155
ShiKahr, Vulcan

AS CAPTAIN JONATHAN ARCHER walked alongside Minister T'Pau through the corridors of the Vulcan High Command headquarters, he considered how very differently they had been received here today as compared to six months ago. The last time he'd been here, T'Pau was the fugitive leader of the Syrrannite political faction, and the High Command, led by the power-mad V'Las, was minutes away from starting an interstellar war with the Andorians.

After Archer had come into the Command chambers then, carrying not only the *Kir'Shara* artifact that contained within it the true teachings of Surak, but also holding the actual *katra* of Surak himself inside his head, things had changed radically for Vulcan and for its ruling body. V'Las was forcibly removed, and his Council disbanded. The new leader of Vulcan's civilian government, and its military affairs, now walked beside Archer.

"Here we are," Minister T'Pau said, coming to a halt and gesturing toward a chamber outside of which two large—and heavily armed—guards stood, their bare, muscular chests mostly exposed underneath wide silver tunics and sashes. She nodded to them, and their stances relaxed only slightly as they stepped farther apart.

"Does the *Kir'Shara* really require a clean room,

Minister?" Archer asked as they stepped through a pair of pressure doors and into a large, brightly lit, circular chamber. In the center of it, on a table, sat the meter-high pyramidal artifact that Archer had carried with him from its tomb underneath the T'Karath Sanctuary. The table was circular, and was ringed by an array of computer banks. Seated at a station in front of each computer screen was a Vulcan in white robes. Each of them were studying the symbols on their screens intently, and sometimes tapping data onto padd controls nearby.

T'Pau turned to Archer, one eyebrow slightly raised. "I would think that you, of all people, should understand the value of the *Kir'Shara*."

Archer smiled slightly. "I guess you're right," he said simply. Despite his long-held animosity toward the Vulcans, and his conviction that they had long held Earth back from making advancements in exploration, his time on Vulcan—largely spent while the soul of its greatest leader had literally lived *inside* him—had made him somewhat more attuned to Vulcan causes than he'd ever been before. He wasn't about to take up *kal-toh*, the bizarre Vulcan puzzle game that T'Pol had once shown him, but he did at least feel that he understood what the *Kir'Shara* represented to the Vulcan people: It was the embodiment of their highest ideals and aspirations, their living link with everything they regarded as noble and true.

"Thank you for showing me," he said. "I'm glad it's in good hands, and not in my backpack—or my *head*—any longer."

"Your aid in retrieving the artifact—however unintentional its cause—has not been lost on me," said T'Pau, her stony face betraying no acknowledgment of his jest as she turned away toward the door. "Nor on the many others who are presently organizing Vulcan's new government. Your actions have done much to solidify positive future relations between humans and Vulcans."

She stopped and looked up at him. "That is no small feat, Captain Archer. You have my thanks, and whenever possible, you will have my support."

"I appreciate that, Minister," he said. He knew she was referring to the twenty-three ships she had sent to help those battling the mysterious Romulan drone ship that threatened to destabilize interstellar politics and start a war between the Tellarites and the Andorians. At the time, he had been slightly annoyed that she had responded so frugally, but upon reflection, he realized that she had been truthful in telling him that this was all they could spare during Vulcan's protracted time of internal political upheaval and reorganization in the wake of V'Las's ouster.

T'Pau leading, the pair stepped back through the pressure doors and into the corridor. Waiting to meet them, as planned, were Trip and T'Pol.

"Is everything loaded, Trip?" Archer asked.

"It's all aboard the shuttlepod, Captain," Trip said. His usually amiable drawl sounded flat and lifeless today.

Archer turned to T'Pau. "Then I guess this is where we say good-bye for now."

T'Pau nodded and held up her right hand, spreading her fingers into an elegant V-shaped formation. "Live long and prosper," she said.

Archer, T'Pol, and Trip each returned the salute, and intoned the ancient Vulcan saying. Archer had always found the hand gesture difficult, but during the last six months it had become a good deal easier. *Maybe a little bit of Surak has rubbed off on me permanently,* he thought.

As the trio moved through the hallways to a docking pad and boarded Shuttlepod One to return to *Enterprise,*

Archer couldn't help noting not only that Trip and T'Pol were not talking much, but also that they both seemed to be going out their way to avoid making any kind of physical contact.

It's to be expected, I guess, Archer thought. He wondered how long the grieving process would take, and how it might affect his two top officers' behavior and duties aboard *Enterprise*. On the other hand, perhaps being back in the shipboard environment—with Vulcan and its newest grave receding light-years into the cosmic ocean—might be just what they needed to return them to normalcy . . . or whatever passed for it these days, given the volatile and unpredictable nature of their most recent missions.

Archer yawned as he studied the report on the padd that Crewman Baird had handed him when he went off shift. Archer had come to the bridge early, to relieve D.O., who had been fighting a stubborn viral infection since just prior to the Terra Prime incidents. He knew that it chafed the no-nonsense officer to have been out of action during that crisis, particularly when he'd left the less experienced Ensign Sato in charge of the bridge in his absence. Though Archer sympathized with D.O., he sometimes wondered idly whether she, like Hoshi, would have held off from firing on Terra Prime's Martian stronghold in those last, critical moments the landing party had needed to disable Terra Prime's weaponry and arrest John Frederick Paxton himself.

Hoshi had proven herself immensely valuable long before then, however, particularly during the time since the Xindi attack on Earth, when the hunt for Earth's alien attackers had been greatly abetted by her ability to decipher never-before-encountered languages. *Maybe it's finally time she got a promotion*, Archer thought, though he felt strongly that handing promotions out as though they were party favors tended to devalue their importance among the crew. *She's earned it. For that matter, more than a few others around here have earned it as well.*

He glanced over at Hoshi, who was working intently at her station. *Yes, maybe it is time for something positive to happen aboard this ship. Especially considering all the doom and gloom we've been facing lately.*

Almost as if on cue, Hoshi did a double take, then turned to look at Archer, her eyes wide.

"Captain, I have an emergency hail . . . from Shran."

Archer stood up and moved toward her. "Coming from where?"

At the helm, Mayweather tapped some controls and responded. "The signal is coming from a small vessel at extreme range, headed this way from Andorian space."

"Put him on the screen," Archer said.

As Hoshi tapped her console, the blue-hued face of the Andorian ex-Imperial Guardsman filled the bridge's forward viewscreen almost instantly.

"This is quite a surprise," Archer said, addressing the screen. "I thought it would be years before we saw you again, not months." The fact that Shran's left antenna evidently had yet to grow back completely reminded Archer of how recently the two men had last encountered one another.

"I'm sorry, pinkskin," Shran said in gravel-strewn tones. *"But it was essential that I leave Andoria and ask for your help."*

"You need *my* help?" Archer said, pacing toward Travis. *"It hasn't been that long. And as I recall, you still owe me a favor."*

Archer sighed. Shran was reminding him that he had saved *Enterprise* from destruction after the Vulcans had fired on the ship on the orders of V'Las. The captain hadn't been aboard at the time, but he owed the debt nonetheless.

"I remember. But this isn't a good time, Shran. It looks like Starfleet Command is planning to keep us pretty busy nursemaiding interstellar envoys over the next three weeks or so. I assume you know why."

Shran seemed almost irritated. *"I may no longer be a member of the Imperial Guard, but I'm aware of the proposed Coalition."*

"It's more than a proposal," Archer said. "We'll be on Earth three weeks from now to witness the official signing of the Coalition Compact."

Shran stared forward intently. *"As you say, the signing ceremony isn't for three weeks. If it even happens. If you give me the help I need, you'll be home in plenty of time."*

Archer laughed under his breath and turned his back to the screen, walking around Mayweather's station and back toward his command chair. "I'm afraid a detour is out of the question right now."

"Jhamel has been abducted . . . taken." Shran's voice was angry, his mien hard, his uneven antennae deployed like twin rapiers. *"You* owe *me."*

Archer turned back toward the screen, recalling the courage and ethereal beauty of the Aenar woman. Without her telepathic assistance, Romulan Admiral Valdore might have succeeded in destroying *Enterprise* with his remote-controlled drone ships last year.

"Who took her?"

Shran leaned forward slightly. *"Old 'mutual friends' of ours. Orion slavers. It's a long story. I'll explain when I meet up with you in person. You need to alter course."*

Archer looked over at T'Pol. Neither of the dealings they'd had with the Orion Syndicate lately had turned out particularly well; T'Pol had even been sold as one of their slaves not so long ago.

He sighed, then spoke to Mayweather, who regarded him expectantly. "Set a rendezvous course."

"Thank you, pinkskin," Shran said just before the

screen replaced his image with that of the starfield ahead.

Archer wondered exactly what trouble the Andorian had *really* gotten himself into, and exactly how much danger *Enterprise*'s crew was going to be in if they helped him out of it. And yet, despite the occasional scuffles, diplomatic errors, and *Ushaan* battles-to-the-death, Shran had always seemed to come out on Archer's side.

Archer could only hope that this time would prove no different.

"And I thought things must have gotten complicated for the Vissians, who had three genders," Trip said, putting his elbows on the table in the captain's mess, which had just been pressed into service as an impromptu conference room. "I'm sorry, I'm *still* stuck on the four sexes thing. Why is it we didn't already know about that?"

Shran, accompanied by an Aenar male whom Shran had introduced as Theras, had docked their small, battered civilian vessel with *Enterprise* approximately fifteen minutes earlier. During the last ten minutes or so, they had attempted to explain to Archer, Trip, T'Pol, and Malcolm the general mechanics of the Andorian marriage bond, in addition to the more urgent issue of the mass kidnapping of Aenar from their subterranean city on Andoria.

Four sexes to mate. Thaan, chan, zhen, *and* shen. *Bondmates.* Shelthreth *ceremonies.* Archer's thoughts were spinning as Theras spoke awkwardly, as though unused to using his voice, but nevertheless refraining from making telepathic contact out of deference to his nontelepathic hosts. All the while, Shran looked on with ill-concealed impatience.

"Wait," Archer said, putting up his hand. "You said that Jhamel was *your* bondmate, Theras, and that the other two were your third and fourth."

The albino Aenar turned toward Archer, his sightless eyes staring in the direction of the captain's voice. "Yes. Shenar and Vishri."

Archer turned toward Shran, puzzled. "Forgive me, Shran, but the last time I saw you and Jhamel, I got the distinct impression that the two of you . . ." He paused, embarrassed as he realized that he had strayed onto a subject likely to offend both his guests.

Theras surprised him by smiling. "Do not fear offending us, Captain," he said. "All of Jhamel's bond-mates are well aware of the feelings she and Shran have for one another. Since we're all telepathic, such emotions would be rather difficult to conceal. Therefore we do not begrudge them."

Shran, however, appeared to have far less equanimity about his relationship with Jhamel than did Theras. The Andorian looked guilty for a moment, his antennae drooping to either side. When he finally spoke, his voice was low. "I fell in love with Jhamel, Captain. But the biology and culture of our people—Andorian and Aenar alike—dictate certain realities. Jhamel had long ago been promised to a *shelthreth* group, and for the continuation of their family line, she needed to be there. But that didn't make our feelings for one other any easier to deny."

He looked over at T'Pol. "Vulcans have arranged marriages as well. Even certain human societies have had them. But sometimes, love between two beings can transcend what society or biology dictates, whether it's taboo or not."

Archer saw T'Pol stiffen slightly in reaction, but his first officer registered no other visible sign that Shran's words had had any effect on her.

Trip was less controlled in his response, sitting back in his chair, crossing his arms, and looking away with his jaw clenched. *Even blind Theras can see that Shran just hit Trip where he lives*, Archer thought. *And that's* without *the telepathy.*

Archer leaned forward and attempted to redirect the subject before it made the mood in the room even more tense than it had already become. "I think we understand what you're saying, Shran. Now tell us more about this Orion attack."

As the Andorian told the story of the interrupted *shelthreth* ceremony at the Aenar city, Archer watched his officers. Trip still seemed distant, and T'Pol stoic, but Malcolm seemed—not surprisingly—to be listening eagerly and expectantly.

After a few minutes of explanation, Shran finally settled back into his chair. "Due to my . . . loss of the *Kumari*, the Imperial Guard has been less than helpful on this matter. They wouldn't even grant me the use of a garbage scow and its crew, much less another military ship."

Theras spoke up. "We also suspect that those to whom we had to appeal may also have resented the time that Shran spent among the Aenar."

" 'Vacation among the pacifists' is not high on most Guard officers' 'to-do' lists," Shran said wryly. "So we used the craft I have now. Not very fast, and no weapons to speak of, but it can still follow a trail. We've been tracking the slavers for six days now. Their vessel has a unique warp signature."

"What I don't understand is why the Orions acted so boldly," Malcolm said, gesturing with his hands as if they were claws descending on prey. "Andoria's military isn't exactly known for its lack of readiness. Why would they directly attack a city there and risk capture . . . or worse?"

Theras turned in Reed's direction. "The relationship between the Aenar people and the Andorian majority is largely one of mutual suspicion. When you add to that the inherent conflict between our pacifistic beliefs and the frequent belligerence of the Imperial Guard, it's not hard to understand why the military isn't highly motivated to help us. During the conflicts against the Vulcans and the Tellarites over the past few years, Imperial Guard protection for the Aenar has waned to almost nothing. Given their predilections, it's highly likely that the Orions have kept abreast of these facts, and therefore saw us as easy prey."

"The Orions also appear to be taking advantage of local peculiarities in Andoria's magnetic field lines," Shran added. "The effect is most extreme at the poles, where the field is weakest and lets some of our star's solar wind actually reach the surface in places. The infall of charged particles obscures Andoria's planetary security sensors, and probably allowed the slavers to bring a small ship into the northern wastes completely undetected by the Imperial Guard."

"So now we know *how* they did it," Archer said. "But we still don't know *why* the Orions are kidnapping Aenar." He had already formulated an answer to that question, but he wanted to hear what the others thought before he articulated it.

T'Pol tilted her head, momentarily regarding him as a parent might an obtuse child. "It is logical to assume that the Aenar are not being used for physical labor, given their lack of a visual sense. However—"

"However, their telepathic abilities certainly give them a fair number of other uses for the slavers and their clients," Reed said, interrupting her in his evident enthusiasm to get to the bottom of the mystery.

Trip cleared his throat, then spoke for the first time in minutes. "What worries me is who the Orions' customers might be. The last time we ran into something like this it was the Romulans. What if these wholesale abductions mean that the Romulans are planning to send their drone ships against us again? With dozens of Aenar telepaths at their disposal instead of the one they had last time, they could do one hell of a lot of damage."

"My thoughts exactly," Shran said in somber tones.

T'Pol looked down at a padd in her hand. "The trajectory the Orion warp signature is following *does* point toward Romulan space."

"And about three dozen *other* star systems along the way," Reed said grumpily.

Archer sighed heavily and considered the points of their discussion so far. The conjecture certainly seemed plausible, and if there was some kind of massed droneship attack being planned, it was certainly going to spell trouble for someone. But for whom?

Which planet would the Romulans attack first, if that's really their plan? Will it be one of the core Coalition worlds? Or will it be a target in one of the nonaligned systems scattered between here and the Romulan Empire?

And therein lay the rub. They had no real proof of anything, other than the scanty evidence that Shran and Theras had provided them.

"Given the circumstances, and the lack of concrete information," Archer said finally, "I'm not sure I can justify devoting *Enterprise*'s resources to helping you, Shran."

Malcolm nodded. "Unless some more definitive evidence pointing to the Romulans emerges, I'm forced to agree."

Trip scowled, shaking his head in silent dissent, while T'Pol sat impassively, keeping her own counsel in typically Vulcan fashion. Archer had no doubt that at least one of them would insist on having words with him about this matter in private, and soon.

Shran stood up, his fists pounding the tabletop, his antennae rigid. "Captain, you *must* help us! If you don't, you will not only have dishonored your debt to me, but you also could be leaving your world and your allies exposed to a potentially lethal series of Romulan attacks."

Archer refused to allow himself to take the emotional bait, though he found it difficult not to respond in kind to Shran's increasingly bellicose tone. "Shran, it's that 'could be' that sticks for me. I will inform Starfleet Command, and report everything you've told me. But unless my superiors order me to pursue the Orions, I simply can't afford to go off on what could turn into a weeks-long interstellar chase. At least, not until after the Coalition Compact business is concluded back on Earth."

Shran's skin blushed a darker blue, and he closed his lips tightly, glaring at Archer. Finally, he said, "I am asking you, as an ally, as someone who has fought beside you, *and* against you, to help me find Jhamel."

Archer glanced briefly at Theras, who seemed to stare at him expressionlessly with those milky, unseeing eyes. He wondered if the Aenar really was as flaccid and lacking in will as he appeared. Though he might well still have been in shock over the abduction of his bondmates, Theras seemed as unmoved by their plight as he'd been by Shran's earlier declaration of affection for Jhamel.

"We have to be back to Earth in three weeks for the signing ceremony," Archer said. "Unless Starfleet issues new orders, that's nonnegotiable. In the meantime, I don't think we can risk doing anything—including provoking the Orions—that might cause a major disruption to the Coalition. But I will *consider* all the facts—as you have presented them—and discuss with my superiors and my officers what can be done about your request. In the meantime, you and Theras should take some time for a shower and get some food in the mess. Trip can also assign you an engineer if your ship needs any repairs or supplies."

Shran continued to glare at Archer as Theras moved his chair back and stood. As soon as he moved aside,

Shran stepped forward and put his hands on the table's edge, then leaned in toward Archer.

"I'd advise you not to waste too much time 'considering,' pinkskin. The slavers already have a six-day head start *now*. They're on the move, heading toward the Romulans, with fresh munitions for their war machine. And one of those munitions—whether I can have her or not—is the woman I love."

Shran strode angrily toward the door, then turned back around to regard the room from the open doorway. "You worry about what you risk by pursuing the Orions." His voice sounded as cold as Andoria's northern wastes. "But be certain that you *also* concern yourself with the danger to the Coalition of Planets should you choose to ignore what I've told you."

Shran stormed out of the captain's mess, with Theras following meekly behind him.

Archer felt himself shudder involuntarily. Shran's final comment could be interpreted either as a warning about the Romulans or as a threat from Shran himself.

He had no doubt that the passionate Andorian, even though stripped of both his rank and his ship, could indeed be quite a formidable foe. . . .

SEVEN

The early twenty-fifth century
Terrebonne Parish, Louisiana

JAKE SISKO REACHED FORWARD with his right hand, tapping a symbol on one of the pair of padds sitting next to each other on the desk. They had already paused the other moments ago. Nog had brought both of the devices with him, since they had sizable holo-imagers built into them. The effect was like having simultaneous mini-holodecks running side by side, like bizarre living dollhouses. Except this time, though the story began the same for both, the divergences were notable.

He turned toward Nog. "Okay, this is *weird*. Not alternate universe weird, but it's not adding up right."

Nog nodded, his mouth full after taking a hefty gulp of his wine. Swallowing, he said, "I knew you'd be intrigued."

Jake shook his head. "I don't know if I'm intrigued, or just plain troubled."

"Well, it's not the first time hew-mon history has gotten distorted," Nog said. "Look at Zefram Cochrane. He's still hailed as a great hero at the Academy, even though Troi's memoir describes him as more of a scared, drunken genius than the larger-than-life figure everybody thinks they know."

"Yeah, but this is *more* than that," Jake said, reaching for his glass. "Cochrane's *personality* was one thing; we're seeing whole sequences of history that are different from the version that just about everybody accepts."

Jake's stomach gurgled suddenly, and he realized that he hadn't eaten yet. Rena often joked that if she wasn't around, he'd starve to death and be eaten by the cat before anyone found him. "Excuse my rumbling," he said. "I'm going to fix myself a sandwich. Do you want anything to eat?"

"What local delicacy would be good with a pinot noir?" Nog thought for a moment, then grinned. "Do you have any fresh nutria?"

Jake blanched. "Ugh! Not unless you want to go out in the bayou and try to catch them. I can replicate you some, if you really have your heart set on it."

"Won't taste quite the same as the wild version, but I suppose it'll have to do," Nog said, his shoulders drooping in mock resignation.

Jake stood up and began walking toward the kitchen, rolling his shoulder to try to work a kink out of it. "You know, Nietzsche said, 'History is nothing more than the belief in the senses, the belief in falsehood.' I wouldn't be surprised if a significant amount of what we think we know to be true in our own histories could be represented completely differently two hundred years from now."

He unwrapped a loaf of bread and sliced two pieces from it with a serrated knife from a wooden rack on the kitchen's tidy counter. "I remember Dad once telling me about the American presidents, pre-World War III. He said that history always told people that George Washington was the father of the United States, and that he had been the first president of this country. But there were actually over a dozen men that preceded him, although their powers were different and they were called 'President of the United States in Congress Assembled.'"

Nog had followed Jake to the kitchen. "You hewmons and your territorialism. You think the history of the Grand Naguses is any different?" He smiled widely.

"You should hear some of the 'facts' about even *recent* history I've been told during my visits to Ferenginar. Some of what's being taught to my younger brother and sisters about Rom sounds almost like a fairy tale."

"Well, you have your world, I have mine," Jake said, slicing some salami he'd pulled from the refrigeration unit. "I knew that World War III had pretty much caused havoc with files and data back in the twenty-first century, but I don't think—I *didn't* think that Earth's history could have gotten so messed up since then."

Nog picked up the salami log and sniffed at it, then wrinkled his nose as if in disgust. "This smells awful." He took another sniff. "Why don't you go ahead and make me a sandwich from it as well?"

Jake snorted a laugh and reached for the loaf of bread. "So, history is being rewritten all over the place, and this is no different, is that what we're saying?"

Nog put his hands up, protesting. "Not *me*. I think there's something more to this."

"Okay, so returning to the mystery at hand, the accepted holoprogram of 2161 says that Shran was a military hero who disgraced himself in private business and had to fake his own death," Jake said as he continued cutting the sandwich fixings. "And that he had a five-year-old daughter with Jhamel, whom he had met in 2154, and that it was their daughter that was kidnapped. The new holoprogram, that is reported to be from data recorded in 2155, says that Shran was disgraced due to the destruction of his ship, wasn't even one of Jhamel's bondmates, and therefore had produced no children with her, and reports that *Jhamel* was actually the one who got kidnapped."

Nog nodded, watching Jake cut the salami. "I don't think Shran is the real focus of this mystery, though. I think it's Commander Tucker. More of the foul-smelling meat, please?"

Jake looked at his friend and affected a perplexed expression. "Commander Tucker has exactly *what* to do with foul meat? Oh, you want more on your sandwich." He gamely sliced off a few more pieces, then began assembling the sandwiches with a graceful economy of movement he'd picked up over the years he'd spent working in his grandfather Joseph's restaurant in New Orleans. "*Thanks* for spoiling the surprise for me, Nog. You, of course, have *seen* all this already, so you know what's coming."

Nog shook his head. "Actually, I haven't seen all of it yet. But I *did* watch and read through enough of it to get the basic gist before I decided to journey out here to see you."

Jake cut the sandwiches in half, then slid the knife under them and transferred them to small plates. He handed one to Nog. "Here. Feed yourself, and *don't* spoil any more surprises for me."

"So, you don't want to hear about the—"

Jake put a hand up over Nog's mouth, and glared at him sternly. "*No.* I've already gotten my history through one filter, and now I'm seeing it through another. I don't need to hear yet another version through the Nog-filter."

He picked up his plate and his wineglass and padded toward the desk, a similarly encumbered Nog trailing after him.

"Boy, you can be as grumpy as your dad sometimes," Nog said, almost under his breath.

"You don't know the half of it," Jake said, sitting down in his comfortable writing chair and setting his sandwich to the side. His hand trembled slightly as he moved to activate the padds again.

"Now hush up, and let's see what comes next."

EIGHT

Day Twenty-One, Month of Tasmeen
Somewhere in Romulan space

DOCTOR EHREHIN WAS AWAKENED in the semidarkness by a hard jolt of confusion. He was unsure for the moment exactly where he was as he rose slowly in his bed, his back protesting as he moved carefully to a sitting position.

"Cunaehr?" he called out, then listened attentively to the silence that answered.

At length he rose from the bed and cinched his robe tightly about his slight frame, tiny lightning bolts of pain assaulting his lower spine. Ignoring the familiar discomfort, he padded barefoot across the thick white carpet toward the heavy curtains that lined the richly appointed bedroom's wide transparisteel window. He pulled on the sash, letting in the wan of light of the dawn that was just beginning to tease the horizon of this arid, relatively undeveloped planet.

Then, all in rush, he remembered where he was: safely ensconced inside one of the secret government villas on Nelvana III. It was the same place in which he had awakened with a quite similar jolt of confusion every morning since the drive-test mishap at the Unroth facility. He was beginning to believe that he would continue to arise each daybreak in temporary bewilderment, at least until such time as his project support people finally finished putting right the Unroth mess, so that the various tests and analyses could begin to go forward again.

Perhaps that time would arrive soon, since at the moment he truthfully could not recall just how many confusing mornings had passed since the Romulan military had brought him to Nelvana to recuperate in this isolated if luxurious estate.

"Cunaehr?" Ehrehin repeated, after turning away from the window to face the door at the broad bedroom's opposite side. Still no one answered. Perhaps none of the staff had risen as yet. But that didn't explain the lack of response of his bodyguards.

"Cunaehr?" Cunaehr, his beloved favorite student and assistant, would never have abandoned him this way.

Ehrehin stopped short, recalling in a sudden wash of grief that Cunaehr would never answer him again. *If that really* was *Cunaehr I saw with his head smashed in back at the lab on Unroth,* he thought.

He raised a withered hand to a throbbing temple. Why was everything becoming so damned confusing?

Ehrehin was startled out of his musings by a noise that seemed to come from the still dimly lit hallway in front of him. A footfall?

Breakfast, perhaps, he thought, suddenly eager to get on with his normal activities.

He crossed the room quietly and entered the plushly carpeted hallway.

And realized with a start that a pair of large, dark-clad figures stood in his way. Behind them an indistinct figure lay slumped between the carpeted hallway and the tile floor of one of the villa's kitchens.

Ehrehin scowled as he looked over each of the men. "You're not Cunaehr," he said finally, addressing them both. "Have you come to bring my breakfast?" It was only then that he noticed that neither man carried a tray, cups, or any other food-related accoutrements.

The man on the left raised a dark, blunt shape that Ehrehin recognized as a military-issue disruptor pistol, after spending a brief beat puzzling over it. The other man carried one as well.

"Are you my new bodyguard detachment?" Ehrehin said.

"Yes," said the man on the right after an awkward pause. "Yes, we are."

Ehrehin took a cautious step backward, but froze when the man on the left brandished his weapon in a menacing fashion.

"Get dressed quickly and quietly, Doctor," he said. "You are coming with us."

When Subcommander D'tran entered Valdore's office, the admiral presumed that he had come to convey the next in D'tran's series of *dierha*-by-*dierha* intelligence updates. Then Valdore spared a quick glance at the wall chronometer that overlooked the desk behind which he had spent so much of his working life. The admiral saw at once that the other man had actually turned up nearly a quarter-*dierha* early.

And from the look on the middle-aged subcommander's pale, lined face, he had come bearing tidings that he wasn't eager to impart.

"Report, Subcommander," Valdore snapped, having no patience with such stalling. "Just tell me what's gone wrong."

D'tran took a deep breath. "It's Doctor Ehrehin, Admiral. We have . . . lost him, sir."

Valdore instantly could see every tactical timetable that he had constructed since his release from imprisonment crashing like an incoming meteor. He rose to his feet, pushing his desk chair toward the weapons-lined wall several long paces behind him. He leaned forward across the desktop, planting both of his muscular arms on the sherawood surface to support himself. "Do you mean to tell me the doctor has *died*, Subcommander?"

Somehow, the cowering subcommander avoided taking a step backward. "No, sir. At least, not that we can determine for certain. But I have just confirmed that Ehrehin has been taken from his secure compound, apparently by members of a Romulan dissident group. We are not entirely certain as yet which group is responsible, since no one has spoken up to take 'credit' for this crime."

Evidently it was an unusually competent *dissident group,* Valdore thought as he released a frustrated sigh. Who knew how far this could set back the development schedule for the new stardrive?

Aloud, he said, "Get me the officers directly responsible for safeguarding Doctor Ehrehin. And see to it that his captors are tracked down. Spare absolutely *no* effort, Subcommander."

"At once," said D'tran, who appeared more than eager to leave Valdore's presence and set about his urgent tasks. "May I take my leave of you, sir?"

Another thought suddenly occurred to Valdore. "Wait," he said, and paused just long enough to let the subcommander realize that another order was forthcoming. "What is the status of the Aenar slaves the Adigeons are brokering for us?"

D'tran regarded him with a somewhat curious expression. "Still en route to our intermediaries on Adigeon Prime, sir."

"But *still* no firm estimated time of arrival?" This was another matter that Valdore was finding increasingly vexing. "What is causing these continual delays?"

"Our intermediaries are blaming the Orions, sir. They are evidently the procurers whom the Adigeons have retained to acquire the . . . commodity in question. And the Orions seem to be making numerous other stops and connections on their way to the delivery point for our cargo."

"I now need those telepaths sooner rather than later, Subcommander," Valdore said in a low growl. "They could well turn out to be our only hope of tracking down Ehrehin and his captors." The time had come to take a few drastic measures.

"Subcommander," Valdore continued, "I want you to explain to our 'esteemed intermediaries' on Adigeon that their continued safe passage through Romulan space depends greatly upon my continued patience and good-will. And have them expedite the arrival of those telepaths any way they can."

"Immediately, sir," the subcommander said, then snapped off a smart salute and exited the office.

Valdore stood alone in the room for a protracted moment, then walked to the wall at the rear of his office where he kept his many edged weapons on display, now that he had retrieved them from the locker where they had been so haphazardly stored during his long confinement. With care and reverence, he took down his *dathe'anofv-sen*—his Honor Blade—which gleamed brightly again now that he had finally found the time to remove the faint patina of tarnish it had picked up in the dank, subterranean storage room. He placed the blade and its scabbard carefully on his uniform belt, straightened his posture, then exited the office to report the latest developments to T'Leikha.

He wondered how much more would be permitted to go wrong before the First Consul required him to allow the Honor Blade to drink deep of his lifeblood.

NINE

Sunday, February 9, 2155
Enterprise NX-01

THE SILVER-HAIRED EMINENCE stared impassively from across the approximately sixteen light-years that separated him from Archer's ready room aboard *Enterprise*.

"That's essentially what happened, sir," Archer said to Admiral Sam Gardner. "Based, of course, on what Shran and Theras told us."

His tie slightly askew, the admiral folded his arms in front of himself, displaying the heavily braided sleeves on his dark uniform jacket. *"Captain, it sounds to me that you aren't entirely convinced by Commander Shran's assertion that the Orion slavers' action against the Aenar represents a prelude to a large-scale Romulan military incursion."*

Seated behind the cramped ready room's small desk, Archer continued to stare straight into his computer monitor, despite the distraction of his chief engineer's fidgeting; Trip was standing just inside the admiral's line of sight, alongside a far more tranquil, but no less serious-visaged T'Pol. Trip had already made it clear that he vehemently agreed with Shran's assessment, and Archer couldn't fault him for that, so long as he maintained respect for the chain of command. And, truth be told, Archer felt no small amount of guilt for allowing his upcoming diplomatic duties to keep him from simply rushing into the breach on Shran's behalf.

Whether or not the Romulans really are about to attack us, Shran is definitely right about at least one thing,

Archer thought. *I do owe him.* After all, he hadn't forgotten the rescue on Coridan, or the Andorian's invaluable help against both the Xindi and the Romulans, or Shran's admirable restraint when V'Las had tried to start a Vulcan-Andorian war.

On top of all that, Archer still felt a small pang of regret for having sliced off one of Shran's antennae with an *Ushaan* blade. The incident had occurred at the time of last November's Babel conference and the previous Romulan crisis—so recently, in fact, that Shran's missing antenna had still only partially grown back. Though he knew that the truncated antenna would probably finish regenerating itself within another month or two, Archer would always suspect that the humiliation associated with the loss would take a good deal longer to heal.

Archer nodded tentatively toward Gardner's image. "Let's just say I'm . . . concerned, Admiral. I think that Starfleet should investigate the matter as thoroughly as possible, if there's any chance at all that Shran may be right—"

"Captain," the admiral said, interrupting. *"Neither Starfleet nor Earth's government—all the way up to Minister al-Rashid, and even Nathan Samuels himself—can afford to risk sending the fleet's flagship off on what could very well turn into a lengthy and distracting snipe hunt. Not with the Coalition Compact signing ceremonies coming up so soon. And* certainly *not on the basis of such inconclusive evidence."*

The longer Gardner spoke, the more Archer felt his spine stiffen—and the more he was coming around to Trip's way of thinking. "Respectfully, Admiral, the signing ceremony is three weeks away—"

Gardner interrupted again, causing Archer to bristle further. *"The galaxy is a* very *big place, Captain Archer. And, unfortunately, the slave trade afflicts a fair chunk of it."*

"Perhaps you've just identified a very good reason for us to stay out here and do something about it, Admiral," Archer said, carefully schooling his tone to a fairly convincing degree of calm.

Gardner nettled Archer still further by grinning indulgently. *"I would have thought that four years out on the frontier would have taught you a little more patience, Captain."*

Archer returned the admiral's grin, but with considerably lower wattage. "Patience. Never had much time for it. Sir."

"Captain. Jonathan." Gardner appeared to be changing his tack, trying to appear reasonable, rather than patronizing or outright authoritarian. *"You've been around long enough to know how lawless most of the galaxy is. You and I both know it's filled to overflowing with slave traders, pirates, gangsters, smugglers, and soldiers-for-hire. The best chance we have of doing anything substantive about that sad reality is the Coalition of Planets. Therefore it's my duty, and yours as well, to do* nothing *that might conceivably make any of the prospective members any more nervous about entering the alliance than they already are—at least until* after *the Compact is finalized and signed."*

Not for the first time, Archer breathed a silent prayer of thanks to the fates that Starfleet Command had seen fit to entrust *Enterprise* to him instead of to Gardner.

The Admiral continued: *"And that includes taking risks that might provoke the Orion Syndicate into embargoing any of the Coalition worlds with which they currently do business, such as Coridan or Tellar. Adopting an overly aggressive posture against the Romulans right now is a similarly bad idea, since we don't yet understand all the repercussions for the allies should hostilities break out within the next three weeks."*

Trip, who was already fairly vibrating with repressed frustration, had apparently reached the limits of his patience. "Admiral, does your list of 'don'ts' include leaving our collective ass exposed to a Romulan sneak attack? That's *one* 'repercussion' that's fairly easy to see."

"Trip!" Archer snapped, turning toward his engineer and rising from his chair.

"You have something you'd like to share, Commander Tucker?" Gardner asked. Though he hadn't raised his voice, he no longer sounded as though he wanted to play reasonable.

"I do, Admiral," Trip said, almost snarling as he stepped toward the computer on Archer's desk. "Sir, have you even *read* the report I filed about the Romulans' invisible mine field? It was a clear and present danger back when we found it, and I'd bet my commission that the Romulans haven't gotten any friendlier in the two and a half years that have gone by since. They've even tried to install invisibility cloaks on their ships, and if they ever perfect *that*—" Trip's anger-besotted features posed a remarkable contrast to T'Pol's expression of slightly surprised calm.

"Commander," Archer ordered, "that's enough."

Though still red-faced, Trip nodded to Archer and looked contrite as he stepped back beside T'Pol.

"I apologize, Admiral," Archer said as he turned back to the screen in front of the desk. He barely resisted an urge to ask the admiral if he *had* actually read Trip's report on the cloaked Romulan mines, though he strongly suspected that he already knew the answer.

"It's already forgotten, Captain," Gardner said, putting on an almost amiable smile. *"We'll chalk it up to garbled communications and leave it at that."*

Archer cast a quick warning glance back at Trip, who took the hint and remained silent.

"Carry on with your present orders, Captain. I look forward to seeing you all at the Coalition Compact ceremonies three weeks from now."

"Thank you, sir." Archer knew when he was being shut up and shown the door without having to hear it in so many words.

"*Gardner out.*" The silver-haired visage abruptly disappeared from the screen, to be replaced by the white-on-blue Earth-and-laurel-leaf insignia of the United Earth government.

Archer turned his chair toward T'Pol and Trip. "Well. That's that. Gardner is obviously taking no chances. He's not going to risk doing anything that might rock the boat." He turned a hard gaze upon Trip. "And he obviously must think I'm running a pirate ship, judging from the discipline around here."

Trip was shame-faced. "Sorry, Captain. I opened my mouth without engaging my brain first. As usual."

Archer couldn't help but smile at that. "I'm not keeping score, Trip. There isn't a tote board big enough. But for what it's worth, I think you're probably right about the Romulans. You had me half-convinced when we spoke after we met with Shran and Theras."

"If you don't mind my asking," Trip said, "what brought you the rest of the way to my side of the argument?"

Archer hiked a thumb over his shoulder toward his computer screen. "Admiral Gardner, and his self-inflicted blind spot. I wonder how many times in history some avoidable catastrophe was allowed to happen only because the leaders at the time were in complete denial about its existence."

Trip nodded, somber. "I suppose the question now is, What do we do about it?"

"Trip, I'm not sure there is anything we *can* do," Archer said with a resigned sigh. "Not without violating direct Starfleet orders."

"But the Romulans are obviously up to no good, Captain." Trip's earlier frustrated tone had returned full force. "And I'd wager that they aren't going to just sit on their hands until the Coalition has finished dotting all its i's and crossing all its t's."

"Do you suppose, Commander," T'Pol said with her customary coolness, "that your opinion regarding the Romulans might have been shaded by your recent brush with death inside one of their drone ships?"

Trip regarded her in contemplative silence for a long moment, frowning. At length, he said, "Well, I won't deny that that incident got my attention, big-time. But it doesn't undercut the possibility that the Romulans have just collected enough Aenar telepaths to pull the same trick again, dozens of times, and in dozens of places. In my book, that fact alone puts them on a very short list of nominees for the next big threat against Earth."

Archer couldn't disagree, though he still had to admit that he, Trip, and Shran still could neither prove anything nor sway the powers that be to take any preventive action.

Recalling the suddenness of the horrific Xindi attack, Archer hoped it wouldn't already be too late by the time his superiors finally became convinced.

Lying on the narrow bed in his quarters, his shoulders propped up by a pile of none-too-soft Starfleet-issue pillows, Archer idly tossed a water-polo ball against one of the four walls of his spartan cabin. Lying in the far corner with his face on his outstretched paws, Archer's beagle Porthos watched the captain intently.

T'Pol was standing beside Archer, resolutely refusing, as usual, to sit in either of the room's two simple, gray Starfleet-issue chairs. He wondered if his first officer found the chairs uncomfortable or if she wasn't simply trying to keep her distance from Porthos, whose scent she had often said she found disagreeable.

"If we're late for the ceremony, it will have far-reaching consequences," she said finally, clearly not content to leave the matter of the Aenar mass kidnapping alone until Archer had resolved it one way or the other.

Archer frowned, annoyed to be reminded yet again of the impending diplomatic event on Earth. "If Shran hadn't helped us, I never would've gotten aboard the Xindi weapon. Have you forgotten that? This alliance is based on friendship and loyalty—exactly what Shran is looking for right now."

After a beat of silence, she said, very quietly, "I don't trust him."

"You don't trust *Andorians*," he said, his annoyance escalating another notch. "The Vulcan Council is a little more enlightened. If *they're* willing to forge an alliance with Andoria, the least *you* can do is give Shran the benefit of the doubt."

Though her Vulcan poise seemed to remain in place, Archer sensed that she was shrinking from his words, rebuked. He tried to soften his tone somewhat as he continued, "When we met four years ago, I didn't trust *you*. For that matter, I didn't trust *any* Vulcans. You helped me get past that, remember?" He paused, struggling for the words that would best explain the decision he'd just made. "I can't turn my back on him, T'Pol. Try to understand."

"I'll try," she said.

Porthos chose that moment to leap up onto the bed and into Archer's lap with an enthusiastic *woof*. The captain tossed the water-polo ball aside and gave the beagle an affectionate scratch between the ears. T'Pol quietly edged away from Porthos, though she seemed to be making a concerted effort to be discreet about showing her persistent aversion to the dog.

Setting Porthos aside, Archer rose from the bed and crossed to the room's small refrigeration unit, from which he extracted several small morsels of sharp cheddar cheese. He tossed them to Porthos, one at a time, and each piece vanished before hitting the deck, like skeet being launched and vaporized on a MACO phase-rifle range. Porthos sat up, his tail thumping against the deck in gratitude, his dark eyes regarding Archer expectantly.

"That's all for today. Phlox says you need to watch your serum cholesterol."

The beagle half growled and half whined in disappointment as Archer walked to the wall-mounted com unit beside which T'Pol was standing. He pushed the large button in the panel's center.

"Archer to Lieutenant O'Neill."

"O'Neill here, sir," came the third watch commander's crisp reply.

Archer's eyes locked with T'Pol's.

"Change our heading, Lieutenant. We're going into Andorian space. Best speed."

"Sir?"

"I want to follow the trail of that Orion slave ship. Ensign Sato will inform Shran and Theras. Commander Tucker and Lieutenant Reed will coordinate our efforts with theirs. Shran will provide us with the vessel's warp-signature profile for our sensor scans."

"Aye, sir."

"Archer out." He pressed the button again, closing the channel, then headed for the door.

"Captain," T'Pol said.

He turned to face her, pausing in the open doorway. "Yes?"

"Permission to speak freely, sir?"

"Always." He stepped back toward her.

"I can't help but wonder whether you had already made your mind up to help Shran before you contacted Admiral Gardner."

Archer allowed himself an enigmatic smile. "I can see how it might look that way."

"Indeed. Especially given the fact that you never came right out and asked the admiral for his permission to investigate the mass Aenar kidnapping."

"I suppose you also noticed that Gardner never exactly ordered me *not* to go after the slavers. All he said was that he couldn't order me to do it."

She raised an eyebrow and a look rather like a smirk twisted her lips. "I will remember to mention that when I appear as a character witness at your court-martial."

Archer couldn't have been more stunned had she drawn a phase pistol on him and fired. "That's remarkable, T'Pol. Did you . . . did you just make a joke?"

"For your sake, sir, I certainly hope so."

Was that another one? he thought as he opened his door again. He let his enigmatic smile glide right into a mischievous grin as he walked back into the doorway.

"Sometimes," he said over his shoulder as T'Pol followed him, "it's a lot easier to beg for forgiveness than to ask for permission."

As he entered the corridor and headed toward the central turbolift that led to the bridge, he wryly considered one day proposing that aphorism as a new Starfleet regulation.

TEN

Monday, February 10, 2155
Enterprise **NX-01**

MALCOLM REED WATCHED as Tucker raised the shot glass toward the broad crew mess hall window as though toasting the still mostly unexplored interstellar wilderness that lay beyond it. He drained it in a single swallow, appearing to relish the way it burned as it went down. He set the empty glass onto the tabletop with a resounding *thwack* beside the bottle of Skagaran Lone Star tequila.

"I think that stuff might do a better job of scrubbing your plasma conduits than whatever it is you're using now, Trip," Reed said. Besides Commander Tucker, Reed thought he might well be the only other off-duty soul still awake at this ungodly hour. Malcolm had also ceased filling his own shot glass perhaps ten minutes earlier, leaving it upended before him in a silent gesture of surrender.

"I think maybe I'll pass your suggestion along to Lieutenant Burch," Trip said, making a sour face as he pushed both the bottle and his own glass closer to the center of the tabletop. "Besides, a hangover probably won't make me any more persuasive to Admiral Gardner, or anybody else in Starfleet Command. Hell, T'Pol didn't want to hear me out even when I was sober."

Reed thought Trip's decision to forgo the remaining tequila was a wise one. But he also knew that the decisions that lay ahead would require a good deal more than just wisdom.

"For whatever it's worth, Trip, I think your analysis of the Aenar kidnapping is spot on, T'Pol notwithstanding. Are you going to keep trying to persuade the brass that the Romulans are the ones behind it?"

"What choice do I have?" Trip said, sounding almost belligerent. "You've done the math the same way I have, Malcolm. What the hell would *you* do in my place?"

Reed held up a placating hand. "I'm on your side, Trip. Remember?"

Trip slumped back into his chair and released a heavy sigh. "I'm sorry, Malcolm. I know you are. It's just that we've shown Gardner that the Romulans pose what could be the biggest threat that Earth or any of our new allies have ever faced—and he just doesn't want to hear it because it's *inconvenient* for him."

Reed completely agreed with the commander's assessment, and he shared his friend's frustration, if not his present level of inebriation. "Do you suppose there's any chance of changing his mind?"

"Not very damned likely. The captain says the only thing that's likely to persuade Gardner is the kind of evidence that swoops in from space and blows up whole cities."

Reed nodded quietly. "What about contacting other admirals in Starfleet Command? Like maybe Douglas or Black? Or even Clark or Palmieri?"

"You mean make an end run around Gardner?" Trip didn't sound very happy at that prospect either. "Well, I suppose career suicide is *one* option, Malcolm. Maybe it'll turn out to be the *only* one." He leaned forward morosely and very deliberately grabbed both the bottle and his shot glass, dragging them toward him across the beads of alcohol he had left on the otherwise spotless tabletop.

Gardner is a blind man, Reed thought as he watched his friend pour himself another drink. *Thank goodness*

Captain Archer is at least conducting a low-profile investigation. But what if next time it's someone who isn't willing to buck the system? It looks like other players will have to become involved in this game if Starfleet Command is going to wake up in time.

Reed decided the time had come to play what might turn out to be Earth's hole card. Speaking quietly, he said, "Before you seriously contemplate charging into Starfleet Headquarters and wrecking your career, I think you'd be wise to call somebody else I know."

Trip paused in mid-swallow, setting his drink down half intact. "Who?"

Reed spared a moment to glance around the dimly lit mess hall, confirming again that no one else was present. When he turned his gaze back upon Trip, he spoke in a voice that was scarcely louder than a whisper.

"Someone who'll probably listen to your warnings very attentively. And might even be able to act on them."

Even though it is *somebody I swore I'd never deal with again if I could help it,* Reed thought. *But desperate times need desperate deeds.*

Trip pushed both the bottle and his half-consumed drink away again. "I'm listening, Malcolm."

Reed nodded, drew a deep breath, settled back into his chair, and told him.

And hoped all the while that he hadn't just made the biggest mistake of his entire life.

Taking a seat behind the desk in his quarters, Trip looked blearily up at the wall chronometer over the door to his quarters. His shift was to start in just under three hours.

He adjusted the angle of the data terminal before him so that he faced it directly, activated it, and inserted the data card Malcolm had given him. Time stretched for several seconds as the black screen briefly turned sky blue while the ship's com system followed the data card's protocols for establishing a secure connection with the particular subspace frequency the tactical officer had provided.

A dark-haired, middle-aged man appeared on the screen, apparently seated in a perfectly ordinary office. Trip could see the man clearly only from the chest up, noting that he wore a tailored deep brown jacket made of a leatherlike fabric. The man appeared far too rested to be completely believable, prompting Trip to wonder which Earth time zone the other man called home.

The face on the screen displayed a look of mildly surprised recognition upon seeing Trip's face. *"Commander Tucker."*

Trip nodded. "Harris, I presume?"

"The very same, Commander. What can I do for you? And why are you contacting me?"

"As opposed to Malcolm, you mean."

"Lieutenant Reed and I have had a long relationship. Since you're on this frequency, I'm assuming he's taken you into his confidence about me."

"According to Malcolm, that 'relationship' is strictly past tense, Harris."

Harris's lips curved upward slightly in an ironic smile. *"I've heard that from him on more than one occasion. It's become quite a familiar refrain by now."* Then his dark eyes narrowed and focused on Trip as though he could see him directly, without the intermediary of a subspace transceiver. *"But I'm sure you aren't contacting me in the middle of your ship's night just to talk about the past. In fact, I happen to know that you're a great deal more concerned about the future."*

"Concerned" is a nice understatement, Trip thought. Aloud, he said, "It's about the Romulans."

Harris's expression turned grave as Trip struggled to organize his thoughts. *"Go on, Commander."*

Here goes, Trip thought, taking a deep breath. "Earth and all the other Coalition planets are in serious danger. The Romulans are planning to move against us in a big way. And soon."

Harris displayed a degree of emotional control that T'Pol probably would have admired. *"Do your colleagues aboard* Enterprise *concur with your opinion?"*

"Malcolm is with me on this. And so's Captain Archer."

"But not Starfleet Command, I gather."

"You must have been eavesdropping on us, Harris."

Harris smiled benignly. *"You're quite the flatterer, Commander. But it isn't all that hard to guess that the brass hats might not want to look too closely at any inconvenient truths for the next few weeks. At least not until the Coalition Compact is finalized and signed. I'm sure Admiral Gardner doesn't want to be responsible for spooking the various Coalition delegations."*

"That's my take on things, too," Trip said, nodding. It hadn't escaped his notice that Harris had never explicitly denied his charge of eavesdropping—and the idea was making all the small hairs on the back of his neck slowly rise to attention even as he continued speaking. "Are you aware of the mass kidnapping of Aenar telepaths from Andoria last week?"

"We are, Commander. And we clearly see a Romulan hand in that action, even though they tried very hard to cover their tracks by going through intermediaries. We have no doubt that the Romulans plan to use those telepaths to revive their telepresence drone warship program, and on a considerable scale.

"But that isn't the end of it. Our intelligence sources show strong indications that the Romulans are on the verge of perfecting a new generation of starships, vessels capable of reaching speeds of at least warp seven."

Trip couldn't keep his jaw from falling open. "Warp

seven," he said quietly. Five years after the launch of *Enterprise*, Earth was still working the remaining kinks out of Henry Archer's warp *five* engine. "That puts them even with the Coridan shipyards."

Harris nodded. *"Even Coridan will be hard-pressed to counter a Romulan invasion of Coalition territory, which we believe is coming soon."*

"A warp-seven drive would use one hell of a lot of power," Trip said, running power-curve calculations in his head.

"Agreed. And that means that the Romulans will need to get their hands on huge quantities of dilithium—which the Coridan system planets have in far greater abundance than any of the other Coalition worlds do."

"So Coridan must be the Romulans' first target," Trip said, swallowing hard. "For lots of reasons."

"Once the Romulans annex the most productive dilithium mines in known space, the Coalition wouldn't stand a chance of resisting strikes from a Coridan beachhead. Tellar, Andoria, even Vulcan would fall like dominoes following a long war of attrition, bolstered by Coridan's captured resources and the Romulan expansion ethic."

"And then Earth." Trip's voice was pitched barely above a whisper.

"It certainly isn't a pretty picture, Commander."

Trip gripped the sides of his desk tightly. His head was spinning, and only in part because of all the tequila he'd just consumed with Malcolm.

"How do you know all this, Harris?"

When Harris responded, his tone remained patient, almost like that of a college professor conducting an introductory lecture. Or perhaps, Trip thought, like a very slick salesman.

"As Lieutenant Reed has no doubt already told you, Commander, I am part of an organization that has access to numerous intelligence networks and other resources,

including some not immediately available either to Starfleet or most of the other agencies of United Earth's government."

"And is that who you represent? Earth's government?"

"I suppose the answer to that question depends upon whom you ask. Let's just say we represent Earth's long-term interests."

Harris's words weren't doing anything to allay Trip's nagging suspicions. "That sounds to me pretty much like what John Frederick Paxton said about Terra Prime."

"Hardly," Harris said with a gentle chuckle. *"Paxton is a xenophobe and a terrorist. And he's exactly where he belongs right now—in prison. He saw Earth's contact with other sentient races as something to be feared, and therefore curtailed. We see that contact as inevitable and beneficial—but we're not so naive as to believe there won't be dangers that have to be managed very carefully along the way.*

"My group is part of Starfleet, Commander, and it's keeping an extremely watchful eye on what's left of Paxton's network, to prevent terrorist acts like those committed by Terra Prime from ever happening here again. But we're keeping even closer tabs on Earth's many potential interstellar adversaries. Most notably the Romulan Star Empire."

They're part of Starfleet, Trip thought, still having a little difficulty digesting the concept, even though Malcolm had already told him as much in the crew mess.

"You say you're an arm of Starfleet, Harris," he finally said aloud. "But you seem to be operating independently of Starfleet's direct control. How is it you can get away with that?"

"You seem to be implying that there's something illicit *about my group's activities, Commander."*

Trip shrugged, and restrained himself from commenting on the trouble Harris's clandestine organization had caused Malcolm a few months back. Malcolm's activities on Harris's behalf had very nearly gotten him court-martialed.

"I'm just saying it's damned irregular," Trip said.

"*Perhaps. But it's also authorized by Starfleet's own charter.*"

"Come again?"

"*I refer you to Article Fourteen, Section Thirty-one. You'll find that it establishes an autonomous investigative agency that holds nonspecific discretionary power over certain security-related matters. I'd say that incipient aggression by the Romulans certainly qualifies as one of those matters.*"

Trip was still digesting the surprising revelation that Harris's spy bureau might have been hidden right out in plain sight, buried in the text of Starfleet's own founding document, when Harris's last remark finally registered.

"So . . . are you saying you can help me do something about the Romulans?"

Harris put on an ingratiating smile that almost convinced Trip there was some real warmth behind it. "*I am, Commander. Our best analysts have already confirmed that the Romulans present a clear and present danger to Earth and her Coalition allies. We're already conducting operations intended to throw a monkey wrench into the Romulans' warp-seven drive program, while also trying to learn as much about it as possible.*"

"It'd be nice to use the Romulans' own research to jump-start a Starfleet version of the same thing," Trip said, nodding. He wondered just how much warp-seven technology Starfleet already had on the drawing board, and hoped it wasn't as sketchy as he feared it was.

"*Exactly, Commander. In fact, I was just about to approach Lieutenant Reed again regarding this very matter. Things are going to begin happening very quickly, and very soon.*"

"I wouldn't bother calling Malcolm again if I were you. He's still not very keen on working with you folks."

"So you've both already said. Regardless, we were also planning to contact you as well. I must thank you for saving me the trouble."

Trip blinked in surprise. "Why contact me?"

"Because your skills could prove invaluable to us, Commander. We need engineers capable of neutralizing the Romulans' plans directly. People like you who already have a hands-on grasp of the inner workings of Romulan technology. I read your reports on the Romulans' cloaked mine field, their flirtation with stealth ships, and their remote-control drone-ship experiments. Very impressive work. It helped convince me that you are an ideal candidate for field work."

Trip immediately felt flattered, then reminded himself of Malcolm's repeated warnings that Harris was a master manipulator. "Thanks. But those reports must have been evaluated by better engineering minds than mine. Besides that stuff, what makes you think I'm your man?"

"Whether you realize it or not, you are already a citizen of the coming galactic confederation. You are a human being ahead of his time, Mister Tucker. You have demonstrated an ability to empathize with and understand the minds of aliens, like the Tellarites and the Andorians."

"Wow. Malcolm warned me that you lay it on a little thick sometimes to get what you want."

Harris's brow furrowed. "I'm not speaking about your gifts hyperbolically, Commander. People skills are just as important to a field agent's success as engineering talent. Perhaps even more important. Case in point: You may be the first human ever to have a serious romantic relationship with a Vulcan."

"In case you missed it, that relationship crashed and cratered." Whatever might lay ahead between him, Harris, and the Romulans, Trip hoped for a smoother trajectory than the one he had shared with T'Pol.

"All that *proves is that there are no guarantees in this life."* Harris paused to close his eyes and rub the bridge of his nose with a steepled pair of index fingers. *"Frankly, I'm a little surprised at your ambivalence about us, Commander. Need I remind you that no one outside of your* Enterprise *colleagues other than us has been willing to listen to your warnings about the Romulans? We, on the other hand, will not only listen, we'll also provide you with whatever resources, cover, and contacts you'll need while working covertly in the 'off-channel' sector. With our resources at your disposal, you will finally have a real opportunity to protect Earth and her allies."*

Trip sat in silence for a lengthy time, evaluating Harris's words as the other man continued studying him from across the light-years. While he thought Harris's praise of his alleged exodiplomatic skills was highly overblown, he knew he couldn't remain on the sidelines while Starfleet continued to do nothing, Malcolm's warnings about Harris notwithstanding.

He's not the devil, Trip told himself. *If he were, then why would Malcolm have suggested I talk to him?*

"All right. I'm in," Trip said at length. "At least until we get done neutering this Romulan invasion.

"Just tell me what I have to do."

ELEVEN

Monday, February 10, 2155
Enterprise NX-01

JONATHAN ARCHER SIPPED COFFEE from a tall metal mug as he shuffled down an E-deck corridor toward the captain's mess. He wasn't a stranger to exhaustion—it often seemed to be a prerequisite for a captain—but last night he'd gotten even less sleep than usual. Something wasn't sitting right with what was going on with the ship, *and* with Shran. He suspected that getting Shran off the ship might help him sleep better for a night or two, but the consequences of that action might be problematic for the crew at a later date. And not just because of the suspicions shared by Shran, Trip, and himself about the purpose and destination the Orions intended for their Aenar captives.

He rounded a corner and was surprised to see Trip waiting for him outside the captain's mess. The commander looked haunted; not a huge step down from his demeanor ever since the Terra Prime incident and the death of his daughter, but he definitely looked wearier than he had when he'd gone off-shift yesterday.

"I need to talk with you, Captain," Trip said, his voice plaintive.

"Sure, Trip," Archer said, patting his old friend on the shoulder. "Come on in. Have you had breakfast yet? I can have Chef whip something up for you."

Trip took the first seat at the round metallic table, opposite the viewport. "No, thanks, Captain. I'm not really very hungry right now."

Archer seated himself at his regular spot, glad to see a covered dish already waiting for him. "Suit yourself," Archer said, lifting the cover. Chef had prepared eggs Florentine and crêpes today, along with three wedges of the multigrain toast that Archer preferred.

Unfolding his napkin, Archer asked, "Now then, what can I do for you?"

"I want to get this all out before you say anything, Captain," Trip said, splaying his hands across the table in front of him. "It's going to be difficult enough to get through this without interruptions—no offense—and I really want to finish."

Archer smiled wanly and cut a bite of crêpe with the edge of his fork. "The floor is yours."

The captain wasn't quite sure what he expected Trip to say, but several minutes later, when the engineer's tale seemed to be winding to a close, Archer's meal had gone cold, and he hadn't eaten anything past the first bite. He'd expected something related to Trip's relationship with T'Pol—perhaps a heartache-heavy request for another transfer—or some news of a discovery about Shran or the Aenar, or even some minor conjectures about the Romulans, but this . . .

"Are you finished?" Archer asked.

Trip sighed. "More or less. For the moment."

Archer fixed his chief engineer with a steely gaze. "So they want to send you into Romulan space as a field operative. Okay, it's a tactic as old as Homer. But even supposing that Harris's intelligence about the Romulans is correct, along with all our suppositions about how they plan to use the Aenar against us, what real *point* is there in having you infiltrate the Romulan Star Empire?"

Trip looked puzzled. "We've got to sabotage their war plans somehow."

" 'Somehow' is pretty damned vague, Trip." Archer felt he had to persist with a few admittedly merciless questions before he allowed his old friend to go any further down such a dangerous road. "How exactly could one agent in disguise stop any attack against Coridan Prime? I'm pretty sure you never took a course in conversational Romulan."

"Maybe I should ask Harris to consider asking Hoshi to go instead," Trip said wryly.

Archer raised a placating hand. "I'm not trying to shoot you down, Trip. But there's a lot to consider here. For one thing, no Coalition ship is likely to be within range of the most powerful transmitter you could carry while you're in Romulan space."

Trip nodded. "I admit, I may have to improvise. Commandeer some of their equipment. Live off the land a bit."

"More than a bit, Trip. And have you really considered the danger? The Romulans can probably detect and destroy any ship you bring into their space fairly easily. And I assume they're security-minded enough to make it pretty difficult for you to 'live off the land.' I'm pretty sure you won't be able to just pop in and out of Romulan space at will, or smuggle secret communiqués to us when you can't raise us over the subspace bands. So what's the real advantage, given all the downside? And how are you even going to *do* it?"

"Harris plans on putting me under deep cover. From the sound of it, it'll involve some surgical alterations, to make me look like a Romulan."

That raised another point that Archer hadn't even considered. "Do they *know* what the Romulans look like?"

Trip shrugged. "Harris says they don't. But they have connections with people who do. People who supposedly can make me look enough like one of them to pass."

"Well, at least we know they're humanoid," Archer said, half under his breath. He'd often wondered how a race that was so feared throughout the known galaxy could have remained so secretive. But as he had learned over the four years he'd commanded *Enterprise*, every race—every *society*—had its secrets, at least to some degree. Like the Coridanites, who for some reason had never allowed outworlders to see the unmasked faces of their diplomats, and guarded their high-warp technological secrets jealously, even from their interstellar allies and trading partners.

"I'll be working alongside one of their most experienced operatives." Trip said. "Our job will be to infiltrate their new stardrive project and sabotage it. They need someone with engineering experience to pull this off. That's why they can't use Malcolm."

"And what about the telepathically piloted drone ships, and the Aenar, and the possible assault on Coridan? You're going to stop those, too?"

Trip rolled his eyes, and breathed out heavily through his nose. "No, sir. It looks like those jobs will be up to *you.*"

Archer snorted. "So this secret intelligence group thinks that *I'll* just do their bidding as well? We're not a defensive first-strike vessel, no matter how many MACOs or new weapons we've taken on since the Xindi attack."

"I really don't think it has anything to do with what Harris or his group wants, Captain," Trip said, leaning forward. "You're already *on* the trail of the Orions. If this is all real—which I believe it is, and I think *you* do as well—you know that events are going to pull you in. And one way or another, you're gonna make sure that the Romulans don't get their way."

Archer spread his hands wide and looked toward the ceiling, as if appealing to a higher power. A tremendous weight seemed to settle squarely upon his shoulders. "'Events are going to pull me in.' Nice way to say either that I'm predictable, or that I'm easily manipulated by outside forces."

"That's not what I meant, sir." Trip sighed and shook his head. "I'm just not saying it quite right."

Archer rose and walked to the viewport and gazed out at the distorted, warp field-streaked stars. *At times like this, I sure could use a sunrise at breakfast time,* he thought. Finally, he turned back toward Trip, who had remained seated, looking up at him with a mixture of trepidation and resolve in his eyes.

"You said it right enough, Trip. I don't trust this Harris, but I've done a little digging, and I know his organization is real, and it *is* sanctioned by Starfleet, even if only the upper brass seems to know anything about it. And the conclusions we're all reaching on this ship seem to support the idea that the Romulans have got some very deadly schemes in the works right now."

He rubbed his temple with one hand and reached for his coffee with the other as he took his seat again. Even lukewarm coffee would help him focus now that his head was spinning. A terrible decision faced him now. And though the likely outcome pained him, he knew there was only one choice he could make.

With no small amount of regret, he spoke that choice aloud. "If you feel that the threat is real enough for you to take a leap like this, Trip, I'll do my best to make it easy for you. I'll approve an extended leave of absence." He tried to sound positive, though he wondered whether it was more for himself than for Trip. "An open-ended leave, so you can return when the mission is over. Although God knows *what* you'll look like by then, or even if you'll want to settle for being a chief engineer once you've gotten a taste of the spy life."

"Actually, Captain, I won't need a leave of absence," Trip said quietly as Archer took another swallow from his coffee cup. "Because I need to die first."

Archer quickly put the napkin over his mouth to avoid reflexively spitting out his coffee. Regaining his composure, he coughed and asked, "Come again?"

"There's every possibility that I could be captured," Trip said. "But since I'll be surgically altered, identifying me will be difficult. *Especially* if Charles Anthony Tucker III is *dead*."

"Now you're talking crazy talk," Archer said, frowning.

"No, think of it as a kind of witness protection plan. If I'm dead, it insulates *Enterprise*, and Earth—and my family and friends—from any sort of retaliation or repercussion. Politically or otherwise."

Archer closed his eyes, trying to damp down the mental warning klaxons that were going off inside his head. "So you intend to fake your own death?"

"Just until this assignment is over," Trip said, his tone earnest. "Or until its *repercussions* die down."

"That could be *years*, Trip," Archer said, unable to filter the exasperation from his voice. He opened his eyes again, fixing his subordinate with a hard gaze. "If the Romulans are a threat *now*, and we manage to stop them, what makes you think that threat is simply going to go away in the future? The Romulans aren't the schoolyard bully who becomes your friend after you give him one hard punch in the nose."

"I know," Trip said, his voice low. "But, if the Romulans succeed . . . it won't be like the Xindi attack. It will be *every* world that loses billions of lives. The Coalition will die . . . I *need* to do this. I need to be . . . someone else for a while. Some*where* else. I need to feel like I'm accomplishing something more than I'm doing here and now."

Archer knew that Trip hadn't meant the statement as a slur on his captaincy or on the accomplishments of *Enterprise*'s crew. But the comment still stung. "You've accomplished a lot here, Trip. You can *still* accomplish a lot here. Hell, I don't know what I'd do without you half the time, and the other half I'm just glad you're by my side."

Trip turned his face away, but said nothing.

"What about your family? They've already lost your sister." Archer hesitated for a moment, knowing he was treading on shaky ground, then decided it would be better to forge ahead. "And what about T'Pol? Are you really ready to give up on her? Do you think they'll all *really* be happier waiting and wondering if you're safe, or if you're rotting in some Romulan prison, or worse?"

Trip wiped the palm of his hand across one cheek, and then the other. His voice was tremulous. "They won't know," he said. "They *can't* know. The more people know, the more they'll be at risk of reprisals if I somehow screw the pooch on this thing. The more at risk *Earth* will be. They *all* need to think I'm dead. They need to *believe* it." He raised his hand again, covering his eyes with his palm, and let out a deep, unsteady breath.

Archer felt tears welling up in his own eyes, and he closed them tightly. They sat together in silence for several minutes, the ever-present thrum of the deck plating making the only audible sound in the room.

Finally, Trip looked up at Archer again and spoke. "There are two people who will have to help me with this, besides yourself. Malcolm is the one that got me into this, for better or worse—better, I hope, eventually—and given his past experience with covert operations, he might figure it all out on his own and try something foolish if I were to try to hide this from him. And he can help make sure that any investigation into my . . . demise gets wrapped up as neatly as it needs to be."

"And Phlox," Archer said, nodding. "He'll have to be the one to sign the death certificate."

"Yep."

"What about . . . ? Are you sure?" Archer let his words trail off, trusting that Trip knew exactly who he was talking about.

"She *can't* know," Trip said, his face creasing as if he was about to weep again. "She'll be fine. She'll control her emotions and meditate and move on. Hell, after what we just experienced together on Vulcan, I think maybe she's already starting to move on."

"How are you going to do it?" Archer asked.

"That's another area I could use your help with, along with Malcolm and Phlox. It has to happen soon. And it ain't gonna be suicide." He chuckled mirthlessly. "And to think I actually worried I might have committed *career* suicide in front of Admiral Gardner yesterday."

Archer smiled gently in response to Trip's valiant attempt to find humor where there really wasn't any. "Should I call Phlox and Malcolm now?"

Trip closed his eyes and let out a long, stuttering breath, his hands clenching into fists, then unclenching. He opened his eyes and looked to Archer, then gave a slight nod.

Archer rose from his chair and tapped the button on the wall-mounted com panel nearby. "Archer to Lieutenant Reed and Doctor Phlox. Please join me immediately in the captain's mess."

As both men responded, each confirming his pending arrival, Archer stared at Trip, who rose from his seat. He still wasn't at all certain that the engineer was doing the right thing. But given the same set of circumstances, he wasn't sure he would do anything differently himself.

"Thank you, Captain," Trip said, his eyes glistening. "For everything."

Seated in the command chair in the center of *Enterprise*'s bridge, T'Pol stopped reading the report on the padd in her lap, and glanced at the turbolift behind her.

Captain Archer had been in some kind of secretive meeting in his private mess for some time this morning, leaving her to take over command of the alpha shift. She certainly didn't mind—as first officer, it *was* her duty, after all—but it seemed strange that Archer had opted not to include her in the meeting, as he had included her in his consultations the previous day regarding the kidnapped Aenar and the possibility of an impending Romulan military incursion.

She wanted desperately to ask Ensign Sato who was in the meeting with Archer, but didn't want to appear to be snooping. Instead, she moved over to her own station and slid her hands swiftly across the controls, accessing the ship's computers.

What she found surprised her. Archer was currently meeting with Commander Tucker, Lieutenant Reed, and Doctor Phlox. She had expected him to be in consultation with Shran, and perhaps one or two of the others. But the Andorian was currently in the ship's mess hall, as was the Aenar telepath Theras.

What could they be discussing? She anticipated that she would find out soon enough; it was certainly illogical for Archer to keep secrets from her.

Mayweather's voice interrupted her thoughts.

"Commander, we have a definite lock on at least one Orion ship that shows the same warp-signature profile that Shran gave us."

T'Pol returned to her seat. "Very good, Ensign Mayweather. Increase speed and set a pursuit course, but keep us just out of their sensor range."

Now she had a reason to speak with Archer, though she resisted the urge to leave the bridge to do so. She tapped the communications console on the arm of the command chair.

"T'Pol to Captain Archer. We've found the Orions."

TWELVE

Friday, February 14, 2155
Enterprise NX-01

IT WAS NOW FOUR DAYS since they had last met here, in the captain's mess, for a much more intensely emotional exchange than they were having at present.

Today, however, all Trip wanted was to spend some informal downtime in the company of someone he'd counted as a friend for the past two decades. *One last drink before marching into the abyss,* he thought, trying to prepare himself for what lay ahead with a little gallows humor.

He hoisted a glass of whiskey poured from Jonathan Archer's own personal stores. "So, you think this alliance is going to hold?"

Archer examined his glass. "We'd better hope so. There are thousands of planets within reach. We've got to start somewhere."

"Who would've guessed: Vulcans and Andorians in the same bed." He put his glass down on the table.

"The Tellarites were never big fans of the Andorians, either," Archer said, nodding slightly.

They both sat in silence for a moment, as the light from the warp-refracted stars skimmed by outside the room's viewport. Despite his enjoyment of this rare, relaxed moment, some part of Trip still felt that they should discuss his "situation" further, even though they had both been strategizing and making contingency plans separately—and together—for much of the day already. Trip knew that the rest of the crew must have really begun to wonder exactly what was going on between him and the captain. *They'd all have to be blinder than Theras if nobody's noticed all these private meetings yet,* he thought.

And there was probably nobody aboard *Enterprise* more observant than T'Pol.

"This is a special bottle of whiskey," Archer said, finally breaking the silence that had settled between them. He lifted the bottle again and refilled the bottom two centimeters or so of Trip's glass. "Zefram Cochrane gave it to my father the day they broke ground at the warp five complex." He poured himself more as well.

"And here we are," Trip said, hoisting his glass, "toasting the future."

Archer raised his drink as well. "May it bring safety from the Romulans, the rescue of the Aenar, the unlocking of the warp seven mystery, the successful launch of the Coalition of Planets . . . and your swift resurrection."

They clinked their glasses together and sipped the amber liquid.

"Written your speech for the Coalition Compact ceremonies yet?" Trip asked, putting his glass down on the silver tabletop. "I heard that Starfleet Command decided to make you the show's opening act."

Archer nodded, frowning. "That was Admiral Gardner's doing. I guess it proves he actually *does* have a sense of humor after all."

"Or maybe he just wants to keep you from missing any of the pomp and circumstance," Trip said, grinning over his glass. "He's probably still afraid you'll get sidetracked out here, chasing after those Orion slavers."

"I still think we'll catch up to them in plenty of time, Trip. We've only been on the trail for the past five days."

"I know you will, Captain. So . . . how about that speech of yours?"

"I always crammed before exams," Archer said, answering Trip's grin with one of his own. "You know that. Besides, I've still got nearly three weeks left."

Trip's grin became a smirk. "Some things never change. It's the biggest day of your life, and you're going to wait until the night before."

"The biggest day of *our* lives," Archer said, raising an eyebrow slightly.

"Well, it's doubtful I'll be there to see it," Trip said. "You'll have to make sure to get me a vid recording of it to watch later. And I'm sure it'll show that *you* were the man everyone there really came to see."

Archer was about to respond when a loud *boom* reverberated through the ship and the deck rocked and shuddered beneath their chairs. Archer tipped back slightly in his seat, grabbing his glass to keep it from sliding off the table.

As the captain hurried over to the wall-mounted com panel, Trip retrieved a padd from where he had left it on the tabletop and quickly studied the readout on its small display. Reed had carefully blocked certain frequencies from Hoshi's station earlier that afternoon, and the padd was one of the few devices aboard now capable of receiving a particular prearranged set of signals.

"Archer to the bridge. What's going on?"

T'Pol's voice crackled over the speaker. *"We're under attack, sir. A small vessel."*

Archer looked to Trip, and the engineer held up the padd, nodding.

"Who are they?" Archer asked, speaking into the com panel. None of them actually knew the answer to that question, but with Trip's confirmation just now, at least four members of the crew now clearly understood the *purpose* of the intruders.

"We don't know yet," T'Pol said.

Enterprise shook again, and a high-pitched, ululating klaxon sounded.

"Intruder alert," T'Pol said, her voice rising slightly in pitch and urgency. *"Unauthorized personnel on E deck, near the starboard docking bay."*

That's convenient, Trip thought. *We're on E deck, too. Good thing I won't have to keep my ride waiting while I'm in the turbolift.*

Trip headed for the exit, but the captain put a restraining hand against his friend's chest before he reached the door. "Whatever we do, we have to make it convincing. Malcolm's already keeping security as busy as he can, but outside of this room, the ship's computers will still record everything we do or say."

"Agreed," Trip said. "I think I've got the script memorized, Captain. And we're both pretty good at improvising when we need to."

They exited the room and ran down the corridor. Ten steps out of the room, Trip realized that neither of them had thought to grab a weapon. Although a couple of phase pistols probably would have made their play more convincing, it was too late to make a run for the armory now.

As they rounded a curve in the corridor, three tall aliens stepped out toward them.

They had most definitely *not* forgotten to bring their weapons.

"We've come for Shran and the Aenar!" the tallest alien snarled, his long dirty hair and gray-green, chalky skin making him resemble a zombie extra from one of the twenty-first-century flatvid horror films Trip enjoyed. His two companions both appeared to have been cut from the same unsavory, not to mention hostile, cloth.

Trip held up the padd, a gesture that not only emphasized the fact that he was unarmed, but also allowed the intruders to see the padd's display, if they looked closely enough. He hoped beyond hope that these were indeed the "pirates" that Section 31 had promised to send to help him fake his death. They certainly looked the part, particularly since they had a pair of what appeared to be energy rifles, as well as a pistol of some sort, trained directly at him and the captain.

If these guys aren't *from Harris's outfit,* Trip thought, *then the captain and I are both in one hell of a lot of trouble.*

The lead "pirate" peered at the padd, then nodded and pulled a device of his own from the sash around his waist. After the alien had depressed a few buttons, Trip heard a telltale beep from his own padd, which was evidently receiving signals from the intruder's device.

"You must take us to them, or we'll have no choice but to cause some damage," said the leader as Trip checked the code his padd had received. It checked out. He gave Archer a subtle hand signal to apprise him of that fact.

Archer nodded, then puffed up his chest in a conspicuous show of bluster. "Shran left six hours ago. You're too late."

"You're lying. His shuttle is still in your launch bay," the leader said. He stepped forward, his weapon trained directly on Archer. "Kill him," he ordered the subordinate to his right, who responded by raising his rifle.

"Hold on!" Trip said, holding up his hands. "Wait a minute!"

"Trip, I'll take care of this," Archer said, putting out an arm to stop him from advancing on the "pirates."

"The hell you will," Trip said, pushing at his old friend's arm. To the lead invader, he said, "*I'll* bring you to Shran. I know where he is."

Archer turned and brought his hand up to Trip's chest. "I gave you an *order,* Commander."

Trip ignored him and continued to address the leader of the intruders. "You heard me. I said I'd bring you to Shran."

"Trip!" Archer pushed his friend against the bulkhead.

The alien leader muttered something about them turning around, but Trip wasn't really hearing him. For that moment, his gaze locked with that of his oldest friend, and absorbed a myriad of emotions. Love, regret, anger, fear.

"Hey, this guy's the captain," Trip said, shouting to the "pirate" leader, breaking the moment.

"That's enough," Archer snarled.

Trip faced the chalk-skinned alien. "He's my *boss*. If I'm gonna disobey his order, I don't want him coming along."

"Trip, that's *enough!*" Archer repeated, shouting this time, shoving Trip again.

An errant thought flickered across Trip's mind. *Everyone's playing their parts a bit* too *well.* But he knew they had to. When the security logs were reviewed, this had to look real. Still, it bothered him that the fingers of these "pirates" really were poised to pull their triggers.

"Listen . . . I won't do this if you kill him. But could you *please* shut him up?"

Trip fully expected one of the boarders to stun Archer with a blast, but instead, on a nod from the leader, one of the other two aliens crashed his rifle's stock into the back of Archer's head. The captain immediately crumpled to the deck, unconscious.

Trip winced. *They* really *didn't need to do* that. Still, he had his part to play, and they were running out of time before Malcolm's security teams would arrive from the armory on F deck.

He began leading the "pirates" down the corridor, trading barbed words with them as they went, all of it concerning the specific whereabouts of their quarry, and the Orion slavers who had supposedly paid these men to bring Shran and Theras to face "justice" for the deaths of some of those who had participated in the recent raid against the Aenar city. Trip felt as though they were being almost *too* arch with these exchanges, but hoped that upon a close investigation of *Enterprise*'s security logs, no one else would notice just how dunderheaded this entire piracy scenario really was.

"Take me to Shran *now*, or I'll send one of my men back to kill your captain," the lead alien said, making a show of his mounting impatience.

Trip affected a nearly panicked tone, but wasn't completely sure he was only acting. "Okay, okay! I've got a better idea. I'll bring Shran and Theras to *us*. We won't have to go any farther."

"Be very careful," snarled the pistol-wielding alien.

They went on a short distance until they reached a narrow hatchway, which he and Malcolm had already rigged for precisely this sort of situation.

"You can all come see for yourselves," he said to the men behind him as he pulled the hatch open and began to climb inside a crawlspace filled with a profusion of cables and conduits. "This is just a com station."

He reached up and began moving a small handle mounted at the top of the cramped chamber. "I'm gonna need to open this so I can bypass the security protocols," he continued. "Is that okay?"

The "pirate" leader approached closely and inspected the equipment. His weapon remained raised and ready. "As long as you keep your hands where we can see them."

"No problem," Trip said as he continued working. The handle turned, opening up an overhead access panel containing still more cabling and circuitry. After carefully bypassing the security protocols, he grasped one end of an open energy conduit inside the panel and pulled it down.

Holding the open conduit out in front of him, he said, "Now, all I need to do is connect this to the relay inside that panel." He gestured toward a second overhead panel, located not far from the first one.

"Stop," the head raider said. To one of his men, he said, "Open it for him." He pointed at the second panel. "If there's a weapon in there," he warned Trip, "you're going to die before your captain does."

Still holding the conduit, Trip watched as one of the rifle carriers reached up and opened the second panel. No obvious weapons were in evidence.

"Satisfied?" Trip said.

The head alien sniffed. "Proceed."

Trip reached up into the second open panel and extracted another open conduit line, the virtual twin of the one he still held in his other hand. Then he joined the ends of the cables, twisting them together, and flipped the toggle switch next to his right hand.

At his signal, the aliens all backed away slightly, getting safely out of harm's way. Trip jumped down and out of the access hatchway, counting the few seconds that remained.

Gotta have some famous last words, he thought. "There's just one other thing I need to tell you," he said, making certain that he spoke loudly and clearly, so that the ship's computer would pick up every word. "You can all go straight to hell."

Trip felt his skin itch, experienced a bizarre, disjointed feeling, and then he was pulled away. In that nanosecond when he was still corporeal, he hoped that the small plasma explosion he'd set up would go off without a hitch—and without blowing a huge hole in the hull on the starboard side of E deck.

* * *

As a slightly disoriented Trip lay on one of sickbay's biobeds, Phlox quickly applied convincing facsimiles of all the appropriate wounds to the engineer's face and chest. Only minutes remained now before Archer was due to call and raise the medical alert, and before the med techs arrived. Phlox had let them go off shift early, but since they all bunked on E deck—the same deck where sickbay was located—they would doubtless arrive quickly once called.

"You will need to breathe as though you're having an extremely difficult time doing so," Phlox said to Trip, who looked quite gory at the moment. Even though he knew it was his own harmless handiwork, the sight of the apparently mortally wounded man—his friend—made the Denobulan physician shudder inwardly.

"I faked being sick at school a whole bunch of times, Doc," Trip said, smiling wanly up at Phlox.

"Yes, well, but this is considerably different," Phlox said, grimacing. He thought the whole plan was outlandish, and felt certain that it would never hold up to close scrutiny. But as long as it was under way, he was determined to do his best; Commander Tucker's scheme wasn't going to fall apart because of *his* actions.

Archer stood by the doorway, rubbing the side of his head and wincing. He'd apparently actually been injured, however slightly, during the subterfuge, but there was no time to treat him now. Suddenly, the captain's communicator beeped. "We're out of time, Doctor."

The captain flipped the communicator's grid open. "We need help in sickbay," he said, his voice now sounding strained. "Trip's been hurt."

"Alerting sickbay personnel now," T'Pol said, her voice issuing from the device. *"What has happened?"* Phlox could hear the concern in her tone as he moved to a nearby com panel to enter the command that would summon his emergency med tech staff.

"The intruders were trying to get to Shran and Theras," Archer said to T'Pol. "Trip tried to stop them. He got caught in some kind of plasma explosion."

Two of Phlox's medical technicians—Garver and Stepanczyk—rushed into the chamber, even as T'Pol's voice issued from the communicator. *"The intruders are no longer aboard* Enterprise. *Their ship is pulling away."*

"What about Shran and Theras?" Archer asked, although he already knew the answer. After all, the reason the "pirates" had come aboard had absolutely nothing to do with *Enterprise*'s two guests from Andoria.

"Still aboard, Captain. Commander Tucker's gambit appears to have succeeded in discouraging them." Had her voiced quavered ever so slightly when she'd said Trip's name?

"Pursue them, but do *not* engage," Archer shouted. "Archer out."

Phlox began barking orders to his med techs, even as Trip put on an award-winning performance for their benefit. He really did seem to be in great pain, as well as unable to breathe properly.

"The plasma was superheated," Phlox said to Archer, counterfeiting a sense of rapidly rising alarm. "It thermalized his lungs." He turned urgently to one of the techs. "Initialize the hyperbaric chamber."

Archer approached the side of Trip's biobed. Between gasps, the engineer said, "Sorry about the rifle butt . . ." He trailed off, his breath apparently beginning to fail him.

"I know, Trip," Archer said. "Just take it easy. Everything's all right."

Trip suddenly began to wheeze violently, as though he could no longer breathe at all.

"We need to get him into the chamber! Now!" Phlox shouted. With Archer's help, the Denobulan and his med techs moved Trip onto a gurney, and then slid the gurney toward the open and waiting cylinder of the hyperbaric chamber.

As they slid Trip inside, Phlox saw the engineer offer a weak smile—and perhaps an almost imperceptible wink—to Archer.

I hope the techs didn't see that, Phlox thought as he pressed the button that closed the door and sealed off the airtight chamber from the rest of sickbay. He turned and regarded Captain Archer, who hadn't returned Trip's smile.

They both knew that in faking his death, Trip had changed whatever remained of his life forever.

And theirs as well.

Although he was reeling from the news, Travis Mayweather knew he still had a job to do, and he did his best to focus on it. Ten minutes ago, they had lost the trail of the pirate vessel when it entered a dense cloud of asteroids, planetesimals, and assorted other space debris that orbited an uncharted, unremarkable F-type star. *Enterprise*'s polarized hull plating was holding up under the barrage, but the ship was taking a battering.

"I still can find no trace of the intruders' vessel, Captain," T'Pol said, sounding grimmer than at any other time he could remember.

Mayweather couldn't even imagine what she must be feeling right now, after absorbing the terrible news of Commander Tucker's sudden death. *Feeling? Is she even allowing herself to experience her emotions right now? Or is she just using her Vulcan training to lock them away?*

"Keep searching," Archer said from his command chair, his tone and manner grave as well.

The ship pitched to one side as something large and solid collided with the polarized hull plates. "Sorry, Captain," Mayweather said, not turning from his post. "We're flying almost blind here."

Almost as if on cue, the forward viewscreen lit up brightly, illuminating the interstellar flotsam and jetsam that surrounded them. Mayweather knew what it was even before T'Pol verbalized it for the entire bridge. He had seen enough accidents in space while growing up on space freighters to recognize a catastrophic collision.

"I'm showing a warp-core explosion approximately four hundred thousand kilometers ahead," T'Pol said. "The energy pattern is consistent with the warp signature of the intruder's vessel."

Out of the corner of his eye, Mayweather saw that Archer had stood up from his chair and approached the helm controls.

"Take us in slowly, Travis," he said quietly. "That *had* to be them. They probably shut down their engines while they were hiding from us, then got creamed by an asteroid. Let's confirm the wreckage."

"Yes, sir," Mayweather said. He half hoped to find escape pods somewhere in the region surrounding the late pirate vessel's mostly vaporized remains.

The possibility that Commander Tucker's killers might have died an easy death didn't sit well with him at all.

THIRTEEN

The early twenty-fifth century
Terrebonne Parish, Louisiana

JAKE STIFLED A YAWN behind one hand.

"You're *bored*?" Nog asked, surprise in his voice.

Jake turned to his old friend and grinned. "Not at all, just tired. Between the sound of the rain, the warmth of the fire, the wine, and my age, I'm fighting the sandman."

Nog tilted his head to one side. "Is that another hewmon cultural idiom, or some other reference I *should* understand but don't?"

Jake smiled again. "It's from an old Earth myth. The sandman was the king of dreams. He's the reason when you wake up you have little bits of grit in the corners of your eyes."

Nog's expression was one of simultaneous enlightenment and befuddlement. "Ah, I remember now. And he also brings women the men of their dreams. Like in that song I heard some of the female singers perform back at Vic's. But I don't ever have 'grit' in my eyes when I wake up."

"Humans often do," Jake said. The mention of Vic made Jake nostalgic for the old days. Some years back, Quark had given him a copy of Vic's holodeck program; he had only played it a dozen times or so since, usually when he wanted to get into an old-timey mood for his writing. Vic didn't seem to care that he wasn't activated often, or at least if he did, he didn't chide Jake about it too much. *Still, it would be nice to visit Vic's again*, Jake thought.

"So, what do you think now?" Nog asked, gesturing toward the two small holo-imagers whose two extremely divergent narratives about Commander Tucker they'd been watching.

"It's very strange," Jake said. "Parts of the story are familiar, but just interpreted differently, and placed five years earlier. It's like the story behind the story."

"Don't they say that history is written by the conqueror?" Nog asked.

"The *victor*. Though either word works about as well as the other." Jake ran his hand over the short, gray hair at the back of his head. "What's so strange about this is that Charles Tucker was one of the better-known martyrs of the proto-Federation, and yet the commonly accepted details of his death are nothing terribly heroic. If anything, the standard 'bad guys invade the ship' scenario makes both him and Captain Archer look sort of unprepared, and makes *Enterprise* security seem so lax as to be laughable."

"Maybe we're going to find out that Tucker's role in early Federation history was more pivotal than we knew," Nog said.

Jake nodded sagely and reached for his now nearly empty wineglass. "The other thing that's really unusual about the revised version is the way Section 31 is depicted. It's smaller than we know it actually became, but the bureau seems to have an almost noble agenda . . . or at least as much nobility as a spy organization can have."

"Maybe the morality of it is colored by what happened to Earth in the Xindi attack of 2153," Nog offered. "Not to mention Terra Prime. And it's not like I supported Thirty-One at the end, but we know that every government in the galaxy has its own spy network. It's not like this was the only one, for poverty's sake."

Jake laughed. Another thought suddenly occurred to him. "What about the parts of the original history that centered on Rigel X, with Shran's daughter being rescued from her kidnappers, and the theft of the Tenebian amethyst, and so on? Is all of that a complete fabrication?"

"Well, given that Shran didn't have a daughter at this point, I'd say that's probably a 'yes,'" Nog said. "But it might also be some sort of amalgamation of other events. After all, for years we've been watching some holodeck programmer's version of these people's lives, based on records and logs; things we now know have been tampered with." He paused and grinned at Jake. "Maybe something interesting happens in the Rigel system in *this* version as well."

Jake regarded his friend with a suspicious eye. "Just how far ahead *did* you watch this?"

Nog grinned and leaned forward, his nimble fingers moving toward the holo-imager controls he'd left sitting on Jake's ancient wooden desk. "Not much further. So, let's see what happens next."

FOURTEEN

Friday, February 14, 2155
Enterprise **NX-01**

WHEN CHARLES ANTHONY TUCKER III was a teenager, he and his friends had dared each other repeatedly to open a hatch door on a grain silo, but Trip had actually been the one who had taken the challenge. He hadn't been paying close enough attention in science class to judge the pressure such materials in a container of that size might be under, and was thus half buried by the flood of grain that spilled out before he could even retreat three steps. If his brother Bert and their friend Bill Hunt hadn't been quick to pull him out, he might well have been entombed on that long-ago day.

Since that time, Trip had been in more than a few tight spots, but none of those had been quite as suffocating as the grain incident.

Until now.

After the pallet on which he lay finished retracting into the hyperbaric chamber, the oval-shaped, airtight door near his feet closed. Its motion was silent, yet forceful enough to make his ears pop. He resumed his normal respiration then, relieved to relinquish the burden of showmanship to Phlox and the captain. Other than his own breathing and the gentle whispering susurration of the chamber's independent ventilation system, he was blanketed in utter silence. Then the cylindrical hyperbaric chamber began to thrum around him, just as the light panels built into its walls began throwing off just enough illumination to call attention to the chamber's disquieting smallness.

Trip fought down incipient claustrophobia by closing his eyes and by trying to regulate his breathing. Beyond the chamber's confines, he could hear muffled voices, though he couldn't quite make out the words.

A com speaker near his head—which allowed sickbay personnel to communicate with patients inside the otherwise sound-opaque hyperbaric chamber—suddenly came to life. Now he could hear what was going on beyond the confines of the hyperbaric chamber, in sickbay, where Phlox and his medical technicians were frantically continuing to respond to a preprogrammed sequence of ever-declining vital signs.

My *vital signs*, Trip thought, swallowing hard. He opened his eyes again, though he studiously tried to avoid staring at his own ghastly reflection.

Of all the personnel now present in sickbay, only Phlox's assistants would not have known that those life readings were utterly counterfeit, mere electronic simulations designed to allow Charles Tucker to die, officially and on the record.

"*What's happening in there, Phlox?*" the captain said through the chamber's speaker, still playing his part to the hilt.

"*He may have inhaled too much of the plasma during the explosion,*" came the Denobulan's precise, professional response, his voice laced with concern and a convincing tinge of fear. "*His lungs are failing.*"

"*Vital signs crashing, Doctor,*" said Crewman Stepanczyk, one of the medical technicians.

Archer: "Do *something!*"

"*I'm afraid, Captain, that there is very little that we can do,*" Phlox said. "*We're losing him.*"

Trip listened quietly to the sounds of his own death. A chill slowly navigated the length of his spine, reminding him of how his mother described that very sensation: "Somebody just walked across your grave."

And now here he was, entombed in a space not much larger than a casket. For better or worse, a chain of events had led him ineluctably into this tiny tube, pretending to be dead, while three of his friends lied to all his other friends and family for him. He thought of how T'Pol would react, especially after the loss of their daughter and their emotionally wrenching journey to Vulcan. And his family, barely over their grieving after the loss of his sister Lizzie, now forced to mourn another death. He hoped that Albert, the final "living" Tucker sibling, would take care of their parents better than he, Trip, had after Lizzie had been killed by the Xindi.

He closed his eyes again, and in the resulting darkness he saw a slow parade of faces.

His mother, Elaine. His father, Charles. His brother, Albert.

T'Pol.

The pain came then, like a barbed lance piercing his heart.

How can I do this to them? The regret was almost overwhelming, nearly swallowing him from the inside.

A part of him wanted to kick his feet out at the chamber door, yelling to them that it was all a mistake, that he wasn't dead, that the whole thing had been a setup. He considered for a moment what the ramifications might be, both for himself and for his coconspirators. *I guess it depends on whether the news got off the ship or not,* he thought. *If everybody who's in the loop agreed to keep quiet, the logs could be fixed or "lost," and we could write our* own *version of history.*

But there in the back of his mind, brooding and snarling like the monster that lived in his childhood closet, was the fear of what would happen if he *didn't* go through with this covert mission. In his mind's eyes, his loved ones' faces were replaced by fleets of Aenar-piloted remote-control drone warships. Each vessel was painted garishly to resemble a hungry, carnivorous bird with talons outstretched, and was equipped with exotic weapons and warp seven-capable engines. He imagined the Romulan fleets arriving in an eyeblink at Earth and Mars, tearing open the vulnerable underbelly of an unprepared Starfleet, destroying the shipyard and spacedock facilities that orbited both worlds. He imagined the invaders laying waste to Starfleet's headquarters on Earth, setting mankind's dreams of exploring the galaxy back centuries, if not destroying them forever.

He couldn't allow that. How many times had he already put his life on the line for the ideals of Starfleet, for the future of his family and friends? How many times had he put everything on the line for her, *Enterprise*, his ship?

He felt her even now, in this claustrophobic enclosure, her engines humming almost imperceptibly, a vibration that was nearly always present but that had long ago become nearly as familiar to him as the sound of his own breathing. For the past four years, the warp drive's gentle but ever-present oscillations had given him comfort, helping him drift off to sleep during most night cycles; the occasional absence of those vibrations frequently led to insomnia, and to extra late shifts in engineering until Trip felt things had finally been put right again.

Soon he would be very far away from the comfort of those engines. He would have to take reassurance instead in the knowledge that he was protecting *all* of this. *For now*, he thought. *I'm coming back. I'll be aboard* Enterprise *again. I'll be with my family again. Laugh with my friends, tell her that I* do *want to find a way to make it work . . .*

How can I not *do this?*

"No response, Doctor." It was of the med techs, Garver this time.

I'm coming back, Trip told himself again. *Back from the dead, once all this Romulan madness is finally over and done with.*

If it could ever be over and done with.

"Phlox!" Archer again, just outside the chamber.

"I'm so sorry, Captain," Phlox was saying in tones that dripped with grief. *"He's gone."*

A pause. Then Phlox spoke again: *"Computer, record that death occurred at nineteen hundred and thirty-three hours, fourteen February, 2155."*

Feeling unaccountably calmed by the knowledge that the deed had finally been done, Trip opened his eyes. He looked up again at his reflection, which looked bizarre and funhouse-distorted in the curved, too-close metal ceiling of the chamber. He could see that the Denobulan physician had certainly managed to make him look gruesome, in spite of the haste with which he'd had to work. A large, livid burn snaked down his neck, and a profusion of other wounds and smudges covered both his flesh and his torn uniform.

So this is what it's like to be dead, he thought, really trying on the idea for the first time. *Funny. Doesn't hurt quite as much as I thought it would.*

Or maybe it hurt far worse; after all, he'd always assumed that dead people couldn't feel pain, or anything else for that matter.

A ratcheting noise near his feet interrupted his reverie. The chamber door opened and sickbay's bright lighting flooded into the relative darkness inside the tube. He shut his eyes quickly, and felt the pallet on which he lay slowly move out of the chamber. He held his breath, pretending to be dead, just in case someone other than Phlox, Malcolm, or the captain happened to be present. He wondered how long he could pull it off.

The pallet's movement stopped.

"It's all right to breathe now, Commander Tucker," he heard Phlox say. "Everyone here knows the truth."

Trip brought his hand up to shield his eyes from sickbay's bright overhead lights, and moved to sit up. He felt someone place a hand behind his back, and knew it was Malcolm, just from the slight smell of his aftershave.

His eyes adjusting as he blinked, Trip saw that Archer was pacing in front of him. Malcolm was standing next to the table as Trip swung his legs down to stand on the deck.

Phlox put one hand on Trip's shoulder, turning the engineer toward him. "This will hurt a little bit," he said, reaching for the horrible fake burn at the side of Trip's neck. He pulled it off, along with what felt like a few layers of skin.

Trip winced. "Did everything go okay?" he asked, looking over to Archer and Reed as he rubbed the sore spot. Glancing toward sickbay's entryway, he saw that Phlox had stretched a white privacy curtain across the transparent aluminum doors that separated the ship's infirmary from the rest of E deck.

Archer sighed. "As well as can be expected. I have a monster headache, but we'll take care of that shortly." He rubbed the spot on the side of his head where one of the "pirates" had clubbed him.

"We've got to get you off the ship now," Malcolm said. "*Enterprise* is going to pursue the pirate ship any moment. I've taken measures to make sure that we don't quite catch them."

Phlox held up a pile of garments. "Get into these, Commander, quickly. Where you're going, you won't want to have any trace of Starfleet on your person. And we'll need your uniform for the . . . burial."

Trip undressed quickly. "Try to make sure there aren't too many broken hearts, please?"

Malcolm managed a slight smile, but Trip could see that there was little humor behind it. "Actually, there will probably be widespread relief among the crew, especially in engineering. They've always said you were a tyrant."

"I'll do my best, Trip," Archer said. "I'll contact your family personally."

Trip was soon dressed again, in a nondescript utilitarian brown jumpsuit.

"The materials I pumped into you while we were trying to 'save your life' were actually several wide-spectrum inoculants," Phlox said, handing him an enzyme-infused medical wipe to clean the burn smudges away. "It's unlikely you would have ever before encountered the pathogens they protect against, but you're venturing into unknown territory now. It's better to be safe than sorry."

Trip turned to Phlox. "Thanks, Doc. For everything."

Phlox nodded, his eyes almost as grief-filled as though Trip had actually died.

Trip moved over to Malcolm, taking a device that his friend offered. "*This* is how they're going to lock onto you," Malcolm said. "And it contains the *only* codes you'll be able to use to communicate with us, if you need to. Wipe them as soon as you have them memorized."

Trip put one hand on Malcolm's shoulder, and stuck his other hand out. They shook hands, looking into one another's eyes.

"Thank you, Malcolm. I'm sorry you won't be with me on this mission."

Malcolm smiled grimly again. "Just remember the first rule of being a spy: Don't fall for the girl. They're *always* working for the bad guy."

"I'll try to remember that," Trip said, turning toward

Archer. He held out his hand again, but was surprised when the captain pulled him into a bear hug instead.

"I've known you too long," Archer said. "You come back to my ship. That's an order."

"I will," Trip said. "You just make sure you do *your* part to save the galaxy while I'm gone." He felt his eyes watering, and pulled back from the embrace.

Trip stepped to the center of the room and depressed a button on the device Malcolm had given him.

"It's been a pleasure and an honor serving with you all," he said. "This isn't a good-bye, though. Just a 'see you later.' "

Even as the words were still leaving his lips, he felt the unnerving tug of the transporter, and the eerie sensation of momentary freefall that accompanied it.

Like a Valkyrie, the beam carried him off to his next life.

It had been three hours since Trip had materialized aboard the "pirate" ship, where he had finally met the men who had been paid to "raid" *Enterprise.*

Wungki was the captain's name, and he was scarcely any friendlier now than he'd been in the corridors of E deck, where he had played the role of the head "pirate." He *had* apologized, however, for having been so rough on Captain Archer. Captain Wungki's crew of eight consisted entirely of mercenaries, all of whom seemed willing to work for just about anyone capable of paying them.

That meant that they tended not to ask questions, and therefore were likely to be counted on to be discreet. "You're not the first person whose death we've helped fake," Wungki had said with an ugly smile, immediately after Trip's arrival on his ship. "There was a Betazoid man once, whom we helped 'kidnap' from his own wedding. Actually, it was a rescue." He snorted. "That was a tough assignment, given those people's empathic talents. And the fact that everybody there was naked really distracted my men."

Trip nodded as though he knew what Wungki was talking about. He assumed the Betazoids were some race he'd not yet encountered, though he had no idea why they would be naked at a wedding, nor whether or not he would find a nude Betazoid wedding party distracting.

Wungki's crew had avoided capture by *Enterprise* through a sort of bait-and-switch operation. They had apparently been carrying a smaller, decommissioned vessel in their cargo hold, which they set to self-destruct via a remote signal, and then released into space. They had then landed their primary vessel in a large crater in the asteroid field *Enterprise* was searching, and shut down all unnecessary power, using some form of dampening device to hide their life signs and residual energy emissions. Trip had attempted to learn more about the dampener, but it seemed that the crew wasn't eager to share their secrets; most of his questions had been rewarded with silence.

Now, with almost three hours having passed since the detonation of the decoy ship, Wungki and his crew finally felt safe enough to power their systems back up and venture out into open space again.

Despite all the excitement he had crammed into this very long day—or perhaps because of it—Trip now found himself sitting on a hard bench in a smelly alcove, on the point of dozing off. With Wungki's crew manning all the shipboard stations, he had essentially nothing to do other than sit in an alcove, waiting. He had no reports to read, and he was stuck among a crew that wasn't about to give him access to their computer system, even to look for entertainment.

He awoke with a start when someone shoved him.

"We're within range of your contact," one of the more grotesque-looking mercenaries said. "We'll be beaming you over as soon as he gives us the signal."

"Oh, thanks," Trip said, shaking his head to clear the fog away.

Minutes later, after a barely acknowledged good-bye to the mercenaries, he felt a transporter beam shimmer around him for the second time in one day. For an instant, he was amazed at how nonchalantly some people seemed to be using transporters these days; even *Enterprise's* crew had come a long way toward trusting the devices over the past four years, when at first they had been used mostly to move parts, tools, or other inanimate material on and off the ship.

He materialized on a small pad in what appeared to be a vessel barely larger than a Starfleet shuttlepod.

A lithe woman, her long black hair pulled back into a ponytail behind her, sat at what appeared to be the ship's helm, which was crammed into a small cockpit area. Trip's mind flashed on Malcolm's warning about women for a moment, until she turned around.

It was not a woman but a man, apparently of Southeast Asian descent. The man stood and approached Trip, moving with an almost sinuous grace.

"Hello," he said, his voice a deep basso. "I'm Tinh Hoc Phuong, field operations, currently assigned to the Romulan theater of operations. Glad to finally meet you." He held out his hand. "Welcome aboard the *Branson*."

Trip shook the other man's hand. "Charles Tucker, uh, Commander, Starfleet. But most people just call me Trip."

Phuong smiled. "Not anymore they don't."

Trip was a bit taken aback, but he tried his best to maintain his composure. "Yeah, well, I haven't quite gotten used to being dead just yet."

"I disappeared off the sensor grid three years ago,"

Phuong said. He gestured to a small alcove to Trip's right. "You want some coffee, or something to eat? We've got a long flight ahead of us."

"Sure," Trip said, moving over to the alcove, where he saw shelves bearing various prepackaged foodstuffs, all arranged in an efficient manner. There was also a tiny kitchen area, with a small sink, and a few nozzles and buttons built into the counter area.

"The green button on the left is for coffee," Phuong said as he crossed back his ship's flight controls.

"So, where's our first stop?" Trip asked. It struck him then that this voyage could take him to a nearly infinite list of possible destinations, virtually all of which would probably be completely unknown to him.

"Adigeon Prime. Not very far from territory claimed by the Romulans."

Trip didn't immediately see any cream or sugar in the kitchen alcove as he picked up one of Phuong's cups and filled it from the spigot under the green button. *Guess I'll just have it black,* he thought as he carried his beverage to the forward section. He sat in the copilot's chair next to Phuong's seat, and found it comfortable.

"We meeting someone there?" he asked, gratified that he had at least heard of Adigeon Prime prior to today.

"No other bureau operatives, if that's what you mean. Just the people—or whatever they are—who've been hired to help us get our mission fully under way."

"So, if you don't mind my asking, you said you disappeared three years ago. Is that how long you've been working for Section 31?"

Phuong looked at him inquisitively. "Section 31?"

Trip felt a cannonball of dread drop into his stomach. Had he somehow been tricked and kidnapped by someone other than Harris's spy organization?

Almost instantly, the other man nodded. "Oh, you

mean the *bureau*. I get it. Article Fourteen, Section Thirty-one of the Starfleet Charter. Catchy name."

Trip relaxed slightly. "Bureau of what?" This was definitely something that Malcolm hadn't briefed him about.

"Of *nothing*. Even though we're authorized to operate by the Starfleet Charter, we don't exist—at least not officially. So, it's just 'the bureau.'"

Trip looked down into the nut-brown depths of his coffee, feeling decidedly uneasy about his radically changed circumstances. Although life aboard *Enterprise* had always had its dangers, the interstellar espionage business seemed a good deal more hazardous by comparison. He couldn't forget what had happened to Malcolm last year when the Klingons had kidnapped Phlox. Malcolm, acting on Section 31's orders, had sabotaged *Enterprise* to slow down Captain Archer's rescue efforts. The incident might well have ended Malcolm's career but for Archer's decision to protect his armory officer rather than having him court-martialed.

Now Trip was growing concerned that the cloak-and-dagger bureau might just bury him as well and as thoroughly as it had buried Phuong. After all, Phuong had apparently been operating undercover for three years already. Remaining "dead" for such a long stretch of time didn't appeal to Trip.

"Having second thoughts?" Phuong asked, looking over at him. "Everyone does."

"Mmmm," Trip grunted noncommittally.

Phuong let out a heavy sigh. "I understand. I was a diplomat, in another life. Not top-level, so you'd never see me at the really world-shaking interstellar functions, but close enough to the top to know who all the players were. I guess that's why they recruited me."

Trip looked sideways at the man in the pilot's seat. "This is my first . . . assignment."

The other man smiled again. "Oh, I know. I've read your file. I probably know more about you than some of your friends do." He grabbed a padd that had been sitting to the immediate left of his instruments, and handed it to Trip. "Read this, then we'll be even. It's my whole boring life story, up to and including what I've done for the last three years."

And I wonder how much of it is true? Trip thought. He wasn't sure he trusted Phuong, but the man seemed disarmingly honest. *An odd trait for a spy.*

"Before you get too far into it, I just wanted to say that I read your reports on the Romulans' use of cloaking technology," Phuong said. "Actually, I've read *all* your reports on the Romulans and their technology. I can even quote them back to you if you want." He put a finger to his temple. "Near-photographic memory. Comes in handy when circumstances in the field force you to purge your data to keep it from falling into the wrong hands. Anyhow, I was impressed. The analysis you wrote about the Romulans' telepath-driven droneship program was fine, meticulous work. I volunteered for this mission because I wanted to work with *you*."

"Thanks," was all Trip could think of to say.

But Phuong apparently wasn't yet finished dispensing praise. "Having you along on this assignment—a trained engineer who's already seen Romulan tech up close—makes me think we stand a real chance of putting the Romulans' warp seven program out of business. Or maybe even of grabbing it for the Coalition."

Despite himself, Trip felt a small smile break across his lips. Whether Phuong's words were mere flattery or were sincere, the fact that Section 31 had paid so much attention to his warnings reassured him that they did indeed take the Romulan threat seriously—unlike Admiral Gardner, who couldn't even be bothered to lock his own back door against the coming hordes.

Maybe sometimes the powers that be really do need somebody guarding that back door for them, he thought. *Whether they know about it or not.*

He set aside his apprehensions, at least for the moment. Being able to believe that he truly was in the right place, doing the right thing—even briefly—was a small comfort after the maelstrom of a day he'd just had, and the cataclysmic changes he'd just introduced into his life.

But it was comfort nonetheless.

Now feeling relatively at ease, he began familiarizing himself with the layout of the *Branson*'s controls, which he recognized right away, thanks to his Starfleet training. The *Branson* was a small *Rutan*-class trading vessel, of a type that hadn't been built since the late 2130s. Designed to support a maximum of six people and to carry several tons of cargo, the *Rutan*s had a top range of perhaps fifteen light-years, and were notoriously slow.

Trip didn't have to spend much time behind the controls before he realized that Phuong had apparently found retrofit remedies for both of those problems.

For the second since he'd come aboard, he smiled. *Adigeon Prime, here we come.*

FIFTEEN

Friday, February 14, 2155
Enterprise NX-01

ARCHER CONSIDERED WAITING, hoping that some kind of glitch—or miracle—would scuttle Trip's espionage mission. But the captain knew waiting could endanger not only the mission but also his friend's life. He had to contact the Tuckers now. Trip had outlined his parents' schedule for the captain, making certain not only that both his parents would be home, but also that his father would already have taken his daily medication.

Although he had first met Charles and Elaine Tucker some twenty years ago, his most memorable encounter with Trip's parents had come in 2143, when they had come to visit the Academy following the successful—if illegal—flight of the *NX-Beta*. Gracie, as she preferred to be called, had pulled Archer aside by his arm, scolding him as if he were her own son.

"Don't you get my boy involved in *any more* of your wild schemes, Jonathan Archer," she had said, waggling her finger in his face. "I don't care *who* your daddy was, or how much Trip worships what he did. He needs to learn responsibility, not how to take joyrides across the solar system."

"Yes, ma'am," Archer had said guiltily.

A moment later, she had slapped him, lightly, as if to make certain she had his full attention. "Don't you 'yes, ma'am' me as if I'm some tawdry Helena. I'm quite *seri-*

ous. My boy looks up to you. You need to make sure you're man enough to *deserve* it."

Archer never had found out what a "tawdry Helena" was, but he had spent the better part of the next dozen years or so as Trip Tucker's friend, confidant, and superior officer. And through it all, he had always tried his utmost to be certain he was man enough to deserve Trip's respect and friendship.

He tapped the buttons on the padd on his desk, and the image on his screen changed from the white-on-blue symbol of Earth's Starfleet to a darker hue with a moving sine wave superimposed, signifying that his signal was transmitting.

Several moments later, the screen brightened, and Charlie Tucker appeared. *"Hello?"* He peered into the screen, and his face was almost instantly split by a smile. *"Jonathan Archer!"*

"Hello, Charlie," Archer said.

The older man put one hand up and turned to yell over his shoulder. *"Gracie, it's Jonny on the line."* A pause, and then he yelled, *"Jonny Archer!"* A few seconds later, a middle-aged woman pulling a housecoat around her shoulders appeared on the screen with Charlie.

"Lordy, you haven't changed a bit!" Elaine said, smiling. *"Must be some alien mojo working to keep you young."*

Archer struggled to keep his composure in the face of such a pleasant greeting. Besides, he knew a polite lie when he heard one, just as he knew how he really looked in the mirror. "Thank you, Gracie. You look as fantastic as always."

Charlie Tucker craned his head from side to side, peering at Archer—or rather, *around* Archer. *"Where's our boy? He couldn't make it to the call?"*

Archer gulped, and blinked hard. "Mr. and Mrs.

Tucker . . . there's no easy way for me to tell you this, but earlier today, Trip—"

Elaine Tucker let out a shriek, her happy countenance crumbling. *"No! Don't tell me . . ."*

Charlie put his arm around his wife's shoulder, drawing her in, muttering something to her that the Tuckers' audio pickup didn't quite catch.

"I'm so sorry to have to tell you," Archer said, his voice low.

Charlie looked toward him across the monitor, his lower lip trembling. *"Is he gone, or just injured?"*

Archer felt his own eyes welling up with tears. "He's . . . gone, sir."

Charlie looked away, his lips tightening inward and outward. *"Was he doing something heroic?"*

"Yes, he was," Archer said. "He was saving me, and the ship. And quite possibly a lot more than that." This felt less like a lie than the rest of it, but *Enterprise's* captain still felt his stomach tying itself into knots over having to deceive the Tuckers.

Elaine let out a deep sob, then shouted something unintelligible through her crying. Charlie pulled her in tighter, and looked back toward the screen.

"All right, Jonny," he said, his voice quavering. *"We . . . we, um . . . we need some time to make some sense out of this. Please . . . uh . . . forward the details to us, and we'll be in touch."*

"I understand, and I will," Archer said. "I want you to know that he was the bravest and best friend I've—"

The screen abruptly went black before he could finish. Even though he had lost his father when he was young, and as *Enterprise's* captain had lost both Starfleet crew members and MACO troopers, Archer could only imagine the grief the Tuckers must be experiencing now. First their daughter Elizabeth had been killed in the Xindi attack on Earth two years ago, and then, only a couple of weeks ago, their sole grandchild—Trip and T'Pol's daughter, also named Elizabeth—had died.

And now, as far as they know, Trip *is gone, too. But their pain is a lie this time . . . a lie made necessary by other lies and secrets and subterfuge.* He hated the Romulans for driving them to this. More than he had ever hated anything, even the Xindi, he hated them, these faceless creatures from the other side of space.

Archer struggled to regain his composure and tamp down his feelings. He still had to call Trip's brother Albert. He recalled that Albert and his husband Miguel also lived in Alabama, not far from Charlie and Elaine. He hoped they'd be able to help the Tuckers cope with their latest dose of grief.

Grief caused by the lie of Trip's death, which we designed and executed so very carefully. Archer wondered what Trip would do once he was free again to resume his old life, if that were ever to happen. Would he find the emotional barriers erected by Section 31's lies as easy to break down as they'd been to construct?

T'Pol reached for the small framed photograph on Trip's desk. The image was of him scuba-diving in Earth's Caribbean Sea. Below him was a manta ray, its flat form belying the danger posed by its venom-tipped tail.

She studied the picture for a moment, recalling Trip's talk of taking her diving. Having grown up on arid Vulcan, T'Pol had had little experience even with swimming, much less underwater sightseeing and adventuring.

She felt sadness welling up inside her again like a towering wave, and stopped to concentrate, willing the emotion to be suppressed. She put the photograph down on top of an open suitcase on the bed. Many more of Trip's small possessions were in the padded enclosure, including other photographs and the harmonica he'd played from time to time.

T'Pol turned and picked up one of Trip's royal blue uniform jumpsuits. After the Vulcan High Command had cashiered her, Starfleet had granted her a commission. Yet she had never donned their uniform. Perhaps the Vulcan uniform she still wore—a garment that now bore Starfleet commander's pips—represented an illogical attachment to the past.

And perhaps Trip's death signified that the time had finally arrived to move past such impulses.

She started to fold Trip's uniform, but found herself, without cause, pulling it close to her face. She inhaled deeply, directing the residual musky scent of her former lover on the garment.

Ever since she'd come on board *Enterprise*, she'd been tolerant of the assault of smells that swirled around her: the humans, Captain Archer's dog, and even from the machinery that ran the vessel. But now, as she smelled the ghosts of Trip's sweat, mixed with the slight ozone tang of the engine room, she found the odors comforting.

The door to Trip's quarters slid open, but T'Pol didn't turn to see who was entering.

"Need any help?" Captain Archer asked, leaning against the bulkhead beside the bed.

T'Pol began refolding the uniform, handling it as though it were a precision scientific instrument. "No, thank you."

Archer gestured toward the case she had been preparing. "For his parents?"

Nodding listlessly, T'Pol asked, "Will they still be coming to the ceremony?"

"We didn't talk long, but I'll try to make sure that they do. I think they know that Trip wouldn't want it any other way."

He chuckled mirthlessly and reached forward, pulling a small Frankenstein monster figure from the shelf. "Don't forget this," he said, holding it out for her.

T'Pol took the figurine and studied it in silence, remembering the first time she and Trip had watched the original film version of *Frankenstein*. He had shown it to her as a thank-you for the Vulcan neural pressure therapy sessions she had been performing on him to help him get over his insomnia. It was during the viewing that they had first touched in a far less formal—and decidedly nontherapeutic—manner. Just Trip's hand over hers, but she had not pulled away, nor questioned his intentions as she might have just days earlier.

Aware that the captain was watching her expectantly, she said, "I'd like to meet them."

"His parents?" asked Archer.

"Yes, I'd like to meet them." T'Pol stared down at the figurine in her hands, stroking it.

Archer moved past her, toward the head. T'Pol could sense that he seemed nervous, as if afraid of saying the wrong thing. "They're a little eccentric. I think you'll see where Trip got his sense of humor."

"My mother was somewhat eccentric, as well," T'Pol said.

Archer stared away from her. "I wasn't around her for very long, but I could see that."

T'Pol placed the Frankenstein monster figure into the case. "Trip told me that as time went by, I would miss her less." She sat down on the bed, feeling her mind clouding with unwanted emotions again. "Though she hasn't yet been gone for a year, I think he was wrong. Because I find myself missing her more with each passing month. Why would he tell me that?"

Archer spread his hands awkwardly. " 'Time heals all wounds' . . . but 'Absence makes the heart grow fonder.' I guess it's a little tricky." He moved over toward her. "Emotions have a way of contradicting themselves."

T'Pol could feel the pain rising again inside her, pushing against her eyes and her sinuses. "And you wonder why we suppress them?" She looked down, forcing herself not to give in to her feelings, pushing back against them as hard as they pushed to escape.

Archer sat on the bed and leaned toward her. "When I took command of *Enterprise* almost four years ago, I saw myself as an explorer. I thought all the risks would be worth it . . . because just beyond the next planet, just beyond the next star, there would be something *magnificent*. Something . . . noble."

He paused, as if searching for the right words. "And now, Trip is dead . . . and we're out here chasing aliens who want to stop our exploration, who don't care about noble ideals, and who never had the good fortune to know Trip."

Archer turned and looked toward the viewport, and into the inky space beyond it. "In a few weeks, I have to go give that speech at the Coalition Compact signing ceremony. I have to talk about how all the risks were worth it, about how worthwhile it's all been . . ."

"Trip would be the first to say it *was* worthwhile," T'Pol said, her voice barely wavering as she swallowed still more of her sorrow.

Archer looked at her and smiled, but his expression contained no joy or mirth. She could see in his eyes that he was conflicted, that something else, something deeper, was troubling him. It was a look of regret and uncertainty. He opened his mouth as if to say something further, then looked away, to the viewport and the warp-distorted streaks of starlight beyond.

Finally, he stood and walked to the door. "I'll leave you to finish here, T'Pol. But if you need to talk to me—even if you need to let down your famous Vulcan guard—you're welcome to. I won't tell."

T'Pol regarded her captain for a moment. She wondered what he would think if she revealed that one of the last things she had told her mother before her death was that she didn't want anything further to do with her. How would Archer feel if he were to learn that when she had first learned of little Elizabeth's mixed parentage, she had wanted nothing more than for the child to disappear?

What would his reaction be if he knew that Trip and T'Pol had decided to break off their relationship completely on Vulcan, but that she had found among his belongings an undelivered letter written *after* their journey to Vulcan—a letter in which Trip had described his deep and full love for her, and the pain their separation was causing him?

And worst of all were her own traitorous thoughts, full of love and other emotions as well, all of which brought her anguish every time she considered life without Trip.

And now, she had no choice but to forge ahead alone. Her mother, her child, her lover. All *gone*.

She swallowed and blinked, masking her shame behind what she hoped was an impassive Vulcan mask. "Thank you for your offer, Captain. But I believe I can deal with such things on my own."

The words seemed to echo in the air after Archer exited.

On my own.

T'Pol lay her head down on one of Trip's pillows. Then, silently, agonizingly, before she could halt them, tears rolled down her cheeks.

SIXTEEN

Saturday, February 15, 2155
Deep space

"ADIGEON PRIME," Trip said as he idly studied the image of the blue-green planet displayed on Phuong's secondary library-computer monitor. According to the *Branson*'s navigational computer, their destination lay some eighteen hours away at their current speed. "Don't know a lot about the place."

Seated in a relaxed fashion in the pilot's seat, Phuong cast a grin in Trip's direction. "That may be because the Adigeons don't like to call a lot of attention to themselves. They're businessmen."

Trip shifted in the copilot's seat, struggling vainly to get comfortable as he turned to face Phuong. "Don't businessmen need to advertise?"

"Not when so much of their business depends on . . . discretion," Phuong said.

Trip nodded, understanding. "So they're criminals."

"That's oversimplifying things quite a bit, Commander," Phuong said, shaking his head. "Let's just say they often act as third-party brokers to many interstellar business entities who value their privacy. Including the Romulans, who are notoriously secretive about their military and civil affairs and their strengths and weaknesses. You might describe the Adigeons as a sort of cultural and intelligence membrane between the Romulans and the other societies with whom they sometimes have to do business. Sort of like the old Swiss banking firms back on Earth."

"So our plan is to use the Romulans' own Adigeon Prime business agents to infiltrate them," Trip said. "I guess the Adigeons' discretion must come with a price, and that it's a price the bureau was able to pay."

Phuong offered Trip a lopsided smile. "Very astute, Commander. The Adigeons also have other talents that we're going to need."

"Ah. Our Romulan disguises."

Phuong nodded. "The Adigeons can provide medical procedures ranging from simple plastic surgeries to genetic alterations that haven't been available on Earth since the Eugenics Wars ended."

"So far, no human has ever seen what a Romulan looks like," Trip said. "So I take it that the Adigeons know a lot more about that subject than we do."

"That's correct, although the Adigeons have been well paid to keep such secrets to themselves. But thanks to a highly bribable Adigeon plastic surgeon, you and I will be going under the knife. We'll not only receive all the appropriate surgical alterations, we'll also be fitted with ear-implanted translation devices to help us communicate with any Romulans we encounter. By this time tomorrow, our own mothers probably won't recognize us."

The thought of his grieving mother almost made Trip wince. But the image also reminded him that the sooner this mission was completed, the sooner he'd be able to return home to comfort her in person.

"And is this process reversible?" Trip said.

"So I've been told."

Trip wished Phuong had sounded a little more confident about that, but decided to table that particular question for now. "So what happens once we're in disguise, Tinh?"

"We will meet with members of a Romulan dissident faction known as the *Ejhoi Ormiin*."

Trip tried to get his lips around the name and failed utterly. "The what?"

"*Ejhoi Ormiin*. According to my intelligence sources, the phrase roughly translates from the Romulan *Rihannsu* language as 'to decide with finality on the best of several options.' It's the name of a group that opposes the Romulan Star Empire's current ethic of expansion and conquest."

Hope warred with suspicion deep in Trip's gut. "And you trust them."

"We have to make our leaps of faith *somewhere*, Commander, or else we'll never get *anywhere*. At any rate, the *Ejhoi Ormiin* already know we are coming to meet with them. They are presently harboring an important Romulan warp scientist, a man named Ehrehin."

"*How* important?"

Phuong's mien quickly took on a more sober cast. "How important was Henry Archer? Or Zefram Cochrane?"

Trip felt a chill of apprehension slowly ascend the length of his spine. *That important,* he thought.

Phuong continued, his tone growing progressively grimmer: "This Doctor Ehrehin's expertise could very well spell the difference between victory and defeat in the coming conflict, depending upon which side gains sole access to him. Imagine what will happen to Earth if the Romulans succeed in building whole fleets of warp seven-capable ships before we can. Ehrehin is the key to the whole thing."

Trip sat in silence, processing what Phuong had told him, imagining one doomsday scenario after another and finding each of them uncomfortably believable. He could feel the forces of history and contingency already in motion all around him, like the faint buzzing of warp-field lines against his skin when he tended *Enterprise*'s engines. How many times before had catastrophes such as the coming one happened, or nearly happened, in human history? He recalled that just prior to Earth's first space age, the finest rocket scientists of the day had been employed by Nazi Germany. Had the United States failed to recruit Wernher von Braun just after the Second World War, the Soviets might well have added his talents to those of Sergei Korolev, thus completely changing the outcome of the U.S.-Soviet space race and the Cold War that had spawned it.

Only this *is even* more *serious,* Trip thought. *Because the safety of the Earth and all her allies is at stake.*

Still, Trip had to cling to the hope that an all-out war with the Romulans was still somehow avoidable. "There's no way around this thing, is there?" he asked Phuong at length.

"A way around war with the Romulans?" Phuong's expression became grave, and he shook his head. "I'm afraid I've come to understand the Romulans a little too well to believe that's possible."

That's saying a lot, considering the fact that he's never even seen *a Romulan,* Trip thought. Aloud, he said, "Don't you think Romulan dissidents—like these *Ejhoi Ormiin* people—might have anything to say?"

Phuong chuckled, but it was a dry, humorless sound. "Passion isn't the same thing as power, Commander. Unfortunately, the *Ejhoi Ormiin* aren't in charge, and that's not likely to change anytime soon."

Trip sat back in silence, staring straight ahead at the starfield through which the *Branson* was headed. He was suddenly struck by the sheer immensity of the implacable forces arrayed against Earth and her allies—and by the Coalition's remote chance of survival, given its apparent blindness to the very real dangers that lay directly in its path.

"Why is it that only a few people can see what ought to be obvious?" he said a few moments later, once he'd found his voice again.

Phuong answered in soothing, encouraging tones. "Maybe certain people can't help but see it—especially if they're trained problem solvers."

That seemed to Trip entirely too facile an answer, and he turned to cast a skeptical eye upon the other man. "There are lots of 'problem solvers' on Earth who have bigger brains than either of us do, Tinh."

"Granted. But a lot of those 'big brains' are pursuing other agendas, too—like struggling to hang onto a high political office or an admiral's pips. Public controversy and fear can work against those sort of agendas, and people like Nathan Samuels and Admiral Gardner damned well know it, especially now that they need to put the Terra Prime attacks behind them in order to keep the public calm and the Coalition together."

"What about the other Coalition worlds?" Trip asked. "Aren't any of them willing to listen and help?"

"Our bureau—Section 31, as you call it—is a secret organization based on Earth, Commander. And it would be a lot tougher for us to *stay* secret if we were to tip our hand to Earth's allies—to say nothing of the damage we might do to interstellar relations if our allies ever got the notion that Earth is either an active or an unwitting host to what some might call a rogue spy network. Not that they don't use similar means and methods themselves, mind you."

Trip nodded. "Like the Vulcan agents who spied on the Andorians while posing as monks on P'Jem."

"Exactly. Besides, I wouldn't count on a lot of help from the allied planets right now anyway. They've each got their hands full. The Andorians and Vulcans are *still* busy spying on each other, even now. Minister T'Pau is still in the process of purging the Vulcan High Command of V'Las loyalists, which has hamstrung Vulcan's military response capabilities, at least for a while. The Coridan worlds have been so close to civil war over the past few years that I doubt Coridan Prime would share its warp-seven technology with Earth in time to provide any tactical advantage over the Romulans. And the Tellarites never seem to get tired of arguing among themselves, or with anyone else, for that matter."

Trip sighed, not sure how to respond, though he was certain that Phuong's analysis was pretty much spot-on, if a bit cynical. "Sounds like you don't have a lot of faith in the Coalition."

"Not true," Phuong said, waving a hand as though to dismiss Trip's words. "I'm just realistic enough not to expect it to solve every problem overnight. The Coalition is only a starting point for Earth's future. It's going to need quite a bit of time to prove itself truly useful to all the parties involved."

"But it won't get that time if the Romulans move before we're ready for them," Trip said.

"Precisely." Phuong nodded and smiled, evidently delighted at Trip's insight. "It's crucial that we prevent the Romulans from completing Doctor Ehrehin's new stardrive prototypes. If we miss on this, there'll be nothing to stop the Romulans from invading Earth itself."

Phuong's dark eyes seemed almost to glow with an inner fervor as he continued: "During the eleven years I served in Earth's diplomatic service, wishful thinkers have treated my take on the Romulans like the ravings of a delusional paranoid. But the bureau saw the Romulan threat with clear eyes. Its directorate was willing to listen—and more importantly, was willing to *do* something. The Xindi attack taught us the importance of being out here, of being proactive. That's why our role in keeping Earth safe will become even more critical as the Coalition moves forward and Earth comes into contact with God only knows how many more new potential adversaries in the years ahead."

Phuong's impassioned speech gave Trip a momentary

chill of recognition. And despite his current extreme vulnerability—being in deep space with a spy who would no doubt kill him if he perceived him as dangerous to his mission—Trip realized that he simply couldn't let it pass without comment.

"The last time I saw anybody look as intense as you do right now was the time I nearly got killed by John Frederick Paxton."

Trip half expected an extremely angry response. But instead, Phuong laughed, the sound coming from deep in his belly.

"Stick with the bureau long enough, Commander, and there's no way you could mistake us for Terra Prime," Phuong finally said once his laughter finally died down. "The bureau doesn't want humanity to shy away from alien contact. Or to expand through the galaxy as exploiters or conquerors. We only want the human race to face whatever's out there with open eyes, open minds, and a pragmatic attitude."

Trip absorbed Phuong's apparently heartfelt sentiments with no small amount of relief. Turning back toward the ever-unfolding starfield that lay before him, Trip resumed studying the image of Adigeon Prime. Although his apprehensions about what lay ahead—particularly about what awaited him in the Adigeons' surgical facilities—hadn't entirely abated, they had at least receded somewhat.

Maybe I really did *make the best decision I could have by agreeing to come out here,* he thought. *And the sooner we get the deed done, the sooner I'll be able to tell my folks and T'Pol that "the rumors of my death have been greatly exaggerated."*

That was assuming, of course, that he'd find a way to survive a sojourn in entirely unknown space, while hiding and spying among deadly adversaries, people that no one from his planet had ever even laid eyes on before. . . .

SEVENTEEN

Monday, February 17, 2155
Enterprise **NX-01**

THE PALE BLUE DOT on *Enterprise*'s bridge viewer gradually resolved itself into a disk, then grew still further until it became recognizable as the frigid, perpetually snow-blown desert that was Rigel X—the planet where the Orion's slave ship's trail had abruptly ended.

Jonathan Archer had been here before, on his very first mission aboard *Enterprise*, in fact, and the recollection wasn't a pleasant one. Since he had hurriedly departed from this place in the midst of a running firefight—and gotten shot while doing so—Rigel X wasn't high on the list of locales he wanted to revisit anytime soon.

"Delightful planet, Captain," Malcolm Reed said, with no small amount of irony. Sitting at the tactical station that faced the bridge's center from starboard, he seemed to have read Archer's mind better than even Theras could have.

"I suppose ending up at Risa was too much to hope for," Archer said dryly as he rose from his command chair and strode toward the image of the dark, frigid world that now lay only a few hundred kilometers beneath *Enterprise*'s ventral hull. Had the star Rigel, visible beyond its tenth planet's limb as a small but bright disk, not been a blue supergiant, this world would have been as thoroughly frozen and uninhabitable as Pluto. Though quite distant from its primary star, Rigel X provided a marginally livable environment that supported a large population of itinerant traders and permanent residents, sentients from at least a dozen worlds spread throughout the several sectors of space—all of whom worked, played, and lived in an enormous, thirty-six-level commercial habitat complex built right into the planet's living rock.

"Travis, put us into a standard orbit."

"Aye, sir," the helmsman said as he deftly worked the controls.

As Archer continued to watch the screen, he saw bright lines intermittently lancing the turbulent indigo atmosphere with delicate and swiftly fading traceries of fire. Too regular and elliptically shaped to be lightning discharges, the brilliant streaks betrayed the ascent and descent of all manner of spacecraft, which must have been taking traders and customers of all sorts to and from the surface of Rigel X.

The captain recalled how he'd felt four years ago, that he didn't want a Vulcan on his ship. Now, he couldn't imagine *Enterprise* without T'Pol. His science officer, quiet, competent, and still able to surprise her captain. This morning he stepped out of his ready room and immediately noticed that something was off. Looking towards the science station, Archer saw T'Pol in a Starfleet uniform. Even now he had to suppress a smile. Turning toward the science station, Archer asked, "T'Pol, have you found any ships in the vicinity that might correspond to the warp trail we followed here?"

T'Pol shook her head gravely. "I've already begun running scans of the surface, and every ship within range of *Enterprise*'s sensors, whether on the surface, in the atmosphere, or in orbit. Nothing conclusive has emerged so far, although I *have* detected a number of Orion ships of various classes, all of them commercial transports and freighters. It is possible that the particular vessel we followed is indeed present on the planet, but has powered down temporarily so as to make itself undetectable."

"What about Aenar life signs?"

"So far I've found no evidence of any Aenar or Andorian life-forms anywhere on the planet, or aboard any of the incoming vessels I have detected."

"But that doesn't necessarily mean they aren't here *somewhere*, Captain," said Reed. "People who peddle flesh the way the Orions do would be highly motivated to keep their activities camouflaged. Absence of evidence isn't evidence of absence."

"Either way," Archer said, "somebody down there must know the location and status of that Orion slave ship we tracked here. I'm taking a landing party down to the trade complex to find out."

"Aye, sir." Ensign Mayweather entered a command into his helm console, then rose from his seat to face the captain. "I'll start preparing Shuttlepod One immediately."

Archer raised a hand in a gentle "slow down" gesture. "Not this time, Travis. We'll be using the transporter, since we need to get in quickly and may need to get out even more quickly." Once again, he couldn't escape the memory of the painful energy-pistol burn he'd received the last time he'd been in a rush to leave Rigel X.

Though Mayweather looked crestfallen as he returned to his station, Archer lacked the time and the patience at the moment to promise the junior officer more exciting piloting duty "next time."

Archer turned back to face the aft portion of the bridge, where T'Pol and Hoshi manned the two stations at his right, while Malcolm looked on from the tactical station at the captain's left. "Malcolm, you're coming, too. I want a pair of MACOs along to watch our backs as well. T'Pol, you have the bridge." He started toward the turbolift, motioning to Malcolm, who immediately followed.

"Shran has already made it abundantly clear that he intends to come along with any landing party we dispatch to the surface," T'Pol said as Archer passed.

He stopped in the open turbolift entrance for a moment, considering. "All right, T'Pol," he said finally. "Shran can come along. I suppose he'd be pretty hard for the rest of you to live with if I were to leave him here. But Theras is definitely staying aboard *Enterprise*."

T'Pol raised an eyebrow. "I'm certain that Shran will be quite pleased by *both* of those decisions, Captain," she said just before the turbolift doors closed.

"Captain, are you certain it's wise to bring Shran along on this mission?" Malcolm asked as the turbolift began its descent toward D deck, where the transporter was located. "If you don't mind my saying so, I've always found him rather lacking in . . . restraint."

"Really, Malcolm. I hadn't noticed."

Malcolm continued, ignoring Archer's jest. "And he's been particularly touchy since he first brought this Orion slaver business to our attention."

"I suppose I'll have to take him aside before we beam down and give him a gentle lecture on restraint," Archer said.

"Good idea, sir. I'd also recommend taking along a third MACO."

"Why?"

Malcolm grinned sheepishly. "Just in case Shran needs a little additional babysitting."

The landing party materialized in near darkness, standing in a tight, back-to-back circle. Archer's eyes weren't yet adjusted to the dim light, but he could feel the penetrating cold of the trade complex's poorer quarters immediately. He could see the flicker of the fires that Rigel

X's homeless, hopeless transients were burning to cook their meals, or perhaps merely to stay warm. He could smell the pungent mixture of smoke and sweat, despair and greed that swirled in the chill air. He could feel the harsh solidity of the metal floor beneath his boots. And in the middle distance, he could hear the roar of a crowd, punctuated by the fast, terse vocalizations of a humanoid speaking into a public address system of some sort, announcing what sounded like quantities and prices in various alien currencies.

Archer ordered the team to move out, taking the point while a pair of MACO troopers—their company leader, the petite and dark-haired Sergeant Fiona McKenzie, and the eagle-eyed Corporal Hideaki Chang—flanked him, their phase pistols holstered to avoid provoking anyone, yet still within easy reach. Reed, Shran, and the remaining MACO, a small, wiry, shaved-headed corporal named David McCammon, watched the rear as the group moved quickly through a twisting maze of causeways, alleys, and ramshackle galleries, toward the source of the sounds.

Although Archer had visited this trading facility before, what he saw when the team finally reached the large, crowded gallery-cum-amphitheater truly shocked him.

Of course, it wasn't as though he'd never seen a slave auction before. Nine months earlier, T'Pol and several other members of his crew had briefly become trapped in just the sort of nightmare that now lay spread before him. Now as then, helpless, shackled people of every imaginable species, and members of more than a few he didn't recognize, were being herded by armed, green-skinned overseers toward a raised dais, where a large, bejeweled, and lightly armored Orion male vended his wares to an equally diverse group of much more finely attired sentients. These obviously well-heeled buyers probably originated from points all over known space, if not from considerably beyond as well.

As his team insinuated itself close enough to the stage to get a clear look at the seemingly endless pageant of chained and nearly naked flesh from countless worlds, the fact that there were no humans among the captives being sold gave Archer only cold comfort. After all, no species had a monopoly on fear; in Archer's experience, all sentient beings experienced that emotion in pretty much the same way. The stage presently abounded with ample evidence that fear was as universal as life was cheap.

At least in places like this, where those who thought that their wealth entitled them to purchase *people* seemed to be as common as hydrogen.

"There are no Aenar here, Captain," said Shran, who was standing at Archer's left. He, too, was studying the stage intently. Archer could see that the Andorian was as disgusted as he was by the flesh market before them.

"I haven't seen any, either," Archer said. The two men had to shout to hear one another over the all-enveloping white noise made by the bidding crowd around them.

Malcolm, who had sidled up to Archer's immediate right, consulted the scanning device in his hand. "Even at close range, I've found no Aenar life signs so far."

"Perhaps they're being sold at another slave market elsewhere on the planet," said Shran.

"Look at the size of this operation, Shran," Archer said. "Do you think there could be another market here capable of competing with *this*? Besides, Rigel X only has *one* central trade complex."

"It's one too many, if you ask me," Reed said. His face was a study in distaste.

"I can certainly agree with you on that, pinkskin," Shran said.

"My guess," said Archer, trying to keep the team

focused, "is that the slave ship we tracked here made a wholesale transfer of all the captured Aenar onto a second ship."

"Makes sense," Reed said. "They could have bypassed the auction block altogether if they already had a single buyer lined up."

A buyer like the Romulan military, Archer thought with a chill.

Shran's antennae flattened against his scalp in a clear display of anger and frustration. "If that's true, then we're not leaving this planet until I find out where that slave ship is now, and *exactly* what became of its . . . cargo."

"Someone in charge of logistics around here would have to be able to shed some light on the matter," Reed said.

"Then let's not waste any more time," Archer said, motioning to Sergeant McKenzie that it was time for the landing party to move on. Chang and McCammon immediately took up protective positions on the team's flank as Archer directed it away from the densest section of the roiling crowd of slave bidders.

Archer stopped when he noticed that Shran was hanging back, and motioned the others to halt as he wended through a small cluster of buyers, making his way back to Shran's side.

"Come on, Shran," Archer said, shouting almost directly into Shran's ear to make himself heard. "We can't stay here."

"We can't let an abomination like this continue, either," said the Andorian, a faraway, almost fanatical look in his icy blue eyes.

Although he could certainly sympathize, Archer didn't like what he was seeing and hearing. "Remember the little chat about restraint we had earlier, Shran?"

"No one should be treated this way," Shran said. He

either hadn't heard Archer's words or had chosen to ignore them.

Archer noted that the Andorian's hand was on the holster of the phase pistol that Malcolm had issued him.

He placed a restraining hand on Shran's arm. The Andorian stiffened, but made no move either to shake Archer off or to draw his weapon.

"Shran, this thing bothers me as much as it bothers you," he said. "I'd love nothing better right now than to shoot this place up and set all these people free. Hell, if I'd seen this the *last* time I came here, I might have actually *done* it."

Shran looked at him, his eyes flashing with passionate outrage. He shrugged off Archer's hand and drew his weapon. Fortunately, no one in the crowd showed any sign of having noticed it, probably because of the obscuring folds of the Andorian's field jacket.

"Shran, suppose you *do* free them all instead of just getting us all killed," Archer said in mounting desperation. "What do you think will happen to these people afterward?"

"What could be worse than *this*, pinkskin?"

Archer knew that once Shran fired his weapon, the landing party would be very unlikely to get back to the ship intact. And getting everyone back to the ship alive was his primary responsibility. His body tensed as he prepared to bring Shran down hand-to-hand should it prove necessary.

In the meantime, he pressed on with an argument of necessity, despite the fact that he didn't truly believe it in his heart. "I'll tell you what would happen, Shran. Some of these people would be shot dead. Some would die after being trampled. A few might even make it outside. Most of those would freeze to death, and the ones that didn't would starve. If we interfere, we make a horrible decision for these people. There'll be no going back for any of them."

Slavery is a terrible life, Archer thought, hating himself for being unable to end these people's all but unimaginable suffering. "Shran, they'll blame us, Earth and Andoria, and the Coalition we've worked for could die stillborn. But someday, together, we could wipe places like this off the face of the quadrant."

Shran continued to stand where he was, angry but vacillating, his weapon in hand, though still concealed. Archer remained poised to body-slam him, despite the very real risk of starting a panic in the crowd. "Shran."

Slump-shouldered with defeat, the Andorian finally holstered his weapon, then began moving toward Reed and the MACOs. Archer followed him, heaving a sigh of relief.

"Let's find Jhamel, Archer," Shran said as the group reached the periphery of the madly bidding crowd, where they could hear each other without having to raise their voices. "I'll save my anger for those who took her—and for anybody who tries to stop me from getting to them."

Thank goodness for Andorian restraint, Archer thought as the slave auction passed from his sight, though not from his conscience.

EIGHTEEN

Monday, February 17, 2155
Adigeon Prime

ALTHOUGH ADIGEON PRIME was an Earth-like planet in most respects, its significantly lower gravity took some getting used to—as did the natives. Trip looked out a window at the expansive city over which flew hundreds of winged Adigeons.

Outside of graphic novels and vids, he had never before seen flying humanoids with his own eyes. He'd heard of a race called the Skorr, but their homeworld was apparently some distance away from the sectors through which *Enterprise* had traveled thus far.

The Adigeons he'd seen so far were all roughly three meters tall or taller, and were made more imposing by the large wings that sprouted from either shoulder blade. Unlike bird wings, however, these were more membranous; an intricate weaving of connective tissue and musculature striated the wings, over which were layered the membranes. The effect left Trip with the impression of fleshy feathers overlaid onto bat's wings.

Other than their wings and their large, lidless, side-mounted eyes, the Adigeons weren't particularly avian in appearance, once one got past first impressions. For one thing, their wings terminated in exceptionally long, slender, and sensitive fingers, which must have accounted for the reputation of their surgeons, as well as going a long way toward redeeming their relative lack of binocular vision. Their skin came in a wide variety of colors, ranging from a mottled gray to deeper browns and purples, while the feathery hair they exhibited seemed to grow mostly on the backs of their skulls, just above their almost catlike, membrane-feather-covered neck ruffs. Their facial features were also striking: their mouths were vertical and lipless, with two gill-like flaps on either side underneath high-set cheekbones.

When they'd docked the *Branson*, Trip and Phuong were greeted by a pair of indistinguishable Adigeons—Trip took them to be females, though he couldn't be certain—who greeted them politely but officiously. They had presented the two humans with small translation devices to attach to their clothing, and some sort of gravity-regulating ankle bracelets that allowed them to walk with some semblance of normalcy in the planet's low-gravity environment, which Trip found reminiscent of Mars.

On their way to the *c'Revno-hibce*—the surgical facility where their physical alterations were to be performed—neither of the females spoke unless spoken to, so both Trip and Phuong had mostly looked out the windows of their hovercab-like transport.

Once they had reached the facility, an apparently male Adigeon went over the financial arrangements with Phuong; when those details appeared to have at last been agreed upon, Trip and Phuong were given a stack of papers to fill out. Another Adigeon, a clerical specialist with skin the color of expensive Beaujolais, sat with them to read the questions on the forms into their translation units and record their answers by hand in the Adigeons' written language.

Trip answered the questions about his medical history as best he could, but a good half of the questions were not only being posed in an imperfectly translated alien tongue, but were also beyond his comprehension of human physiology.

Phuong had instructed the clerk that personal information about either of them—such as names, relatives, and other facts—was classified and therefore unnecessary. Although he knew that the subterfuge was appropriate for their mission, the words had jarred Trip at first. *My life is "classified and therefore unnecessary,"* he thought. *Not exactly comforting.*

Finally, they were shown into a smaller room, issued some loose-fitting, pastel-colored garments, and told to prepare themselves by taking medical decontamination showers. As they cleaned themselves with globular balls of squishy, foul-smelling stuff that the Adigeon medical technicians had described as "active abiotic astringents," Trip noticed that Phuong's entire back, as well as his left side under his arm, was laced with a faint but easily discernible network of old scars. He wasn't yet comfortable enough around the other operative to ask about them, but he hoped they hadn't been the result of some past mission that had gone badly awry.

Once they were scrubbed and partially dressed in the garments that were clearly *not* made for non-Adigeons, Trip waited in the preparation room with Phuong. He turned away from the window and saw his companion on his knees, his arms crossed at the wrists, his palms resting on his chest. Trip watched him for almost a minute, then cleared his throat. Phuong opened his eyes.

"Praying before the operation?" Trip asked with a slight smile. "Does this mean I should, too? You seemed less nervous before about all this . . ." His voice trailed off as he gestured around the room.

"Don't read too much into my actions," Phuong said. He didn't rise, but stayed on his knees. "I pray *often,* and almost never entirely out of fear. I was raised in a strictly religious family, and I believe that God watches over me, no matter where in space I may find myself."

Trip nodded. "My family went to church a lot, too, but I haven't kept up with it as much as my parents have." He sat in a nearby chair—rather awkwardly, because it was made for Adigeons, who were far taller than most humans—and tugged at the billowing Adigeon medical garment to keep himself covered. "What I learned in Sunday school sometimes seems kind of weird to me these days, because we've been traveling to all these strange new worlds and meeting up with so many new civilizations. Most of them have their own version of God, or gods, or goddesses, or even whole pantheons. . . . It makes it seem a little silly for me to keep praying to the God I grew up being taught about."

Phuong tilted his head, an inquisitive look on his face. "I'm not sure why it would be silly. It's only a question of faith. I have faith in my God, just as the Vulcans and the Andorians have faith in theirs."

Trip squinted, hoping that his next statement wouldn't offend the other man. "Yeah, but what about the whole 'God created everything' proposition? Does that mean that the Vulcan and Andorian deities don't exist, and only Earth's God does? And what about all the religions on Earth that don't worship the same God?"

"In all your years in Starfleet, I'm certain you've seen many things that might have seemed inconceivable to you at one time," Phuong said, now standing up. "The universe is full of things beyond our ken. We *know* that time travel is possible, we know that some phenomena can defy the laws of physics as we think we understand them, and we know that beings live and exist in dimensions just beyond ours."

He drew closer to Trip. "I'll tell you something that will *really* make you appreciate the mind of God—or at least the mysterious nature of the multiverse. The bureau has proof of the existence of an alternate universe that is virtually identical to our own—*almost*. But in *that* universe, significant changes have occurred throughout history. Some of the people there are *us*, only us raised in an alternate environment that forced them to make different choices in their lives." He paused for a moment. "We doubt that this 'mirror universe' is the only one of its kind."

He turned away, looking toward the window. "So with all of the knowledge you have gained aboard *Enterprise*, can you really fault the idea that the God we were both taught about might exist—right alongside other planes of existence in which *all* Gods might be real? Or that in certain other realities, *none* of them exist?"

Trip wasn't sure how to respond to such deeply metaphysical questions—or to the mind-boggling scientific revelation Phuong had just made—but he was saved from having to do so when a trio of Adigeons entered the chamber.

"I am Carver MoulMa's," the lead creature said—at least according to Trip's translation device—his vertical mouth undulating as he spoke. "I will be the principal carver in your operation. I see you have been prepared, so we will proceed."

A jolt went down Trip's spine as he heard the words. He hoped that "carver" was just the translator's way of saying "doctor" or "surgeon."

"I trust our instructions remain clear," Phuong said, a slight edge to his voice.

"Certainly," MoulMa's said. "When your operation is complete, you will be fundamentally indistinguishable from a Romulan."

"Which means we'll look like what exactly?" Trip asked.

The three Adigeons made some noises that sounded like glass being crunched beneath a hard boot heel. On one hand, Trip hoped he was hearing whatever passed for laughter on Adigeon Prime; on the other hand, he was worried at least a little that they might actually *be* laughing.

"You will look much like you do now," MoulMa's said. "Only with the superficial distinguishing characteristics of a Romulan rather than those of a Terran." He then gestured back toward the direction from which the trio had come.

"Your financial arrangements are nonreversible. Your carving is scheduled to commence in *selb dakkiwso*. So, unless you wish to abandon your plans, we should proceed presently."

"No refunds," Trip said, aiming a wry smile at Phuong. "Guess we'd better stay and get our money's worth."

Phuong met Trip's gaze steadily. Then he stepped toward the Adigeons. "I will be the first to be . . . 'carved.'"

Trip had remained within the confines of the surgical theater's observation gallery for as long as he could stand it, watching the three Adigeons and their various assistants "carve" into Phuong. Unlike the medical procedures he'd seen Phlox undertake in sickbay, this one seemed almost brutal, and was definitely far more bloody. He exited the room swiftly and threw up in what he hoped was a trash receptacle, then returned to his solitary viewing post, where he kept his eyes either closed or averted for the duration of the procedure.

After what seemed to be several hours, the assistants began wrapping Phuong in regenerative bandages. With so many surgeons and their assistants crowded around Phuong at the moment, Trip couldn't see precisely what his fellow operative looked like, but he was heartened to note that no limbs appeared to have been discarded. *Of course that doesn't necessarily mean they haven't attached a new limb or two,* Trip thought with a small shiver.

Minutes later, the assistants gently placed Phuong

into a hovering antigrav chair, then carefully pushed him out of the surgical theater and into an adjacent sterile white area that Trip guessed was some sort of recovery room. The patient was definitely conscious, but seemed unsteady. Bandages entirely covered his skin, making him look like the Mummy in one of Trip's favorite series of monster films. With the addition of a hat and a pair of sunglasses, he would have been a dead ringer for Claude Rains in *The Invisible Man*.

"Can I talk to him?" Trip asked one of the Adigeons.

"You appear to be capable of speech," the creature said, and the others made the crushed glass sound in response.

Now Trip was sure that this was the sound of Adigeon laughter. He did his best to ignore having made himself the butt of one of their alien jests.

"Tinh?" He kept his voice low. "Are you all right?"

Blinded by the bandages, a woozy Phuong turned his face in Trip's general direction. "This hurts like hell, but they're taking me in for dermal regeneration now. Can't wait to see what I look like afterward."

"Yeah, me too," Trip said. He resisted the urge to pat the Section 31 operative on the shoulder, since he was unsure just where it might be safe to touch him.

"I'll see you on the other side of the gauze," Phuong said as the three Adigeons pushed his hovering conveyance away.

My turn now, Trip thought as he entered the operating chamber, which had been sterilized by some sort of mist during the brief time he had been talking with Phuong in the other room.

MoulMa's and the other doctors entered the room again, with three new assistants in tow. All of them were clad in fresh, unbloodied surgical apparel. "Disrobe and place yourself on the table," MoulMa's said crisply and emotionlessly.

Trip shivered as he dropped the blouselike garment to the floor, then approached the table. Sitting on it and lying back, he was pleased to find that the padded surface was warm to the touch.

MoulMa's hovered over him, looking down. The effect of the surgeon's sideways mouth and gills and dinnerplate eyes was even more disorienting from below, and Trip's already racing heart began to beat even faster.

"Shkt'kooj will administer some *farron* gas to you as an anesthetic," MoulMa's said. "You will feel nothing until you wake up after our carving is complete."

Yeah, and then I bet it'll hurt like hell, Trip thought, remembering Phuong's words.

"One question before we start, Doc," Trip said aloud. "I just want to be *certain* that this operation is reversible. I'm not going to be stuck looking like a Romulan forever, am I?"

MoulMa's tilted his head, his eyes widening. "Your agency has paid us to reverse the carving after you return. The amount they paid is significant enough to make certain that your current . . . countenance will be restored with an extremely high degree of fidelity."

Trip let out a breath, not quite certain if the Adigeon had reassured him or not. "Just wanted to be sure," he said.

With a flick of a long wingtip, MoulMa's signaled to one of the assistants, and Trip felt a tiny prick at the side of his neck a moment later. Almost instantly, he felt his muscles go completely limp, and his mind began to fog.

As if from a great distance, he heard MoulMa's, but he wasn't even sure if the carver was talking to him or to the others.

"Not that we expect to actually perform the *later* carving," MoulMa's said, his voice distorted. "Our work today will be utterly flawless and discreet, of course, as compelled by our agreement with your superiors. But we expect that the two of you will never return once you pass the borders of the Romulan Star Empire."

Too groggy to be alarmed, or even to comprehend what he'd just heard, Trip felt himself sinking into darkness. In his last moments of consciousness, he reverted almost reflexively to the prayers he had learned as a child.

NINETEEN

Monday, February 17, 2155
Rigel X

THE HUGE MALE ORION the team had waylaid wore a uniform that marked him as a fairly high-ranking logistics clerk, an Orion Syndicate underling charged with responsibility for many of the comings and goings of captives as they wended their way through the slave market's complex and circuitous vending process.

Among the things Shran expected this man to know were the comings and goings of the many ships that picked up and delivered the market's countless sentient cargoes.

Luckily enough, the fellow hadn't raised a hue and cry when Shran, flanked by Captain Archer and Lieutenant Reed, had confronted him while a trio of MACOs cut off any possible avenue of escape. The team had caught the Orion walking alone through a darkened and empty side passage, and gently "encouraged" him—with the muzzles of their energy weapons—to enter a small nearby storeroom that both Shran and Archer had already agreed would be ideal for conducting interviews with some of the less forthcoming locals.

Once the team had escorted the Orion into the poorly illuminated and ventilated room, safely out of sight of the slave market's roving security troopers, Archer and Reed began inquiring about the present whereabouts of the ship that had recently come to Rigel X to take custody of a large contingent of Aenar captives.

The Orion had only laughed. After repeated questioning, and after several suggestions that the human soldiers might soon take stern measures to loosen the clerk's tongue, he actually *spat* at Archer. Again, the greenskin laughed.

Because he knows *where that ship is,* Shran thought, fuming in silence. So far, he had bowed to Archer's earlier insistence that his participation in this mission was to be contingent upon his, Shran's, restraint.

But now he could restrain himself no longer. The Orion's intransigence, along with his dismissive laughter, sparked an icy blue rage within Shran's breast, a passion so intense that he could think of nothing other than beating the man to a bloody, senseless green pulp.

The fact that the Orion was nearly twice Shran's size mattered to him not at all.

Shran charged, hitting the Orion hard in his thick midsection, knocking the flabbergasted slaver onto his back, slamming him to the concrete floor with a nearly bone-shattering impact. Shran landed on top of the supine Orion, wedging a knee tightly into the hollow of the big man's throat while pressing down with all his weight.

"You know where the ship carrying the Aenar was headed," Shran snarled into the Orion's face, his uneven antennae lashing forward like a pair of hungry vipers. "Now you're going to *share* your knowledge."

The Orion coughed and sputtered as he grabbed for Shran's throat with his huge, spatulate hands. The Andorian slammed both of his fists into the other man's face in quick succession, and the large green hands faltered.

"Shran." Archer's voice, behind him, urgent. Shran ignored it and continued bearing down on the slaver's throat.

"Talk to me!" Shran said. He pummeled the Orion again, left-right-left.

"Shran!" Lieutenant Reed this time.

Shran felt hands grabbing him roughly, two pairs of arms on either side of him. He turned, snarling, and saw that the intrusive arms and hands belonged to Archer and Reed. They dragged him off the stunned Orion, around whom now stood the three MACOs, their weapons poised to counter any surprise move the slaver might make.

Shran didn't think the Orion would be doing a lot of moving in the foreseeable future, however. But he believed that the green giant was probably still able to speak.

"Release me, pinkskins!" Shran bellowed, shaking off Reed and spinning toward Archer, who did indeed release him. Archer stood his ground, facing Shran—who had instinctively adopted a half-crouching combat stance, without showing any trace of fear.

"Why did you interrupt my interrogation?" Shran demanded.

"Interrogation?" Archer said, his expression one of incredulousness. "It looked more like an attempted grudge killing to me. We can't learn anything from dead men, Shran."

"When *your* loved ones are those whose lives hang in the balance, I'll play by your rules."

"Shran, when you're part of *my* landing party, you'll play by *my* rules. *Regardless* of whose lives hang in the balance. Now stand down, before you force me to take off your *other* antenna."

Why did he have to bring that *up?* Shran thought, his rage now almost entirely redirected from the greenskin to the pinkskin. The still incompletely healed stump of his left antenna throbbed to the beat of his racing pulse.

"I've already been down this path a time or two

myself, Shran, during the Xindi crisis," Archer said. "All it ever got me was blood on my hands, and stains on my conscience."

"Until Jhamel is safely returned to me, a conscience is a luxury I can't afford."

"Can you imagine what *Jhamel* would have to say about that?"

Shran *did* imagine it then, and his cheeks burned with sudden shame. As suddenly as the fury had come upon him, it dissipated.

He stood staring at Archer, abashed.

"So, what's *your* idea for making him cooperate with us?" Shran said at length. "Do we prepare him dinner?"

Archer smiled that cursedly reasonable smile of his. "Let's start by asking him a few more polite questions."

"Polite. Wonderful. This should be *very* enlightening."

Shran took a step back, allowing Archer to approach the man who lay sprawled and in pain on the concrete floor. The Orion seemed to be whispering, trying to speak, though his swollen, bloodied lips and damaged windpipe were obviously giving him no small amount of difficulty.

"What's he saying?" asked Reed, who stood at the captain's side, far closer to the Orion than was Shran.

" 'Adigeon Prime,'" said Archer. "The slavers rendezvoused with a ship bound for Adigeon Prime. Looks like the Aenar captives were to be delivered to their . . . buyers through an Adigeon business agent."

"The Adigeons are nonaligned," Reed said. "They could act as a third-party broker between anybody and just about anybody else."

"Including the Romulans," Shran said, his anger stoked anew, but not yet to the point of frenzy. "Who better for the Romulans to use to cover their traces than both the Orion slavers *and* Adigeon Prime's paper-pushers?"

"Let's get back to *Enterprise*," Archer said, nodding in agreement. "We'll head straight for Adigeon Prime, and there we can—"

Archer was interrupted by an amplified, mechanically augmented voice that rattled the storeroom's steel-and-concrete walls. *"Freeze right where you are!"*

Shran glanced at the Orion, who was trying to sit up. Although Shran's blows had evidently cured the clerk of his laughter, he was smiling triumphantly, his outsize white teeth smeared liberally with his own green blood. It occurred to Shran then that choosing an empty storeroom equipped with only one way in or out had been a spectacularly bad idea.

No wonder the Orion showed so little fear, he thought. *He must have summoned help with a concealed transmitter of some kind.*

"Throw down your weapons," said the voice from beyond the storeroom's closed door. *"Come out of the room with your hands raised, and kneel in the outer corridor. You are in violation of Orion Syndicate Economic Protocols, and are therefore subject to immediate arrest and confiscation."*

Shran quickly took up a low defensive position along the wall beside the door, while Archer, Reed, and the dark-clad MACOs spread out across the small room, taking cover behind the various crates and boxes. None of those objects amounted to any serious protection, though they might serve to obscure everyone's position for the few crucial moments the team would need to effect their escape.

Archer pulled his com device from his belt and flipped its grid open. "Archer to *Enterprise*. Emergency beam-out. *Now.*"

"Commander T'Pol here, Captain," came the Vulcan woman's crisp response. *"Request acknowledged. Stand by for emergency beam-out."*

" 'Confiscation,' " Shran said to Archer. "Do you understand what that means?"

He nodded. "I think so, unless something's gone haywire with our translators. Sounds like they're looking to add to their slave inventory."

"When *aren't* they?" Shran said.

Shran tried to adjust the setting on his phase pistol, but found that it had been locked into a stun setting. He shook his head in disgust. Coddling slavers such as these made no sense to him whatsoever. *Pinkskins,* he thought. *I hope this Coalition they're trying so hard to build doesn't fall victim to their own timid natures.*

"T'Pol already tried a stint as an Orion slave, Captain," Reed said dryly. "I don't think she enjoyed it all that much."

"It's not a job I'd recommend, either," said Archer. Addressing T'Pol again through the com device, he said, "T'Pol, where's that beam-out I asked for?"

"*Please stand by, Captain. Lieutenant Burch is presently trying to establish a positive transporter lock. However, the Orions appear to be attempting to deploy some sort of scattering field to prevent it.*"

"Then tell Burch he'd better hurry it the hell up," Archer said.

"*Unless you present yourself for confiscation within the next* alik, *we will use lethal force,*" intoned the harsh voice from outside the storeroom.

"It would be a shame if they damaged otherwise perfectly salable stock that way," Reed said. "Think they mean business, Captain?"

Archer shrugged. "I don't intend to stay here long enough to find out, Malcolm."

"Then let's just hope we don't discover exactly how long an *'alik'* lasts," Reed said.

Wearying of the battlefield banter, Shran raised his

weapon with one hand and held it pointed directly toward the door. With his other hand, he reached into his sash and withdrew the gleaming *Ushaan-Tor* blade he reserved for occasions such as this.

"If I am to be enslaved, then the slavers will purchase my servitude with large volumes of their own blood."

"They won't want you," Archer said, scowling at the blade. Gesturing with his com device toward Shran's truncated left antenna, he added, "After all, you're still damaged goods."

Shran's angry response was interrupted by the roar of an explosion. The blast broke the door into several neat pieces and swiftly began to fill the room with thick, black smoke. Fortunately, the initial blast had caused no one any apparent injuries, which confirmed Shran's belief that the Orions were more intent on capturing than on killing—at least for now.

Through the choking haze of smoke, Shran saw a pair of armed Orions dash in via the suddenly open doorway. Before Shran could fire, the pinkskin soldiers mowed them down, apparently stunning them rather than killing them outright. Though Shran was sorely tempted to finish the slavers off with his *Ushaan* blade, he concentrated instead on remaining vigilant for the next wave of intruders.

The hum and shimmering light of *Enterprise*'s transporter cheated him of even that small satisfaction. After a brief moment of disorientation, he was standing on the narrow, circular transporter stage along with the other five members of the landing party, all of whom had been begrimed at least to some degree by their close call.

Shran's eyes swept the transporter stage while everyone else stepped off into the small corridor alcove that housed it. He approached Archer, who had walked to a com panel in the corridor to instruct his bridge crew about the ship's new course and heading. The tension in the deck plates beneath Shran's boots changed immediately, signaling that *Enterprise* was already on its way toward Adigeon Prime.

And Jhamel.

"You should have brought along the Orion," Shran said to Archer as he walked beside him toward the turbolift, with Reed following along behind. "In case he lied to us."

"I don't abduct people, Shran. I'll leave that sort of thing to the Orions."

"Your softness will be your undoing one day, pinkskin."

Archer nodded. "That's entirely possible, Shran."

"I don't think the Orion was lying to us," Reed said.

Shran stopped and turned to face Reed, his antenna undulating forward in curiosity. "Why do you say that, Lieutenant?"

"Because I think you really frightened him. I'm quite certain I heard him say, 'Keep that blue lunatic away from me' right before he broke and told Captain Archer about Adigeon Prime. I believe on Earth the interview technique is known as 'good cop, bad cop.'"

Or perhaps it's 'good captain, bad captain,' Shran thought.

The trio resumed walking, then entered the turbolift, which immediately began making its swift ascent toward the bridge. Shran beamed triumphantly at Archer. "It seems that my preferred interrogation method has been vindicated after all."

Archer scowled, shaking his head ruefully. "No, Shran. It hasn't. You would have killed him."

"It would have been no less than he deserved, Captain. But I know I wouldn't have killed him," Shran answered with certainty. "You see, I may lack Jhamel's kindly instincts, but I always know my limitations."

"I saw blood in your eye, Shran. How can you be so sure you would have stopped short of killing him?"

"Because you were with me." Shran smiled. "And I know that you would never have permitted it."

TWENTY

Tuesday, February 18, 2155
Somewhere in Romulan space

TRIP AWAKENED TO A SENSE of mounting panic.

For starters, he seemed to be blind. He struggled to get into a sitting position from the hard yet yielding surface on which he lay in the darkness, and began clawing at his eyes. He calmed slightly when he realized that they were covered with some sort of cloth or gauze.

A hand gently clasped his shoulder, and he tried to shove it away. "Easy, Commander," a voice said. Soothing. Familiar.

Trip stopped trying to pull at whatever it was that was covering his eyes, and fell back onto his elbows. "Phuong? Where am I?" *And why does my voice sound so different?*

"We're both back on the *Branson*, Commander," Trip heard Phuong say. "We left Adigeon Prime a couple of hours ago. We're already headed for Romulan space."

"I hope that means that the surgery was a success," said Trip, his bare feet finding the deck plates as he worked himself into a sitting position. He realized he must be sitting on one of the narrow cots in one of the *Branson*'s small aft sleeping areas.

"One thing's for sure, Commander; their anesthetics are certainly effective. Evidently more on you than on me. Let me help you get this bandage off your face."

Trip felt Phuong's hands gently set about doing just that. "Why'd they have to cover up my eyes?"

"The Adigeons said something about having to install a protective inner eyelid. Something unique to Romulans, apparently. They wanted it left covered for at least an hour after they gave us the last of the tissue regeneration treatments."

The bandages abruptly fell away from Trip's eyes and he suddenly found himself blinking against a swirl of harsh light. Although the light fixture in the sleeping area seemed a little too bright to his dilated pupils, his eyes seemed to adjust very quickly to the abrupt disappearance of the darkness into which he'd awakened.

"Looks like the Adigeons do pretty good inner-eyelid work," Trip said, his gaze lighting on the face from which Phuong's voice had evidently come.

While the face in question was still clearly humanoid in appearance, it was one that Trip almost didn't recognize— but for certain unexpectedly familiar features. One of these was Phuong's thick black hair, which had been severely shorn down to a stark bowl cut. Another was his dark eyebrows, which swept sharply upward at their outer edges.

But the most striking change visited upon Phuong was to the tips of his ears, which now tapered gracefully upward into points. Except for the presence of a subtle but clearly noticeable brow ridge, Trip could have sworn he was staring into the face of a Vulcan.

Trip rose to his feet, and his words came out in a hoarse whisper. "Tinh, are you sure the Adigeons got your order right?"

Phuong's right eyebrow rose and he grinned in a decidedly un-Vulcan way. "We'd both better hope so, Commander." He placed a hand on Trip's shoulder and steered him toward the head at the rear of the cabin.

Trip saw his reflection in the mirror over the gunmetal gray washbasin and came to an abrupt stop. He raised his hands to a face that he doubted his own mother would have recognized.

He couldn't tear his gaze away from his own set of distinctly Vulcanoid ears, which were accented by a prominent brow ridge, a thick mane of dark brown hair, and nearly black eyebrows canted at a steep angle that reminded Trip of the windshield-wipers on some of the old gasoline-powered ground vehicles his grandfather used to spend his summers restoring and repairing.

If only T'Pol could see me now, he thought, approaching the mirror more closely in order to study his new face in greater detail. After concluding that he looked like a Vulcan with a forehead concussion, he examined the rest of his face with an intensity he usually reserved for complex technical diagrams. His eye color had been darkened almost to black, the width of his nose and mouth had increased slightly, and even his skin color had subtly changed, taking on an almost pale green cast.

"So the Romulans must be kissing cousins of the Vulcans," Trip said at length, his eyes still riveted to the face in the mirror. "Wonder if the Vulcans have known it all along, but decided to keep it to themselves." *After all, that's the way they handled "sharing" their warp technology with us for years.*

"Can't say I'd blame them for not being eager to put all their dirty laundry on display," Phuong said.

Trip nodded, still watching the dour-faced alien who was staring back at him from the mirror. "I suppose that'd be especially true on the eve of the signing of the Coalition Compact."

Does T'Pol know anything about this? Trip thought, feeling adrift.

"Exactly," Phuong said. "Regardless, the Adigeons have surgically altered you not just to make you look generically Romulan, as I do. You have, in fact, been made to resemble a *particular* Romulan, right down to your voice prints—specifically, you are now a junior warp scientist named Cunaehr, who was Doctor Ehrehin's most trusted assistant."

"Was?" Trip asked, turning to face Phuong. "Past tense?"

"He's dead," Phuong said, nodding. "Killed in a recent warp-test accident."

A worm of suspicion was beginning to turn deep in Trip's gut. "You knew beforehand what they were going to make us look like?"

Phuong held up a placating hand. "I knew about Cunaehr and his relationship to Ehrehin, thanks to our intelligence dossiers. But as far as what Romulans look like in general, I'm as surprised as you are. The Adigeon surgeons seem to have their own sources regarding the exact likenesses of prominent Romulans."

Trip stroked his own now very alien-looking cheek. "Well, let's hope they did a good enough likeness to fool this Doctor Ehrehin."

"Ehrehin might not be all that hard to fool, if our dossier on him is correct," said Phuong.

Trip's enlarged brow crumpled inquisitively. "What do you mean?"

"Doctor Ehrehin is an elderly man, Commander. And he's reportedly been only intermittently lucid during recent weeks. As far as I know, this hasn't affected his theoretical and mathematical work, and it may even make him tractable enough to allow Earth and the other Coalition worlds to benefit from his expertise—provided he's comforted by the presence of one of his most trusted assistants."

Comforted by a dead man, Trip thought. He was beginning to feel that he was about to participate in something exceedingly ugly. "All I have to do is pretend to be Ehrehin's beloved apprentice. Then take advantage of a feeble old man's vulnerabilities."

Phuong scowled and folded his arms across his chest. "This is war, Commander."

"Sure it is, Tinh. Never said I had to like it, though." Trip turned back toward the mirror and looked once again into the face of Cunaehr. As important as he knew this mission was, he now felt determined not to allow it to completely swallow his real identity—at least, not forever. He couldn't let the role of Cunaehr, or for that matter Phuong's apparent tendency to allow the ends to justify the means, to engulf the man he still was at his core.

After all, Trip thought, *I'm going to have to go home sometime and be able to put all this behind me.*

Running his index finger along the side of one of his oddly natural-feeling pointed ears, Trip asked, "What did the Adigeons do to us *exactly*?"

"The details?" Phuong said. "Well, the bureau spared no expense, Commander. The Adigeons not only performed all the necessary cosmetic alterations, they made quite a few temporary internal changes, all of them reversible. They even resequenced our genes."

Trip turned back toward Phuong, his fists clenching involuntarily. "That's illegal."

Phuong shrugged. "It's illegal on *Earth,* Commander. But the Adigeons weren't a party to either the Augment tyrannies of the twentieth century, or to the Eugenics Wars. So they're a little less squeamish about such stuff than we are."

"But why change our DNA?"

"Because it's our best chance of fooling suspicious Romulans—particularly those equipped with medical scanners. Cut yourself shaving and you'll even bleed green. Only an extremely deep tissue scan will reveal the truth."

Or an autopsy, Trip thought, though he tried very hard to push that unpleasant notion aside.

"Besides, the Adigeons say we may even receive some ancillary long-term health benefits as a result of these alterations," Phuong continued. "An extended life-span, for instance."

Trip shook his head incredulously, then moved even closer to the mirror until he was almost nose-to-nose with the reflected image of Cunaehr.

"Tinh, if we foul up on this mission, figuring out how to spend a few extra years of retirement pay won't be at the top of our list of problems."

TWENTY-ONE

Thursday, February 20, 2155
Enterprise **NX-01**

THE SWIRLING, BLUE-GREEN CLOUD bands of Adigeon Prime displayed on *Enterprise*'s central bridge viewer abruptly gave way to the image of a vaguely humanoid creature. The being's long brown wings, feather-covered epidermis, and outsize, apparently lidless eyes gave it a more than passing resemblance to a gigantic barn owl.

"Universal translator engaged, Captain," said Hoshi from the communications console located at the periphery of the bridge's forward portside section. T'Pol stood at the station to Hoshi's immediate left, attentively watching the readings on her science console.

"Captain Archer," said the avian creature on the screen, the stridulations of its nonhuman vertical mouthparts rendered into intelligible speech by Hoshi's linguistic algorithms. *"I am given to understand that you have been trying to reach me."*

Archer tried his best to offer the Adigeon official a safely diplomatic smile, and to maintain at least the appearance of patience. *Yes I have,* he thought. *The whole damned day.*

Aloud, he said, "Thank you taking the time to speak with me, Administrator Khoulka'las."

Archer heard the turbolift doors whisk open behind him, and a quick glance over his shoulder revealed the arrival of a stern-faced Shran, who was followed out of the lift by Theras. The Aenar seemed intimidated by the very notion of being on the starship's bridge, although Archer knew he was incapable of seeing it.

Turning back toward the Adigeon on the viewer, Archer said, "We're trying to find a group of people who were recently kidnapped from Andoria by Orion slavers."

"How unfortunate," the administrator said, *"that anyone should fall unwillingly into the hands of Orion slavers. How many Andorians were taken?"* Archer thought he could hear a note of sympathy in the synthetic voice, though he wasn't certain whether to attribute it to the administrator's goodwill or to the emotional subtext recognition subroutines Hoshi had written into her translation matrix software.

"Thirty-seven individuals in all," Archer said. "And strictly speaking, they're not exactly Andorians as such."

"Not Andorians? But from Andoria?" The administrator's synthesized voice registered confusion, even though the creature's body language, which largely consisted of many frequent, small jerky movements, remained obscure.

"The captives are Aenar, Administrator. A subspecies of the Andorian race. They're pacifists, unable to defend themselves. And they possess strong telepathic abilities, which is probably what made them such attractive targets for the Orion slavers."

"Indeed."

"Administrator, we've obtained information indicating that the slavers transferred the Aenar captives to a ship bound for your world, and that Adigeon business agents were facilitating a sale of the Aenar to a third party."

"Such third-party business arrangements are commonplace on Adigeon Prime, Captain. Businesses in three sectors rely on our world's customary unbreakable, duranium-clad confidentiality agreements." The note of sympathy

Archer had heard earlier appeared to have faded away, if he hadn't merely imagined it in the first place.

He took a deep breath, centering himself before speaking again. "I respect the confidentiality of Adigeon Prime's brokers, attorneys, and business agents, Administrator. But a terrible crime has been committed, and we must investigate it. We need to learn the details of the slavers' business arrangements—including the identity and location of the . . . final purchaser."

"Kidnapping is indeed a terrible crime, Captain. However, so is breaching Adigeon Prime's sacred veil of privacy."

Archer's patience was rapidly nearing its breaking point. "Administrator, there has to be *some* provision in Adigeon law that permits you to access transaction records in a case like this."

"Indeed there is, Captain."

Better, Archer thought, swiftly damping his frustration back down. Aloud, he said, "What do I have to do, Administrator?"

"You must demonstrate reasonable suspicion that an Adigeon business agent has knowingly participated in a transaction that is either fraudulent or otherwise prohibited under Adigeon law."

Now we're finally getting somewhere, Archer thought as he nodded to the Adigeon official. "Administrator, a member of the Orion Syndicate has informed us that Orion slavers have arranged to ship a group of thirty-seven Aenar telepaths to an anonymous client, using an Adigeon business agent as a broker. Because of a previous encounter between Starfleet and the Romulan military, we have good reason to believe that the Romulan Star Empire is the client slated to receive those telepaths. Unless the Adigeon agent brokering this transaction is found and stopped, Administrator, your world could be party to a serious crime against the Aenar people, and the world of Andoria."

I knew those Stanford law courses would pay off eventually, Archer thought, proud of the case he'd just made.

After Archer had finished, the bird-creature regarded him in silence for perhaps an entire minute; the administrator's rapidly nictitating ocular membranes provided the only evidence that the avian being was still alive.

Finally the administrator said, *"Do you claim that the Aenar telepaths procured by the Orions do not possess the abilities required by the brokerage agreement, or have not been delivered in the contractually mandated condition?"*

"No, Administrator Khoulka'las," Archer said, his frustration roaring right back to where it had been moments ago, just beneath the surface. "And I don't understand the relevance of any of that. What I *am* claiming is that the abduction of these people is what constitutes the crime needed as a pretext to allow us access to the relevant business records."

The administrator assayed a barn owl's version of a shrug. *"That is as may be, Captain. But it is also irrelevant. So far you have described no crime that has occurred within the bounds of my jurisdiction. You have presented no evidence that an Adigeon broker has misrepresented his services to a client, nor committed any other act of business malfeasance or misfeasance. Adigeon Prime's sacred veil of privacy must therefore remain in place. I'm afraid I cannot help you."*

"Administrator Khoulka'las, if you'll just—"

"Good day, Captain," the administrator said, interrupting. His image vanished from the screen half an instant later, the connection broken from the other end.

"Dammit," Archer muttered as he stared at the viewscreen's depiction of the blue-green world that continued making its stately rotation hundreds of kilometers below.

"I should have mentioned the Coalition," Archer said, half to himself. "Complicity in an attack against one member world is the same as complicity in an attack against all the member worlds. Khoulka'las might have ice water in his veins, but I doubt that even *he* would want to get sideways with *five* other planets all at once."

"Unfortunately," T'Pol said, "the Compact's mutual defense provisions will not be in force until *after* the document is signed. The Aenar abduction, and all crimes related to it, have so far been committed prior to that time."

Archer suddenly remembered exactly why he'd decided to change his major from prelaw after his freshman year at Stanford.

"Perhaps you should simply have offered him a bribe." Archer was momentarily startled by Shran's voice, which had come from directly behind him. "I hear they like platinum here. As well as something called latinum."

Archer turned to face the Andorian, who stood beside Theras in the bridge's upper aft section. "I'm surprised to hear you say that, Shran. I thought you'd have preferred that I offer him a brace of photonic torpedoes instead."

Shran appeared somewhat stupefied by that remark, as though he himself had just realized that he had indeed said something out of character for him. "Perhaps I've finally begun to take your incessant calls for 'restraint' to heart, pinkskin," he said at length as a smirk played at the edges of his mouth.

"Or it may be that Jhamel's agreeable nature is influencing you," Theras said to Shran. "That's a good sign."

"I'm delighted that Shran is finally starting to mellow," Archer said, addressing Theras. "It might even make life around here a bit more pleasant for the duration. But it won't go a long way toward helping us find those missing telepaths. And without the help of Adigeon Prime's authorities, we're at an impasse."

"I certainly hope not, Captain," Theras said, his blind eyes settling eerily upon Archer's sighted ones, no doubt guided by the Aenar's telepathy. "I have to allow myself to hope that Shran's . . . attitude adjustment may mean that we may be closer to Jhamel and the other captives than we think."

Archer found the blind telepath's elliptical remark both confusing and intriguing. "I don't understand, Theras. Are you saying that you've begun to . . . home in on her telepathically?"

"No, Captain." Theras turned his milky eyes upon Shran. "But I believe that *your* mind may have begun to react to the presence of *hers,* if only unconsciously."

Shran's face abruptly lost its prior, almost convivial expression, immediately collapsing back into a far more familiar frown. "Ridiculous, Theras. *I* possess no telepathic talents."

"No," Theras said. "But such gifts aren't necessary for one to share a permanent mind-link with a true telepath."

"That is true," T'Pol said in a voice that sounded almost wistful to Archer's ear.

"Theras," said Archer, "Are you telling us that Shran and Jhamel are telepathically linked somehow?"

Theras nodded. "Yes. I believe they are."

"That's ridiculous," Shran said flatly.

"You love her, Shran," Theras said, though his tone remained even, matter-of-fact, and completely nonaccusatory. "You've already admitted as much."

Shran flushed a deep indigo. "Theras, it isn't wise to put Jhamel's allegedly calming influence over me to the test."

Theras continued, undeterred by color cues and body language that he couldn't see. "You share a bond with her, Shran. And it's deeper than anything she and I could ever share."

"You are a part of her *shelthreth* quad, Theras. And that is something that *I* can never share."

"Only because our *shelthreth* was arranged long ago, Shran. Before another conflict involving the Romulans brought the two of you together, binding you in shared loss and shared triumph."

The "why" of the notion made some degree of sense to Archer, even if the "how" still eluded him. Jhamel had lost her brother Gareb during the Romulan drone-ship crisis, while a Tellarite diplomat had killed Shran's beloved Talas; Jhamel and Shran had also worked in tandem to help Archer's crew stop the Romulan drone affair.

"Even if you're right, Theras," Shran growled, "the bridge of a pinkskin starship is no place to discuss the matter."

Archer had to agree. Noting Shran's obvious discomfiture, he tried to steer the conversation away from the Andorian's personal feelings and back toward the mechanics of Aenar telepathy.

"I still don't quite understand this, Theras," Archer said. "If we were actually anywhere near any of the Aenar captives, wouldn't *you* be the first to notice? After all, you're the only telepath we have on board, if you don't count T'Pol."

Archer noticed that T'Pol had raised an eyebrow in response to his last remark. Though she was capable only of touch telepathy—and therefore possessed far less esper ability than Theras—it was certainly possible that she was miffed at being summarily excluded from *Enterprise*'s current extremely short list of psi-gifted individuals. He made a mental note to apologize to her later.

"If we were extremely close to my fellow Aenar, I

would almost certainly detect their thoughts," Theras said. "I wouldn't even have to be particularly close to them, for that matter. But I'm assuming that their captors would have drugged them to prevent them from revealing their location telepathically, particularly to other Aenar who might come looking for them."

"That is a logical assumption," T'Pol said.

Archer frowned in his first officer's direction. "So wouldn't those drugs also disable Shran's link with Jhamel?"

Theras shook his head. "Only death itself can interrupt such a profoundly deep connection."

"Then it's a pity I'm not an Aenar," Shran said. "If I were, I suppose I could telepathically trace Jhamel and the others straight to their exact location via this supposed mind-link, whether the slavers had drugged them or not."

"It's a pity that I cannot test that idea with my own deep link to Jhamel," Theras said sadly. "But if you were an Aenar, Shran, I think you probably could do just that."

"But if I *were* an Aenar," Shran said, hostility audible in his voice, "I'd have been captured right alongside you and everyone else the Orions took, because I wouldn't have been able to put up enough of a fight to stop it."

Theras quailed before Shran and even took a step backward. And although Archer sympathized with Shran's obvious and justified frustrations—his ongoing inability to rescue Jhamel had to be hard for him to take, particularly now that he'd been informed that he possessed a mental connection to her that was tactically useless—he couldn't allow the Andorian to get away with taking those frustrations out on the gentle Aenar any further.

"As I recall, Shran, the fight you put up didn't end up making all that much difference, as far as the Orions and their business partners are concerned," Archer said, stepping toward Shran. He hoped his body language was communicating the wordless pick-on-somebody-your-own-size message he intended to convey.

Perhaps because he wasn't a bully by nature, Shran seemed to receive the message without comment or complaint. He merely fumed in silence, his antennae lancing forward in undisguised but undirectable anger. *Now that's the Shran we've all grown to know and love so much these past few years,* Archer thought before turning toward Theras.

Malcolm Reed, who'd been sitting in silence at his starboard station until now, chose that moment to speak up, raising the very question that Archer had been about to ask: "Theras, why haven't you mentioned Shran's mind-link to Jhamel before now?"

"I suppose I never considered it relevant," Theras said, turning so that his glassy eyes pointed in the tactical officer's direction. "It had always seemed to me merely a personal oddity, and certainly nothing to worry about. Since I have always trusted Jhamel's judgment, I had no reason to resent either her or Shran because of the link. And because Shran lacks sufficient esper capacity to even consciously sense the mind-link's presence, I could think of no practical way to use it to aid in our search. So I assumed that it wasn't noteworthy enough to talk about."

"That's because it wasn't," Shran said flatly.

"Perhaps," T'Pol said. "Or perhaps not."

"You have something?" Archer said. He couldn't help but notice that her reserved exterior was being betrayed by the slight olive flush that had risen in her cheeks. For a Vulcan, it was the equivalent of shouting "Eureka!"

T'Pol turned toward her science console and began punching in strings of commands with a dexterity that would have put the most nimble blackjack dealers on Risa to shame. "I'm not entirely certain yet, Captain."

"Forget certainty," Archer said, approaching her console and watching over her shoulder as she worked. "At this point, I'm willing to settle for wild speculation."

"Very well, Captain. Shran can't use his mind-link with Jhamel to locate her. Correct?"

"So I keep hearing. Endlessly," Shran said as he came up beside Archer, also clearly curious about T'Pol's emerging hypothesis.

T'Pol turned her chair slightly so that she could look up at both Archer and Shran. Addressing the Andorian, she said, "I believe it may be possible to use your link to Jhamel as a means of actually locating her—by using some outside assistance."

Archer thought he was finally beginning to see where she was going with this. "You're proposing a Vulcan mind-meld."

Shran took a step back. Archer turned toward him, and saw an unmistakable look of dread cross his face. "You want me to open my *brain* up . . . to a *Vulcan*?"

"Settle down, Shran," Archer said. "Hear her out first before you run away."

"Don't push your luck, pinkskin," Shran muttered.

T'Pol shook her head and adopted a long-suffering expression that was clearly intended for both men. "Actually, I am proposing no such thing." She turned back toward her console and silently entered another command.

An image appeared on the monitor screen at the center of her console, a depiction of a small, delicate mass of improvised-looking wiring and circuitry. Archer recognized it immediately, and understood. The device made him think somberly of Trip.

Archer glanced at Shran, whose approving nod showed that he understood T'Pol's plan as well.

The Vulcan rose from her chair and stood for a moment at crisp attention beside her station. "If you'll excuse me, Captain," she said, "I have some work to do elsewhere."

Archer grinned. "Agreed." She nodded once, turned on her heel, and disappeared into the turbolift.

"Perhaps you won't need to offer the administrator that bribe after all," Shran said, his azure face split by a fierce gird-for-battle smile.

Archer chuckled, then headed back for his command chair.

Before he could settle into it, he noticed the look of horror that had colonized the death-white features of Theras, whose antennae both sagged toward his shoulders, displaying his obvious emotional distress.

"Theras, what's wrong?" Archer said.

"I fear I have erred grievously in not informing you earlier about Shran's link to Jhamel," Theras said. He appeared to be on the ragged edge of tears. "In the name of Infinite Uzaveh, what have I done?"

"What have you done?" Archer said as he laid a hand gently on the albino's slight shoulder. "Theras, you may have just saved the day for us all."

TWENTY-TWO

Thursday, February 20, 2155
Somewhere in Romulan space

AN ALARM ON THE HELM CONTROL of the *Branson* suddenly began blaring, causing Trip's sleepily drifting attention to focus like a mining laser.

"We've got *trouble!*" he yelled to the aft part of the vessel, where Phuong had lain down to rest several hours earlier.

Even as the other agent ran forward, the communications light flashed. Trip tapped a control in the center of the instrument panel.

"*Ullho hiera, mos ih ihir nviomn riud ih seiyya!*" The voice was stern and angry. The translator implanted within Trip's ear immediately translated the warning. "*Unidentified vessel, prepare to be boarded or destroyed!*"

Phuong put a finger to his lips and tapped the communicator off as he sat down hurriedly in the main pilot's seat. "We don't respond to them," he said. His newly elevated eyebrows enhanced his look of surprise.

Trip's eyes widened, both surprised and alarmed himself. "What do we *do*, then?"

Phuong began manipulating verniers and toggles and tapped the buttons at the helm. "We polarize the hull plating and run like hell. And find a way to shake them."

Trip felt the ship accelerate, and strapped himself into the copilot's chair with the seat's safety harness. He tapped the console, activating a small screen, which displayed an image of a semi-familiar ship. It was gracefully curved, with two struts on either side holding up the engine nacelles. The hull of the ship was greenish and had an intricate design painted on its ventral surface: the stylized image of a swooping predatory bird.

"It's a Romulan warship," Trip said, remembering the encounter that *Enterprise* had had with two similar ships two years earlier. "I don't know where the hell they came from."

"They're opening fire," Phuong said, sliding his hand over the controls. A moment later, the *Branson* shuddered from what must have been at least a glancing impact, and the two men braced themselves against the helm as the hull plating and the inertial dampers struggled to keep the ship intact and level.

Trip's eyes were drawn to a red warp-engine warning light that began flashing urgently as the demands of the hull-polarization relays began redlining the warp core. Realizing he had only seconds to act, he swiftly entered a command into his console.

"What the hell are you *doing*?" Phuong said, looking at him as though he'd just lost his mind.

"Taking us out of warp. Slowing to impulse until the warp core cools down."

"*Now*?" Phuong was beside himself.

"It's better than redlining the antimatter containment system and blowing ourselves to quarks," Trip said in the calmest tones he could muster.

"It's not all *that* much better, Commander. Look at the rate they're gaining."

"We can't outrun them," Trip said. "And we can only dodge them for another few seconds. So unless you've got some kind of new souped-up hull plating folded up in your back pocket, what the hell are we going to do?"

Phuong paused momentarily to study some readings, then tapped another control. An old-style aviation joystick rose up from a recessed panel at the helm in front of Trip.

"I hope you can steer manually," Phuong said, a grim smile on his lips.

Probably not as well as Travis can, Trip thought. He grabbed the stick. "Where are we going?"

Phuong tapped on the controls, and a viewscreen located just below the forward windows magnified the section of space directly in front of the ship. "There," Phuong said, pointing to a field of space debris that lay ahead, faintly illuminated by the glow of the nearby orange star around which the debris field orbited. "That's where we'll lose them."

It never failed. It often seemed to Trip that hot pursuits through space involved a nearby debris field or nebula or other such sensor-obscuring cosmic feature far more frequently than dumb luck alone could account for. He wondered if the Romulan military staked such places out, watching and waiting the way the highway cops of previous centuries used to trap speeders, and the *Branson* had merely had the bad fortune—or her pilot and copilot had exhibited the poor judgment—to fly too close to such a place.

Keeping his eye on the image of the pursuing ship, Trip jammed the control stick hard to the right, then forward. The two blasts of energy the Romulans had fired at them shot off into space, missing them entirely.

"That's something like four million kilometers away," Trip said. "While we're stuck at impulse, we aren't going to get there in time to do us any good."

Phuong got up from his seat and moved to some wall-mounted controls. "We will if we go back to warp."

Trip's eyes widened. "Not a good idea while the core's still this hot. It could be an hour or more before I can verify that the containment field won't collapse under the stress of a fully operational warp field."

"So let's go to warp *without* a fully operational warp field."

Trip was beginning to see where Phuong was going, and he was a bit embarrassed that he hadn't seen the solution first. "We'll set up a warp burst, just enough to kick us forward a few million klicks, then drop back into normal space."

"We can lose them in there," Phuong said. "These engines are tough. They can take it."

"As long as we don't overshoot the mark," Trip cautioned. "Or smash into any debris too big for the hull plating to handle."

Phuong shrugged. "We don't have time to be choosy, Commander. They're powering up their weapons again. Hit it!"

Trip jammed the controls to the side again, spinning the ship away from another pair of energy blasts.

"You ready?" Phuong asked, returning to his chair.

"Do I have a choice?" Trip answered.

"They're my engines, Commander, so maybe I ought to be the one to handle the warp burst. Get ready to do some fancy flying."

"I'd rather you fly while I handle the engines, Tinh. But she's your ship."

Phuong didn't respond to Trip's comment, either because he was ignoring it or because he was intent on the data spooling onto the console at his left. "I'll take us to warp for approximately zero point seven one seconds," Phuong said. "And then you'll get us lost among the rocks and asteroids."

Phuong's finger hovered over the controls for a moment, as if he were having second thoughts. Then he pushed the button.

Trip felt the familiar slight tug of warp acceleration, visually exacerbated by the brief streaking elongation of the stars and debris visible through the forward window.

He felt a cold trickle of sweat running down his neck and wondered for an instant if his sweat had changed color the way his blood had.

In a fraction of a second, the *Branson* had traversed some four million kilometers. Both men were thrown forward as the ship abruptly returned to low impulse, their restraining straps taut until the inertial dampers caught up with the abrupt velocity change.

"*Shit!*" Trip exclaimed, wiping sweat from his brow. "We're still in one piece." They also appeared to have dropped out of warp only a few hundred kilometers from the densest region of the debris field.

Suddenly, the ship rocked violently, and an alarm klaxon filled the cockpit with a shrill wail.

"There's *another* one of the Romulan ships!" Phuong shouted excitedly as he frantically tapped his controls. The viewscreen beneath the forward window responded by revealing the presence of a second birdlike vessel, this one apparently larger and better armed than the first.

"Get into the debris field, *now!*" Phuong said.

Trip ignored his instincts and pushed the lever to the left, sending the *Branson* directly into the most debris-cluttered portion of the space ahead that he could find. Almost immediately, a proximity alarm began sounding, adding to the general din in the cockpit. With the help of the sensors and the viewer, he attempted to dodge a large chunk of rock, but evidently not quite quickly enough. He saw a boulder-sized meteoroid flash across the top of the viewscreen before it vanished, and the *Branson*'s hull transmitted the reverberating sound of the glancing impact into the cockpit, which seemed almost to ring like a bell for several seconds afterward.

"Between that hit and the Romulan blast, the hull plating is down to forty percent," Phuong said, concern evident in his voice.

"I don't suppose it would do any good to try talking with them, would it?" Trip asked, twisting the controls to avoid the debris field's profusion of tumbling chunks of rock, metal, and ice. "We do *look* like them now, and these translator gadgets in our ears will let us speak their language."

"We're too suspicious all alone out here. If they didn't kill us outright, they'd question us for weeks, and *then* kill us," Phuong said. "No, we have to get integrated into their social structure before we start trying to bargain with Romulan military officers, and we need to reach our friendly contacts inside the Empire to do that. Which means our top priority right now is to avoid these two ships."

One of the viewscreens showed a brilliant explosion behind them, as a large portion of a small asteroid suddenly became superheated vapor, evidently because of Romulan weapons fire.

"They're shooting into the field!" Trip said. He wondered again, for perhaps the six-hundredth time in the past minute or so, exactly what had made him decide to take on this assignment.

"Then we've got to go in deeper," Phuong said. The *Branson* rattled and shook. "And try not to get ourselves killed in the process."

Commander Nveih i'Ihhliae t'Jaihen roared in anger and stabbed his *kaleh* into the neck of the controller. Centurion S'Eliahn clutched his neck, crying out in terror and pain as his emerald blood pulsed out in jets. He crumpled leadenly to the deck.

"Get over here and find them," Nveih yelled to Tanekh, the female decurion who presently cowered at the communications station.

He stepped over the dying S'Eliahn and moved back to his command chair. He'd always found the young officer incompetent, but his attractiveness had made up for it. But last *khaidoa*, when the centurion had refused Nveih's overtures to engage in carnal pursuits with him and Nveih's wife, S'Eliahn's fate had been sealed. All the Romulan commander had needed was any small excuse to rid himself of the party who had so insulted him.

The pursuit of the unidentified vessel into the asteroid field near the Galorndon sector had provided just that excuse, though S'Eliahn might well have been spared had he not bungled so badly in carrying out his orders to either cripple or destroy the fleeing vessel.

How did they get this far into Romulan territory without being caught? They were clearly *vaehkh*, aliens from beyond the Empire's farthest-flung *Avrrhinul*, or Outmarches; Nveih could tell *that* from the configuration of their ship alone. He wondered if the small vessel had received help penetrating this far into imperial territory, possibly from dissidents. *Or perhaps they're just smugglers who've ventured too far from the customary lanes of galactic commerce for their own good*. He didn't really care. Either way, it was his duty to see to it that they neither escaped nor got any closer to Romulus than they already had.

"Commander, I'm showing that their ship is losing power," Subcommander Vosleht reported from his post on the bridge's port side. "Unfortunately, they've entered the densest part of—"

The bridge viewscreen of the *Lha Aehallh* suddenly flared brightly, and Vosleht paused in making his report to look. The explosion could really only mean one thing.

"They collided with an asteroid," Decurion Tanekh said from her new station. "Initial scans show that they've been destroyed." She had apparently gotten her nerves under control, and now sat above the pooled blood of her predecessor, whose body she appeared to have rolled just out of her way.

"Make *sure* of it," Nveih snarled. "Find their wreckage and learn who or what they were." He stalked toward the exit, then turned back to his crew and pointed toward the barely twitching S'Eliahn. "And have that piece of *hnaev* cleaned up."

He wasn't looking forward to telling Commander T'Ihlaah about losing the vessel. The only positive thing about it was that T'Ihlaah's ship, the *Qiuu Nnuihs*, had bungled the capture first.

Perhaps he would be able to persuade T'Ihlaah that it was in their better interests to keep the incident out of both of their reports.

TWENTY-THREE

Thursday, February 20, 2155
Enterprise NX-01

"I BELIEVE THE ADJUSTMENTS are now complete," T'Pol said, setting the dynospanner down on the console beside her. She turned the chair—and the jury-rigged titanium helmet that sat atop the chair's backrest—toward the three men who stood near her in the small alcove in sickbay.

"It doesn't look much different than it did the last time we used it," Shran said as he stepped in front of Doctor Phlox and Theras, then gingerly touched the device's headpiece, obviously taking care to avoid touching the heavy cables that led from the helmet's crown to the new power coupling the engineers had hurriedly installed in the bulkhead. "This appears to be the very same telepresence unit Commander Tucker built."

T'Pol wasn't eager to waste time giving Shran a detailed technical report—reassembling the device with Lieutenant Burch was difficult. A competent engineer, who kept repeating, "Call me Mike." His very presence was a painful reminder of Trip's death.

"It *is* the same device," she said. "At least in essence. With some assistance from Lieutenant Burch, however, I have given it a considerable boost in both power and sensitivity, particularly at the most relevant brainwave frequencies."

Theras stepped forward, his gray, blind eyes focused at some invisible point straight ahead of him. Although

T'Pol knew that Theras couldn't see in a conventional manner—his Aenar telepathy made a highly effective substitute for the normal visual sense—she thought he was being quite careful not to come into direct contact with any part of the nearby telepresence equipment, as though he feared it might shock him.

"Are you saying you can locate Jhamel with your device?" Theras asked, sounding even more anxious than usual.

"Yes, in a manner of speaking," T'Pol said. "I believe that this equipment might succeed in enhancing the mind-link that Shran evidently still shares with Jhamel, thus enabling us to follow it to her, as well as to the rest of the Aenar captives."

"Assuming," Phlox said from a corner of the alcove, "that the device proves safe to operate."

T'Pol couldn't help but notice the look of abject hurt that had crossed Theras's face at her mention of the mind-link between Shran and Jhamel; she could almost have sworn that the albino Aenar had just gone another half-shade paler. It was obvious to her now that Theras had been less than truthful when he had claimed not to be bothered by the fact that Shran, an outsider to the Aenar people, shared a deep and intimate psionic connection with a member of Theras's marriage-bond group—a connection that Theras obviously had yet to forge with Jhamel, otherwise *he* would be the one about to be strapped into the chair rather than Shran.

T'Pol could also see that Shran failed to notice—or perhaps didn't care—about Theras's discomfiture. His antennae pushing forward aggressively, the Andorian moved toward the chair and raised the helmet from its backrest, picking it up with both hands.

"Let's stop wasting time and get started," he said in a deep, almost feral growl.

Very carefully, T'Pol took the helmet from Shran in

order to allow him to get into the seat without becoming entangled in the cables. Once he was seated, she set the headpiece onto his cranium, taking care not to restrict his antennae, which appeared to be recoiling instinctively from the edges of the helmet. She set about methodically attaching and tightening the straps that held the headgear in place, then turned to enter a series of commands into the adjacent console.

A faint hum instantly filled the air, which almost immediately carried the faint scent of ozone. T'Pol hoped she hadn't already routed too much power through the telepresence unit's relays.

"Please tell me everything you're sensing, Shran," T'Pol said.

"Nothing so far," Shran said. "Perhaps you need to increase the gain." T'Pol sincerely hoped she wouldn't have to run much more power through the apparatus than it was already accepting.

"Do you understand," Phlox said, addressing Shran, "that your nervous system will be at progressively greater risk as the power levels increase?"

"Of course, Doctor," Shran said, and sounded irritated that Phlox would even ask that question. "But I want Commander T'Pol to use as much power as it takes to find Jhamel."

Though T'Pol wasn't prepared to go quite that far, she inputted the command to bring the power levels up higher still. She looked up from the indicators and saw that Theras's chalk-white face was a study in anxiety, while Shran simply seemed to be growing increasingly impatient. Phlox stood by, observing the proceedings in silence, reminding T'Pol of a vigilant *ferravat* bird of the Vulcan deserts.

"I've increased the power by ten percent," T'Pol said.

The whine of the telepresence unit ascended a half step in pitch, and T'Pol thought she could smell something burning. A lengthy beat elapsed, after which Shran said, "Still noth—"

"Shran?" T'Pol said, moving closer to the Andorian. A combination of trepidation and anticipation swirled behind her brow, though a lifetime of Vulcan training kept it safely invisible.

Phlox had begun running a small medical scanner through the air above Shran's head. "I'm reading some synaptic instability, Commander. It's intensifying."

"Understood, Doctor," T'Pol said.

"I'm sensing . . . *something*," Shran whispered.

"Jhamel?" T'Pol prompted.

Shran appeared to try to nod his head, but the helmet and the cables attached to it restricted his movements. "Yes," he said finally.

"Can you tell where Jhamel is?" T'Pol said.

"A ship. Perhaps a cargo hold. So much . . . fear. Despair. . . ."

"Can you tell us the ship's location?"

"No. Light-years away from here, at least. No." Tears of frustration and pain were beginning to roll down Shran's azure cheeks.

"His synaptic connections are in extreme danger, Commander," Phlox said tersely as he continued to scan the Andorian. "He can't sustain much more of this."

"Acknowledged, Doctor." T'Pol realized that Shran's intense emotions were becoming increasingly difficult for him to rein in, which wasn't a surprising phenomenon in such a violently passionate race as the Andorians. *Keep the questions specific and to the point,* she reminded herself.

"Can you estimate the ship's range from our current position?" T'Pol asked, speaking slowly and with exaggerated patience.

"Raise . . . raise the power levels," Shran said, now openly weeping. His body was beginning to shake, almost convulsing. "Then I might . . . might be able to . . ." His voice trailed off, as though he was in too much pain to continue speaking.

"That could very well damage you permanently, Shran," Phlox said.

"The loss . . . of Jhamel . . . would damage me more, Doctor. *Do it,* Commander!"

"Very well." T'Pol leaned across the console and deftly entered another command.

"Commander, I must advise against this," Phlox said, his tone uncharacteristically prickly.

"Noted," T'Pol said, choosing to ignore Phlox's warning as Shran had demanded. "I have increased power levels another ten percent."

The whine of the apparatus was rising inexorably into a frantic shriek. Alarm lights flashed on the console, and the acrid scent of ozone from the overheating power leads intensified.

"Jhamel!" Shran cried out, his shaking body tensing in the chair as though absorbing a lethal jolt of electrical current.

"Commander!" Phlox shouted, sounding utterly appalled.

T'Pol was about to cut the power back when Shran added, "I can see her!"

T'Pol's attention was suddenly drawn to yet another alarm that had begun flashing on the console, this one warning of imminent neurological trauma, as well as the impending burnout of several key circuits in the telepresence system.

"He's killing himself, Commander," Theras said, his voice taut with fear.

"You have to stop this *now,* Commander!" Phlox said.

"Tell us Jhamel's range and direction, Shran," T'Pol said, working hard to keep her own rising anxiety levels out of her voice.

"Almost have it," Shran said, his voice weak and strained. "I can . . . *feel* it!"

"Shran, I'm going to have to cut power soon." Although recovering the Aenar captives was a vitally important military objective, T'Pol knew she couldn't allow Shran to die, or be made a vegetable, in pursuit of it.

"No! Let me—"

Shran's plea was interrupted by a sudden rush of sparks and flame, erupting simultaneously from both the console and the cables that trailed from Shran's scalp. The Andorian screamed as T'Pol slammed the abort button with the bottom of her fist, abruptly engaging the breakers that cut the telepresence unit off from the ship's power. The pyrotechnics instantly ceased, and Shran slumped forward in the chair, restrained from tumbling onto the sickbay deck only by the helmet and its attached cables. His eyes were rolled up into his head, displaying only a disconcerting blue against the more ashen hue his usually cerulean skin had begun to take on.

T'Pol and Phlox quickly unsnapped the helmet's straps, pulled Shran free of the apparatus, and carefully carried him onto one of Phlox's diagnostic beds, with some assistance from a very jittery Theras.

"He's alive," Theras said from behind T'Pol, his voice sounding very small and fearful. A moment later, the readouts above the bed confirmed Theras's blind observation while Phlox busied himself injecting various neurological agents into Shran's neck.

T'Pol was surprised a moment later when Shran's eyes fluttered open and focused upon her. Amazingly, he now seemed none the worse for wear, other than some prominent singe marks on his clothing and a few white hairs that were curled and scorched.

As Phlox continued working over him, Shran began speaking to T'Pol in a weak voice. "You . . . shut down the telepresence unit, Commander. *Why*?"

"She was attempting to save your *life*," Phlox said acidly, running a scanner over Shran's chest. The doctor paused long enough to turn and cast a critical eye in T'Pol's direction. "Though not quite as quickly as I would have liked."

"I nearly had Jhamel's location," Shran snarled before T'Pol could respond to Phlox's barb.

"Perhaps we can make another attempt soon," T'Pol said, addressing Shran. "Once Doctor Phlox confirms that you are medically fit to do so, of course." She gestured toward the various seared electronic components that now lay strewn about the sickbay deck. "And once Lieutenant Burch and I effect whatever repairs the telepresence unit now requires." *If that's even possible now*, she thought, her nostrils recoiling from the pungent ozone smell that now filled the room.

Shran simply glowered at her in hostile silence, and she met his stare with a wall of Vulcan impassivity. *His passions may get him killed*, she thought. *As well as Jhamel.*

Phlox intervened a moment later, ending the nonverbal showdown by stepping between T'Pol and the bed on which Shran lay. "If you don't mind, Commander, I'd like my patient to have an opportunity to rest for a while."

T'Pol nodded, picking up immediately on the Denobulan's none-too-subtle hint, and gestured toward the wreckage of the telepresence apparatus. "Very well, Doctor. I will send Lieutenant Burch down shortly to collect our equipment."

Phlox smiled solicitously, as though trying to make amends for his earlier display of brusqueness, however justified it might have been. "Thank you, T'Pol. I would very much appreciate that."

With that, T'Pol turned and exited the sickbay. A moment after entering the corridor, she realized that she wasn't alone when a shaky voice spoke from directly behind her.

"Why do you suppose the device failed?"

She turned to face Theras, somewhat surprised that the faint-hearted Aenar had the presence of mind to ask such a probing question. "It is difficult to say," she said. "There could be some unforeseeable difficulty on Jhamel's end of the mind-link. Or perhaps the problem is that Shran possesses no innate telepathic abilities of his own, in spite of the psionic link that Jhamel established with him."

Perhaps, she thought, *we could adjust the device so that it can be used in tandem by both Shran and Theras—*

"T'Pol." It was another familiar voice. She turned again and saw a somber Captain Archer standing behind her, evidently having just exited a nearby turbolift.

"Captain."

"I was on my way to sickbay to check on your telepresence experiment," he said.

She shook her head. "The results of the first attempt left much to be desired. However, I am confident that we will be able to try again soon, perhaps as early as tomorrow. Once Phlox declares Shran medically fit, and after our equipment undergoes some repairs."

Archer nodded sadly. "I see. Well, I suppose that means you can afford to put it aside for a while."

T'Pol found that she was having difficulty suppressing a scowl. "I would prefer not to do that, Captain. It is vitally important that we prevent the Romulans from gaining access to any more Aenar pilots."

"Of course it is, T'Pol. I'm only asking you to set it aside an hour so." The captain paused momentarily before continuing in a quiet, strained voice. "It's almost time for Commander Tucker's memorial service."

TWENTY-FOUR

Thursday, February 20, 2155
Romulan space

"IT'S LIKE I ALWAYS SAY, COMMANDER," Phuong said, "nothing says 'my ship was completely destroyed' better than a cargo module blown to tiny pieces across an asteroid field."

Trip watched the cloud of metallic debris slowly expand as its millions of constituent parts—all of which had been essentially a single piece bolted to the *Branson*'s belly only minutes earlier—drifted and tumbled through space, occasionally colliding anew with each other and the multitudes of irregularly shaped rocky bodies that called this region of space home.

"Let's just hope that those Romulan bird-of-prey captains are in the mood to buy what you're selling," Trip said, his throat dry with apprehension. *Otherwise, pretty soon we won't need a ship to fly through space.*

"Don't worry," Phuong said in a voice that brimmed with so much confidence that Trip wondered if his associate wasn't a better actor than a tactician. "This is the same tactic we used to cover the escape of your 'assassins' from *Enterprise*."

Trip could only shake his head at that, since he preferred to believe that the *main* reason that the maneuver had worked when employed against *Enterprise*'s crew was the fact that Captain Archer and Malcolm Reed were both in on Section 31's plot to fake his death in the first place.

An hour passed with agonizing sluggishness while the *Branson* continued to cling to the deep shadows of one of the larger bodies in the system's extensive asteroid field. While Phuong effected repairs to the ship's various damaged systems—he'd insisted that he knew the ship better than anyone, including its many one-off modifications, and therefore declined Trip's offer of assistance—Trip continuously checked the passive scanning devices, only to find no evidence that any Romulans were still present. But he knew that there was no guarantee that a bird-of-prey wasn't simply hanging out there somewhere, using yet another asteroid for cover as it patiently waited for its prey to reappear. . . .

It was Phuong's patience that wore out first. "Well, we can't stay here forever, Commander," he said, breaking the near total silence that had engulfed the cramped cockpit for more than an hour. "Let's move out."

Trip nodded, and the two men began silently entering commands into their respective sections of the conn and navigational consoles, quickly powering up the little *Rutan*-class ship and getting her back under way through the asteroid field and into the emptier spaces that lay beyond its orbit.

Trip was tempted to use the *Branson*'s active sensors to determine whether or not the Romulan patrol vessel was still lingering nearby, but decided against it. Such a move might risk giving away their position, even if the other vessel had already moved on but was still near enough to detect the *Branson*'s presence.

"See any sign of sensor contact?" Phuong asked.

Trip studied his console readouts yet again and shook his head. "Nobody seems to be scanning us."

"Then it's Rator II or bust," Phuong said, laying a new heading into the navigational computer with quick, practiced motions.

It occurred to Trip that Phuong was once again taking him to a destination that he knew next to nothing about. *I hope I don't start getting used to this*, he thought as the little ship shuddered and lurched into warp.

Fortunately, Rator II wasn't far away from where the *Branson* had been waylaid by the Romulan patrol; it took only the better part of a day to reach at the *Branson*'s maximum speed of warp 4.5.

On the other hand, the fact that this obscure Romulan colony world was so easy to get to filled Trip with worry that the very patrols they thought they'd eluded were quietly following, just waiting to pounce on them as well as on Phuong's local *Ejhoi Ormiin* contacts, whom he assumed would be harboring the much sought-after Doctor Ehrehin.

Trip watched the pleasantly blue world as it grew in the forward viewports until the warm radiance of its cloud-dappled sunlit side dominated his view. The planet seemed extraordinarily Earth-like, although its ocean-dominated surface was punctuated by long chains of volcanic islands rather than large continental masses. The view became distorted for several minutes as Phuong guided his vessel into the atmosphere on a landing trajectory, atmospheric friction superheating the air around the craft until it ionized and gave off an almost blinding orange glow. Then, almost like a light turning off, the inferno dissipated, replaced by a view of a steadily approaching ocean, replete with a chain of black, mountainous, and vegetation-rich islands.

Following an apparently preprogrammed approach path, Phuong set the *Branson* down on a relatively flat stretch of obsidian-like rock, only a few hundred meters from what appeared to be a concrete Quonset hut-type structure that seemed almost to have been extruded directly from the glassy stone that surrounded it.

"The local *Ejhoi Ormiin* union hall, I presume?" Trip asked wryly, gesturing through the front viewport toward the nearby structure.

"So say our best intelligence files," Phuong said, nodding.

Trip powered down the console in front of him and rose from his copilot's chair. "Let's hope your best turns out to be good enough." Instinctively, Trip moved aft toward the weapons locker Phuong had showed him shortly after he'd first come aboard and opened it.

"We won't be needing those," Phuong said.

Trip turned toward the other man and scowled. "You've got to be kidding."

"No, Commander, I mean it. We're talking about the *Ejhoi Ormiin* here. They may be trustworthy, but they're also extremely careful and more than a little justifiably paranoid. The best we can hope for is that they'll politely relieve us of any weapons we're carrying while we're here. The worst is that you'll panic them and get us both shot."

Trip had to concede that Phuong had a point. He clearly had a lot to learn about the world of espionage, and suspected that Phuong's diplomatic background had served him well. After another moment's hesitation, he closed the locker.

Without any further conversation, the two men each ran a quick systems check on the special travel garments they'd picked up on Adigeon Prime. Once they were satisfied that everything was as it should be, they exited the *Branson* through the port hatch and descended to the dark, glassy-looking surface, which turned out not to be anywhere near as slick and slippery as it had appeared from the air. Trip supposed this surface must have been laid down countless millennia ago, and had since been subject to various weathering processes that had roughened it up over the eons. They began crossing the ancient lava field, which Trip thought smelled vaguely like gunpowder, and moved steadily toward the Quonset hut; Trip tried to take the lava's apparent great age as a hopeful sign that they probably wouldn't have to contend with a volcanic eruption during their stay here, which he sincerely hoped would be brief. *I like a tropical island paradise as much as the next guy,* he thought. *But I can do without the constant worry about Romulan patrols popping up. Or whether or not we can really trust these* Ejhoi Ormiin *characters.*

When they were still perhaps fifty or so paces away from the hut, a door slid open in the structure's side, and a trio of dour-looking, paramilitary-clad figures stepped out into the white afternoon sun.

Romulans, Trip guessed, judging by their distinctly Vulcanoid appearance. They were all males, and he could see at once that at least two of them were armed with heavy pistols of some sort. Whether these weapons turned out to fire directed energy beams or ballistic metal pellets, he had no choice other than to assume that they were lethal. Following Phuong's lead, Trip stopped in his tracks and raised his arms high over his head, keeping his hands open to demonstrate that he posed no threat.

As one of the trio of Romulans—the one that wasn't carrying any visible weaponry—stepped ahead of the other two, Trip thought, *Let's hope we get our money's worth out of these Adigeon translation devices.*

"*Jolan'tru,* Ch'uihv of Saith," Phuong said. "I am Terha of Talvath, from the Devoras cell." Thanks to their implanted translators, both Phuong and Trip could converse fluently in the language they now knew was called *Rihannsu.*

When Trip got a close look at the face of the man whom Phuong had addressed as Ch'uihv, he experienced a sharp, undeniable sensation of déjà vu. All at once he was convinced that he had seen this man before, although the precise context of that previous encounter eluded him.

After taking a lengthy beat to look both Phuong and Trip up and down, Ch'uihv finally turned to Phuong and said, "Your reputation precedes you, Terha. *Jolan'tru.*" He made a polite half-bow in Phuong's direction, and Phuong casually copied the gesture as though it was something he had done all his life.

Realizing not only that their translators were working as promised, but also that their surgical alterations had at least passed visual muster, Trip forced himself not to heave an audible sigh of relief. But he almost took an involuntary step backward when Ch'uihv abruptly turned to face Trip.

"And you, Cunaehr—I truly never expected to see *you* again, especially after that accident on Unroth III."

Once again, Trip was rattled by that same feeling of déjà vu. Even the man's voice sounded familiar.

He suddenly realized why, and that abrupt awareness very nearly caused him to lose his composure. *But he really thinks I'm Ehrehin's assistant, Cunaehr,* Trip thought, his mind racing. *So he hasn't seen through my disguise the way I've seen through his. At least, not yet.*

Trip was determined to cling to that slender advantage for as long as he possibly could. "It was a very near thing," he said finally, trusting his Adigeon-altered vocal cords, as well as his translator, to complete the illusion that he was, indeed, Cunaehr. "I look forward to seeing Doctor Ehrehin again."

The man named Ch'uihv broke out into a smile, an occurrence that Trip gathered was probably rare. And seeing a smile on such a Vulcan-like face struck Trip as extremely odd. "And I am sure that Doctor Ehrehin will be delighted to see you. It's extremely fortunate for us that you are here, in fact; your presence may make him easier to handle. Please, come inside with us."

The stolid presence of the armed men by the door made it crystal clear to Trip that Ch'uihv wasn't making a request.

"Lead the way," said Phuong, his voice betraying no fear.

Instead of taking them straight to Doctor Ehrehin, as Trip had hoped, Ch'uihv and his men led them into a comfortably appointed sitting room or waiting room, where yet another Romulan—a youngish-looking female this time, also clad in paramilitary garb, and looking every bit as dangerous as any of the men—brought them refreshments before leaving them alone together in the room.

Trip and Phuong sat at a small, round table, both of them eyeing the tray of exotic-looking fruits, meats, and breads that the woman had left for them.

Phuong immediately grabbed a plate and some silverware. He heaped some food on a plate and started to eat.

"Hey!" Trip said. "You sure that's safe?"

Phuong paused for a moment, then spoke around a mouthful of food. "You think they'd bother poisoning us? If they really wanted us dead, I think they'd just shoot us."

Trip had to admit that Phuong had a point. Besides, he couldn't deny the insistent growling of his own stomach, and he quickly began digging into the food before him with gusto, though he studied the tall, clear carafe that accompanied it with some suspicion. It contained an intensely blue liquid that reminded him uncomfortably of something called a Blue Hawaii, an alcoholic beverage with which he'd once had an unfortunate experience back on Earth many years ago.

Phuong noticed Trip's discomfiture immediately. "It's called Romulan ale. It's got quite a kick, but I can guarantee that it's nonlethal."

Trip shrugged, then began filling a pair of squared-off drinking glasses with the sapphire-hued fluid. "If you say so." He handed one of the glasses to Phuong, then took a single cautious sip of his own before deciding that he liked a smooth Kentucky bourbon a lot better.

"Something's bothering you," Phuong said, setting his cutlery down momentarily.

Trip nodded. "I'm not sure it's safe to talk about it here, though."

"The electronics woven into our clothing would have let us know if there were any bugging devices trained on us now. Go ahead and speak freely."

Trip looked furtively about the room for a moment, as though he expected to see a hidden microphone embedded in a wall, or a chair, or perhaps even in the food. Feeling foolish, he forced himself to focus all his attention back upon Phuong.

"It's about our host," Trip said quietly. "This Ch'uihv character. He's not who he seems to be."

Phuong chuckled and appeared almost to aspirate a swallow of his Romulan ale. "In case you haven't noticed, neither are we."

Trip felt his irritation beginning to rise. "From the moment I first laid eyes on him, I knew I'd met him before. It was over three years ago, during one of the civil conflicts on Coridan Prime. His name was Sopek back then, and he was the captain of a Vulcan military ship."

Phuong blanched. "You're saying you think he's some sort of Vulcan-Romulan double agent?"

"Looks that way to me. Anyhow, I don't trust him. There's no knowing whose side he's really on."

"There's no way to really know that about anybody, especially in this business," Phuong said. "The question is, what does he know about *you*?"

Trip shrugged again. "As far as I can tell so far, only what we want him to know."

Phuong drained his Romulan ale in a single quaff, making Trip wince involuntarily in sympathy. "Regardless of the espionage activities of Ch'uihv—or Sopek—we don't really have a good alternative to trusting him. He's still our only link to Doctor Ehrehin. We'll just have to treat Ch'uihv with a great deal of caution."

Trip shook his head resignedly. "Caution. Good idea. Now, why didn't *I* think of that?"

Now it was Phuong's turn to sound irritated. "Look, Ch'uihv represents a breakaway Romulan faction that wants to assist Doctor Ehrehin in defecting to Vulcan before the Romulan military can catch up to him."

"We hope," Trip said. "Ch'uihv's people could just as easily be planning to use Ehrehin's technology for their own purposes—which could pose just as big a danger to Earth as the Romulan military does."

Phuong set his empty glass down on the tabletop with a loud clatter. "We *have* to take Ch'uihv at face value. Because if he isn't for real, then we're probably both dead already—along with all the worlds of the Coalition, which will fall one by one to Romulan fleets powered by Ehrehin's new stardrive.

"But only if we fail."

Or if we're just plain wrong, Trip thought, then drained his own glass, stoically ignoring the blazing sensation as the bright blue stuff burned its way down his gullet like the sea floor sinking into a fiery subduction zone.

Though he didn't like it, Trip knew that Phuong was right. Regardless of whether or not Ch'uihv—or Sopek—proved trustworthy, there really was no choice at all other than to trust him. But that didn't mean that they had to trust him *blindly*.

Remembering that, Trip thought, *just might give us the upper hand.*

TWENTY-FIVE

Thursday, February 20, 2155
Enterprise **NX-01**

AS THE SLEEK TORPEDO CASING was launched into space, the majority of *Enterprise*'s crew who had assembled in Shuttlepod One's launch bay stood silent, while some wept or sniffled. At the forefront of the crowd, near Captain Archer and the other command staff, T'Pol neither cried nor sniffled, nor even felt the strong need to suppress the emotions that were no longer battling within her.

The feelings that had so wracked her mental disciplines when she had been in Trip's quarters had given way to an almost preternatural calm. She had wondered at first if she were in shock, but earlier in Trip's memorial service, when she had touched the smooth surface of his metal coffin, another thought had sprung into her mind.

For some reason she couldn't properly identify, touching the torpedo casing had given T'Pol a gnawing disquiet, a suspicion that something was not right. But the precise nature of that something, however, remained frustratingly obscure to her.

Now, as Trip's casket drifted away into trackless space, T'Pol wondered idly if the decision to jettison his remains here, so far from his native Earth, was really what Trip would have wanted. But when she had brought this objection to the attention of Captain Archer and Lieutenant Reed, they had both assured her that the action had been taken to honor one of Trip's final requests. Apparently he had indicated in his will that he'd wanted to be interred in deep space, among the stars, should he happen to die in the line of duty.

Oddly, not only was Archer adamant about following Trip's wishes, he also seemed particularly intent on carrying out the memorial ceremony and services quickly, weeks before *Enterprise* was due to return to Earth. It seemed to T'Pol that the logical course of action would have been to wait until Trip's remains could be taken to Earth, so that his family, friends, and colleagues could commemorate him, and then launch Trip into space afterward. But the captain had disagreed.

T'Pol looked to the side of the launch bay, where she noticed Doctor Phlox studying her intently. She stared back at him, and they locked eyes for a moment before the Denobulan physician turned away.

For some reason she could not identify, the doctor's inquisitive stare made her apprehensive. She decided then and there that the best way to pursue these accumulated oddities might be to question the chief medical officer directly.

How much has she figured out? Phlox thought, more than a little concerned.

"Thank you for coming to see me, T'Pol," he said, doing his best to sound casual as he gestured toward one of the sickbay's biobeds. "I was going to request that you pay me a visit anyway, so I'm pleased that you've saved me the trouble."

T'Pol leaned against the bed, keeping her hands at her sides. "Why did you wish to see me, Doctor?" she asked, one eyebrow slightly raised. She seemed to be making no effort to conceal her curiosity. "Might it be related to the reason you were staring at me during Commander Tucker's memorial service?"

Phlox could have kicked himself now for having stared. He had clearly further roused suspicions that she had developed when she'd gotten close to the torpedo casing.

The casket that most definitely did *not* contain the remains of Commander Tucker.

He chuckled, temporizing as he decided on the best way to allay T'Pol's suspicions. "In addition to my role as a general physician, I often function as a *mental* health practitioner, in lieu of any other officer aboard this ship acting in that capacity—other than Chef, I suppose." He spread his hands and smiled widely. "I don't know if that's because of my bedside manner, or because doctors are bound by their medical ethics to hold *anything* their patients tell them in strictest confidence, as long as it doesn't endanger the ship."

He paused, letting his words hang in the air for a moment, but T'Pol merely stared at him curiously, making no immediate effort to step into the conversational breach. After thirty seconds or so, she finally opened her mouth as if to speak, closed it again, then spoke at last.

"Are you saying that you believe that there is something confidential that I wish to share with you?"

Phlox tilted his head, returning her curious stare with one of his own. "I didn't say that, Commander, but if you *were* burdened with such a secret, I'd be more than willing to hear it—and I'd be obliged to be discreet about it." He folded his hands in front of his stomach, waiting. Beyond his genuine concern, he also hoped to gauge exactly how much T'Pol might really suspect about the truth behind Trip's "death."

T'Pol dipped her head, then spoke again in a much quieter voice than usual. "I have had difficulty controlling my emotions ever since Trip's death." She began twisting her hands together, evidently unconsciously. "I had a very difficult . . . breakdown of my emotional barriers last week, while I was packing up Trip's personal effects."

"That isn't surprising," Phlox said gently. "Losing a compatriot is difficult enough, and losing a . . . lover is wrenching, to say the very least. But when one factors in the extraordinary emotional strain you've been under lately, on Vulcan, and on Mars, this . . . event might be— as the humans put it—the proverbial 'straw that broke the camel's back.'"

She stiffened, as though offended. "I am a Vulcan."

"T'Pol," he continued, "Vulcans are most certainly not *devoid* of emotions, however adept you have become in the practice of suppressing them. Vulcans experience feelings as full and rich as those of any species. But suppressing emotions tends to put them under pressure. And when something is under too much pressure for too long, it can erupt unexpectedly, sometimes with rather alarming results."

He turned and grabbed one of his handheld medical scanners, then approached T'Pol more closely. "Lift your head, please." He began scanning her, holding the glowing, whirring device next to her temple. "Were there any *physical* side effects to your . . . breakdown? Other than your eyes, I mean." He had noticed that her nictitating inner eyelid had suffered multiple broken blood vessels, which gave their normally clear membranes a slightly lime-colored tint.

"Ironically, I have been having difficulty getting to sleep," T'Pol said.

Phlox understood that she was referring to more than a year earlier, when Trip had been unable to sleep after his sister had died in the Xindi attack on Earth. Phlox had referred Trip to T'Pol for Vulcan neuropressure; since that time, the two had become increasingly—if sometimes combatively—involved with one another romantically.

"I can prescribe a mild sedative for you," he said, sidestepping the neuropressure issue. He backed away slightly to study the readings on his scanner, then set it down on a countertop and turned back to her.

"Beyond recent events in your life, I can think of another possible causal factor for your recent . . . emotional lapse," he said. "The aftereffects of the trellium." While *Enterprise* was searching for the Xindi in the hazardous unknown region known as the Delphic Expanse, T'Pol had become addicted to a mineral known as trellium, a substance that had enabled her to escape the restraints of logic, at least temporarily. Phlox had helped T'Pol end her addiction, but the physical repercussions of her chemical dependency were still measurable.

"I *have* been able to control my emotions since that time," T'Pol said, a hint of defensiveness in her voice. "Until now."

Phlox nodded. "Have you? Or were you *struggling* to control them on a deeper level?" He approached her again, staring into her eyes. "I've seen you fighting your emotions, T'Pol. More and more. Understand that *I* don't consider emotions to be a negative thing. Denobulans revel in them, as do humans. So I cannot compare my situation to yours. But if you are susceptible to emotional outbursts due to a residual chemical imbalance in your body, it may be more harmful to you *not* to give in to your emotions, at least from time to time."

T'Pol nodded, but Phlox could see that she had discarded his advice the instant he had voiced it. He stepped away and pretended to tidy up his counter.

"There is something else," T'Pol said, her voice clearer. "Something that I do not believe can be blamed on the trellium, or on my present lack of emotional restraint."

Phlox stiffened slightly. *This is where she tells me her suspicions,* he thought. He turned back toward her.

T'Pol crossed her arms across her chest and shifted her

weight from foot to foot. Despite these telltale signs of nervousness, her face remained an all but inscrutable mask.

"I believe that Commander Tucker is still alive."

Phlox carefully masked his own responsive body language, glad that the first officer was only a touch telepath and couldn't read his thoughts just now.

"That's an interesting notion," he said at length.

"I know that it's a logical impossibility," T'Pol said, gesturing with one hand. "If Trip isn't dead, that would mean that you and the captain, and perhaps Lieutenant Reed as well, would have to have faked his death for some unknown reason. An alternative possibility is that I am becoming delusional."

Phlox clasped his hands behind his back tightly. "Putting aside the absurd notion that there has been a conspiracy to make Commander Tucker only *appear* to have died, the second notion strikes me as equally absurd. At least until you exhibit other symptoms of having experienced a break with reality.

"I must also point out to you that *denial* is one of the stages of mourning that people commonly experience after the loss of a loved one." He paused, and modulated his voice. "Why do you think he *isn't* dead?"

"There are . . . things we shared, which have forever linked us," T'Pol said.

He could tell that she was holding something back, and wondered if she was talking about a mind-meld between Trip and herself. He stayed silent, though, and resolved not to pry into that deeply personal aspect of their relationship, even though he found the Vulcan practice of telepathic linkage and fusion a fascinating concept, one that he hoped to explore for a future medical paper now that mind-melders were becoming more socially acceptable on Vulcan under Minister T'Pau's new government.

"Beyond that, perhaps it is because I was not allowed to see the body—"

"At Commander Tucker's request," Phlox said, interrupting.

"And today, when I touched the torpedo casing that contained Trip's remains, I felt nothing but . . . cold. Absence. Though I know it is not logical, all my instincts told me that he was *not* inside the torpedo."

"He wasn't," Phlox said.

T'Pol looked at him inquisitively.

He stepped closer to her. "The body that was in that tube was *not* Commander Tucker. The essence of what Trip was still exists out in the universe. He *is* still out there," he said.

"More importantly, Trip is also here," he said, touching a finger to T'Pol's forehead. "And here." He touched the right side of her ribcage, where he knew the Vulcan heart to be located. "And he *will* be with us forever."

T'Pol stared at him, the area between her eyebrows twitching and wrinkling as she struggled with the maelstrom of emotion that was clearly roiling within her. And then, abruptly, her forehead smoothed, and she nodded.

"Thank you, Doctor," she said.

Half an hour later, alone in sickbay, Phlox looked up from feeding his Aldebaran mud leeches. He realized, in a flash, that although he had managed to talk to T'Pol without telling her any bald-faced lies, she, too, might have pulled a canny maneuver on *him*.

Not only had she never said whether she actually believed that he, the captain, and Lieutenant Reed really had conspired to fake Trip's death and conceal the truth from her, but she had also avoided revealing whether her discussion with him had allayed her fears, or confirmed her suspicions.

He considered the conundrum that T'Pol presented for several more minutes, then smiled.

"Whatever she knows or believes, I think I can trust her to do what's best," he said to the hungry leeches squirming in the liquid-filled container below his fingers.

TWENTY-SIX

Friday, February 21, 2155
Rator II

"THE GOOD DOCTOR IS IN HERE," Ch'uihv said, pressing his thumb on the biometric keypad mounted on the wall beside the door. The door slid open obediently.

Beside himself with anticipation, Trip stepped toward the open door, with Phuong a step or two behind him, when the Vulcan double agent suddenly stepped into the open aperture, blocking their path.

"I must caution you, Cunaehr: Ehrehin has been rather withdrawn of late, and he has been only . . . intermittently rational. I fear that he has begun having second thoughts regarding his defection."

Trip nodded, not much liking the way the other man seemed to be scrutinizing his face. Had he finally noticed that he wasn't actually Cunaehr?

Or worse, was he finally remembering him, the way Trip had remembered Captain Sopek?

"I understand," Trip said at length. "Perhaps seeing me again will help Doctor Ehrehin become . . . better grounded emotionally."

Ch'uihv—or Sopek—nodded, though his expression remained as grave as any Vulcan's. "That is my hope as well," he said before stepping aside.

Trip led Phuong through the open doorway and into the darkened chamber that lay beyond. The door whisked closed behind them, and Trip squinted as his eyes slowly adjusted to the lower light levels inside the room, which carried the heavy scents of medicines and cleaning chemicals.

He came to a halt as he saw the silhouette of what appeared to be someone seated in a chair that was facing obliquely toward the small room's far corner.

"Doctor Ehrehin?" said Phuong, who had come to a stop beside Trip.

The form in the chair stirred slightly, but made no move to rise to greet his visitors. A gruff, aged male voice emanated from the corner. "Who wants to know?"

"My name is Terha," Phuong said.

"Never heard of you. Go away."

Phuong continued in a gently insistent tone. "Sir, I've brought someone with me whom I believe you will be very pleased to see."

The old man touched a control of some sort on the arm of his chair. With a faint mechanical *whirr*, the chair slowly turned to face Trip and Phuong. Trip could see the old man's white hair and wizened features fairly clearly now, despite the obscuring semidarkness of the room.

"Do you know what I'd be very pleased to see right now?" Doctor Ehrehin said in a querulous tone. "The inside of one of my laboratories, for a start."

Trip noticed that the old man seemed to be studying his face carefully. *Looks like it's finally showtime*, he thought. *Better knock him dead with the first performance, or else we're* both *liable to end up that way.*

Aloud, he said, "Don't worry, Doctor. Soon you'll have all the lab resources you could ever want."

Ehrehin responded with an almost cackling laugh. "You mean after I defect to one of those so-called Coalition planets? Is *that* what they've told you?"

Trip felt confused, and noted that his discomfiture was slowly escalating. This man wasn't speaking like a defector. In fact, he sounded more like a prisoner. Of course, Ch'uihv had warned them that Ehrehin might not be entirely rational. But still . . .

He took a few more steps toward the aged scientist, as did Phuong. Trip saw that Ehrehin had continued squinting up at him all the while.

A look of recognition, mixed with equal parts hope and fear, crossed Ehrehin's face as Trip came to a stop less than a meter away.

"Cunaehr?" Ehrehin said in a quavering voice. "Is that you?"

Trip swallowed hard and nodded. "Yes, sir. It's me."

The old man looked toward the ceiling. "Computer, turn up the lights by twenty percent." Fixing his gaze back upon Trip as the light level increased, he said, "Come closer. Let me get a better look at you."

Trip knelt beside the old man's chair and let the scientist examine his face more closely. With a tremulous hand, Ehrehin gently brushed his rough, gnarled fingertips across Trip's cheek. *Here's hoping the Adigeons gave us our money's worth,* he thought, his heart in his throat.

"It *is* you," the old man said at length, leaning back in his chair so as to get a better look at his visitor. "But how is that possible, Cunaehr? I saw you die."

Trip put on the most disarming smile he could muster. "Are you sure about that, Doctor? I'd like to think of my presence here as empirical evidence to the contrary." *Sure hope I sounded enough like a scientist to fool a scientist,* Trip thought.

Ehrehin squinted up at Trip for another protracted moment, then shrugged. "I suppose I can't argue with empirical evidence." He pushed against the arms of his chair, rising to his feet with what Trip judged to be a good deal of pain. "Now help me get out of here."

Trip rose and allowed the frail scientist to lean on his arm. "Ch'uihv says that a transport will be coming for you in just a few *eisae*."

"A few *eisae*," Ehrehin repeated, almost mockingly. "I suppose that bastard Ch'uihv thinks that'll give him all the time he needs to finish getting what he wants out of me."

"I don't understand," Trip said, though he feared that he did indeed understand what was really happening here all too well.

Ehrehin stared at Trip as though he were a willfully obtuse schoolchild. "You really don't think he intends to just hand over my knowledge of *avaihh lli vastam* to others without first taking it for himself, do you?"

It took the electronics mounted in Trip's inner ear an additional moment to process the unfamiliar term Ehrehin had used: *avaihh lli vastam*, which translated from the Old High Rihannsu still sometimes used by academics as "warp-seven capable stardrive" in the current vernacular.

"You have to help me get away from these people, Cunaehr," the old man continued. "Before they finally *do* succeed in breaking me. It's really only a matter of time, and Admiral Valdore's forces might not find me before it's too late."

Trip exchanged a brief glance with Phuong, whose expression revealed as much perplexity as Trip himself felt. Focusing his gaze back upon Ehrehin, Trip said, "I don't understand, Doctor. I thought you'd gone willingly with the *Ejhoi Ormiin.*"

Ehrehin's eyes were now wide and pleading. "I'm sure that's what they told you, Cunaehr. Just like they also must have said that I might start raving, saying things that don't make sense."

Trip nodded. "They warned me that you might not be . . . quite yourself."

"If that's true, then you can no doubt chalk that up to my having been kidnapped from what was *supposed* to be a secure military safe house, then interrogated night and day ever since. They've even been using psionic probes on me." Ehrehin pulled back the sparse white hair that hung across his forehead, displaying a series of overlapping, vicious-looking circular scars that were scabbed over with dark green blood.

"The *Ejhoi Ormiin* want to take the secret of the *avaihh lli vastam* for themselves," Trip said, suppressing a horrified shudder at the repeated, brutal violations that the old man had revealed. How much more punishment could the fragile scientist take before his sanity—or perhaps even his life—was in real jeopardy? It came as something of a surprise to feel such compassion for a Romulan—until he realized that the impulse probably spoke rather well of his own humanity, even if no one in the Romulan Star Empire ever came to appreciate it.

Finger-combing his hair back over his scars, Ehrehin scowled deeply and disgustedly. "Didn't I just *say* that?"

"We thought that the *Ejhoi Ormiin* were primarily interested in keeping the new stardrive out of the hands of the Romulan military," Phuong said, his brow furrowed almost as deeply as Ehrehin's was. "In order to halt the Praetor's plans for conquest and expansion."

"That's only about half right. They certainly don't want the military to possess the advantage of the new drive, because that would interfere with their *own* plans for conquest. Once the technology is in Ch'uihv's hands, he plans to use it to oust the Praetor and have the *Ejhoi Ormiin* stage a coup that will place them firmly in control of the imperial government."

"I thought you weren't all that comfortable with the Praetor's ambitions yourself, Doctor," Phuong said.

"That's never been a secret," said the old man. "If the military hadn't needed my expertise so badly, I would almost certainly have been imprisoned or executed for having spoken my mind on the matter. But at least the Praetor always had the virtue of a certain . . .

predictability. There's no way to know for certain exactly what the *Ejhoi Ormiin* radicals would do with my technology."

Trip looked over to Phuong while Ehrehin was speaking. The Section 31 operative seemed almost to deflate before his eyes as he no doubt was coming to the awful realization that the intelligence the bureau had gathered concerning the *Ejhoi Ormiin* was at best badly incomplete, or at worst flat-out wrong.

It was easy for Trip to imagine what Phuong must be thinking, since the shock of the same realization was settling over him as well. *I guess this is the kind of intelligence failure that's toughest to avoid,* Trip thought. *Especially when you've got to run all your information through the filter of secondhand facts and bribable third-party information brokers like the Adigeons.*

"Help me, Cunaehr," the old man said, almost begging. "Help me get out of here, and back to the protection of Admiral Valdore's fleet."

Trip exchanged another wordless glance with Phuong, who gestured with his head toward the door. *He needs to talk with me, but he can't do it in here,* Trip thought, understanding that the room had to be crawling with listening devices.

"I promise you that we'll do whatever we can to help you, Doctor," Trip told the old man. "But first, I'd like to know exactly what you've revealed to Ch'uihv so far."

With tears pooling in his eyes, Ehrehin nodded, then began speaking in a low, halting voice. . . .

"I *did* warn you that Doctor Ehrehin might not be entirely rational," Ch'uihv said, his expression dour as he and a pair of his grim uniformed guards escorted Trip and Phuong back to the quarters they had been issued for the duration of their stay at the *Ejhoi Ormiin* facility. "I wouldn't be at all surprised if he blamed us for the harsh treatment the Romulan military visited upon him in order to 'motivate' his research."

Trip nodded to Ch'uihv as they walked, but he schooled his face into blank impassivity. He simply wasn't buying Ch'uihv's story; the old man's wounds had appeared far too recent to have been inflicted by the Romulan military to which he was so eager to return.

Trip was absolutely convinced that Ehrehin was indeed here entirely against his will, just as the old man had said.

And as he followed Phuong into the spacious guest suite they were sharing, Trip was just as certain that Ch'uihv—or Sopek—had listened to every word of their exchange with the elderly scientist, no doubt hoping that he and Phuong would unwittingly function as *Ejhoi Ormiin* interrogators, using Cunaehr's privileged relationship with Ehrehin to entice him to divulge some previously hidden fact regarding the new stardrive.

"Well, what do we do now?" Trip asked Phuong once they were alone together in the suite's common area.

Phuong tipped his head to one side, as though listening to voices that no one else could hear. Trip realized that he must be consulting the microelectronic gear sewn into his clothing, checking the room for listening devices.

"At least we can speak freely here," Phuong said at length. He looked Trip squarely in the eye, his face pale even for a Romulan. "I think we screwed up badly in trusting these people."

Trip's brow furrowed. "'We'?"

"I mean the whole bureau. All right, *me*. They followed *my* recommendations, after all."

Holding up a placating hand, Trip said, "I'm not keeping score. At least we were *both* completely right about at least one thing."

"And what's that?" Phuong wanted to know.

"The fact that the Romulan Empire really is the biggest danger facing Earth right now. The only real question is *which* Romulan regime is going to take charge of going to war against us."

Phuong chuckled, but the sound contained no mirth. "That's pretty cold comfort."

Eager to rescue his partner from a funk that wasn't going to do either of them any good, Trip decided to change the subject. "At least we're pretty sure we know how much *Ch'uihv* knows so far."

Phuong shrugged. "Thanks presumably to Ehrehin's contacts in the Romulan military, we know that a Romulan admiral named Valdore is planning to launch an attack against some unspecified Coalition planet—most likely Coridan Prime—in the very near future. One of their goals is no doubt to discourage the upcoming signing of the Coalition Compact. But that really isn't much more than we knew or suspected already."

"At least the old man hasn't drawn diagrams of the new space drive for Ch'uihv's people," Trip said. *Yet,* he added silently, feeling a distinct chill at the notion.

"That's according to Ehrehin," Phuong said, still sounding disconsolate.

Determined to keep Phuong focused on keeping them both alive, Trip said, "As I think I heard *somebody* say not very long ago, we have to make our leaps of faith *somewhere*. Speaking of which, I'm guessing you're taking the rest of Ehrehin's claims at face value."

Phuong nodded emphatically. "I don't believe what Ch'uihv says about Ehrehin being only 'intermittently rational.' I've seen enough prisoners—hell, I've *interrogated* enough of them—to know the difference between a lie, a delusion, and the plain truth. That man is as rational as you or I, and I believe he's telling the truth."

For a moment Trip wondered how much that opinion was worth; after all, it was obvious that Phuong had begun to question his own ability to read people accurately. *And we* both *voluntarily marched right into this situation,* he thought. *Just how "rational" does that make either one of us?*

And something else was gnawing at Trip as well. "At least he seems rational *now*," he said. "And frankly, I have one major doubt about even that."

Phuong raised an eyebrow quizzically. "What do you mean?"

"I mean that it seemed a little bit too easy to convince him that I was his assistant, miraculously returned from the dead. If Ehrehin was really on top of his game, wouldn't he have asked a few more questions? If it were *me* in Ehrehin's situation, I'd just assume I was dealing with somebody who'd been disguised as Cunaehr."

A thoughtful look crossed Phuong's face, then he shrugged. "Sometimes it's better to be lucky than to be good. Maybe we were just fortunate enough to stumble onto an advantage that we can exploit once we get Ehrehin out of here."

Trip nodded, though his engineer's instincts rebelled against the whole concept of relying on luck. On top of that, he wasn't feeling at all sanguine about taking advantage of the grief and hope of such a frail, vulnerable old man—especially someone who had already suffered such barbaric treatment as Ehrehin had already endured at the hands of the *Ejhoi Ormiin*.

But he knew he didn't have any alternative, especially not when the stakes were as high as they were right now. *Maybe having 'Cunaehr' at his side for a while will give the poor old guy some comfort after everything he's been through,* Trip thought, trying to assuage his conscience with only partial success.

Evidently distracted from his earlier self-recriminations—and slipping back into his mission-planning mode—Phuong interrupted Trip's ruminations. "So we now have two extremely urgent reasons to get Ehrehin out of here as quickly as possible." He began ticking points off on his fingers. "First, there's Ehrehin himself, and the knowledge he's carrying. Second, we have to warn Coridan Prime about our new intelligence that corroborates our suspicions that they will be the Romulans' first target. But I seriously doubt we'll be able to do that from here without tipping our hand to Ch'uihv."

It all made sense to Trip, particularly the point about alerting the Coridanites. It would be a disaster of immeasurable proportions if the Romulans—whether they answered to the Praetor or to the *Ejhoi Ormiin*—were to succeed in seizing control of Coridan's vast dilithium reserves. After all, if Ehrehin's new engine really proved capable of reaching and sustaining a speed of warp seven—as Coridan Prime's ships were rumored to do routinely these days—it would no doubt be one of the most dilithium-hungry technologies ever devised.

But Trip could see at least one glaring problem—perhaps an insurmountable one—with Phuong's plan. "Somehow, I don't see Ch'uihv just letting us take Ehrehin back to the *Branson*."

"That's why we're not going to use the *Branson*," Phuong said with a grin. "But I'm betting we'll find something suitable in Ch'uihv's own vehicle pool—after I get out and do a little reconnaissance work, that is. After all, Ch'uihv never told either of us that we weren't allowed to stroll the grounds a bit during our stay."

Trip shook his head, not quite sure he was believing what he was hearing. "Are you serious?"

"This is what spies do: improvise," Phuong said as he moved toward the door, where he paused for a moment, looking back at Trip. "Stay here and get some rest. You look like hell." And with that, he vanished into the corridor beyond.

The door whisked closed again, and Trip stood staring at it incredulously.

That turncoat Sopek was way, way *off base about who's really "intermittently rational" around here,* Trip thought, shaking his head.

TWENTY-SEVEN

Friday, February 21, 2155
Enterprise NX-01

T'POL SAT IN SHUTTLEPOD TWO with the others. Ensign Mayweather was at the helm, and a pair of MACOs sat at the ready. The cabin was dimly lit, and the ship rocked sharply as they entered the troposphere of the planet.

"I went to see Phlox this morning," the man sitting next to her said.

She turned, and was startled to see a Vulcan sitting there. *Had he been there all this time?*

And yet, he was not a Vulcan, despite the dark hair, arched brows, gracefully pointed ears, and slightly green-tinted skin. Something about him was different, yet comfortably familiar.

"I saw the doctor today as well," T'Pol said, unsure of what else to say.

The man turned toward her. "Did he talk about me?"

T'Pol's eyebrow rose reflexively. "You?"

"Us?"

"What *about* us?" T'Pol asked. "This is illogical."

"Why'd you bring it up, then?" the man asked.

The shuttle continued to rock around them, but none of the others present were speaking, as if they were frozen in place. Exasperated, T'Pol turned and looked more closely at the man. There was something in his eyes . . .

He smiled and winked, and then reached up to tug on

the zipper at the top of his head. His skin unzipped down his forehead, over his nose and lips, down his chin, and to his chest.

T'Pol reached over and pulled apart the skin, revealing the far more familiar face underneath. Trip smiled at her, his expression both sweet and haunted.

He was most certainly not dead.

"Wherever you are, do you ever miss me?" she asked, pitching her voice low to prevent the others from hearing. It didn't matter, since it appeared that they were no longer aboard the shuttlepod anyway; they were in his quarters aboard *Enterprise*.

He looked surprised. "You mean . . ."

She nodded shyly. "Yes."

He picked up the toy armadillo from above the bed and idly played with it as he looked out the viewport at the stars, which looked like so many twinkling lights set against a black velvet curtain. "You know how long it's been?" he finally asked.

"That's not what I asked you," she said, standing, nude, and approaching him from behind.

He bent forward as she began applying neuropressure to his shoulders. "Well . . . uh . . . yeah . . . I guess, sometimes."

The remainder of the green-tinted Vulcan skinsuit began to slough away under T'Pol's ministrations, exposing more of Trip beneath it. She grasped it in the center of his back and tore it away. The remnants fluttered to the floor and became fine gritty sand, like the parched red soil of Vulcan's Forge.

"I haven't thought about those days in a long time," T'Pol said, reaching around his sides to hug him from behind.

He turned around and looked down at her, smiling slightly. "Benefit of being a Vulcan."

She lay back on the bed with him, sweat beading on

her collarbone and forehead. A wave of ecstasy moved through her. His skills were so different from the savage couplings of *Pon farr*.

"After speaking with Doctor Phlox, I realized that we might never see each other again, dead *or* alive," she said finally, the warm glow ebbing.

He climbed on top of her, pressing her down into the mattress as he placed his hands against her temples, spreading his fingers and placing his thumbs beside the bridge of her nose. "I can guarantee you that we're not going to lose touch. *My mind to your mind.* Stop thinking like that. *My thoughts to your thoughts.*"

The tears flowed out of her again, pouring over his fingers and down her face in rivulets, filling the bed, submerging them both in seconds. Trip pulled her close as they sank into the warmth, his mouth coming to hers, his eyes seeing into her soul.

However long it may be . . . I believe I'm going to miss you, she thought.

And in her dreams, the tears and regret and happiness and love caused T'Pol no pain at all.

TWENTY-EIGHT

Friday, February 21, 2155
Rator II

TRIP COULD SEE T'POL lying on the bed beside him, although he knew that her presence here was a physical impossibility. Even so, *there she was*, warm against his body, speaking with him, making love to him. It was obvious that she was no phantom image from some transient dream; she was every bit as tangible and real as he was.

Then Trip felt something grab his shoulder.

He awakened with a start to see a smiling Phuong standing over him. The visual effect was startling: a Vulcan—no, a Romulan—smiling. His heart racing, Trip sat up on the low sofa where he had evidently fallen asleep after Phuong had left.

"You okay?" Phuong said, his smile folding into a look of concern.

She was here with me, right in this room, Trip thought, still unable to relinquish the sense of reality the absurd dream-reality had carried with it. *I* know *she was here*.

"I'm fine."

Phuong's smile returned, and he patted Trip on the shoulder. "Well, I'm glad to see you decided to take my advice and get a little shut-eye while I was out scouting."

"Scouting?" Still unnerved by the sudden transition from deep sleep to bleary wakefulness, Trip rubbed at his aching eyes. "What . . . what did you find?"

Phuong's smile broadened into a triumphant grin.

"Our way out of here. Once we collect Doctor Ehrehin, that is."

Trip rose from the sofa and paused momentarily to consider his partner's ad hoc plan, or lack thereof. While he knew he could have done with a few more hours of sleep, there wasn't much to be gained by waiting. They were, after all, among hostiles who might see through their disguises at any moment and then turn on them. And every passing hour might give Ch'uihv the opportunity he needed to break Ehrehin once and for all, and plunder the dangerous secrets he carried.

Despite his unease about what lay ahead, Trip tried his best to match Phuong's insouciant grin.

"What are we waiting for?"

"Have you come to get me out of here?" Ehrehin asked earnestly.

After pausing to check the charge on the pistol he'd taken from one of the two unconscious guards in the corridor—Phuong had identified the weapon as a "disruptor"—Trip met the elderly scientist's gaze squarely. "As a matter of fact—yes, we have."

Ehrehin beamed at him. After helping the old man out of his chair and onto his feet, Trip turned toward Phuong, who displayed a somewhat worried expression.

"What's wrong?" Trip asked as he carefully walked Ehrehin toward the chamber's single door.

"I'm afraid my surveillance jammers won't last much longer," Phuong said, his head tipped as he listened to electronic inputs from his clothing that only he could hear. "And if somebody opens the storage lockers down the corridor and finds those guards before we can get away . . ."

Using the palm-sized electronic key he'd taken from one of the guards, Trip opened the door to the outer corridor while Ehrehin continued to lean on him. "Then let's get a move on."

Per Phuong's clever introduction of several specialized computer viruses into the facility's systems, the corridor beyond the door suddenly plunged into near-total darkness, making it difficult for Trip to see Phuong as he led the way through a complex series of bends and turns that he had obviously committed carefully to memory a few hours earlier when he had reconned the building. Trip supported most of Ehrehin's weight while continuously turning and dodging the various *Ejhoi Ormiin* personnel who hustled past them in all directions; fortunately, they were apparently confused and thus far utterly oblivious to the jailbreak that was occurring right under their noses.

A seeming eternity later, Trip briefly leaned an exhausted Ehrehin against a wall while Phuong manually cranked open a door that led to yet another darkened chamber. Once the trio was inside, Trip inferred from the loud echoes of their footfalls that they had entered a vast, cavernous space.

An underground hangar, he realized.

"This way!" Phuong hissed, and led the way to a nearby shape that became clearly visible only after Phuong manually opened an exterior entry hatch, which automatically activated a set of dim interior lights. Trip saw that they were about to board a sleek yet battered-looking space vessel, a vaguely cylindrical craft equipped with twin outboard engine nacelles. The ship was positioned horizontally on several landing struts, and Trip estimated her to be about as large as the *Branson,* or about three times the size of one of *Enterprise*'s shuttlepods.

Let's hope those nacelles will make this bucket as fast as she looks, he thought as Phuong helped him walk Ehrehin toward the open gangway. Trip couldn't help but notice that Phuong seemed imbued with renewed strength, as though he had redeemed himself for whatever mistakes he and Section 31 might have made earlier.

A loud explosion to Trip's left, accompanied by a bright shower of multicolored sparks and flame, shoved him unceremoniously to his knees. The blast would have sent Ehrehin sprawling had Phuong not caught and steadied him.

"Stay where you are, all of you!" called a stern male voice behind Trip, who guessed it was coming from near the very same entrance that he, Phuong, and Ehrehin had just used. The vast hangar was immediately filled with the staccato reports of many loud, echoing footfalls, and the din swiftly surrounded them.

Aw, crap, Trip thought.

The hangar's overhead lights came on, triggered by what Trip assumed was an emergency power circuit designed for occasions such as this. Though Trip's eyes were momentarily dazzled by the brilliance, he could make out the ring of armed, uniformed figures deployed all around them. One of those figures stepped directly toward him, carrying a large black pistol in one hand.

It was Ch'uihv. Or Sopek.

Trip decided it didn't much matter what the man chose to call himself.

The former Vulcan ship captain came to a stop perhaps two meters away from Trip—close enough for Trip to catch the full brunt of the man's angry, hostile glare.

"I am very disappointed in you, Cunaehr. Some of my associates counseled me initially not to trust you, but I ignored them because of your relationship to the esteemed Doctor Ehrehin." Ch'uihv paused to favor the old man with a respectful nod before fixing his angry glare again upon Trip. "But it is clear to me now that you are most likely either a spy for Admiral Valdore and the military, or an operative for one of the Romulan Star Empire's intelligence services."

He raised his weapon and leveled it straight at Trip. *Think fast, Tucker,* he thought, struggling in vain to find the right words to buy at least a little more time before his assailant opened fire.

"Cunaehr had absolutely nothing to do with this," Phuong said in a loud, confident voice as he stepped directly between Ehrehin and Ch'uihv, his hands raised over his head. "This was entirely *my* doing, not his. I merely thought it prudent to bring Cunaehr along to calm Doctor Ehrehin should he become emotionally overwrought."

What the hell does he think he's doing? Trip thought.

A thoughtful look crossed Ch'uihv's face, and he lowered his weapon momentarily. Then he took Trip's weapon, walked past him, and stopped within a meter or so of Phuong, who had just dropped his own weapon onto the floor. Ch'uihv raised his weapon once again.

And fired it point-blank at Phuong, who was instantly reduced to a pile of incinerated flesh and clothing. The sickening stench of immolated flesh filled the hangar, and Trip had to work hard to suppress his suddenly buoyant gorge. In the distance, he heard at least one of the armed guards retching. A fleeting hazy memory, now suddenly crystal clear, danced through his mind: the Adigeon surgeon warning him that this voyage into the Romulan Star Empire would probably be a strictly one-way affair.

Ch'uihv stood almost directly over Phuong's smoldering mortal remains. Strangely, Trip thought the look on his violence-hardened face strongly resembled pity. "Such a noble soul," he said. "And such a filthy liar." He raised his weapon again.

This time, he pointed it directly at Trip's head.

TWENTY-NINE

Friday, February 21, 2155
Enterprise NX-01

STANDING ALONGSIDE CAPTAIN ARCHER, Phlox watched anxiously as T'Pol adjusted the power levels on the telepresence helmet yet again. Against his better judgment, the doctor had allowed Shran to be rewired to the device, but only after Shran, Theras, and T'Pol had all had six hours of desperately needed sleep.

He still thought that the machine was likely to cause irreparable damage to Shran's cerebral cortex, but the Andorian was adamant, and the device did seem to represent their one tangible hope of finding the kidnapped Aenar. However, Phlox's current concerns were exacerbated by the unpleasant whine of the machine and the ugly burned-flesh-and-ozone smell that once again permeated his sickbay.

Shran ground his teeth, his hands alternately and repeatedly flexing and extending, perhaps because the helmet restricted the unconscious, emotionally driven movements of his antennae. "I think . . . I sense something," he said. "The ship that's carrying Jhamel. It *is* in Romulan space."

T'Pol's expression showed more concern than surprise. "Are you certain?"

Tears rolled down Shran's face from underneath the helmet, leaving indigo streaks against the backdrop of the Andorian's sky-blue skin. "Yes. I . . . recognize some of the constellations."

Archer and T'Pol exchanged determined glances.

Suddenly, Shran's expression took on a look of fear. "Jhamel! I'm . . . *losing* her. Something is wrong with her!" His vision blocked by the helmet, he pointed in T'Pol's general direction, his arm shaking violently. "Turn up the gain!"

Phlox studied the readings on his scanner. "You are already experiencing severe nerve and cellular damage, Shran. Any more power, and you will be unable to physically function."

"*Do it!*" Shran shrieked, his body convulsing. "I'm losing her!"

T'Pol looked at the console, then back at Shran, apparently considering the warrior's plea. Her hand hovered over the control for an instant that seemed to stretch into minutes, then pushed down on the cutoff control.

Phlox was glad that things hadn't gone as far as they had the first time, and immediately began scanning Shran for further damage.

The Andorian slumped forward in his chair, still twitching violently. Phlox and Archer moved to hold him up, as T'Pol unlatched the telepresence helmet from his head.

"Why didn't you turn the gain up higher?" Shran asked, his anger-laced voice barely more than a whispery rasp.

"Because you cannot save Jhamel if you are in a vegetative state, or dead," T'Pol said.

"Can you tell us the heading of the vessel she's on?" Archer asked.

"If I can see some star charts," Shran said, his breathing labored. "I've traveled a bit more than most Imperial Guardsmen."

"You need to be treated first," Phlox said. He didn't like some of the readings his scans were showing, but with some medicinal cocktails, he felt that the Andorian might be restored to his usual strong and aggressive state.

"Help me get him to the bed," Phlox said, gesturing toward one of the medical bays.

As the quartet transported Shran to the bed—Theras taking his feet and following the lead of the others—the wall-mounted com unit let out a loud whistle.

"Bridge to Captain Archer." The voice belonged to Ensign Sato.

The four of them hurriedly put Shran down on a biobed, and Archer sprinted to the device, depressing a button on its lower edge. "Archer here."

"You have a priority one communication from Admiral Gardner."

Archer blanched visibly, then looked back at the others. "I'll take it in my quarters in one minute," he said, then let go of the button.

"I'll make certain that Shran is able to function again as soon as possible, Captain," Phlox said, trying to reassure him. "He'll be examining star maps in no time." He wished he was as certain of that as he sounded.

"Thanks, Doctor," Archer said. "I've got to go figure out how much trouble I'm in now. After that, I'm probably going to need Shran's help more than ever."

"How do you mean?" Phlox asked.

"I just might end up having to apply for a job on his ship," Archer said dryly as he crossed quickly to the door.

Phlox watched his superior officer exit. Given Admiral Gardner's reputation, he thought, I'm not entirely certain he's joking.

"Come again, sir?" Archer wasn't quite certain he'd heard the admiral correctly.

"I said that our intelligence sources are reporting some

new rumblings of war from Romulan space," Gardner said, the expression on his face both officious and annoyed. *"It's possible that the warnings that you and Commander Tucker gave may have had some validity. Of course, we still need to find significantly more proof before we can take decisive action."*

Had the situation not been so dire, Archer might have been amused. What Gardner had said was the closest thing to an apology he'd ever heard from the man.

"What about my request to pursue the kidnapped Aenar, Admiral?"

Gardner shook his head. *"I find pirates and slavers just as reprehensible as you do, Captain. But I'm not still sending Earth's flagship halfway across the galaxy to catch them. Especially when doing so might rouse the Romulans into an active state of war."*

Though Archer wasn't surprised, he found it difficult not to keep the anger out of his voice. "What about Coridan, then? The intelligence *we* received indicates that Coridan Prime is the likely first target of any coming Romulan attacks." Of course, he wasn't about to reveal his Coridan information was based on the Section 31 reports that Reed had relayed to him. "I'm prepared to take *Enterprise* there at maximum speed once the word is given."

Gardner stroked his salt-and-pepper beard as he leaned forward toward his own screen. *"Captain, you will proceed back to Sector Zero Zero One, where you will assist in preparing a defense of Earth. There may be any number of attacks against us in the days leading up to the signing of the Coalition Compact. That event could be a lightning rod for the discontented across the quadrant. We need you here."*

The Admiral leaned back again in his chair. *"The Coridanites have ample ship and weapon resources to repel any Romulan attack. These . . . rumors you have heard may well be a feint by the Romulans intended to draw Starfleet resources to Coridan, thereby leaving Earth largely vulnerable. I'm certain that I don't need to remind you what happened the* last *time we let ourselves get caught with our pants down because our flagship was parsecs away."*

"Sir, Earth's defense systems have been significantly improved since the Xindi attacks," Archer said, irked by Gardner's cheap shot.

"They've not been improved anywhere near enough to suit me," Gardner said brusquely, barreling forward before Archer could say anything further. *"At this juncture in the Coalition's development, now is definitely* not *the time to put our faith in rumors and scraps of information about Coridan, or to second-guess Romulan intentions in a way that leaves our flanks exposed."*

He pointed toward Archer. *"Let me be blunt, Captain. You are to get* Enterprise *back to Earth, double-time and posthaste. Do I make myself clear?"*

Archer wasn't happy with Gardner's decision, nor with his chiding tone, but he nodded his assent to a superior officer, as he was trained to do. "You do, sir."

"Good. Then I will expect to see you by this time next week. Gardner out." A moment later, the viewscreen replaced the admiral's frowning image with the blue-and-white logo of Earth's Starfleet.

Archer's stomach churned as he examined his ever-narrowing set of options. Because of everything they'd learned so far, he was convinced that the Aenar were indeed en route to the Romulans—if they weren't already in the clutches of their military—and that one way or another, they were going to be used as deadly weapons against the Coalition. Beyond those concerns, and his debt to Shran, he was also keenly anxious about Trip's covert spy mission into Romulan territory.

A part of him fantasized that Trip would find out

some vital piece of information, break protocol, and contact *Enterprise*, and that they would swoop in not only to save the day, but to save Trip as well. He smiled ruefully at the thought, knowing it was as implausible as the plot to any bad holovid adventure he'd watched as a boy.

The door to his quarters chimed.

"Come in," he said. He was surprised to see that it was T'Pol. "I didn't expect to see you quite so soon. How's Shran?"

"Still recovering in sickbay, Captain, though very quickly, according to Phlox," T'Pol said.

"That's good news," Archer said, feeling real relief at the news. He hadn't realized until this moment just how important it was to him to see the Andorian survive and succeed in his personal quest.

"His capacity to recall stellar cartographical details is evidently quite prodigious. He was also determined to relay the information to us as quickly as possible, regardless of the pain he was experiencing. Most importantly, he was able to pinpoint for us the exact region through which the transport ship was traveling when he made contact with Jhamel's mind."

She handed him a padd that displayed a navigational heading. "My calculations show that the slavers are less than a day ahead of us at our maximum speed. If Shran is correct, we should have little difficulty catching up with them."

Archer rubbed his chin as he considered his next move. "The heading they're on takes them right toward the heart of the Romulan Star Empire. In another day, they'll be even closer. Going after them is *incredibly* risky." He put the padd down on the table and looked up at T'Pol. "But that's not the *worst* of our problems."

The Vulcan first officer raised her eyebrow inquisitively, but said nothing.

"Gardner just ordered us back to Earth," Archer said. *"Now."* He related the rest of his conversation with the admiral, while T'Pol listened without comment.

"This puts us in a bit of a bind. We know that the Orions took the Aenar, but we have no solid proof yet of why. The only clear information we have on the Aenar's current whereabouts comes from Shran's psychic link to Jhamel."

T'Pol moved one of the ready room's other chairs out and sat down in it. "Captain, given everything we now know about the Aenar abductions, and the information you obtained on Rigel X about the Adigeons, the only logical answer is that the Aenar are being delivered to the Romulans. The Romulans have only one purpose for the Aenar: to pilot their telepresence drones in attacks against their enemies.

"So the question becomes, which world will be their first target? Will they attack Earth, in an attempt to disrupt or even destroy the Coalition? Or will their initial target be Coridan, a prospective Coalition member that possesses more dilithium wealth than the rest of the Coalition combined, and which reportedly has much faster ships?"

"Which do *you* think it is?" Archer asked.

"The answer to that remains unclear, given our current information," T'Pol said. "But we *are* relatively certain that stopping the delivery of the Aenar to the Romulans could greatly hamper whatever plans the Romulans *are* making, *whomever* they are making them against. Securing the Aenar would therefore be an offensive tactic rather than merely a defensive one."

Archer interlaced his fingers behind his head and leaned back in his chair. "If we go to rescue the Aenar, we're disobeying a direct order. Which could have serious repercussions, even if we're right."

T'Pol tilted her head slightly, and the merest hint of

mischief crept into her eyes. "Did the admiral give you explicit directions to begin your journey to Earth as soon as you broke contact?"

Archer smiled broadly. "Not *explicitly*. He said it would be in our best interests to do so, and noted that he'd see me within a week."

"Then you still have some six days and twenty-three hours in which to arrive," T'Pol said, looking out the viewport, her expression changing from mischievous to calculating. "We are within a day of catching up with the ship carrying the Aenar. If all goes well, that diversion should prove to be a brief one." She paused for a moment, then turned to look directly into his eyes. "Should you decide to *make* that diversion, of course."

"I'm sure we'll still catch hell for this, but Gardner *wasn't* all that precise in his orders, now that I come to think of it," Archer said, tugging the waist of his jumpsuit down as he rose to his feet. "I don't see any reason we can't make a *brief* course diversion. We'll just have to make up for the lost time double-quick on the way back home."

Archer pushed one thought into the back of his mind. *All of this supposes that we're the ones who come out on top in the fight to free the Aenar. Can't assume that the Romulans on that ship will be pushovers.*

On the bright side, if we don't *win, I probably won't have to worry all that much about the wrath of Sam Gardner.*

THIRTY

Friday, February 21, 2155
Rator II

TRIP STARED, GRIMLY FASCINATED, as the barrel of the disruptor pistol swung in his direction and remained leveled directly at his face. Switching his grip so that he held the weapon in both hands, Ch'uihv regarded him through narrowed eyelids.

This is it, Charles, Trip told himself. Time seemed to slow down precipitously, the way clocks did aboard space vessels that accelerated nearly to light speed without actually going to warp. He was hyperaware that within another elastic moment or two he would be just as dead as Phuong, whose still smoldering corpse he had to continue studiously ignoring in order to avoid becoming violently sick.

Soon, he would be as dead as almost everyone in his life already believed him to be.

He judged the distance between himself and his executioner—about two meters—and decided he had nothing to lose by leaping straight at him. Maybe Ch'uihv would be surprised just enough to give him a fighting chance. Of course, he knew that wouldn't save him from the armed guards.

But what the hell, he thought. Trip tensed his leg muscles and bent his knees slightly, preparing to take what would very likely be the last long-odds gamble of his life.

"Stop this!" came a shout from behind, disrupting

Trip's concentration and causing a look of mild surprise to cross Ch'uihv's normally stoic features.

It took Trip a beat to recognize the frail Ehrehin as the source of the cry.

"Don't take your foolish rage out on Cunaehr, you execrable coward," Ehrehin said, his voice astonishingly calm and resolute. "There's no reason for you to do any more killing."

Ch'uihv chuckled and shook his head. "On the contrary, Doctor. There is indeed a very sound reason. I want something very badly, and unless you provide it immediately I will demonstrate precisely *how* badly by killing your beloved Cunaehr—if that's really his name—right where he stands."

The new stardrive, Trip thought.

"Don't do it, Doctor," he said, turning toward the elderly scientist. Before he could react, a crushing blow came down against the side of his head, and he crumpled to the deck, stunned but still conscious.

"Give me detailed schematics of your *avaihh lli vastam* work, Doctor. Or else I will apply more than the butt of my weapon to your aide's skull."

Sprawled prone on the unyielding hangar floor, Trip felt the cold barrel of Ch'uihv's weapon pressing painfully into the back of his neck.

"Choose, Doctor," Ch'uihv growled. *"Now!"*

"Ehrehin, don't—" Trip said, his voice muffled by the deck and his words interrupted by a bout of nausea, no doubt caused by the blow to his head.

"I will begin counting now, Doctor. *Sei.*" Thanks to his internal translator, Trip recognized the Romulan word for "three."

"This is absurd," Ehrehin said.

"Kre."

Two, Trip counted. The weapon continued jabbing painfully into the back of his neck.

"There's no reason this has to happen."

"*Hwi.*"

One.

Ch'uihv's pistol clicked loudly, sounding to Trip like the rattle of a guillotine blade being drawn upward. He tried to persuade his body to roll to the side, even though he still felt stunned and nauseated from the blow he'd just taken. Besides, he knew there was no way he could outrun Ch'uihv's weapon, even if he were in perfect condition.

"*Lliu.*"

That's "zero," Trip thought. The stench of Phuong's charred flesh assaulted his nostrils, like a portent of what was to come. He closed his eyes tightly, preparing as best he could for the inevitable.

"If you kill him, I shall kill myself," Ehrehin said impatiently. "And my knowledge will die with me."

Trip opened his eyes and saw that the scientist was now standing so close to him that there was no way to hit Trip without taking them both down.

"Is that what you want?" Ehrehin continued, haranguing their captors. "Or would you prefer that we all sit down like civilized people, so that I can properly satisfy your curiosity about my work?"

At first, Trip had thought that Ehrehin had stood up to Ch'uihv; then he suddenly realized that the old man had just done the exact opposite, though he clearly had little choice in the matter.

The pistol withdrew from Trip's neck, and a pair of Ch'uihv's men hauled him roughly to his feet, manacling his wrists behind his back without showing an excessive amount of gentleness.

Though he was grateful still to be alive, he knew that Ehrehin had just made an enormous mistake—and very likely the final one of his long career.

* * *

A trio of guards dragged Trip unceremoniously out of the hangar, into the now brightly illuminated corridor, and finally into a nearby conference room, which was equipped with a large table, a half-dozen chairs, and several small desktop computer terminals.

Without exchanging any words with him—or so much as looking at him—the guards shoved Trip down into one of the chairs. He wasn't sure whether the manacles that secured his wrists behind his back were making him more uncomfortable than the disruptor pistols that were now trained on him.

Scant moments after Trip's entrance, the conference room door slid open to admit Ch'uihv and another pair of guards. The men, who were half carrying and half dragging Ehrehin between them, deposited their charge somewhat more gently into the seat beside the one Trip occupied.

Ch'uihv took the seat directly across the table from Trip and Ehrehin as the guards looked on vigilantly. The *Ejhoi Ormiin* leader turned one of the computer terminals so that it faced him. He quickly entered several commands, apparently activating both his own terminal and the one closest to Trip and Ehrehin.

"There is an electronic stylus attached to the terminal in front of you, Doctor," Ch'uihv said, his intense gaze locked upon the elderly scientist. "You will use it to enter whatever formulae or diagrams my people will need to master in order to replicate your latest work on *avaihh lli vastam.*"

The elderly scientist sighed in resignation, though he didn't seem quite able to pick up the stylus before him.

"Doctor. I thought I had made myself clear back in the hangar. Please do not force me to do to your assistant what I was forced to do to his associate, Terha." To illustrate his point, he unholstered his weapon and set it down on the table before him, tantalizingly out of Trip's reach.

He's going to kill me anyway, Trip thought. *Hell, he'll probably give Ehrehin the very same treatment once he thinks he's got what he needs from him. There's just no trusting this bastard.*

"Don't do it," Trip whispered, leaning toward the scientist. A large, rough hand shoved him hard against the back of his chair.

"I will be watching your every entry most attentively, Doctor," Ch'uihv said.

You're not the only one, pal, Trip thought, his engineering reflexes kicking in nearly as strongly as his instinct for self-preservation.

Ehrehin looked at Trip, a deep sadness in his rheumy eyes. With obvious reluctance and a trembling hand, the old man took up the stylus, then began slowly sketching directly on the monitor screen on the tabletop in front of him.

Trip watched in growing fascination as a detailed technical diagram began to take shape on the screen—an image that Ch'uihv seemed to be studying intently on his own terminal. Trip hoped that before Ch'uihv finally killed him, he'd develop at least a partial understanding of this new technology that purportedly allowed starships to reach warp seven.

Unfortunately, it was a technology that would soon be in the hands of a breakaway Romulan faction that was probably at least as dangerous to Earth and her allies as all the military power of the Romulan Star Empire itself.

THIRTY-ONE

Friday, February 21, 2155
Enterprise NX-01

ARCHER LEANED FORWARD in his command chair, staring straight ahead at the screen. The long-range scanners were showing him exactly what he wanted to see.

"You're *certain* they haven't detected us?" he asked.

"They've shown no sign of it so far," Reed said from his station to the captain's right. "They apparently aren't making any active proximity scans, and they've neither sent nor received any outside messages since we found them."

Ten minutes earlier they had finally almost caught up with the transport ship—thanks to Shran's continued use of the telepresence unit—only to discover that what they were chasing was not an Orion ship, as they had assumed, but rather a completely unfamiliar class of transport vessel, presumably one of Romulan design. The prevailing theory among the bridge crew was that the Romulans had picked up their Aenar cargo from the Orions somewhere outside of Romulan territory, and had then headed back toward their homeworld.

"Cocky bastards," Archer said. "They think that because they're in their own space, they won't have to worry about being brought to book for their crimes."

"They may well be correct," T'Pol said. "While we appear to be the only other vessel in the vicinity, we should remain alert for other countermeasures the Romulans may have deployed nearby."

"We're already scanning for cloaked mines," Reed said. Archer saw him shudder, and knew he must have been recalling the time he'd been impaled by a Romulan mine attached to *Enterprise*'s hull, just months into the lieutenant's tenure aboard the ship. Reed very likely would have lost his life in that incident, had Archer not rescued him.

"There could be other Romulan weapons of which we are unaware," T'Pol said.

"Are we sure that the Aenar are aboard that ship?" Archer asked.

T'Pol studied her scanner's readings, the bluish light from its hooded display brightening the area around her eyes. "We are still too far away for our sensors to identify individuals, but I can confirm the presence of several dozen humanoid life signs, some of them Aenar and some unidentified."

Archer sighed heavily, considering whether to tell Shran the news. *Better to keep him in plain sight so he doesn't try to use his own ship to ram the Romulans, or do something else equally stupid,* he thought. He looked to Hoshi. "Call Shran up here to the bridge, Hoshi. Make sure he's escorted. Unobtrusively."

He turned back to face the forward viewscreen. "All right, people, we've planned this out, now let's make sure we pull it off perfectly. Travis, make certain that we're on top of them before they know it. Malcolm, transfer as much energy as you need to our ventral hull plating. And ready all weapons."

He turned his chair toward the other side of the bridge. "Hoshi, be sure to keep that translation program running, just in case we need to use it. But we are *not* going to announce ourselves or give them time to find a way to hang onto the Aenar."

He raised his voice so that everyone on the bridge could hear it clearly. "Everyone, stay on your toes. We get in, we get dirty, we get the Aenar out, and we head back home. No mistakes."

He tapped the intercom button on his chair arm. "Ensign Moulton, are you ready with the transporter?"

"Yes, sir," the young officer said crisply. *"We've calibrated the transporter to retrieve* only *live Aenar. Anything else will be left behind."* He could hear the excitement in her voice; a transporter specialist, she was one of the new crew members who had come aboard after the conclusion of the Xindi crisis.

"Excellent," Archer said. He kept the com channel open, and leaned forward again.

In his peripheral vision, he saw the others looking at him expectantly, as if they all stood poised at the starting blocks of a foot race, and he was the odds-on favorite.

"Take us in, Travis," he said. "Full impulse."

The ship trembled slightly beneath his boots. Archer stared at the viewscreen. He knew that this maneuver was physically dangerous for both the ship and the Aenar, and also represented a serious political risk for Earth's Starfleet, which he represented. But he also knew that it was the *right* thing to do.

"Twenty-five seconds to our mark," Mayweather said, the tension in his voice almost palpable.

"Readying weapons," Malcolm said.

"Scanners are resolving addition life-sign data," T'Pol said. "Thirty-seven Aenar, and twenty-two others."

As if on cue, Archer heard the turbolift doors open behind him. He turned and saw Shran walking somewhat unsteadily onto the bridge, escorted by Corporal David McCammon, one of the MACOs. Theras accompanied Shran on his other side, a hand placed supportively on Shran's shoulder.

"Five seconds," Mayweather said. "Four, three, two—"

"Fire!" Archer said. An instant later, two reddish

directed energy blasts lanced out in unison from the forward ventral phase cannons. The image on the viewscreen showed the beams striking the aft end of the Romulan transport vessel, causing a pair of silent explosions.

"Targeting again," Reed said, then depressed a button.

The viewscreen image changed to a reverse angle as a quartet of phase cannon blasts ripped into the Romulan ship even as *Enterprise* zoomed past the other vessel.

"Their engines have been crippled," Reed said, his tone exultant. "Their defensive hull plating is down to twenty percent of capacity and is failing quickly."

Archer flashed a grin at Malcolm, then shot a quick glance in Shran's direction. Despite his apparently depleted condition because of his repeated use of the telepresence apparatus, the Andorian was smiling broadly as well. Theras wore a stricken expression, no doubt unused to being in the presence of such violence.

"Bring us about, Travis," Archer said, then looked down at the intercom on the arm of his chair. "Ensign Moulton, prepare to beam out the Aenar."

"Aye, sir," Moulton said.

"Captain, I'm showing two other ships coming into range, closing fast." T'Pol's voice rose. "They're Romulan war vessels."

Damn, Archer thought. *That's what I get for letting myself get cocky.*

"On-screen," he said.

Even as the image on the viewscreen showed two sleek, greenish craft arcing quickly toward *Enterprise,* Hoshi called out.

"Receiving a transmission, Captain."

"You have made an illegal incursion into territory controlled by the Romulan Star Empire," a woman's voice said menacingly, her words rendered into precise En-

glish by Hoshi's translation matrix. *"And you have fired upon a Romulan vessel. That was your final mistake."*

"They're charging their weapons, Captain," Reed said. He hit the tactical alert alarm with his left hand, and klaxons began to blare throughout the ship.

Simultaneously, a pair of energy bolts lanced out of the forward sections of both of the Romulan vessels.

"Reinforce dorsal hull plating!" Archer yelled, bracing himself for an impact he could only hope wouldn't vaporize them outright.

THIRTY-TWO

Friday, February 21, 2155
Rator II

AFTER EHREHIN HAD laboriously completed his fourteenth diagram, Ch'uihv—whom Trip thought had been listening and watching both patiently and attentively until now—began to look distinctly restless.

"Is this presentation of yours really going anywhere, Doctor?" the man Trip had once known as Sopek asked Ehrehin flatly, the outer edges of his slanted eyebrows rising steeply in clearly evident anger. Trip still found it odd to see emotions displayed on such an apparently Vulcan face.

Despite the danger he was in, Ehrehin displayed an exasperated expression, looking like a college lecturer being asked yet another in an endless series of stupid questions by a none-too-bright undergraduate. "*Wherever* this presentation is going," the old man said in a waspish tone, "it would get there a good deal faster were you to refrain from interrupting again until I *finish* it."

Ch'uihv scowled deeply. "I know something about engineering, Doctor. And if I didn't know better, I might think you were merely stalling for time."

The hard-faced guards posted around the prisoners looked skeptical as well, making Trip—still seated beside Dr. Ehrehin with his hands bound behind his back—decidedly more nervous than he already was.

"Ridiculous," Ehrehin said with the sneer of an

eminent academic who was growing weary of casting pearls before swine. "Now, if I may resume?"

Ch'uihv gestured toward the computer terminals on the tabletop. "By all means, Doctor."

Of course, Trip knew very well that Ehrehin was indeed stalling for time, though precisely what the old man hoped to accomplish by continuing to do so eluded him. Whether it happened in the next ten minutes or was delayed for another two hours, the scientist was marked for death.

Just like me, Trip thought, eyeing the disruptor pistol that Ch'uihv had left lying on the tabletop beside his computer terminal, still well out of Trip's reach. Though the weapon might as well have been a parsec away, Trip couldn't help but wish for telekinesis, imagining the gun making a swift leap into one of his manacled hands.

After deleting his current technical diagram—which had no doubt been captured along with all the previous ones by Ch'uihv's information network—Doctor Ehrehin quickly began constructing another, which made Trip grateful for the interruption to his fruitless reveries. He wondered how much longer the old man could keep Ch'uihv at bay by essentially restating information that any competent novice engineer would already have known.

Then he noticed that this latest diagram was entering what appeared to be entirely new territory—at least to Trip, who was well aware that his own knowledge of the intricacies and nuances of Romulan technology was far less voluminous than Ehrehin's.

The diagram at first appeared to be a flow-chart description of a fairly standard method of continuum distortion propulsion, which was catch-all engineer-speak for every variation of warp drive known to Earth's science and engineering experts. But the drawing had taken an abrupt left turn, forcing Trip to work hard to find any familiar reference points.

Okay, that's the space energy/matter sink, Trip thought, his mind reeling in a way it hadn't since his first grueling year of Starfleet training. *And that dingus has to take care of the warp drive's magnatomic flux constriction functions, and maybe most of the other asymmetrical peristaltic field manipulations.*

But he knew that this explanation didn't take into account the large numbers of warp-field layers Ehrehin's rapidly growing string of marginal equations were postulating. Trip found it next to impossible to visualize that many cochranes of raw power coursing through the system without violently shattering every piece of dilithium hooked into it.

Continuing to watch in silence from his chair, Trip ignored the escalating discomfort of his manacled hands, mentally returning to the beginning of the flow chart as Ehrehin continued his deliberately vague and circuitous lecture. As before, the old man wasn't showing enough to give away his secrets entirely. But he was handing over some tantalizing hints, assuming that either Ch'uihv or any of his people were bright enough to pick up on them.

There's the deuterium supply. Standard stuff. It goes into the matter reactant injector, then into the magnetic constriction segment. Easy-peasy. But the dilithium crystal articulation frame ought to come next, and it's missing. What the hell?

To Trip's surprise, the next destination for the drive's deuterium fuel and its reaction products was a black box that would have corresponded to a standard matter/antimatter reaction chamber were it aboard *Enterprise*—except that *this* chamber apparently wasn't equipped with the high-gauss magnetic bottle that was *always* used to prevent stored antimatter from experiencing a catastrophic, mutually annihilative reaction with the positive matter out of which the entire ship was composed. Instead, the reaction chamber contained something that yielded a mysteriously powerful stream of tightly focused particles that Trip figured for either high-energy gravitons or chronitons, or maybe even both, which was apparently being deposited into yet another intermix chamber.

From the look of this thing, it ought to go "boom" big-time right after the "on" button gets pushed.

But there had to be more to it than that; after all, Trip was well aware that his knowledge of Romulan technology was far from complete. And Ehrehin's presentation would have to ring true enough to prevent Ch'uihv from picking up his disruptor pistol, which he would do if the old man were just weaving a tapestry out of pure, extemporaneous gibberish.

He's not Scheherazade, for Christ's sake, just making all this stuff up as he goes, Trip thought.

Making an intuitive leap based on Ehrehin's deliberately incomplete presentation, Trip could see that such immense energy flows—assuming they were possible—might indeed accelerate a starship to warp six or seven. But how that could be done with neither a textbook matter/antimatter reaction nor a dilithium crystal array through which to channel it lay beyond his grasp.

Until the epiphany hit him with the intensity of an old-fashioned Louisville Slugger swung straight at his forehead. All at once, he understood what *had* to be in the black box that was spilling forth so many gravitons and chronitons. As weird as the notion was, there was no way it could have been anything *else*.

Oh, God. It doesn't even use dilithium, Trip thought, fighting down his incipient panic but failing utterly. He suddenly felt light-headed, and hoped nobody in the room had noticed, especially the guards. *The Coalition worlds will* have *to change their entire approach to defending themselves against this thing now. If they have the time, that is.*

Though he was securely planted in his chair as Ehrehin droned on before the increasingly fidgety Ch'uihv, Trip felt as though he was about to pitch forward, rolling right over a precipice of utter despair.

Because once he was dead, there would be no one left alive to warn Coridan Prime's billions of inhabitants of the horrors that awaited them.

THIRTY-THREE

Friday, February 21, 2155
Enterprise NX-01

THE BRIDGE ROCKED VIOLENTLY, and Archer clutched the arms of his chair to avoid sprawling onto the deck. Shran, Theras, and McCammon, standing beside a science station console, were all thrown into the railings, as was Reed at his tactical station. Fortunately, no one appeared seriously hurt.

"Hull plating at eighty-three percent," Mayweather said, urgency in his voice. "We managed to reinforce hull plate power by the time they hit us."

"They're charging weapons for a second salvo," T'Pol said.

"Head right for them, full speed, and reinforce all forward hull plating," Archer ordered, then turned toward the tactical station. "Malcolm, target their engines."

Back on his feet, Reed studied his console, his hands trembling slightly from battle-generated adrenaline. Archer studied the viewscreen and watched the image of the two ships grow ever larger as the enemy vessels continued their approach. He could see that the ventral hulls of the warships were adorned with a garish design that resembled a predatory bird.

"Targets locked and . . . firing at full power!" Reed exclaimed.

The viewscreen image tracked their progress as *Enterprise* flew past the two ships, her phase cannons blasting away in rapid bursts. Archer was happy to see that several of the blasts were having demonstrable effects on the nacelles supported by struts on either side of the Romulan ships' horseshoe crab-shaped central hulls.

"Bring us back about," Archer said. "Divert power to our aft starboard plating."

Even as *Enterprise* looped back toward the crippled transport ship, Mayweather yelled "Incoming fire!"

This time the volley of shots rocked the ship harder, but a quick look around the bridge showed Archer that nearly everyone had secured themselves into chairs this time, including Shran and Theras. Only Reed remained untethered, standing at the firing controls, his knuckles white as he gripped his console for support.

"Plating at sixty-two percent," Mayweather said.

"We've partially crippled their propulsion," Reed said, a touch of triumph in his voice. "They can't go to warp, but they still have impulse capability. And weapons."

"Charge *our* weapons again, but don't fire just yet," Archer said. "If we can get out of here with the Aenar *without* destroying any of the Romulans' vessels, maybe we can keep the political fallout down to a minimum. And if they can't follow us once we're at warp, all the better."

He spoke into the intercom unit on his chair. "Ensign Moulton, have you been able to beam over any Aenar?"

"*I got five of them,*" Moulton said. "*All males, apparently, and they all seem to have been sedated. But I can't seem to get a lock on any of the others.*"

Archer scowled and looked toward T'Pol. "What's the problem?"

"It would appear that the Romulans have employed some kind of sensor shroud aboard their vessel," T'Pol said, frowning slightly at her scanner. "It is preventing our maintaining a transporter lock. We cannot beam anyone else out unless they're carrying a signal enhancer of some kind."

"Can we take out the shroud?" Archer asked.

"The transport has deployed almost all of its remaining power to the device, including life support," T'Pol said. "If we attempt to break the shroud, we could easily overload their warp core and kill everyone aboard."

"Incoming!" Reed shouted.

The ship rocked again. One of the consoles at the back of the bridge whined, then shot out a volley of sparks. A nearby ensign quickly began spraying flame-retardant foam on the console.

"Plating at fifty-three percent and falling," Mayweather said.

"We have a hull breach on D deck," Hoshi said. "Guest quarters."

"That's also engineering," Reed said. "They're trying to cripple *our* engines."

Archer wasn't at all pleased with the turn this mission was taking. "Travis, continue performing evasive maneuvers, but keep us as close to the transport ship as possible. We need to stay within transporter range."

He tapped another button on his chair's com unit. "Engineering, sorry about all the rough stuff. See if you can divert any extra power to the transporter."

"Yes, sir, Captain," said Burch. The young officer was Tucker's obvious replacement, but Archer had yet to make the assignment official. He knew he would have to do so soon, or else find another permanent chief engineer, should Trip's sojourn in the land of the dead continue much longer.

Archer turned toward his armory officer. "Malcolm, can we target their weapons systems? Keep them from firing on us for a while to buy us a little more time?"

Reed frowned, studying a newly mounted tactical viewer that now stood above his other control console screens. "I don't believe so, Captain. Any serious attempt to disable their weapons tubes will more than likely destroy the ship outright."

"*Do* it, pinkskin," Shran shouted from his seat at the back of the bridge. "They're trying to destroy *us!*"

"Only because *we* started it," Archer shouted back. He looked over at Reed. "If we destroy their ship, the Romulans could use that fact as justification for mounting an attack against Earth, or even the rest of the Coalition."

"But the Romulans have *already* committed acts of war against *us,*" Reed said.

"Technically and legally, they have not," T'Pol said. "At least not yet. The *Orions* abducted the Aenar, which makes *them* responsible for those crimes. And the Romulans are legally entitled to regard us as invaders in their territory, and therefore as the aggressors."

"*Preposterous!*"

Archer turned around in his chair. "Shran, *shut up!*" The azure-hued warrior did just that, though he glowered angrily at Archer with eyes like blue-white suns.

"Hold on to your chairs," Mayweather said. "Incoming!" He pushed hard at several of the helm controls, and Archer felt *Enterprise* turning hard to port as the inertial dampers and the artificial gravity running through the deck plates struggled to cope with the sudden velocity change. Archer held his breath and braced for impact, but none came.

"Good flying, Travis," he said a moment later.

"Sir, we can't evade their weapons forever," Malcolm said, his tone plaintive. "And sooner or later reinforcements will arrive. We have got to withdraw."

"Any luck on getting the Aenar, Moulton?" Archer asked, directing his voice toward the open-channeled com unit.

"*No, sir.*" Moulton's tone sounded stressed. "*We still can't break through their shroud. I thought I had a pattern lock on one of them, but it broke apart during transport. I . . . lost him.*"

"I'm sure you did your best," Archer said, feeling queasy at the idea that they had just killed one of the Aenar in the midst of what had begun as a fairly straightforward rescue mission.

He had to face the fact that they had run out of options. "Prepare to withdraw. We can't stay here any longer."

"No!" Shran unbuckled himself from the chair he had occupied and moved swiftly toward Archer.

"We don't have much of a choice, Shran."

"Yes, you do," the Andorian said, his antennae ramrod stiff with anger. "You destroy both of the warships, we retrieve the Aenar, and then you destroy the transport as well. Leave no trace that we were ever here."

"Do you really think they haven't transmitted information about us back to their base already?" Archer asked. "If we destroy them, that *will* be an act of war."

"Captain?" Reed looked uncomfortable. "There is another factor we have to consider. If we can't rescue the Aenar, and they remain in the hands of the Romulans, we *know* they will be used as weapons. Weapons against Earth, or another Coalition planet, or even some non-aligned world. We can't let the Romulans keep them."

"What are you suggesting?" Archer asked, though he was certain he already knew the answer.

"We *can't* let the Romulans keep them," Reed repeated, more emphatically this time. "We can't destroy the transport ship for political reasons. But we *can* use the transporter to stop the Aenar from being used against us."

"You can't be serious!" Shran snarled at the tactical officer.

Theras approached them, his hand on the shoulder of the MACO trooper who had drawn near to Shran. "Captain, as much as it pains me to say this, your companion may be correct," Theras said, his voice quavering. "I know that my people would rather be . . . *sacrificed* than used as weapons to destroy others."

"You know *nothing*, you coward!" Shran snarled, his fists clenching in rage. McCammon reached for him, but in that second, Shran drove the palm of his hand up and under the MACO's chin, driving him back off his feet.

Before Archer could get to his feet, T'Pol had come between him and Shran. The Andorian swung at her, but she caught his hand, forcing it backward despite the powerful momentum of the blow.

Sometimes I forget how strong Vulcans are, Archer thought in a flash.

"*Stop,*" T'Pol said, speaking in a low growl. "I believe I have an alternative."

THIRTY-FOUR

Friday, February 21, 2155
Rator II

TRIP THOUGHT CH'UIHV was finally about to pick up the disruptor pistol that lay on the table before him and end Ehrehin's lengthy presentation with the finality of the grave.

Then the ground shook and the lights overhead dimmed, and a distant rumbling roar reverberated through the entire *Ejhoi Ormiin* complex.

Ch'uihv leaped to his feet and began barking orders into an intercom unit built into the desktop—to no evident effect—then began ordering the guards in the room to find some answers, immediately. As Ch'uihv's men scattered, Trip's first thought was that one of the island's volcanoes had conveniently decided to get frisky.

Then the floor beneath Trip's chair shook again, with a hard, sharp impact that reminded Trip more of a phase-cannon strike than any natural phenomenon he'd ever encountered.

Admiral Valdore, he thought, shoving himself out of his chair and rising awkwardly to his feet, his hands still bound tightly behind him. As unlikely as it was that the Romulan military had suddenly found this obscure world and mounted a rescue raid to recover Ehrehin in the proverbial nick, it was certainly a more believable scenario than that of an eons-dormant volcano suddenly rising up in wrath at precisely the appropriate moment.

Trip moved toward the old man, concerned that the

current situation might be too much for him. Despite the dim lighting, he could see that Ehrehin appeared to be only a little shaken. But he also knew that circumstances could very easily take a turn for the worse, and in no time flat. *If Valdore doesn't get his hands on Ehrehin, he's going to make damned sure that nobody else gets their hands on him either.*

He could hear the sharp reports of weapons fire echoing through some distant part of the complex, growing steadily louder as they approached. All at once, getting out of his manacles became a priority very nearly as urgent as breathing.

"Get back into your chair," ordered a harsh male voice. A moment later, once of Ch'uihv's guards, his dark paramilitary uniform making him nearly invisible in the low lighting, resolved himself from the surrounding shadows.

Trip could only hope that the other guards in the room, not to mention Ch'uihv himself, were too distracted by what was going on elsewhere in the complex to notice what he had just decided to do. *I'm going to get killed anyway*, he thought. *Either by this guy or by Ch'uihv or by Valdore. So I guess this is the perfect time for a completely stupid and futile gesture.*

"Sorry," Trip said, taking a single backward step away from the approaching guard and the fragile scientist, moving toward the chair he'd just left behind. The guard continued moving in Trip's direction.

Trip suddenly leaped forward, twisting his legs toward the guard, kicking him hard in the abdomen before both men went down hard. The guard's head made a sickening thump against the unyielding floor, his body mostly breaking Trip's fall, which could have injured him severely since his hands were still manacled behind him.

Looks like he wasn't quite expecting a completely stupid

and futile gesture, Trip thought, relieved that the guard wasn't moving, at least for the moment. He immediately turned around and began fumbling with the fallen man's belt, awkwardly seeking anything behind him that might be a set of manacle keys.

Damn. Damn. DAMN! At least a full minute ticked by with no results. On the plus side, he was reasonably certain now that neither Ch'uihv nor any other guards had remained in the room. Buoyed by that small boon, he continued fumbling with the guard's belt while the sounds of the approaching firefight steadily intensified.

"Allow me," said a familiar voice directly behind him.

"Ehrehin?" Trip said, trying to turn so that he could face the voice.

"Hold still, Cunaehr. If you move right now, this could turn out extremely unpleasant for both of us."

The old man, still behind him, was evidently shoving something hard and metallic against Trip's wrists. "Hold on, Doctor," Trip said, suddenly realizing what Ehrehin was about to attempt. But despite his protestations, he knew better than to try to move.

An instant later, a blast of intense heat singed Trip's wrists, the searing pain accompanied by a brief flash of ruddy light. Trip's hands fell away from each other, and he brought them both toward his face to survey the damage, which seemed to be minimal, at least so far as he could tell in the dim light, although the skin on both wrists hurt like hell. The manacles remained on each wrist, but they were now separated, burned completely through the middle.

Trip turned toward Ehrehin, who immediately pressed a still-warm disruptor pistol into his right hand.

"I took this off the guard while you were doing whatever it was you were doing just now. It was the most efficient solution I could find, under the circumstances."

Trip felt the solid heft of the weapon in his hand, and

realized that he would very likely have to put it to use, and probably very soon. "I'm just relieved that you know how to handle one of these things so well, Doctor."

Ehrehin chuckled. "Me, too, Cunaehr. Because I've never so much as held a weapon like this before in my life."

Trip was glad he hadn't known that fact *before* the old men blew apart his manacles. "Well, then let's hope *I* know how to handle one of these things." The sound of the running battle outside the conference room was growing louder still.

"I am counting on that, Cunaehr. You know that Admiral Valdore will try his best to kill me if his forces fail to rescue me."

Trip shook his head. "That's not going to happen, Doctor."

The elderly scientist's tone became grave. "Listen to me, Cunaehr. If it appears that these *Ejhoi Ormiin* are about to succeed in preventing either my rescue or my honorable death, then *you* must intervene." Ehrehin paused to place a hand on top of the weapon Trip held. "Using *this*."

"I can't do that, Doctor," Trip finally said at length. Ehrehin's hand fell limply away from Trip's, and the darkness did little to conceal the crestfallen look on the old man's deeply lined face.

"Then you have broken an old man's heart, Cunaehr. You must understand that I will *not* be forced to assist these people in their war against the Praetor's government. Too many innocent lives would be forfeit if these terrorists actually get what they want from me."

Trip held the disruptor close to his face in order to check its displays. Though he couldn't read the text, he was relieved to note that the graphics showed it to be almost fully charged.

Lowering the weapon, Trip said, "I'm not about to let

that happen, either, Doctor." He took the old man's arm in order to lead him to the exit, but Ehrehin pushed Trip's hand away.

"I have to get you to safety, Doctor," Trip said, trying to rein in his mounting impatience by sounding reasonable.

"So does Valdore. I believe I shall wait right here for his arrival."

Trip could feel the floor shake yet again. Coupled with the noise from out in the corridor, the sensation strained his patience that much closer to its breaking point. "Valdore's men could easily kill you accidentally with a stray disruptor blast, Doctor. I'll be *damned* if I'm going to let that happen." He took the old man's arm again, grasping it more authoritatively this time.

Ehrehin's tone mellowed as he weighed Trip's words. "That makes a great deal of sense."

"Come on," Trip said, holding his weapon at the ready as he led the old man out into the corridor, which reverberated with the sounds of combat. Trip was thankful that none of the fighting was in sight as yet. The dim emergency lighting challenged his memory of the facility's layout, which looked oddly different to him, like a familiar city landmark seen at night for the first time.

He belatedly realized just how much he had become dependent upon Phuong's talents during this mission. *You'd better figure out where you're going, Charles, and right now,* he told himself silently. *Or else you and the good doctor both are going to end up just like Phuong.*

After spending another few moments coaxing his memory, he guided the old man down the left branch of the corridor.

As they turned at a T intersection, a hulking shape stepped directly into their path. Trip saw the golden gleam of the man's polished metal helmet a split second before he raised his weapon and shouted "Halt!"

Trip fired, and his disruptor burned a ragged hole in the other man's torso. He crumpled to the floor in flames, just as Phuong had.

As he hustled Ehrehin past the charred and stinking corpse, he hoped that the old man hadn't noticed that the dead man was not attired in quite the same manner as Ch'uihv's men.

He had been wearing what Trip guessed was a regular Romulan military uniform.

Looks like I'm fighting on Ch'uihv's side after all, whether I like it or not, Trip thought grimly as he and Ehrehin made haste back toward the *Ejhoi Ormiin's* hangar area—with what sounded like all the hordes of hell drawing near them, front and rear.

THIRTY-FIVE

Friday, February 21, 2155
Romulan *Transport Vessel T'Lluadh*

THE ROMULAN SHROUD had evidently been established to prevent *Enterprise* from removing anyone from the transport ship. As Malcolm Reed materialized in a darkened chamber, he rejoiced that the shroud apparently hadn't been devised to keep anyone from beaming *in*. He turned to check on the rest of the boarding party.

Since the lights that flanked his faceplate were turned off, Malcolm activated the night-vision capabilities built into his helmet's visor. Although he couldn't see their expressions, or even facial details, he could tell from body language that the other members of the team—Commander T'Pol, MACO Corporals Hideaki Chang and Meredith Peruzzi, as well as Shran and Theras—had arrived safely. On *Enterprise*, they'd hurriedly donned environmental suits against the possibility of hull breaches or other dangers, and to facilitate scrambled communications that with a little luck wouldn't be overheard by the Romulans. Like Malcolm, they had kept their suit's lamps dark, operating in stealth mode.

Each team member carried a set of twenty transponders, devices designed to enhance the transporter's ability to establish a positive lock, even in the presence of signal jamming, or countermeasures such as the Romulan shroud. They'd brought three times as many of the small devices as they knew they needed, just in case the team got separated—or worse. Everyone but Theras also carried a phase pistol, set for heavy stun. As on Rigel X, Malcolm had double-checked that Shran's pistol was locked on that setting just before the team had beamed over.

All that was missing was an open channel back to *Enterprise*, which the Romulans' shroud appeared to have made impossible at the moment; fortunately, the signals sent by the transponders appeared to be strong enough to breach the Romulans' security barrier and to permit everyone, rescuers and rescuees alike, to be beamed safely back to *Enterprise* once the devices were distributed.

"I can hear them," Theras said over the com unit in his helmet. *"They're so very frightened."*

"I can feel Jhamel," Shran said. *"She's alive."*

Chang moved to the door, his weapon raised. Seen through the night-vision feature in Malcolm's helmet, the MACO appeared as a dark green silhouette set against a backdrop of slightly lighter green. Chang pried the door open slowly with one gloved hand, then pushed it into its wall recess with his foot. Peruzzi crouched to the side by the door, her weapon's barrel tilted upward.

Malcolm saw people stumbling through the hallways, but couldn't quite tell who or what they were. Their silhouettes were completely humanoid, but lacked antennae, so he was certain they weren't Aenar. *Romulans, then,* he thought as he tried to take a scanner reading of the crew, only to discover that the Romulan shroud was obscuring his scan.

As he signaled the team to move out into the corridor, a large figure stepped into the room, his hands groping along the wall for purchase. Before either of the MACOs could respond, Shran had savagely smashed his pistol into the side of the figure's head. As it crumpled to the ground, Shran muttered some phrase that Reed imagined to be a pungent Andorian curse.

They edged into the corridor, carefully dodging the shadowy figures, half a dozen of whom were moving along the walls. Reed found the situation almost surreal, as if he were caught in a dream in which no one had faces except for him.

"They're in the chamber down there," Theras said, pointing down a second corridor. *"I've just made telepathic contact with Lissan. She's been drugged to keep her telepathy in check, as have all the others."*

"Just as you anticipated," Reed said. "But it's a lucky turn for us that the Romulans aren't keeping them so comatose that you can't reach them at all."

"Still, none of the Aenar minds I'm sensing are entirely lucid. I will do my best to explain to Lissan that we're coming to rescue them. Perhaps she can keep the others calm, and prepare them for us."

"Thank Uzaveh you're finally good for something," Shran said acidly.

Instinctively, Reed looked over at the Andorian, then realized that even if Shran could see his glare of disapproval, he wouldn't have cared anyway. Still, Shran's unfairness rankled him. After all, Theras had *asked* to come along on this mission, insisting—perhaps because he had something to prove to Shran—that his telepathy could prove indispensable to the rescue effort. Although Reed himself had wanted to leave Theras behind, he now felt that Captain Archer had been correct in deciding to include him on the boarding team.

Ahead of them, two large, round-helmeted humanoids stood in front of the doorway, brandishing weapons.

As the quintet approached close enough for their booted footfalls to be clearly heard, one of the men said *"Vah-udt,"* his rising inflection on the final syllable suggesting that he was asking a question. *"Dhaile hwai rhadam!"* he added, raising his weapon without aiming it directly at anyone in particular.

"He can only hear us," T'Pol said quietly over her suit's com system.

Reed wished they'd had time to install Hoshi's Romulan translation program into their environmental suits, but it simply hadn't been possible under the circumstances. He hoped the men weren't surrendering, but given their aggressive postures and their weapons, he sincerely doubted it.

"Take them out," he said. "Quietly and nonlethally." Reed saw T'Pol put a hand on Shran's shoulder, holding him back, and then turned to look to the group's rear. So far, it appeared that they'd yet to be discovered, or surrounded.

He heard a pair of sharp energy-weapon reports, and turned back around to watch the shadow-cloaked men slump limply to the deck beside the sealed doorway, the silhouettes of Chang and Peruzzi standing above them, their phase rifles still held at the ready, parallel to the deck.

T'Pol moved to the door's control panel. *"The controls are nonfunctional. The power source is down."*

"Help me pry it open," Reed said. Everyone except Theras moved to help. After several seconds, the doors cracked open slightly, then widened to a gap that was just barely wide enough to squeeze through with a bulky environmental suit.

Inside the chamber, an eerie sight awaited. The Aenar were all standing, or supporting those who could not stand, and staring toward the boarding party with their sightless eyes. Their whitish skin gave off a strange phosphorescence in the glow of the night-vision gear, making them appear almost to be apparitions of some kind. The fact that their clothes were uniformly torn and ragged only enhanced the creepy image, sending a chill down the length of Reed's spine.

"I see you got them all calmed down," Shran said to

Theras, his tone still edged with condescension. The Andorian scanned the crowd, and Reed assumed he was most likely searching for Jhamel.

"Theras, please tell them that we are going to distribute the transponders now," Reed said over his suit's com. "Each of them should have two, just in case one of them fails." He thought it more likely that some of the drugged, frightened, and trembling Aenar would drop their transponders before any of the devices failed, but he wasn't about to say that aloud.

"Tell them they don't need to fear the transport process," T'Pol added. *"And that they'll be safe again once they're aboard* Enterprise."

"Understood," Theras said. Reed could see from Theras's profile that his antennae were pressed forward, touching his helmet's faceplate as though trying to escape.

After the first several drug-numbed Aenar had received their transponders, Reed sent a burst transmission from his com unit to *Enterprise,* hoping the signal would penetrate the shroud. Long seconds elapsed, and suddenly, a shimmering light enfolded one of the Aenar.

As she sparkled into nothingness, the beam cast a glow that made the holding cell clearly visible for a moment. Reed was disgusted by the filth he saw around him, and felt relieved that the abductees were about to leave it behind.

Time seemed to stretch to an eternity, and he tried not to consider what would happen if their plan were to fail. Had the transporter just sent another Aenar's atoms into oblivion? If so, the *Enterprise* was not likely to beam anyone else out, the boarding party included, at least not before weighing the risks further. And there was precious little time for that.

Before gloom could descend over him completely, another Aenar disappeared in a glimmer of light. Twenty seconds later, another, then two, then another pair, vanished.

"Yes!" Corporal Peruzzi exclaimed over her suit's com system. *"It's working."* He rarely heard the attractive young woman say anything; Reed noticed much earlier that whenever she *did* speak, she tended to communicate about half of her thoughts via her restlessly gesturing hands.

"Where is Jhamel?" Reed asked, not specifying whether he was asking Shran or Theras. He didn't want to seem to have taken sides in that particular affair of the heart.

"She's still here," Shran said.

"As are my other bondmates," Theras added.

Reed turned his back on the door and tried to count the number of remaining Aenar. Three seemed to be the limit for simultaneous beam-outs so far. *Moulton is smart not to overtax the system*, he thought. But as he watched, the next beam-out only took two, then after long seconds, one other was transported away. He counted about nine remaining Aenar, in addition to the six-person rescue team. Jhamel was standing with Shran and Theras, but Reed thought their other two bondmates might have been among those last few who had just transported. He wasn't sure.

"What's happened to the transporter?" Shran asked as the seconds stretched out in silence.

Chang broke in before Reed could respond. *"Lieutenant, I'm hearing some—"*

A small but bright flash came from the doorway as Reed turned, and he heard a cry of pain. Even as he raised his own weapon, he saw that Chang was down, and Peruzzi was diving for cover.

"Everyone down!" Reed shouted into his com as a brace of muzzle flashes lit the room. The sudden brilliance played havoc with his night-vision sensors, but he couldn't shut them off for fear of becoming blinded completely once the detention area plunged back into darkness.

He aimed his phase pistol in the direction from which the flashes had come and squeezed off multiple bursts, and was gratified to note that T'Pol, Peruzzi, and, behind him, Shran were doing the same.

More muzzle flashes from the doorway had Reed belly-crawling to the side of the room, where Chang lay. He heard a shriek behind him from an Aenar, and wondered who it was, and whether he or she was merely injured, or worse.

"*Why aren't they . . . beaming us out?*" Chang asked, his voice suffused with pain.

"I don't know, Chang," Reed said, breathing a silent prayer of thanks that the MACO was still alive. "Maybe the Romulans found a way to jam our transponder signals as well as our communicators." That seemed to be the most likely explanation.

A hot disruptor blast from the doorway nicked the heel of the boot on Reed's environmental suit, and he shuddered at the closeness of the blast.

Another explanation for the sudden failure of the transporter was one he really didn't want to consider, but it crept into his mind unbidden regardless. *Enterprise* might have been captured . . . or worse.

Gritting his teeth in grim resolve, he took aim at the doorway. And, he hoped, at their shadowy, faceless attackers.

THIRTY-SIX

Friday, February 21, 2155
Rator II

TRIP ALMOST HADN'T BELIEVED that they would actually make it to the hangar before Valdore's forces descended upon it, killing everyone in sight.

I guess it really is better to be lucky than good, Trip told himself as he helped a winded Ehrehin through the passage from the corridor into the large hangar that housed the *Ejhoi Ormiin*'s vehicle pool. Although the doors whisked shut behind him, they only muted slightly the noise and tumult of the running firefight that was swiftly engulfing the entire facility.

In the dim light, Trip saw the pair of guards stationed just inside the hangar at the same instant that they appeared to notice him.

He fired twice, sending both of the black-clad men—who had either been ordered to avoid the fight in order to defend the *Ejhoi Ormiin*'s small complement of space vessels, or else were about to make their own unauthorized escape from the bedlam outside—flaming to the deck, their weapons clattering impotently beside them.

In the light cast by their sickeningly burning bodies, Trip saw the corpse of Phuong, which still lay where it had fallen after Ch'uihv had so brutally cut him down. Evidently, between the distraction Ehrehin had created when he had conducted his long-winded warp-drive clinic—and the confusion that had engulfed the entire

Ejhoi Ormiin facility ever since—no one had yet been detailed to dispose of Phuong's body.

Trip regarded the weapon in his hand with disgust. *Haven't these bastards ever thought about carrying guns that come with a stun setting?*

"Just a minute, Doctor," Trip said, and walked quickly toward his late associate's still, charred form. Carefully, and with no small amount of revulsion, he reached inside the dead man's ruined jacket and felt around for the inner pocket.

"What are you trying to find?" said Ehrehin, who had come up quietly behind Trip, his question tinged with as much revulsion as curiosity.

Using two slightly shaking fingers, Trip extracted a black, oblong-shaped object about the size of the palm of his hand. "This. There's a data chip inside."

"Hmmm. A data chip doesn't seem likely to have survived such an intense disruptor blast."

"Ordinarily, it probably wouldn't have," Trip said as he opened the small black box along its hidden hinge. The gleaming amber rod inside appeared to be intact. "But this container is made of pretty tough stuff."

While recovering the chip, Trip had studiously avoided looking closely at the ruined corpse that he'd been forced to search, and he continued breathing carefully through his mouth so as to avoid the sickening, acrid-yet-cloying smell of burned flesh that suffused the hangar. Now, he forced the focus of his attention back onto the problems of the living, and onto their solutions.

One such solution now loomed directly ahead of him, in the form of the micrometeoroid-pitted hull of a cylindrical, twenty-meter-long spaceship whose design Trip didn't immediately recognize—the very same vessel onto which Phuong had been about to lead him and Ehrehin before Ch'uihv had interrupted their escape and ended Phuong's life.

Trip walked to the starboard hatch located approximately amidships, and quickly found the exterior control pad that would extend the gangway that someone had closed after Ch'uihv had made his appearance. A moment later, the open hatchway beckoned, and Trip helped the old man begin ascending the entry ramp, which was slanted at an almost forty-five-degree angle.

Trip cast a mournful backward glance at Phuong's still form, which thankfully was visible only in silhouette thanks to the interior lighting now streaming from the ship's hatchway. *I can't just leave him here,* Trip thought. He knew that far more than simple human decency was at play here; if the Romulans were to autopsy Phuong, they might determine that he was in fact a human infiltrator, and the consequences for Earth could be dire. He also understood that while there was no stopping an acquisitive Empire from going to war as it pleased, there was also no good reason to provide it with any after-the-fact justifications for its actions.

The ground vibrated in response to a particularly loud exchange of disruptor fire elsewhere in the complex. The jarring sound ascended above the general background wash of combat noise that suffused the place, reminding Trip that time was growing short. At any moment, Ch'uihv and his people could come streaming in, expecting to use the various small vessels housed here to make a hasty escape.

Trip also surmised that Admiral Valdore's patience wouldn't be infinite either. Sooner or later, once Valdore finally realized that he wasn't going to recover Ehrehin, he'd simply order his ships to obliterate the *Ejhoi Ormiin* compound from orbit. *So we've got not one but two ticking time bombs to race against,* Trip thought, desperately wishing to be anywhere but here.

Once he was certain that Ehrehin wasn't going to take a bad fall and tumble down the gangway, Trip ran back to Phuong and dragged the dead man's surprisingly light body up the ramp and into the vessel. He left it lying in a narrow passageway just aft of the entryway, then sealed the hatch before making his way forward to the cockpit.

He was more than a little surprised to see that Ehrehin had already begun running the pilot's and copilot's consoles through what could only be a standard preflight checklist.

"Thank you, Doctor," Trip said, taking the pilot's seat after the old man relinquished it to him and took the copilot's station on the cockpit's port side.

The elderly scientist smiled beneficently. "Seeing all the trouble you've gone through to keep me safe, Cunaehr, warming up the helm for you seemed like the very least I could do. I flew one of these old scout ships during my military days. I was once a pretty fair pilot myself, you may recall."

In fact, Trip *didn't* recall, but he made no response, busying himself instead with the various controls that were arrayed before him. As the vessel's numerous interlocking systems continued powering up, Trip continued to study the consoles, hoping against hope that he wouldn't reveal his imposture to Ehrehin by appearing hesitant or bewildered by the flight instruments and indicators. Fortunately, Romulan instrumentation was fairly streamlined and straightforward, lacking an excess of confusing redundancy. While he knew all too well that this deficiency might pose other potentially fatal problems after they got under way, Trip was grateful at the moment for anything that might enable him to get away quickly, and without unduly raising Ehrehin's suspicions.

But could this battered little ship produce enough speed to evade Valdore successfully? Trip knew that he needed to do everything possible to make certain that she could—*before* he got her off the ground, and onto any of Admiral Valdore's sensors.

Or weapons locks. With that alarming thought, Trip rose from the pilot's seat, his hope and fear confronting each other like opposing armies. The vessel shuddered and rocked slightly, as though something had just exploded violently elsewhere inside the *Ejhoi Ormiin* complex, perhaps not far from the hangar. *If I'm going to get Ehrehin out of here and keep him away from Valdore, I'll have to be ready to divert every last millicochrane of power this tub can produce.*

And some of that just might have to come from life support, Trip thought, experiencing a chill at that moment that reminded him uncomfortably of the icy cold of space.

"Where are you going?" Ehrehin called to Cunaehr's retreating back. He hadn't expected his assistant to leap up at the precise moment the ship needed to get under way. They hadn't even opened the main hangar bay yet in preparation for launch.

"I thought I passed some equipment lockers on the way to the cockpit," Cunaehr said over his shoulder just before disappearing into an accessway located near the middle of the vessel. The ship rocked yet again, and an ominous rumble was faintly audible through the hull plates. Ehrehin wondered if Cunaehr hadn't been far too correct earlier in voicing his worries that Valdore's forces might kill them both entirely by accident.

How very strange, Ehrehin thought, feeling his apprehension slowly increase the longer Cunaehr was out of his sight.

After a seeming eternity passed, Cunaehr returned, awkwardly carrying a helmet and chestplate in each hand. What appeared to be a pair of heavy, rust-and-silver-colored garments, each of which had clumsy-looking boots and gloves attached, were draped over each of his broad shoulders.

"Pressure suits?" Ehrehin said, frowning. "Cunaehr, why are you wasting our time with those?"

Cunaehr appeared more uncomfortable than he had since he'd been one of Ehrehin's callow young graduate students taking his final exams back at the Bardat Academy on Romulus. "I didn't like the look of the life-support system readings, Doctor. We need to suit up as a precaution before we launch."

Ehrehin felt his frown deepening involuntarily. "I didn't notice anything wrong with the environmental systems." On the other hand, the old man knew that his vision was no longer what it used to be. . . .

"Please trust me, Doctor. This is for *your* safety more than mine. I'll help you get suited up quickly." Cunaehr had begun donning his own suit, getting into it with surprising ease and grace, as though he'd had a good deal of practice. That, too, struck Ehrehin as very strange.

"We'll check each other's seals and connections to make sure everything is working properly," said Cunaehr. "Then we'll strap in and take off."

Ehrehin reluctantly accepted the main tunic piece of one of the two suits. He reflected that Cunaehr had never given him any cause to seriously doubt his judgment before—not even when the younger man actually *had* been a callow young graduate student nervously taking his exams at Bardat. Besides, hadn't he always taught the lad that a good, cautious engineer *always* wore both a good, stout *daefv* sash and heavy *fvalo*-straps if he wanted to make certain that his trousers stayed up?

"Very well, Cunaehr," the old man said at length, then began slowly donning the oddly alien-looking pressure suit the younger man had handed him. As he worked his way into the suit with Cunaehr's gentle assistance,

Ehrehin noticed that a gauge on the copilot's console was announcing with a cool, blinking orange light that the ship was now ready to fly.

Ehrehin only hoped the entire hangar wouldn't come down around their ears before they finally got themselves strapped in and headed for orbit—and for the safety of Valdore's fleet.

THIRTY-SEVEN

Friday, February 21, 2155
Romulan *Transport Vessel T'Lluadh*

THERAS COWERED ON THE DECK as blast after blast slammed into the metal surfaces all around him. He imagined he could feel the fierce heat of the disruptor beams singeing his back through his heavy environmental suit. He hadn't felt such terror since the day the raiders had invaded the Aenar enclave nestled beneath Andoria's northern wastes.

Recollections of how those freebooters had mercilessly ripped his beloved Shenar, Vishri, and Jhamel from his life—and during their sacred *shelthreth* ceremony, of all the days they could have chosen—helped him to focus his thoughts and steel his courage against the ongoing fusillade that was keeping him pinned to the floor.

I must not let fear sunder our shelthreth, Theras told himself, his smoldering outrage fanning itself into an incandescence that he hoped would consume his all but debilitating dread. *I cannot allow it.*

Not wishing to fumble for the external controls of his suit's com system, Theras spread his mind out across the wide interior spaces of the transport ship, his telepathic senses once again "feeling" the locations of his colleagues and protectors. Shran and Lieutenant Reed were positioned closest to him, both hunched behind a dense metal pillar to Theras's left as they returned their assailants' fire. Commander T'Pol and both of the Earth soldiers were slightly farther away in the other direction, all three lying on their bellies and returning fire despite the much scantier cover they had at their disposal. He could feel the pain of the wounded human soldier as though it were a dull ache of his own.

Theras also searched about telepathically for each of the armed Romulan troopers, noting with some sadness that two of them had been hit by the Earth soldiers, their bodies now lying just inside the chamber's doors. He couldn't be certain from their pained, disordered thoughts whether their injuries would prove fatal.

But he knew with visceral certainty that someone—or perhaps *several* someones—in the boarding party would soon be very dead unless the situation rapidly changed for the better. *They'll kill us all if they can,* he thought, tapping into the keenly honed martial savagery of the Romulans' thoughts; the painful intensity of that contact allowed him only a thankfully brief glimpse.

How can anyone harbor such ugliness in his soul? Theras's ingrained Aenar sensibilities barely allowed him to frame the question. He couldn't help but hope that such monstrous violence didn't loom quite so large in the psyches of the Earth soldiers, or anyone else in the boarding party, including Shran, whose anger and impatience Theras could often feel palpably.

Another blast came disconcertingly close as the firefight continued inconclusively. *I have to do* something, Theras thought. *Yet I cannot fight. I am Aenar.*

He felt Shran's rage, which was no doubt being intensified by the fact that Jhamel remained trapped aboard this cursed slave ship.

An inspiration seized him.

I am Aenar. I cannot fight.

But neither am I helpless.

Theras smiled grimly to himself and carefully reached out once again with his mind. . . .

Centurion Rhai had unexpectedly ceased firing, making Decurion Taith fear that one of the interlopers shooting at them from out of the darkness had scored a lucky shot and killed him.

Taith paused for a moment to ascertain his superior's condition, creeping toward him cautiously on knees and elbows. Reaching the centurion's supine form, he placed a hand on his shoulder, preparing to turn the body over in order to check for injuries.

The centurion swung into motion at Taith's touch, bringing the muzzle of his disruptor aggressively up toward the young decurion's face.

"Hold!" Taith whispered.

"Don't sneak up on anyone like that!"

"I thought you'd been killed, like Decurion T'Rheis. Why are you not firing?"

"Why aren't *they*?" Rhai asked.

Taith suddenly realized that the intruders had indeed ceased firing. He had been so intent upon reaching the centurion that he hadn't noticed the abrupt silence of their adversaries' weapons.

"They must be on the move," Taith said, fumbling for the scanner at his belt. "They found the other exit from the holding pens."

"Where are they?" Rhai wanted to know.

Taith's eyes went wide when he saw the reading on the stealth-shielded, backlit screen. "I can't detect them, Centurion."

"*Fvadt!* They must have used their material transmission device to escape us."

Taith adjusted his scan, attempting to confirm his superior's idea. A moment later, he shook his head in confusion. "I don't think so, Centurion. Their teleportation equipment left a telltale energy signature. But I'm not detecting it now."

But Rhai seemed unconvinced. "Perhaps they've adjusted their equipment somehow."

"Or else they're still aboard, Centurion, and are cloaking themselves somehow," Taith said.

"We must be prepared for either eventuality, Decurion. Scan our remaining prisoners. What is their status?"

Taith hastened to do as his superior had bid. When he saw the reading, his heart sank as though it were in freefall in a gas giant's atmosphere. He quickly ran the scan a second time.

"Well?" the centurion asked impatiently.

Taith realized that he had to tell Rhai what he least wanted to hear. "I can't even *find* any of them, sir. They're *gone!*"

"All right, Theras," Shran whispered into his suit's com channel. *"Your plan had better work. The more we prolong this standoff, the more vulnerable we'll be."*

Theras smiled in the direction of Shran's voice. He could feel the attentive presence nearby of Commander T'Pol, Lieutenant Reed, and the two Earth soldiers. "In order to have a standoff, the Romulans would have to know where we are."

"What do you mean?" asked the Vulcan woman.

"I mean that I have used my telepathy *defensively.* They cannot see us now. Nor can they see their prisoners. I've made us all . . . disappear from their conscious minds."

"Good work, Theras," Lieutenant Reed said, both his voice and his aura brimful of admiration. *"If we really are invisible to the Romulans now, maybe we can stay aboard long enough to use their own transporter to send the rest of the Aenar over to* Enterprise."

But Shran sounded and felt far less admiring. *"Then*

we'd better get on with it—before the Romulans figure out that we're using parlor tricks against them instead of real weapons."

As the group slowly made its way forward, moving directly into what had been the active line of fire only moments earlier, Theras wondered just what he would have to do to gain the hard-bitten Shran's acceptance.

Uzaveh take him, Theras thought, concentrating instead on recovering his beloved *shelthreth* bondmates.

He tried, without success, to shut out Shran's intrusive, passionate thoughts about Jhamel; he was clearly prepared to do just about anything to rescue her.

Far more, apparently, Theras thought sadly, *than* I *ever could.*

"The intruders are still here," Rhai said, his words still pitched at a whisper. "And unless I miss my guess, so are the remainder of our prisoners as well."

Taith felt confused, even though he had been the first to raise the possibility. "The scanner cannot confirm that, Centurion."

"Of *course* it can't, Decurion. Not if our prisoners have reached into our minds to alter what we can see—or *think* we can see. Had they teleported away like the *first* prisoners that went missing, they would not have bothered covering it up. Therefore, they *are* still aboard this ship, and are hiding that fact from us. As are their would-be rescuers."

Like all the soldiers serving aboard the transport vessel *T'Lluadh*, Taith had been well briefed on the danger posed by the Aenar prisoners. Although they seemed possessed of far too gentle a temperament for their own good, they were powerful telepaths who could indeed tamper with the minds of their jailers, were they so inclined—and were they given the barest opportunity to do so.

"I thought we had sedated each of the prisoners, Centurion," Taith said. "To blunt their telepathic abilities during their passage to Romulus."

"That was *my* belief as well," Rhai said. "But suppose our prisoners had planted the notion into our minds? Suppose we never actually sedated them, or were deceived into leaving even a few of them with their mental abilities still intact?"

Taith shivered slightly, as though the spirits of Erebus were coming for him. *If we can't even trust our own memories* . . . He allowed the thought to trail away like an errant wisp of smoke, though he could do little to shake the vivid image of the *T'Lluadh* suddenly erupting in all-consuming gouts of flame and venting atmosphere because an Aenar had influenced the control room crew.

"What can we do, Centurion?" Taith whispered.

Rhai raised his disruptor pistol. "If the intruders are still aboard, they may be trying to get the prisoners to freedom right now. Contact the rest of the security contingent, and tell them to concentrate their fire on the detention area's aft exit."

Taith put his scanner away and pulled his communications device from his belt, then raised his own weapon. "What about the prisoners, sir?"

"Our orders are clear, Decurion. They are not to come into the possession of anyone—save the Romulan Star Empire. Perhaps if one or two of them are hit, the remainder might be motivated to behave themselves for the duration of their voyage to Romulus."

As Taith began signaling the rest of his fellow soldiers, he hoped that they would be able to trust that any Aenar suddenly observed "behaving themselves" wasn't actually a ruse of the deadliest kind.

Shran and T'Pol led Jhamel and the remaining handful of sedated Aenar captives through the transport ship's darkened, winding passageways, while Lieutenant Reed and the MACOs—one of whom now walked with a pronounced limp, thanks to a stray disruptor bolt—guarded the group's moving perimeter. As the team made its way toward the vessel's central core, Shran had to acknowledge his grudging admiration of Theras, who was actually taking the point in the pitch-black corridors.

He's a pacifist, Shran thought with no small degree of wonderment; it was, after all, a philosophical stance that stood at odds not only with Shran's own personality, but also one that flew in the face of nearly all of his own often bitter personal experience. *And he's obviously terrified. Yet he's willing to help us fight a very dangerous, unscrupulous foe.*

Because he must want to save Jhamel just as much as I do. Though he was unable to see Jhamel clearly in the darkness, Shran was nevertheless haunted by a vision of the icy gray eyes of the woman he had been quietly in love with for the past several months. A woman whose great strength, despite her own innate pacifism, had been evident to Shran ever since the Romulans had forced her to deal with her brother's death. He clung to the slender lifeline of the psychic bond her telepathic talents had tethered in his mind, drawing comfort from it even as he worried about the incoherence and fear he sensed in her mind. *They've drugged her,* he reminded himself yet again. *Of course she's incoherent.*

A sizzling energy beam interrupted Shran's reverie, passing close enough to scorch his helmet's faceplate. The boarding party and the Aenar immediately split into two groups, which flattened against the walls on either side of the narrow corridor.

Shran found himself standing almost nose to nose with Theras. He grabbed the startled Aenar's tunic, momentarily lifting him a couple of centimeters off the deck. "I thought you said they couldn't see or hear us!"

"They can't!" Theras said, almost stammering in fear. *"At least, they* shouldn't *be able to, even on their scanning instruments."* Once again, Shran felt a wave of loathing for the pasty Aenar, and extended his left arm to shove him up against the same cold metal wall into which he himself was trying to blend.

Another blast bisected the corridor, missing both halves of the team by about a meter.

Theras gasped, making Shran fear for a moment that he'd handled him too roughly. *"They're just firing blindly!"*

"But these passageways ought to look empty to them," Shran said.

Theras nodded, his features taking on an almost hysterical cast. *"They should. But the Romulans must know that there are only two ways in or out of this section of the ship."* Large tears pooled in the Aenar's gray, sightless eyes; he appeared to be in intense physical pain, but it was clearly not because of anything Shran had done to him. *"They've cut us off. And they're determined not to let anyone take their prisoners away from them. They'll kill us all before they permit that. I—"*

Yet another disruptor blast illuminated the corridor for a split second. It struck lower than had the previous shot, but came no closer to hitting anyone.

"Even firing blind, they're bound to start hitting us sooner or later," Shran said, addressing nobody in particular. He supposed that even if the Romulans hadn't actually somehow pierced Theras's psionic veil of selective blindness, they must have intuited the boarding party's continued presence aboard their vessel by some other means.

Of course, none of that would matter a whit if the Romulans managed to score only a handful of lucky, random shots.

"What have I done?" Theras said, breaking down into

shoulder-racking sobs that were amplified grotesquely by his suit's com pickup.

Shran wanted to strike him, but restrained himself when he realized he'd only succeed in injuring himself on the Aenar's helmet. "Shut up, Theras. Remember, they still can't see us. Otherwise they wouldn't be lobbing their fire at us at random."

"There is another problem," T'Pol said. In the dimness, and with the suit's apparently damaged night-vision functions disorienting him somewhat, Shran could just make out the fact that the Vulcan woman, flanked by Reed and a pair of rifle-wielding MACOs, was holding a small scanning device before her face. *"We apparently cannot determine the precise location of any of the Romulans aboard this vessel. Therefore we cannot return their fire with any degree of accuracy."*

Shran felt as though a physical blow had abruptly slammed all the air from his lungs. He grabbed the hard carapace of Theras's suit, keeping both their bodies close to the wall as he caught his breath.

"Why might *that* be, Theras?" Shran whispered.

It took Theras a protracted moment to rein in his sobs and find his voice. *"It may be . . . that using my telepathy defensively has created a . . . blanket effect."*

"Are you saying," Shran said, the words leaving his mouth in a snarling rush, "that you've blinded *us* as well as the Romulans?"

Theras nodded, weeping again. *"Forgive me, Shran. Forgive me, all of you. I am . . . unused to the ways of war."*

Pacifists, Shran thought disgustedly. *Beautiful.* He felt his psionic bond with Jhamel jangling uncomfortably at that thought, momentarily filling his mind with an unpleasant sound not unlike an inexpertly plucked high string on an Andorian *zharen'tara.*

Still another stray blast briefly ionized the air, once

again coming uncomfortably close to Shran's back. Theras winced as the beam passed and struck a distant wall with a momentary spray of bright orange sparks. In that instant, Shran saw Jhamel clearly, her gray eyes staring and sightless, her mien sedated and confused.

She was in mortal danger, as were they all. *Why couldn't Theras have just tricked the damned Romulans into shooting at each other instead of at* us?

"I suggest you *get* used to the ways of war," Shran said, no longer trying to hold back the contempt he felt for this weakling. "And *quickly*, Theras. Otherwise, you've probably condemned Jhamel and all the rest of us to death."

THIRTY-EIGHT

Friday, February 21, 2155
Rator II

"HANG ON, DOCTOR," Trip said, though he could see that Ehrehin was securely strapped into his seat, just as Trip himself was. "I'm taking us out."

"Perhaps we should wait until the hangar bay doors open completely," the elderly scientist said, a note of apprehension causing his voice to quaver slightly.

Trip grinned at him. "Trust me." He pulled back the throttle, and the small vessel shot forward. Trip was slammed backward into the pilot's seat for a second or two, before whatever passed for the scout ship's inertial damping system compensated for the g-forces generated by the sudden acceleration. Like Ehrehin, Trip had not yet donned the helmet of his pressure suit—both pieces of headgear were wedged securely beneath their respective seats, where they would remain until they were needed—so his pressure suit's titanium neck ring bit briefly into the back of his neck as the little ship whipped upward at a steep-angled roll through the only partly opened hangar dome, narrowly missing the still spreading doors. Trip imagined the hangar bay filling with armed troopers, all of them vainly firing their disruptor pistols at his quickly vanishing stern.

Trip opened the throttle further, and the vessel swiftly arced high into the deep cerulean skies above the *Ejhoi Ormiin*'s secret island fortress. The paradisiacal blue of Rator II's atmosphere quickly gave way to a deep, brooding indigo, passing within moments into the star-flecked blackness of space. The cold vista of the cosmos made Trip grateful for the pressure suit he was wearing, even if he was helmetless at the moment.

When he and Ehrehin had first come aboard the little scout ship, Trip had marveled at his good fortune in having found environmental suits constructed so similarly to the standard Starfleet-issue vacuum garb used by *Enterprise* personnel. He could only wonder how these suits had made it aboard. Perhaps Ch'uihv—or Sopek— had acquired a few of them through his espionage connections on Vulcan, or maybe the *Ejhoi Ormiin* had obtained them by raiding an Earth outpost or by hijacking an Earth ship. Wherever the suits had come from originally, it was easy for Trip to imagine that Phuong had found them elsewhere in the hangar while reconnoitering the place, and then had stashed them aboard the scout ship before leading Trip and Ehrehin into their initial—and catastrophically failed—escape attempt.

An alarm on Trip's console suddenly flashed a deep sea green; he reminded himself yet again that to a Romulan, green was the color of blood, and therefore signified the presence of imminent danger.

"We're being pursued," Ehrehin said, leaning forward and to his left to observe the readings on Trip's console.

"I'd be surprised if we weren't," Trip said.

"We need to hail them, Cunaehr. Otherwise, Valdore's forces may kill us inadvertently, as you say."

Trip shook his head, wondering how long he could continue dissembling, stringing the elderly scientist along—and when Ehrehin would finally figure out that he'd disabled the ship's receiver to prevent the reception of any hails from their pursuer, which would certainly reveal the identity of the vessel that nipped at their heels.

"We don't know for certain that the ship on our tail is one of Valdore's," Trip said.

Ehrehin fixed him with a hard stare that seemed to Trip to fairly ooze with suspicion. "Who in the name of Erebus could it possibly be if not Valdore?"

"It could be Ch'uihv's people, Doctor. And hailing them would only confirm our escape for them."

"If he's pursuing us," Ehrehin said, shaking his head. "Ch'uihv already knows we've escaped in this ship."

Trip shrugged, pressing on even though his extemporaneous yarn-spinning was beginning to sound ridiculous even in his own artificially pointed ears. "Maybe, Doctor. Maybe not. If Ch'uihv is the one who's chasing us, then all we know for sure that he knows is that *somebody* took off in this ship without any launch clearance."

Ehrehin leaned back in his copilot's chair and sighed. Trip spared a glance at him and saw that he was staring straight ahead at the distant, uncaring stars. The old man was scowling deeply, apparently becoming lost in thought.

He must suspect by now that I don't have any intention of taking him to Valdore, Trip thought as he leaned forward, entering commands intended to coax still more thrust out of the impulse drive, while simultaneously laying in his desired heading: Coalition space. *So I'd better do whatever I can to keep him preoccupied.*

He touched a few of the cockpit's other thankfully simple controls. The deck plates beneath his feet began to rumble with a gratifyingly familiar vibration. That sensation alone told Trip that the warp drive was beginning to warm up to operational temperatures, pressures, and intermix ratios.

The little vessel suddenly shook and rattled intensely, as though it had been punched by the fist of an angry god.

"They've opened fire," Ehrehin said dryly, one eyebrow arched upward as if to announce that he found making declarations of the obvious to be darkly amusing. He calmly studied the readouts on his copilot's board. "At the rate they're gaining on us, they'll be in weapons range in only a few *siure*."

Trip considered the grim fact that it could all be over for them both in a matter of only a few short minutes. He felt a knot of fear twisting in his stomach.

Fortunately, Trip often regarded his own fear as a wonderful source of motivation during a crisis.

"Put on your helmet, Doctor," he said as his hands flew across the console. "We're going to warp."

Ehrehin scowled again, then reached under his seat and drew up his helmet with a pained grunt. A moment later, he was fitting it clumsily over his head and trying to mate its collar to his suit's broad neck ring.

The vessel shook again, though not quite as roughly as on the previous occasion. Trip hoped that meant that their pursuers had scored only a glancing blow this time.

After noting the temperature and power-level readings, displayed graphically as well as in unreadable Romulan text on the warp field gauge, Trip heaved a brief sigh of relief that the weapons fire hadn't disabled the warp drive.

Yet.

Eager to deny their pursuers another opportunity to strike, Trip wrapped his gloved left hand around a pair of levers. *Here goes.* He pulled the levers down quickly, then punched a button beside them.

A moment later the starfield that lay before them distorted into streaks around the edges, with the light of the stars near the center shifting toward the blue portion of the visible spectrum.

"We are now at warp," Trip announced. *I'm not the only one who gets to state the obvious around here.*

"And I'm sure Valdore's ship is still pursuing us, only much faster than before. Do you think it was really wise to go to warp so close to the planet?"

Trip knew very well that certain types of warp fields could unleash catastrophic gravimetric and subspatial effects if activated too deep inside the gravity well either of a star or a planet. Once again, he had no choice other than to defend his decision to gamble for the sake of his mission.

"Seemed like the best option at the time, Doctor," Trip said as he unstrapped himself from his seat restraints.

He rose to help Ehrehin hook up the hoses that led from the back of his helmet to the environmental pack mounted on the back of his suit.

"Indeed," the scientist said, obviously unconvinced.

Once he was satisfied that Ehrehin's suit was completely sealed and functioning properly, Trip reached behind his own helmet, attaching his own air hoses and checking his suit's seals in a series of swift, practiced movements.

Then he noticed that Ehrehin, who had already strapped himself back into his seat, was staring daggers at him through their helmet faceplates.

"These *particular* pressure suits were an interesting choice on your part, Cunaehr," the old man said, his voice distorted slightly by its passage through two helmets before reaching Trip's ears; Trip had taken the precaution of disabling the com systems in both suits, so that Ehrehin wouldn't be tempted to find a way to use them to communicate with their pursuer.

Trip shrugged as he strapped himself into the pilot's seat once again. "You have to use what you have on hand."

"Indeed you do."

Trip looked across his console's orderly bank of gauges and monitors, noting with some apprehension that the pursuing vessel was steadily gaining on them. Although the scout ship's sensors lacked the resolution to settle the matter definitively, Trip had no doubt that

Ehrehin was right about their pursuer being one of Valdore's military ships. Therefore the other vessel had to be more than capable of catching up with them at their present speed, which both the console gauges and the vibrations of the deckplates told Trip he had already pushed to within a millicochrane or two of maximum.

It's time to push this baby a little bit past spec, Trip thought as he carefully began entering a new command string into his console.

"Tell me, Cunaehr: Are there no other suits aboard this ship?" Ehrehin asked.

He knows, Trip thought. *He* is *a genius, after all.*

Aloud, he said. "There are, Doctor."

"Suits of Romulan manufacture, rather than these . . . *alien* garments?"

Trip was becoming increasingly certain that it wasn't going to matter much longer how he answered the old man's questions. "I think so."

"Yet you chose *these* suits instead. And you seem quite expert in their operation, I might add."

"The environmental packs on these suits were more fully charged than any of the others were," Trip said. Whether his answers continued to matter or not, he found he couldn't resist offering plausible-sounding explanations whenever possible. "And you know what a quick study I am." He punctuated his words with what he hoped was a disarming smile.

The scientist did not return it, however, either because he couldn't see it through both of their faceplates, or because he simply was no longer quite so easy to amuse.

"I had no idea you were so fluent in reading the gauges and instrumentation on non-Romulan pressure suits."

You have no idea, Trip thought as he examined his

pilot's console, confirming that the other ship was still inexorably creeping up on them. Would it be able to open fire on them in two minutes? Three?

"I'm going to have to coax a bit more power out of her," Trip said just before entering yet another command into his board.

The cabin lights instantly shut off, and the resulting total darkness was replaced a beat later by dim, green emergency lighting. Trip could hear the sudden, conspicuous absence of activity in the air-circulating system as the ventilator fans abruptly died. He imagined he could feel the icy vacuum beyond the hull caressing his spine with delicate, chill fingers, although he knew it was far too soon for either of them to start feeling the cold of space through their heavily insulated suits.

Even as the life-support system gasped and died, Trip could feel a qualitative change in the vibration rising from the deck plating beneath him into his thick-soled boots.

The scout ship's warp drive was now receiving considerably more power, and the weakly glowing console display confirmed it. *Warp five point three, and still not quite redlining*, Trip thought, barely succeeding in restraining himself from letting out a jubilant warwhoop—at least until *after* he learned a little bit more about their pursuer's maximum speed.

To his pleasant surprise, Valdore's ship was no longer gaining on them. It wasn't falling behind either, but the purloined scout ship didn't appear to be in any danger of being overtaken now, at least not during the next few minutes.

We're still well out of weapons range. And we'll stay that way as long as the ship tailing us doesn't suddenly sprout an extra nacelle.

Of course, Trip knew that there was no way he could be certain that their pursuer wouldn't find some method of sharply increasing its *own* power output, and thus its speed. But he was reasonably sure that her commander wouldn't shut down her life-support system to accomplish it.

Just as he was absolutely certain that Valdore wouldn't give up the chase while any breath remained in his body, or ships in his command.

But a respite was a respite. Trip knew he now had the luxury of thinking about the future, such as it was, at least for a brief while. In addition to having Doctor Ehrehin in his custody, he also possessed information that was absolutely crucial to the defense of the Coalition of Planets in general, and to the welfare of Coridan Prime in particular. He had to get it to Starfleet as quickly as humanly possible. With a few deft movements of his gloved hands, he restored the components he had removed from the com system a little earlier.

Now which one of these babies fires up the transmitter? Trip thought as he studied his console, as well as all the smaller panels adjacent to it. Fortunately, within a few moments he was pretty sure he'd identified the appropriate controls.

He entered a command intended to open a Starfleet channel on the subspace bands. He waited for at least a minute.

Nothing.

The faintly glowing blue pictogram that had appeared in response to his commands told him either that he hadn't, in fact, accessed the com system, or that the com system had sustained just enough damage during their escape under fire from Rator II as to be completely inoperable.

He had a slow, sinking feeling that the latter scenario was the correct one.

"Why are you running away from Admiral Valdore, instead of toward him?" Ehrehin asked in an accusatory tone. "And why were you tampering with the communications components just now? Who are you, really?"

Though he realized now that his imposture had finally fallen apart completely, at least in Ehrehin's eyes, he nevertheless clung to it, unable to shake his initial impression of the old man as fragile and vulnerable—and therefore unable to handle the brutal truth that his beloved Cunaehr was, in fact, dead.

He turned from his console to face the scientist, doing his best to make direct eye contact through the slight distortion created by two helmet faceplates. "What are you talking about, Doctor Ehrehin? It's me: Cunaehr."

"But you *can't* really be Cunaehr. I can distinctly recall having seen Cunaehr die during the mishap on Unroth III. That is, I can do so on those rare occasions when I *can* recall things distinctly."

Trip sighed, then regarded the old man in thoughtful silence. While Ehrehin still seemed terribly frail to him, the old man also exuded a dignified, determined resolve that commanded respect. It occurred to him that the real Cunaehr had been fortunate indeed to have had such a man as his mentor.

"How can you be so sure I'm not Cunaehr?" Trip said at length.

Ehrehin smiled. "I ran an analysis of some tissue traces that either you or your late associate Terha inadvertently left behind in my quarters. At first, I attributed the strange results I obtained to the rather unreliable state of mind in which the *Ejhoi Ormiin* interrogators had left me. But your actions since then have not only confirmed that you are not, in fact, Cunaehr, but also that you aren't even a *Romulan*.

"What I'd like to know, my *kaehhak*-Cunaehr," Ehrehin continued, "is how an alien like yourself could ever have expected to pass himself off for very long as a genuine Romulan, especially so deep inside Romulan territory."

Unless things go really south on me again, Trip thought, *we won't be anywhere near Romulan territory by this time tomorrow.*

Trip decided then to answer the old man's accusations and questions as honestly as he could, figuring that admitting the truth now could harm him very little at this point. After all, either he would make it back to Coalition space with Ehrehin, and they would both live to tell the tale, or else he'd end up dead—and then the Romulans would move decisively against an utterly unprepared Coridan Prime.

Nevertheless, he instinctively glanced down at the side of his suit to make certain his weapon was still there, even though the scientist posed no physical threat to him.

"All right, Doctor. My real name is . . ." Trip paused, distracted. Besides the obvious lack of a functioning life-support system, something else aboard the ship no longer felt quite right.

The deck plates. The vibration from the warp core had changed, and was continuing to change.

To his horror, Trip realized that it was fading steadily away.

He faced front, abruptly turning back toward the pilot's console. It took only a fraction of a second for the status displays to confirm his worst fears.

Something had gone badly amiss with the little scout ship's overtaxed engines, and she had consequently dropped out of warp.

And the vessel that pursued them was closing very rapidly.

Trip knew with the certainty of gravity that he had a scant handful of minutes to fix the problem, if he was to have a prayer of getting the old man out of Romulan space. After that, Ehrehin and his vast store of knowledge and expertise would fall back into Valdore's hands. Trip knew that his own death would become reality rather than ruse very shortly thereafter.

And no one would remain alive to warn the Coridanites that the gates of whatever hell they might believe in were about to swing wide open.

THIRTY-NINE

Friday, February 21, 2155
Romulan *Transport Vessel T'Lluadh*

DECURION TAITH SAW A DIM but definite shape moving furtively toward him through the darkened passageway. With but a moment's hesitation, he raised his disruptor and fired directly toward what was now clearly discernible as an armed, uniformed alien. He felt certain that he had never seen this species before, despite the creature's superficial resemblance—it possessed a head, a torso, and one pair each of both arms and legs—to the overall shape of a male Romulan.

The initial shot apparently missed. Holding his weapon before him with both hands, Taith fired a second time, and the bright, sizzling beam struck the creature almost directly in its center of mass, forcing it backward as though it had been kicked by a wild *hlai* from the Chula wilderness. Wreathed in flames, the figure crumpled heavily onto the deck in a lumpen heap. Moving cautiously, Taith approached the fallen creature, hoping to examine it a bit more closely and make certain that he really had neutralized the threat it posed.

He cried out in anguish when he suddenly realized that the dead form that lay before him was not, in fact, the corpse of an alien interloper.

It was Centurion Rhai, whose still and lifeless chest was now a charred, bloody ruin.

He heard several other volleys of disruptor fire originating from different areas of the ship, each of them ending abruptly, and each punctuated by the all-too-brief silences that preceded the next salvo. Then the barrages ceased, and the entire ship was suddenly wreathed in a tomb-like silence.

Taith couldn't look away from his commanding officer's vacant, staring eyes. A feeling of despair more profound than any he had ever experienced before engulfed his every sense, swamping his soul as though it were the flood plain of the Great River Apnex.

Weeping, he raised his disruptor, placed its muzzle firmly against the base of his chin, and squeezed the trigger.

Theras wept like a disconsolate child after the echoes of the final blasts died away.

Shran could see the Aenar's tears glistening even in the near darkness of the Romulan vessel's narrow passageway. The sound of the other man's sobs was sorely trying what little remained of his patience.

"Well, did it work?" Shran asked, addressing the entire team through his suit's com system. The psionic bond he shared with Jhamel suddenly stretched taut, then sounded such a deep note of grief within his mind as to inform Shran that his question had been unnecessary.

I need to know for sure, Shran thought. *We can't risk exposing ourselves to their weapons again until I do.*

"Give him a moment, Shran," said Reed, who was standing at Theras's other side. *"Can't you see he's been traumatized by what you've asked him to do? He's a pacifist, for pity's sake."*

Shran took a step toward Reed, his fists clenched and his antennae thrusting aggressively toward his faceplate like enraged eels from one of the Zhevra continent's cold and brackish lakes. "Don't remind me, Lieutenant."

"Gentlemen, I suggest you both give Theras a moment

of quiet to enable him to collect his thoughts," T'Pol said in an infuriatingly calm, reasonable tone, a mannerism that vividly reminded Shran why his people distrusted hers so viscerally.

Just before Shran succumbed to a nearly irresistible impulse to grab Theras by the shoulders and shake him, the Aenar spoke, *"The Romulan soldiers . . . will not trouble us further."*

"You telepathically deceived them into firing upon one another," T'Pol said, not asking a question.

Theras sobbed again. *"Yes. And the last of them . . . just took his own life. Moments ago."*

Reed laid a comforting hand on Theras's shoulder. *"I'm so sorry this was necessary, Theras."*

Shran felt his antennae rising in surprise and pleasure. *He did it. The coward actually* did *something.* It suddenly occurred to Shran that he might have very badly misjudged Theras; he pushed the thought aside, however, in favor of making it his absolute top priority to complete Jhamel's rescue, along with that of the other remaining Aenar captives.

After that, the boarding party itself would still have to get off this ship and return safely to *Enterprise;* he knew that this might prove challenging, since this ship's bridge crew remained alive, and still could potentially put up a fight should Theras's telepathy somehow cease concealing the rescue team from their notice.

"Let's not waste any more time coddling him," Shran said, addressing both Reed and T'Pol. Then he turned to face the nearest of the two pressure-suited MACOs. Though their faces were shrouded in darkness, Shran knew they must have been as eager as he was to get the group moving again toward the Romulan vessel's transporter, from which Jhamel and the others could be sent to *Enterprise.*

"What will become of us now?" Jhamel said inside his

brain, her mind still uncharacteristically disordered because of the sedatives she'd been given, her thoughts feeling jumbled and chaotic. *"Too, too much dying here."*

"We still have a job to finish here," Shran added as he tried to ignore the unfathomable sadness that now flowed freely into him from Jhamel's obviously still drug-muzzled brain.

Theras trudged on with the rest of the group. He felt completely dead inside. And wasn't he, really, so far as his society was concerned? After all, he had become something that his people regarded as anathema: he was now a killer.

A murderer.

He struggled to keep his concentration focused on the twists and turns of the corridors and passageways that he recalled from the minds of the dead Romulans. The route that led to the ship's transporter.

Theras was thankful, at least, that the boarding party had not come close enough to any of the slain Romulans who now lay scattered throughout the vessel so that his suit's night-vision apparatus could reveal them in any amount of detail. But he knew that he would be unable to escape absorbing the horrible visual imagery of what he had done from the thoughts of the other members of the boarding party. Although he recognized that it was cowardly, he nevertheless hoped that the Romulan corpses would never become more than death-sprawled silhouettes in his memory; even that, he suspected, would be nightmare enough to last for the rest of his days.

He was beginning to be distracted, however, by the feelings of grave apprehension he sensed coming from *Enterprise*—in space, somewhere near the transport ship—as her crew bravely held the line against the weaponry of two Romulan warships, risking death to enable the rescue party to complete its mission. He wished he could further influence the crews of the Romulan warships, inducing them to believe that *Enterprise* had departed, but he was growing steadily more tired, and even now felt wearier than he had in recent memory. He felt that he had already stretched his telepathic talents to their limits, and perhaps even a good deal past them.

Another thing he found disturbing was the sluggish nature of the thought-auras of the Aenar captives, especially those of his bondmates, Vishri, Shenar, and Jhamel. Had the Romulans drugged them because they feared they might contemplate taking actions such as those he, Theras, had eventually taken?

Defensive actions, such as temporarily "blinding" the Romulans to the presence of the boarding party.

And offensive actions—such as causing the Romulans to slaughter one another while believing they were striking down invaders.

Would Shenar even have contemplated doing such a thing, had the Romulans left him able to do it? Theras thought as the team finally reached the darkened Romulan transporter room and herded him and the rest of the Aenar inside. *Would Vishri?*

Would Jhamel?

Malcolm Reed had expected to have to spend perhaps a few minutes puzzling out the Romulan transporter's scanning, range, targeting, and transmission controls, after which he expected to execute a short series of swift beam-outs back to *Enterprise.*

What he *hadn't* expected was to discover that the now-deceased Romulan guards had utterly destroyed the transporter with their disruptors, melting both the console and the stage to slag, no doubt to prevent their Aenar prisoners from getting off the ship once they had gotten free of the ship's detention area.

"What now?" Shran said, exasperated.

Reed sighed. "What about Theras? Can't he send our coordinates to *Enterprise* telepathically?"

"Perhaps," said Shran, gesturing toward the environmental-suited Aenar. *"If he hadn't gone catatonic right after the firefight, that is."*

Reed turned and saw that Theras had slumped next to one of the walls. He sat motionless and limp, resembling an empty environmental suit that someone had neglected to stow properly.

"Firefight," Reed said with a humorless laugh. "It was a slaughter."

"Without their *slaughter, it would have been* our *slaughter. He'll just have to learn to deal with—"*

"Gentlemen," Commander T'Pol said, stepping suddenly between them, interrupting. *"There are still other alternatives."* T'Pol held up one of the small transponders. *"I believe we still have a number of these, Lieutenant. Perhaps we can use several of them in tandem to restore our communications with* Enterprise, *and establish a transporter lock as well."*

Reed grinned. "Let's get to work."

"Continue evasive maneuvers!" cried Jonathan Archer, tightly gripping the arms of his command chair as the bridge rumbled and tipped all around him.

Archer wondered just how much more pounding *Enterprise* could take before the constant barrage forced him to withdraw from weapons—and transporter—range. The forward viewer displayed an image of one of the two Romulan war vessels that had continued aggressively defending the transport vessel that carried the Aenar prisoners, despite the fact that *Enterprise* had crippled the engines of all three ships.

The bridge shook and rattled again, and Archer was very nearly thrown from his captain's chair. However crippled their adversaries' engines might be, their complement of weaponry was in decidedly better shape. He knew he'd been lucky in managing to take out the engines of both escort ships while evading what could have been critical damage to *Enterprise*; he also knew that his luck was in very finite supply, and that it would run out entirely should the Romulans score many more hits.

"Sorry, Captain," said Travis Mayweather, seated behind the helm, just ahead of the captain's chair. "The hull plating can't take much more of this. It's down to forty-three percent and falling."

"Understood, Ensign. Keep trying to evade their guns as best you can. But maintain maximum transporter distance."

Archer knew that the time was rapidly approaching when he would have to make a painful and final decision, weighing the lives of his boarding party, Shran, and the few Aenar who remained to be rescued against the safety of his ship and her entire crew.

He knew that only one decision was possible.

The ship rocked again. Archer spoke toward the intercom pickup in the arm of his chair, into the channel to D deck that he'd left open. "Ensign Moulton, if you can't reestablish a transporter lock now, we're going to have to withdraw."

"Understood, sir. I'll keep trying." She didn't sound confident.

Rising from his chair, he walked to the side of the helm. "Travis, take us out of their weapons range."

The helmsman nodded grimly. "Aye, sir—"

"Captain!" The voice coming from the arm of the command chair belonged to Ensign Moulton. Mayweather's hand hovered over the helm throttle control.

"Go ahead, Ensign," Archer said as he ran back to his chair.

"I've reestablished a transporter lock, sir. I don't know how, or how long it'll last, but—"

"Save the explanations, Ensign. Get busy!"

"Our transporter circuits have been taking a beating from the Romulans," Ensign Moulton said over the com channel in the boarding team's suits, her words nearly lost in an intermittently oceanic wash of interference. *"But I can't risk transporting more than one of you at a time."*

"Take Jhamel first," said Shran, who watched soberly as Commander T'Pol and Lieutenant Reed nodded in agreement. Now that Moulton had just finished transporting five Aenar, only Theras and his bondmates remained to be transported, along with three humans, one Vulcan, and Shran.

"—ust a moment," Moulton replied, continuing to fight a losing battle against the static still being generated by the Romulan shroud field. Because all attempts to shut the field down from inside the transport ship had failed, Shran had become convinced that it was actually originating from one or both of the warships currently harassing *Enterprise*.

Several anxious moments later, the hum of *Enterprise*'s transporter effect reverberated through the ruins of the Romulan transporter room, and a sheet of sparkling blue engulfed the groggy Jhamel, who had been sitting disoriented on the deck. Though he didn't want to do anything that might put her safe transit to *Enterprise* at risk, it had been all Shran could do to refrain from offering her a steadying arm to enable her to stand while she'd awaited transport.

The dematerialization effect seemed to labor more than Shran had ever seen before, as though it were having difficulty drawing sufficient power. He offered a silent prayer to all four of the First Kin to ensure that Jhamel emerged from the process unharmed.

"Got her," Moulton said. The com channel hissed and fritzed around her words. *"Powering up for another."*

"Take Theras next," Shran said.

"Very well," T'Pol agreed.

"No," Theras said, once again surprising Shran.

Surprised or not, Shran couldn't suppress a scowl. He approached the wall against which the Aenar *thaan* was leaning. "We can't risk splitting up your *shelthreth,* Theras."

Jhamel's shelthreth, he thought, *which she made you a part of, for whatever reason.*

"Can there be room in any Aenar shelthreth *for one who has taken lives?"* Theras said over the com channel.

Shran had no response to that. He had once dared to hope for a positive answer to that question himself, before he had discovered that his beloved Jhamel's future was already spoken for.

"Let's start with the two other Aenar while you two finish sorting this out," Reed said.

Shran nodded in response to Reed, though he continued studying Theras's blind, pain-weary face, which was limned in the intermittent green glow of Shran's damaged night-vision gear. The transporter continued its increasingly difficult work, taking Shenar first, then Vishri, followed by the injured male MACO, and finally by the female.

Then Reed and T'Pol had vanished as well, leaving Shran and Theras alone together in the darkness.

"I will go last," Theras said. *"I have . . . touched Ensign Moulton's mind to make certain that you will be her next passenger."*

Clutching his modified transponder device nearly hard enough to shatter it, Shran searched the darkness for the other man's milky, sightless eyes. He realized now that he had fundamentally misjudged Theras.

He raged at the realization.

He had mistaken a death wish for courage, self-flagellation for heroism.

"You have no intention of leaving this ship, do you?" Shran said, making a blunt observation rather than asking a question.

His lips unmoving, Theras spoke inside Shran's mind. *"Good-bye, Shran. Promise me that you will take care of Jhamel. And her bondmates."*

Shran started to protest, but the words caught in his throat as the transporter's shimmering blue light and whining din enfolded him. A moment later he stood on *Enterprise's* circular transporter stage, wobbling slightly from a thankfully brief wave of vertigo.

After he removed his helmet, the first thing he noticed was the absence of the rest of the boarding team except for the female MACO, who stood in her now-helmetless pressure suit beside a white-smocked human whom Shran assumed was a medic of some sort. He assumed that T'Pol and Reed were absent because Archer would have needed them urgently up on the bridge, and that the rescued Aenar and the injured MACO had already been taken to the ship's infirmary, or elsewhere aboard *Enterprise.*

Shran launched himself off the stage, stopping in front of a small nearby console, behind which stood a human female whom Shran assumed was Ensign Moulton. The startled MACO raised her weapons defensively, but Shran ignored her.

"Beam Theras over, now!" Shran barked, unwilling to let the Aenar sacrifice his life merely for having defended himself and his teammates.

And for defending Jhamel, whose telepathic bond with Shran seemed to be growing stronger from moment to moment. *Sickbay,* Shran thought, listening to her presence as best he could along the subtle, diaphanous channel that connected them. *She's been taken to sickbay.*

"I'm trying to establish a lock," Moulton said, scowling alternatively at Shran and the console before her. She began toggling switches that Shran couldn't recall ever having seen before, apparently trying to divert still more power to the already overtaxed system.

Then a small explosion sounded behind him, making his ears pop and his antennae retreat as though seeking cover. He turned to see a cloud of acrid-smelling black smoke slowly rising and spreading over the transporter stage.

"Dammit!" Moulton shouted, still examining the readouts before her. "The Heisenberg compensators are completely fused." She focused a hard stare upon Shran as she snapped open an intercom switch. "Ensign Moulton here, Captain. I'm afraid I have some bad news about the transporter. . . ."

As he made his way toward the bridge, escorted by the female MACO, Shran couldn't help but wonder whether the machine had failed all on its own—or if Theras's telepathic influence had had something to do with it.

They quickly reached the turbolift that Shran presumed ran directly through the primary hull's midpoint, and therefore connected to Archer's bridge along the most direct route. Shran felt his bond to Jhamel increase greatly in intensity as the lift doors slid obediently open before him.

A haggard but determined-looking Jhamel was inside the lift, leaning unsteadily against one of the walls.

"We can't let the Romulans have Theras," she said.

Then her eyes rolled shut and she collapsed into Shran's arms.

"Captain, I'm afraid the transporter won't be beaming anybody anywhere for at least a week," Moulton said, frustration coloring her normally phlegmatic manner. *"I'm sorry, sir."*

"It's not your fault, Ensign. I'm sure you did everything you could." Archer now could no longer see any choice other than to withdraw immediately. He rose from his chair and stared at the pair of raptorlike Romulan spacecraft that loomed ahead like an augury of death, grimly aware that T'Pol, Malcolm, Hoshi, and Travis were all looking in his direction, anxiously awaiting his next order. Once again, he had no real choice, though it pained him to admit it.

"Travis, get us out of here. Maximum warp."

"With pleasure, Captain," the helmsman said with an unconcealed sigh of relief. He immediately began entering commands into his console. "Course laid in. Executing."

Archer felt the subtle shift of vibration in the deck beneath his boots, which told him that *Enterprise* had just gone to warp. Even as the image of the two semicrippled warships vanished from the viewer, the turbolift doors at the bridge's aft port side whisked open. Archer turned toward the sound.

He watched a gaunt, careworn Aenar woman whom he recognized as Jhamel step unsteadily onto the bridge, with Shran—still partially clad in a Starfleet-issue environmental suit—gently guiding her arm, balancing her. A MACO exited the lift behind them, then took up a vigilant posture by the turbolift doors.

"*Enterprise* mustn't leave yet, Captain!" Jhamel said breathlessly, her gray eyes focusing directly upon his, despite her inability to see. Archer found the effect disconcerting.

Striding out of the command well toward the Aenar woman, Archer took her other arm and glared at Shran. "Why did you bring Jhamel up *here*? She belongs in sickbay, or in one of the emergency wards down in the launch bays."

"I told her the same thing, Captain," Shran said

mildly, displaying a somewhat grim smile. "But she insisted on speaking to you immediately. I know better than to stand in her way when she's being insistent."

T'Pol rose from the seat in front of her science station, allowing Archer and Shran to guide Jhamel gently into it.

"Theras is still aboard that transport vessel, Captain," said the Aenar woman, her skin as white as scrimshaw, her antennae flailing in slow motion like a pair of anemones.

Archer nodded sadly. In measured, sympathetic tones, he said, "I know he is, Jhamel. But I'm afraid we have no way of rescuing him."

"I am not asking you to rescue him, Captain. And neither is Theras."

"You're in telepathic contact with him now?"

A single fat tear rolled down her ice-hued cheek. "Yes. Please, Captain. Do *not* allow the Romulans to take him. Theras is *begging* me to help him prevent this. He wants you to kill him."

"Kill him?" Archer was appalled by the suggestion, although he had to admit that he could see no good alternative. He was beginning to feel sick to his stomach.

Jhamel nodded. "He wants you to destroy the transport ship, Captain."

Archer shook his head in disbelief. "There are still Romulan personnel alive on that ship, Jhamel, and they'll die if I do that. And the Romulan government won't be very happy about it either. They might even use it as a pretext to justify war. Frankly, I'm surprised that an Aenar would want me to do such a thing."

But I can't let the Romulans use Theras as a weapon, Archer thought. *The way they used her brother Gareb.*

"Theras will give the Romulan crew some warning, Captain. They will escape their ship's destruction. Theras has pledged to see to it."

"If the Romulans can get to their ship's escape pods, then so can Theras," said T'Pol.

"He's not going to do that," Shran said, shaking his head, an incredulous expression on his azure face. His antennae lay flat against his scalp, which Archer interpreted as a sign of grief. "And we can't force him."

"For God's sake, *why*?" Archer wanted to know.

"Because he killed a number of Romulan guards during the rescue mission, Captain," Jhamel said. "He believes he must atone for this."

"And what do *you* believe?" Archer said, chafing at Jhamel's apparent willingness to abet a photonic torpedo–assisted suicide. "Let me fill you in on an ugly truth, Jhamel: Sometimes it's *necessary* to kill in order to defend the lives of others. Sometimes there's no choice other than to deal death in the name of peace. How can you just . . . *abandon* him for recognizing that fact, and acting accordingly?"

Jhamel's brow crumpled in anger, her antennae thrusting forward almost belligerently. This was the first such emotion Archer could recall ever having seen on Jhamel's ordinarily smooth, unlined face.

"Captain, you may not believe this, but pacifists can be very pragmatic people—just as you humans believe yourselves to be, particularly when you are 'dealing death in the name of peace.' So far, you've prevented the Romulans from turning the rest of us into weapons of war, and I sincerely thank you for that. But now you must do the same for Theras—or else they *will* make a weapon of him, just as they did with Gareb."

If the Romulans have even a single Aenar telepath in their possession, Archer thought, *they'll force him to operate another one of their telepresence ships. Or maybe they'll use him for something even worse.* Recalling how Gareb had been used, and how he had bravely sacrificed himself in order to bring his involuntary servitude to an end, Archer realized that Jhamel's thinking was every bit as pragmatic as his own.

Still, he didn't much like where that realization would inevitably lead him. Regardless, he came to a decision, quickly if not easily.

"Travis, belay my last order. Dead stop." *Enterprise* shuddered slightly as she responded to her helmsman's deft touch on the helm console.

Mayweather regarded him with a slightly puzzled expression, but complied nevertheless, dropping *Enterprise* out of warp. "Dead stop, Captain."

"On my order, bring us back to just within weapons range of the Romulan transport vessel," Archer said, turning toward the tactical station overlooking the command well on the bridge's starboard side. "Malcolm, get a pair of photonic torpedoes ready. Maximum yield."

"Aye, sir." Malcolm said, nodding affirmatively as he entered a string of commands into his console. A few moments later, he nodded at Archer to signal that the weapons tubes were ready to fire at his discretion.

"Travis, engage new course."

"Aye, sir."

Within moments, the Romulan transport vessel was displayed front and center on the bridge's main viewer.

"The warships are locking their weapons again," said Malcolm. "We'll probably lose our warp drive if they score a direct hit this time."

"A chance we'll have to take, Malcolm," Archer said, thinking of Theras, and the additional violence the Romulans would surely force upon him.

Then Archer heard Jhamel speaking very gently inside his head. *"You are doing the right thing, Captain. Theras has just warned the Romulans to abandon their vessel, and they are leaving it now. I thank you for what you are about to do, Jonathan Archer. And Theras thanks you as well."*

The disembodied voice was steeped in the deepest sadness that Archer had ever known. *I hope you'll forgive me if I don't say, "You're welcome" to either of you,* Archer replied wordlessly.

"Good-bye, Theras," Jhamel thought, prompting Archer to wonder if everyone else on the bridge had also heard her mournful farewell. He looked toward her and saw that her tears now flowed freely, if silently.

"I salute you," Shran said, facing the viewer, his face frozen into a somber rigidity that seemed almost Vulcan.

A second voice spoke directly in Archer's head. It took a moment for Archer to realize that it belonged to Theras. *"The escape pods are launching, Captain. Please do what you must do."* Unlike Jhamel, Theras's mind seemed to carry no excess of grief or regret. Instead, Archer thought the doomed Aenar's telepathic essence radiated a sense of . . . vindication.

His throat dry, his eyes burning, Archer said, "Fire torpedoes, Malcolm. Then get us out of here, Travis. Maximum warp."

A beat later the transport ship erupted in two spectacular conflagrations, one per torpedo. The molecular fires slowly began to spread, pulling the hull apart in several places. Archer saw the first of the escape pods launch moments later, just before the tableau of destruction vanished from the viewscreen as *Enterprise* leaped to warp.

Jhamel slumped in her seat, weeping violently.

Archer could only hope that she wouldn't feel the need to seek atonement the way Theras had.

FORTY

Friday, February 21, 2155
Romulan space

TRIP WATCHED AS THE BLIP on the sensor display continued its slow, steady progress toward his stolen ship, which remained effectively dead in space. "Becalmed" was how his father—an avid Gulf Coast sailboater—would have described their current condition.

There's got to be a way to get some wind behind our sails again, Trip thought, wishing he could feel as "becalmed" as their ship had become.

He turned his pilot's seat toward Ehrehin, who still occupied the copilot's position. The old man regarded him darkly through the faceplates of their twin environmental suits.

"You mind giving me a hand getting this beast flying again?" Trip said, feeling he had nothing to lose by asking.

The elderly scientist favored him with a drop-jawed look of pure incredulity. "First you kidnap me, then try to keep me away from my would-be rescuers, and now you ask for my *help*? I certainly have to credit you with audacity, my young friend. Whoever you *really* are."

Trip paused for a moment, still struggling to calm himself, though it wasn't easy at the rate their pursuer continued to gain on them. "When did you figure out I wasn't really Cunaehr?" he finally said in a quiet voice.

Wondering if his helmet had muffled his words too much to allow Ehrehin to have heard him, Trip was about to repeat his question when the scientist said, "Frankly, it was always difficult to accept you at face value, although I must confess that you *do* bear an astonishing resemblance to Cunaehr. But it was far too convenient for Cunaehr to reappear precisely when I needed his encouragement the most."

Trip sighed, feeling like an utter failure. *So the only people I've managed to fool on this spy mission of mine are all the people back home who think I'm dead. Peachy.*

"If I really *were* Cunaehr, Doctor," he said aloud, "I think I'd still ask for your help. We need to get the com system back up at least."

"Why? So you can bargain with Valdore for your life? I must caution you: The admiral is not renowned for his willingness to take prisoners."

You're afraid of him, Trip thought. He'd noticed a new tremor in the scientist's voice that couldn't have been attributable to old age alone.

Aloud, he said, "I'm actually thinking about *your* safety, Doctor."

Ehrehin smiled, and Trip saw an amused gleam in the old man's eye. "*My* safety? I should think that the arrival of one of Valdore's ships should more than ensure that."

"Unless Valdore decides to kill you because he believes he's caught you in the act of defecting."

"The admiral would never believe such a story— especially if it were told by a spy."

Trip tried to summon up everything he could remember from the briefings Phuong had given him on Romulan politics. "The question isn't whether Valdore believes *me* or not, Doctor—it's what he *already* believes about *you.*"

Ehrehin's smile collapsed, swept away by another dark, forehead-crumpling scowl. "What are you talking about?"

Another glimpse of the fast-approaching blip on the

console sent a large bead of sweat racing down Trip's back, and pushed his words out somewhat faster than before. "It's no secret that you have differences with the Romulan military. You've even been known to criticize the Praetor himself from time to time. But I suppose that's one of the privileges of being too important to the Romulan war machine—whose goals you haven't been all that happy with over the years—to make you worry too much about ending up with somebody's nice, shiny Honor Blade sticking out of your back.

"And then there's what your military is about to do to Coridan Prime. I might not be Cunaehr, Doctor, but I think I've gotten to know you well enough to believe that you wouldn't want anything to do with that."

Trip could see that he had finally gotten Ehrehin's full attention. He had no choice other than to press on, keep pushing any advantage he could find. "You don't *have* to be a part of that. You don't *have* to keep looking over your shoulder. You don't *have* to live in fear of what will happen to you after the Praetor finally decides that you've outlived your usefulness to the Empire's expansion plans.

"You could live among *my* people instead. Balance out the Empire's need for conquest by helping us stand against their military machine. You know what will happen if you don't: More planets will get rolled over by Valdore. Millions of people could end up dead, or as slaves. And it'll be because *you* helped make it happen. In fact, maybe it can't even happen at all *without* your help. Can you live with that?"

He fell silent then, and simply watched the play of emotions that crossed the old man's deeply lined face— or at least as much of it as Ehrehin's stubborn self-discipline and two sturdy helmet faceplates would reveal.

Trip seriously doubted that he had completely convinced Ehrehin to throw in his lot with him. But the thoughtful look in the old man's dark eyes made it clear that he had upset the scientist's earlier pretense of equanimity about going back to work for the Romulan military machine.

Ehrehin reeled his gaze back in from the middle distance where he seemed to do his deepest thinking, then stared at Trip with large, soulful eyes. "Cunaehr or not, you have been kind to me, *whoever* you are."

"You can call me Trip." He started to extend a gloved hand, but stopped himself, remembering that Vulcans, being touch telepaths, disliked being touched. He decided to assume that their cousins, the Romulans, might have similar habits.

The old man nodded, an awkward maneuver in the bulky pressure suit. "Very well, Trip. I will see what I can do about assisting you in getting this vessel up and running again."

For the very first time, Trip began holding out a real hope that Ehrehin would voluntarily offer to protect the billions of innocents who lived on Coridan Prime, as well as Earth and the rest of the Coalition worlds. The notion buoyed Trip's spirits greatly, because he knew it meant that he might soon have the opportunity to return from the dead to see his parents, his brother, T'Pol, and the rest of his *Enterprise* family again.

Trip glanced again at the pilot's console, where the blip that represented Valdore's doggedly pursuing ship was growing dangerously close to its quarry.

"We'd better get busy, then," he said, then rose from his seat and headed for one of the tool kits he'd seen earlier in the aft section, moving as quickly as his bulky environmental suit would permit.

FORTY-ONE

Friday, February 21, 2155
Enterprise NX-01

SHRAN STOOD AT THE FOOT of the biobed, feeling an overwhelming sense of familiarity as he watched Jhamel sleep. Other Aenar were resting throughout sickbay, while some recuperated in the makeshift medical facilities in *Enterprise*'s two shuttlepod launch bays, or in hastily rearranged crew quarters; the ship's guest cabins were still uninhabitable because of the hull breach sustained during the recent battle.

Enterprise was currently hurtling toward Earth at top speed, so repairs, and a return to Andoria for the Aenar, would have to wait. Archer had apparently already jeopardized his command by undertaking the mission to rescue the Aenar, but Shran felt sure that the compassionate human leaders would forgive him.

He studied the face of the beautiful *zhen* who lay on the biobed, heartened to see her condition had visibly improved, even in the last six hours. With the nutrients and medications Jhamel and the other Aenar had taken in since their rescue by *Enterprise*, they were beginning to lose their color once again. Excepting the bluish highlights she normally had, the only rose-colored portions visible on Jhamel's skin were the fatigue-generated wrinkles and pouches around her eyes.

He looked over to the neighboring beds, where Shenar and Vishri both slumbered, thanks to some sedatives and dream suppressants provided by Doctor Phlox.

He wondered idly how the three surviving bondmates of Jhamel's *shelthreth* group would get along in life now. Without Theras, the *thaan* of the group, they would be unable to reproduce. Given the declining population on Andoria, and the even sharper decline of the Aenar people's numbers, the loss of any member of a potentially fertile *shelthreth* quad was unutterably horrible and tragic.

Because of that tragedy, he took small comfort in the fact that nearly every one of the other Aenar had been rescued, with the exception of the one who had run afoul of a transporter malfunction . . . and, of course, Theras.

He realized only now how completely he had misjudged Theras. *I was as blind as he was*, Shran thought, *but in a completely different way.* The gentle Theras, who had seemed to be such a melting icicle throughout the entire abduction ordeal, had instead shown himself to be the furthest thing from a coward that Shran had encountered among the Aenar. He had overcome his very *nature*, the pacifistic ideals by which he had always lived, in order to help free his fellow Aenar.

Shran had never enjoyed apologizing, but he sincerely wished for a chance to do so to Theras. He'd treated Theras abominably; he'd acted like a bully, intimidating a mild, gentle being every chance he'd gotten. He was trained to be a warrior, and was therefore used to putting himself into harm's way. There was no heroism to much of what he did; it was mostly done out of duty, or a love of the accompanying adrenaline rush, or perhaps just plain orneriness.

"You're wrong, Shran."

Jhamel's voice was speaking inside his mind. He turned to see her looking toward him, her sightless eyes now open, but as blind as always. *"You* can *be a hero when you want to be. It wasn't that long ago that you helped me defeat the Romulans that first time. As well as my grief over Gareb's death."*

"Just as you helped me lay the ghost of Talas to rest," Shran thought back to her.

But he wasn't interested at the moment in rehashing the past; he was already far too focused on the future. He moved closer to the bed, and took her pale hand in his. "How are you feeling?" he asked aloud.

She smiled weakly, and spoke aloud as well in a voice that was hoarse from disuse. "Tired. Hungry. Relieved. Sad." She turned her face toward his. "We have to stop meeting when one or the other of us is confined to a bed."

Shran allowed a short laugh to escape his lips. Their attraction to each other had first sparked when she'd visited him while he'd been recovering from being impaled on an icicle and was troubled by the death of his beloved Talas, and she was still hoping beyond hope for the rescue of her doomed brother, Gareb. He had been lying in bed, and awakened to see her then. Later, when Jhamel was recuperating after having used the telepresence helmet in an effort to help her brother, he had watched over her as she slumbered in a different biobed, and had held her hand, just as he was doing now.

"I'm glad you're well," Shran said.

A troubled look crossed her face. "And Vishri and Shenar? How are they?"

"Resting comfortably," Shran said, casting another glance in the direction of Jhamel's bondmates.

"They're only resting because their minds aren't linked with yours," Jhamel said inside his mind. *"Lucky for them: the agitated state of your mind could wake a hibernating frost boar!"*

"I'm sorry," Shran said, even though he saw her smile, and felt her affectionate, unvocalized laughter. "I can leave if it will help you rest." He started to pull his hand away.

"No, stay!" Jhamel said aloud, pulling his hand back to hers, though weakly. "I was only teasing."

"I liked what you were thinking about Theras a few moments ago," she told him with her mind. *"Please forgive me for eavesdropping."*

He smiled gently. *"I have no secrets from you, Jhamel,"* he thought in reply. At least, he didn't *want* to keep any secrets from her. How she felt, of course, would have to remain to be seen.

"The path Theras chose was agony for him," Jhamel thought. *"But he did it to save us, and ultimately, to preserve the essence of himself."*

"I think I understand that now," Shran said aloud, his voice soft.

"I'm not certain you do," Jhamel thought. *"Even I don't think I understood it until the very end. He provided a future for me . . . for us."*

"What do you mean?" Shran thought back to her.

"We spoke aboard the transport ship, Theras and I, mind to mind. He said that during the entire time of our . . . captivity, he studied you quite closely. Mentally, physically, emotionally."

Shran was alarmed, and lapsed back into speaking aloud. "Why? For what purpose?"

"It is possible that he had some inkling of what was to come," Jhamel said, opting to use her voice again, perhaps in an effort to calm Shran. "He sometimes had premonitions. Perhaps he even saw his own death coming."

Shran shuddered. He'd certainly stared death in the face many times, and had come away stronger each time. But he didn't know the *hour* of his death, and would never want to.

"In his last moments, he told me," Jhamel said, moving very gently back inside his mind.

He looked down at her, aware that his antennae had

been unconsciously mimicking the movements of hers. *"Told you what?"* he asked.

"You are a thaan. Your genetics are compatible with those of our shelthreth. He gave us his blessing."

Shran felt the wind rush out of his lungs in one great whoosh, and he sat down quickly at the edge of the biobed.

"Are you . . . are you asking me to join with the three of you? To *bond*?"

He couldn't believe he was allowing himself to *think* these words in Jhamel's presence, much less say them out loud. In all his years, he had never entered a *shelthreth* quad, having devoted himself instead to his homeworld's defense. His relationship with Talas, a similarly isolated soul, had been the most intimate one of his life, even though they both had known that without another pair of compatible bondmates, procreation—as well as social acceptance on Andoria—would forever be denied them.

"Yes. If you will have us," Jhamel said, a hint of apprehension in her voice.

Shran bent over and nuzzled his forehead to hers, their antennae wrapping around each other.

He whispered in her ear.

"Yes. If the three of *you* can stand *me*."

FORTY-TWO

Friday, February 21, 2155
Romulan space

"ALL FLOW REGULATORS are finally showing orange," Ehrehin said, his breath slightly fogging up his faceplate as he pulled the hydrospanner out of the open relay-circuitry drawer located near his booted feet. "Try it again now."

Orange is good, Trip thought, reminding himself yet again that the instrumentation on Romulan ships differed from that of Earth vessels in sometimes unsettling ways.

"It's now or never," Trip said, glancing nervously down at the console's tactical display, which showed that what they'd both assumed was Valdore's lead ship was almost right on top of them, with a trio of other pursuers—the first vessel had evidently summoned reinforcements—trailing very close behind. The closest of these ships could drop out of warp at any moment, perhaps with Trip's vessel already within range of its weapons.

Trip held his breath and engaged the throttle lever, pulling it slowly and deliberately toward him so as not to overload it.

The starfield ahead of the ship immediately smeared and turned slightly blue. The deck plates vibrated and shuddered violently before quickly settling down to a familiar subaural frequency that Trip supposed reassured warp engineers all across the galaxy.

Once the velocity gauge had finished climbing back to where it was before the engines had failed, Trip turned toward Ehrehin and said, "Think maybe you can spare a moment to help me with our subspace transmitter?"

The elderly scientist stared at him inscrutably, and Trip thought he saw the slightest of smiles flicker across his face. He hoped it wasn't just a trick of the starlight he saw reflected in the man's helmet.

Although the gap between pursuer and pursued remained too narrow for comfort, Trip was relieved to note that Valdore's ships—there were still four in all—were no longer gaining on them. *If we don't have any more engine trouble between here and home,* he thought with no small amount of trepidation, *we both might actually get out of this alive.*

Trip was also thankful for another uncanny stroke of luck: the damage the subspace transceiver had sustained hadn't been nearly as serious as he had feared. Nevertheless, getting the thing back into operational condition—with audio only, at that—had involved more than a little jury-rigging and swearing, as well as the diversion of precious power reserves that he was loath to divert from the drive systems while Admiral Valdore's forces were still nipping at their heels.

But there was no alternative. He had to send a warning about the specifics of the coming attack on Coridan Prime, even if doing so landed both him and Ehrehin right back in Valdore's lap.

Trip patched an optical cable that led from his suit's com system into the microphone/speaker jack he had just discovered on his pilot's console. He then punched in a particular subspace audio frequency and boosted the gain as much as he dared. At that moment, he noticed Ehrehin watching him from the copilot's station, his once rheumy eyes now brimming with undisguised, almost youthful curiosity.

"Whom are you contacting?" the old man asked, apparently almost succumbing to his old habit of addressing Trip as Cunaehr before catching himself and changing his next utterance to "Trip."

Trip smiled at the scientist. "I'm calling the one man who'll do whatever it takes to help us."

Touching the control on his chest that opened his helmet microphone, he said, "Lazarus to Captain Archer of *Enterprise,* Priority One and Coded. This is Lazarus, calling Captain Jonathan Archer. . . ."

FORTY-THREE

Friday, February 21, 2155
Enterprise **NX-01**

"Captain, I have a priority audio communication for you," Hoshi Sato said, swiveling in her chair and touching the com device she sometimes wore clipped to her ear.

Archer looked over to her, his attention diverted from the padd onto which he'd begun entering his speech. After the events of this week, he didn't know if he'd even be allowed to present it at the Coalition Compact ceremony, but he wanted it to be ready nonetheless. "Who's the message from, Hoshi?"

"Your ears only, sir." She frowned slightly. "The only other word in the subspace burst is the name Lazarus."

Archer immediately stood and moved toward his ready room. "I'll take it in here," he said.

Trip's alive, he thought, trying hard to stifle a big grin as he breezed past several of the bridge crew. He hoped that the message would contain good news, perhaps with the engineer telling them he was ready to come in from the cold of his spy mission. He slid into his chair in the ready room and tapped the console on the desk in front of him.

"*Lazarus to Captain Archer of* Enterprise," the voice said over the speakers. The sound was full of static, and distorted slightly, but it was undeniably Trip's voice.

"Archer here. It's good to hear your voice. You ready to come home?"

"Thanks, Captain, but not quite yet. There's been a whole mess *of complications."*

"Are you all right?" Archer asked, frowning with concern as he leaned forward. He wished there was a visual component to the message, so that he could see his old friend's face again.

"I'm okay, but Coridan's in trouble. The Romulans are definitely *targeting the planet. But it doesn't seem to be an invasion. It's more of an annihilation."*

Archer was stunned. "You're *sure* about this?"

"Absolutely. Some time in the next seventy-two hours, they're striking Coridan. You've got to warn them."

"Any idea how they'll attack?"

"No, sir. What I—" the rest of Trip's reply was cut off in static.

Archer hit the com button. "Hoshi, I've lost the signal. Boost our reception."

"Aye, sir," Hoshi said.

The wait for Trip's signal to be regained was torture. Archer's mind reeled with the news. *The annihilation of Coridan in the next seventy-two hours.* The thought was ghastly almost beyond imagination.

"I can't reestablish the signal," Hoshi said. *"Whoever it was, they'll have to start sending to us again."*

"Okay, thank you." Archer couldn't wait any longer. He knew that he had to warn the Coridanites, *and* inform his superiors on Earth. "Hoshi, raise the highest Coridan government official you can, and pipe them onto my screen."

While he waited to speak to the Coridanite government, he tapped in the emergency code to contact Admiral Gardner on Earth. At the moment it was 4:50 A.M. Pacific time on Earth, but the news he'd just received certainly qualified as an emergency.

Archer's desktop screen jumped to life as a weary Gardner appeared on it, yawning as he pulled on a robe.

Archer saw the ready light that Hoshi had sent from the bridge, and his finger hovered over the appropriate button.

"*This had better be damned important, Captain,*" Gardner said grumpily. "*I have some crucial meetings first thing in the morning.*"

"It's *vitally* important," Archer said. He tapped the button, and the screen split in two. Half of the screen now showed the face of a Coridan official, someone in the diplomatic corps, Archer thought, judging from the Coridanite's ceremonial mask. "Admiral Gardner, I've patched us in on a conference transmission with the Coridan official . . ." His voice trailed off.

"*Legate Hanshev,*" the Coridanite said. It sounded like a female voice, but Archer couldn't be certain that the mask wasn't electronically altering Hanshev's speech.

Gardner composed himself quickly, his bearing changing almost instantly. "*All right, Captain Archer. You have our attention.*"

Time to put on my best game, Archer thought. "We have been given intelligence indicating that the Romulans are planning some kind of strike against Coridan in the next *seventy-two* hours. We've been told that this will *not* be an invasion, but rather an attempt to destroy as much of the planet and its resources as possible."

The Coridanite's face was completely hidden behind the inhuman-looking mask, but her body language clearly registered shock. "*How did you come upon this information?*"

"We had heard rumors of such an attack being planned," Archer said. "I aided in arrangements to send . . . trustworthy people to investigate the rumors firsthand." He leaned forward, trying to look as serious as he could. "Let me be plain. I trust the person who gathered this information *implicitly*. I would stake my life on the truthfulness of this person's data."

Gardner seemed to be gritting his teeth, and his eyebrows had both furrowed down into a deep scowl. *"And what are you proposing to do about this, Captain Archer?"*

"Well, my immediate step was to contact you both," Archer said. "This will give Coridan Prime's government as much time as possible to evacuate its people, or mount an attack, or erect defenses. I'd recommend all three. Secondly, I request permission to divert *Enterprise* to the Coridan system immediately. Perhaps we can help Coridan Prime stop this attack, or at least provide support for Coridan's defense and evacuation efforts."

Gardner's eyes narrowed. *"We need you back here at Earth, Captain. I thought I had made that crystal clear before."*

Archer pushed his temper down. "That was when all I had was *rumors*. We now know them to be facts."

"You believe *them to be facts,"* Gardner said, his voice rising in volume.

Before Archer could argue his point further, the Coridanite legate spoke again. *"Admiral, I believe your captain's words. We, too, have our sources, and the threat from the Romulans has been an ongoing concern for some time. Now, it would appear that the threat is finally imminent.*

"As to your offer of aid, Captain, while it is generous, I believe that there isn't anything further you can do that our own ships cannot," Hanshev said. *"If your superior says you're needed on your own homeworld, I will release you from your promise to assist us."*

Archer's mouth dropped open. He knew that the Coridanites were an intensely private and proud people, but refusing aid during such a time of crisis seemed beyond the pale.

"Do you have any further information that might aid the Coridanites?" Gardner asked, a slight smile hidden underneath the edges of his salt-and-pepper mustache.

"Or should we allow them to get on to the vitally important tasks ahead of them, while you fulfill your own mission?"

Inwardly, Archer was seething, but he swallowed his anger. "That's all the information I have. Seventy-two hours."

"I thank you for your warning and your offer," Legate Hanshev said, bowing his head slightly. *"We will make the best possible use of your warning."* The Coridanite's image disappeared, allowing Gardner's to take up the entirety of the screen's frame once again.

"That would have been an excellent play, if it had worked, Captain," Gardner said, his expression returning to its earlier fury.

"That was no 'play,' sir, it was—"

"It was an attempt to circumvent my direct orders!" Gardner shouted, interrupting him.

Archer, his tone dangerously close to insubordination, countered, "People's *lives* will be lost. *War* is on its way."

Gardner glared at him for a moment, then finally spoke. *"The Coridanites don't want your help. And you are due back on Earth."*

On the screen, the admiral lifted his hand, clearly ready to end the communication, but paused just before doing so. *"Let me make one thing clear, Captain. This stunt you just pulled . . . if anything remotely similar ever happens again, I'll have you cashiered out of the fleet."*

The screen went black for a moment before the Starfleet logo reappeared.

Well, that didn't go all that well, Archer thought, his ire up and his ego bruised. He wished for a moment that Porthos were here beside him, instead of in his quarters. He could use some nonjudgmental canine company right about now.

Although his mind whirled with emotions and questions, he seemed to fixate on one thing: No matter how much Coridan Prime might not want *Enterprise*'s assistance, Archer felt that they could stop the oncoming devastation threatened by the Romulan attack.

But it all depends on exactly how I decide to spend the next seventy-two hours, Archer thought. *Gardner's orders notwithstanding.*

The door chime sounded, startling Archer out of his unhappy reverie. He pressed the comm button on his desk.

"Come in."

The door slid open with a quiet hiss. T'Pol stood in the threshold, her hands behind her back and head tipped inquisitively. The intensity of her gaze, however, far exceeded mere curiosity.

She knows I've been keeping her out of the loop, Archer thought as she stepped inside the ready room as the door closed behind her. A frisson of guilt clutched at his heart as Archer considered how much he had kept from her. The fact that circumstances justified his secrecy made him feel a little better about having misled a first officer who had served him so loyally for the past nearly four years.

She raised an eyebrow. " 'Lazarus,' Captain?"

Archer rose from behind his desk. Deciding that she deserved to know as much of the truth as possible, he said, "It's the code name of a covert intelligence source working inside Romulan space. One that I trust implicitly."

"Indeed. And I presume from the raised voices I heard through the door that this source has just imparted some rather important information."

Her remark rattled Archer, until he reminded himself of the uncanny acuteness of Vulcan hearing—and that her frankly inquisitive demeanor meant that she probably hadn't actually heard any of the details of the exchanges he'd just shared with Legate Hanshev and Admiral Gardner.

Speaking in quiet, even tones, he brought her up to date about the doom that now hung suspended, like some cosmic sword of Damocles, over Cordian Prime.

T'Pol sat on the low sofa near his desk, her back ramrod-straight as she stared pensively through the ready room's viewport at the warp-smeared stars beyond. Archer remained standing, watching her uneasily.

"Seventy-two hours," she said finally, her gaze remaining light-years away as she continued to consider the ramifications.

He nodded. "More or less."

"And neither Admiral Gardner nor Legate Hanshev will sanction our involvement in trying to prevent it."

He chuckled, but without any real humor. "That's a wonderfully understated Vulcan way of summing up the situation."

Her only reaction to his good-natured jibe was to turn away from the stars and fix her gaze upon his.

"What are you planning to do, Captain?" she said.

He sighed. "That depends on what my exact options really are. How soon can we reach Cordian Prime at maximum warp?"

"Approximately forty-nine hours." Her answer revealed that she, too, had been giving the subject of Coridan Prime a great deal of thought ever since it had first come up eleven days earlier.

"So I might actually be able to do something to stop this," he said, cautiously allowing a small flame of hope to kindle itself in his breast. "Assuming that the Romulan attack arrives later rather than sooner, that is."

"And also assuming that *Enterprise* can successfully locate and intercept the attacker. Of course, in order even to make the attempt you will have to violate Admiral Gardner's direct orders. For the third time, I believe."

"I wasn't keeping score," Archer said. He could see now that he really had no choice at all, or at least no good ones. Meekly following Gardner's orders simply wasn't an option. His career in Starfleet was important to him, but it couldn't compare to the billions of lives that would be forfeited should the Romulan attack succeed.

Archer wished fervently that Trip was at his side right now. It was only after his chief engineer's departure that he had begun to appreciate how reliant he'd become upon his old friend, particularly when truly difficult decisions loomed directly ahead.

Then he glanced at T'Pol's Starfleet-blue collar, where three bright commander's pips glinted beneath the ready room's white overhead lighting.

He looked up into her eyes, which were set into an attentive yet inscrutable Vulcan mask.

"What do *you* think I should do, T'Pol?"

Her answer came after only a moment's hesitation. "While there's still any chance at all of success, I believe you should do what you've more than likely intended to do since before this conversation even began."

Archer felt a grin begin to spread itself slowly across his face. "That's the 'logical' decision you'd make if you were in my place?"

Something not quite identifiable disturbed the tranquil surface of her features, like a tiny pebble tossed into a still pond. "Captain, some things are . . . larger than logic."

He smiled at her. "I promise not to spread around what you just said."

T'Pol nodded in quiet dignity, then rose from the sofa. She walked directly past him and came to a stop at his desk, where she placed her hand beside the desktop comm button.

She turned and regarded him with a deferential expression. "If I may, Captain?"

He made a simple be-my-guest gesture toward the desk.

She punched the comm button. "T'Pol to Mayweather."

"Mayweather here."

"Ensign, bring the ship about. Set a course for the Coridan system. Maximum warp."

"Aye, Commander."

In for a penny, in for a pound, Archer thought as he and his first officer moved toward the ready room door. Both *of us.*

Whatever happened, they would face it together.

FORTY-FOUR

Sunday, February 23, 2155
Enterprise NX-01

"THERE!" Malcolm Reed cried.

Archer turned his command chair toward the tactical station, watching his armory officer's intense expression as the lieutenant moved his hands rapidly across his console.

"Put it up on the screen, Malcolm."

Looking forward over Travis Mayweather's shoulder toward the main viewer, Archer saw a computer-rendered diagram of the ten planets of the Coridan system. A deceptively delicate red line was rapidly inscribing itself across the diagram, beginning outside the system, from the general direction of the Romulan Star Empire.

As the line grew, extending itself forward, the gentle parabola it described put it on a direct course for the most populous world in the system.

"No answer to our hails, Captain," Hoshi said, seated at her communications station on the bridge's port side. "No sign of an identification beam. No navigational beacon, either. Whoever they are, they don't want anybody to know they're coming."

Belligerency confirmed, Archer thought, gripping the arms of his command chair tightly as he studied the tactical diagram on the screen. This was the engraved invitation to war that Admiral Gardner had evidently been waiting to receive. The attack on Coridan Prime had come, just as Trip had warned him two days earlier.

"Intercept course, Travis," Archer said. "Maximum warp." He felt in his gut that they were probably too far away to stop the attacker, but that wasn't going to stop him from trying.

"Aye, Captain," Mayweather said as he hastened to enter the appropriate commands into the helm console. The vibration of the deck plates suddenly intensified, growing more urgent as *Enterprise* responded obediently to the ensign's spurs.

"That thing is moving *fast*," Mayweather said, studying his console's readouts. "My navigational sensors are still having trouble clocking it accurately."

Archer rose from his command chair and faced Malcolm again. "*How* fast is it going?"

Reed consulted his displays. "It's definitely superluminal. If I hadn't been scanning for it in the subspace bands, I wouldn't have been able to make sensor contact with it at all."

"So it's definitely a ship," Archer said. "I've never seen any natural phenomenon that could break the warp barrier."

T'Pol rose from the science station, where she had been hunched over her hooded scanner a moment earlier. "The object is moving at nearly warp five," she reported.

Slightly less than *Enterprise*'s maximum speed. So there was still at least a theoretical possibility of intercepting it.

"Can you identify it?" Archer said.

T'Pol briefly consulted her scanner's display once again, then said, "Negative, Captain. This ship's configuration and warp signature match nothing currently in our database, including anything known to be used by the Romulans."

Damn, Archer thought. *This ship must have come from some Romulan client world whose ships we've never encountered before. These sneaky sons of bitches really can do a fine job of covering their tracks.*

Archer turned back toward the helm. "Travis, how soon can we engage the intruder?"

Mayweather glanced down at his console. "Approximately two minutes and fifteen seconds, sir."

Glancing back toward the science station, the captain saw T'Pol shaking her head bleakly as she anticipated his next question. He slammed his hand on the intercom button on his chair. "Archer to Burch."

"Burch here, Captain," answered the interim chief engineer.

"Lieutenant, I want you to give me all the power you've got."

"Aye, sir."

But even as he listened to the escalating whine of the engines and felt the increasingly agitated quaking of the deck beneath his boots, he knew he was engaging in a useless exercise. *Enterprise* simply wasn't going to reach Coridan Prime in time to stop what was coming.

All he could really do was watch.

He knew that he had tried his best, just as Trip had done. Just as every member of this crew had done, as always.

Only this time, everyone's best simply wasn't going to be good enough.

Centurion R'Kal i'Rrhiol ch'Chulla finished locking down the *S'Task's* helm controls with shaking, sweaty hands. Then she said a final prayer to all the gods of Erebus.

Now there could be no turning back, no matter how strongly her fear assailed her. Her duty to the Empire discharged, R'Kal quietly committed her *daeinos aehallh*—her immortal soul—to the sacred destination that awaited it in the next world. . . .

* * *

Unencumbered by the ceremonial mask that tradition demanded he wear at all diplomatic functions, Ambassador Lekev sagged wearily against the railing in one of the small, private observation chambers aboard the Coridan Defense *Frigate Krekolv*. For the duration of the current crisis, Lekev and other key officials in Coridan Prime's government—including Chancellor Kalev herself—would remain aboard the *Krekolv*, high above the devastation that could rain down on Coridan Prime at any moment.

Lekev looked out the wide window at the planet far below. For now, Coridan Prime clung to its familiar appearance of serenity. As ever, the cloud-streaked blue world continued turning slowly on its axis, basking in the rays of Coridan's single red dwarf star. But the planet, neatly bisected by its nightside terminator so that half of the hemisphere facing Lekev was draped in darkness—relieved in tiny bright spangles and glowing gossamer streaks by the lights of distant cities and highways—seemed to be holding its collective breath, as though anticipating the unthinkable.

Almost directly between the planet and the *Krekolv* lay the complicated array of interlocking modules, docks, and mechanical armatures that comprised Coridan Prime's principal starship construction and repair facility. Several vessels, ranging from small to quite large—all of them evidently not being used in the current planetside evacuation efforts because they were either under repair or still being built—were currently docked at the huge complex, which was slowly drifting across the terminator toward the planet's night side as Lekev watched.

Lekev had never been so weary before in his life. But he had also never before felt as though his labors had been so thoroughly worthwhile. Ever since Jonathan Archer's warning of an imminent, massively destructive

Romulan attack had reached the news media and Coridan Prime's Chancellory, Lekev had become an integral part of Chancellor Kalev's defense and evacuation team. He had spent the past two days helping to coordinate the government's evacuation efforts, personally herding thousands of children, women, and elderly people onto transports for much of that time.

Of course, even a world as wealthy as Coridan Prime lacked the resources to conduct a full-scale planetary evacuation in a matter of mere days. The central world of the Coridan system, which supported more than three billion people, was simply too populous to allow such a plan to be carried out effectively. However, it was at least conceivable to move many millions of people to the regions of the planet considered least vulnerable to the aftermath of a catastrophe like the one about which Archer had warned them.

Though he felt some justifiable pride in the government's alacrity in handling the crisis, the ambassador was well aware that factors other than the welfare of Coridan's people had influenced the chancellor's quick response to the looming disaster. With her government now on extremely vulnerable footing because of Coridan's ongoing civil upheavals, Chancellor Kalev had no choice other than to appear to be decisive and strong.

And although Lekev wasn't at all sanguine about Chancellor Kalev's self-serving political motivations—Lekev had always considered her an inveterate opportunist, forever pandering to her people's lowest common political denominator—he harbored no doubts about his own purpose: he had simply been determined to do everything he could to save as many lives as possible.

"Ambassador."

Lekev turned toward the voice, leaving Coridan Prime slowly turning behind his back.

"Yes, Chulev?" the ambassador said to his unassuming young assistant, who seemed to have conjured himself out of thin air just inside the observation chamber's door.

Chulev bowed his head deferentially. "The last of the chancellor's cabinet members are finally on board, Mister Ambassador. Captain Solnev plans to move the ship to a higher orbit now, as a safety precaution."

"Thank you, Chulev."

"Sir, do you think the Coridan Defense Fleet stands any chance at all of intercepting the attack?"

Lekev offered his aide what he hoped was a reassuring smile. "There's *always* a chance, Chulev."

Certainly there was a chance of detecting and stopping this lethal but so far invisible threat that was now headed straight for Coridan Prime at many multiples of light-speed. A threat that could arrive at any moment, and from any direction, far faster than any eye could register it.

There was indeed a chance. But even with two full days of advance warning, that chance was as infinitesimally small as the Coridan system was gigantically large.

"Is there anything else, Chulev?" Lekev said.

Chulev nodded. "I also came to see if there was anything further you required of me before I retired for the evening."

Lekev hadn't thought about it until just now, but he imagined that faithful young Chulev had probably not gotten any more sleep than he himself had over the past two days.

"No, no, nothing, Chulev. Thank you. Go now, and get some rest." *If you can,* he thought.

Chulev nodded again, then turned back toward the door.

Another thought suddenly occurred to Lekev. "Wait, Chulev."

Chulev paused in the doorway. "Yes, Mister Ambassador?"

"Your family, Chulev. Do you know if they were able to get out of Uridash City?"

Chulev's normally bland, businesslike mien grew bleak. "I haven't been able to reach them, sir. I can only hope they made it onto one of the evacuation transports and got themselves to safe ground."

Safe ground, Lekev thought. The phrase referred to the relatively few land regions on Coridan Prime's surface that weren't so laced with subsurface deposits of dilithium, pergium, and other energy-rich minerals as to become potential deathtraps when the attack finally came.

"You and your family have *my* hopes as well, Chulev," Lekev said before dismissing his assistant again.

Once more alone in the observation chamber, Lekev turned back toward the world of his birth, with nothing to do except wait.

He didn't have to wait long.

The next instant, a klaxon blared at an earsplitting volume. Lekev recognized the sound from Captain Solnev's security briefing. It meant that something unauthorized had just passed sunward through at least one of the Coridan system's two outlying asteroid belts, and at multiwarp speed.

He couldn't remember whether that meant that death would come to Coridan Prime in the space of heartbeats, or sooner still.

Centurion R'Kal's heart raced as the *S'Task*'s computer read off the final countdown. Her mind cast back to memories of a man with hair and eyes as black as space, and the plump, laughing girlchild she had created with him, both of whom First Consul T'Leikha had promised lives of privilege and wealth for the rest of their days.

"Rhi.

"Mne.

"Sei."

A quick glance at her flight console told R'Kal that *S'Task* was moving at its maximum possible speed—and confirmed that her target remained squarely centered in the little vessel's flight path. She had deactivated her viewer as soon as her target had come into range. She had no need—or desire—to see the sapphire world that lay at the end of her trajectory.

"Kre.

"Hwi.

"Lliu."

The impact came so quickly that R'Kal never even saw the flash.

Lekev watched from the sky in fascinated horror as everything he knew and loved instantly changed forever.

The first thing he noticed was the silent orange fireball, the signature of the impact, as it began spreading quickly across the darkened half of Coridan Prime, setting the equatorial continent known as Idanev awash in furious amber flame.

The next thing he noticed was that the starship construction facility was gone. Not drifted out of sight, not lost in the darkness that marked the nightside terminator, not orbited over the horizon, but *gone.*

The *Krekolv* shuddered and lurched. Alarms shrieked. The captain's voice came over the shipwide comspeakers, warning everyone to get to the reinforced sections deeper inside the ship. Lekev saw gleaming metallic debris spinning crazily near the observation port, and knew at once that this was all that remained of Coridan's proud shipyards; whatever had just passed through two asteroid belts on the way to its deadly collision with Coridan Prime had taken out the orbiting facility on its way in, narrowly missing destroying the *Krekolv*—as well as virtually the entire central government of Coridan Prime—in the process.

Lekev ignored the shrieking klaxons and the captain's warning to withdraw to the better-protected sections of the ship. He stood transfixed at the observation port, watching the fireball on the planet's surface spread, no doubt fueled both by the antimatter stocks on the ship that had struck the Idanev continent—what could the missile have been, other than a warp-driven ship?—and by the extensive subsurface deposits of dilithium and other such ores for which Idanev had long been famous. As he watched, even the waters of the vast Idanev Sea seemed to ignite like dry kindling, touching off a blaze that rivaled the brilliance of Coridan's great red sun.

The ambassador didn't want to think about the sheer enormity of this horror, the scale of this act of pure murder, while he hovered above it all, safe.

Safe ground.

Lekev began to sob, and then to weep. He knew that the government's response teams were on the move now, preparing to deploy rather deadly fire-smothering chemicals—materials that would not have been usable if not for the mass evacuations he'd worked so hard to carry out. But he also knew that the death toll would have to be in the hundreds of millions already, in spite of the evacuation program. Additionally, much of Coridan's volatile, energy-bearing mineral wealth would doubtless be consumed completely by subsurface thermal chain reactions long before the spiraling ecological disaster on the ground could be brought to heel—if such an outcome was even possible now.

Lekev watched his charred, wounded world from space, and knew that no matter how hard he worked, it could never be the same again.

FORTY-FIVE

The early twenty-fifth century
Terrebonne Parish, Louisiana

JAKE SETTLED BACK into his chair, his mouth hanging open. "So that's the *real* story of what happened with Coridan?"

"If we believe *this* version of history," Nog said, rubbing his left eye with the back of his hand. He was clearly tired, but seemed intent on finishing the records. Jake knew that he himself couldn't stop watching either.

"We knew that Coridan was hit hard," Jake said, "but the records have always been vague about exactly how it happened. Although this certainly explains why the Coridanites did what they did during the Romulan War."

"According to some of the files that accompanied this, there *were* news stories filed, but they were quickly pulled or denied," Nog said.

"This is a cover-up of *major* proportions," Jake said, looking over at the nearly empty wine bottle and silently deciding that he'd had enough. Between the late hour, the wine, and his age, he was barely keeping a clear head as it was.

"Maybe Gardner pulled some strings to save his own reputation," Nog said. "Wouldn't be the first time an admiral made a boneheaded choice and tried to save face later. I mean, making the decision not to send *Enterprise* to Coridan is . . . well, stupid, at best."

Jake nodded. "The whole rescue of the Aenar is missing from history as well. Was that Gardner, too?"

"I suspect that omission was probably a combination of work by the Andorians and Section 31," Nog said, staring down into the wine at the bottom of his glass. "The Andorians had enough problems back then; they didn't need the whole galaxy knowing that they had a race of powerful telepaths ripe for the picking. They'd kept quiet about them for generations, so why not continue to do so? And if Section 31 helped them, they might have had access to the Aenar when they needed them. We *know* they used telepaths in their later work. Perhaps this was the genesis of that."

Jake sighed heavily. "It's a shame what eventually happened to the Aenar."

Nog nodded silently, a sad expression crossing his face.

"The most galling thing about all of this is that Tucker was erased from these events," Jake said, steepling his hands under his chin. "Even the ones that haven't been tampered with. I mean, he saved countless millions of lives on Coridan that wouldn't have been saved otherwise. And it was *his* warnings—and his decision to help Section 31—that led Captain Archer to rescue the Aenar. Who knows what would have happened if the Romulans had developed a whole fleet of those drones? Or got their hands on a warp-seven drive, either from Ehrehin or the Coridanites?"

Nog smiled. "I always wondered why Tucker had such a great reputation. I mean, he *was* a good engineer, and he *was* an important part of the crew of the first *Enterprise* in Starfleet history. But there was always an aura about him, as though he'd done something *legendary*. But it never made sense to me before."

"Maybe enough of the truth leaked out back then to influence his place in history," Jake said. "After all, anyone with the power to rewrite history can use that clout for *good* purposes, too."

"So, did he survive, or was this really his last hurrah?" Nog asked.

"You don't know?" Jake said, teasing. He cuffed Nog on the arm, the way they used to do when they were kids.

"I told you I hadn't watched it all the way through, hew-mon," Nog brayed, giving Jake a good-natured shove. "You don't believe me?"

Jake held up his hands in surrender. "That's all the roughhousing these old bones can take."

Nog snorted. "Oh, you're *such* an old man."

Jake realized now how much he'd missed the banter and teasing he used to share routinely with his old friend. It really had been too long since they'd been in touch, and he resolved not to let so much time pass between their reunions in the future.

"All right, let's see what happens next," he said, his hand moving to reactivate the holo. "And let's hope for the best."

FORTY-SIX

Sunday, February 23, 2155
Near Romulan space

TRIP REJOICED WHEN THE INSTRUMENTS confirmed that their ship had actually made it past the known boundaries of the Romulan Star Empire. Of course, his joy was mitigated by the grim realization that Admiral Valdore's ships weren't about to be stopped by a border arbitrarily drawn onto some stellar cartographer's maps.

Trip could be thankful at least that he and Ehrehin had managed to widen their small lead over their pursuers, albeit only modestly. *Or until the next time this rust bucket's warp drive conks out,* he thought, hoping he wasn't tempting fate by visualizing that scenario.

Perhaps a minute later, as he spared as much power as he dared to scan the subspace bands, Trip's earlier elation vanished entirely.

God, no. No, no, no. Trip's heart plunged abruptly into a headlong freefall as he continued putting together stray bits and pieces of the farrago of highly agitated chatter that was coming through the console and echoing inside his suit's helmet. A relatively small number of words and phrases predominated, and thanks to the translation gear the Adigeons had installed inside his ears, Trip heard them distinctly in what had to be at least a dozen human and nonhuman languages:

"—*Coridan Prime*—"

"—*struck*—"

"—*Coridan Prime*—"
"—*projectile*—"
"—*Coridan Prime*—"
"—*impact*—"
"—*catastrophe*—"
"—*Coridan disaster zone*—"
"—*continents ablaze*—"
"—*dilithium fires*—"
"—*Coridan Prime*—"
"—*devastation*—"
"—*conflagration*—"
"—*Coridan Prime*—"
"—*billions dead*—"
"—*burning dilithium*—"
"—*Coridan Prime*—"

All Trip could do was sit and imagine the ignition of the mother of all nuclear core meltdowns, touched off by a collision containing orders of magnitude more energy than the asteroid impact that killed off Earth's dinosaurs. Coridan Prime's rich veins of dilithium would have ignited as a result of the Romulan ship's impact, a disaster accompanied by an enormously destructive, uncontrolled release of antimatter from the vessel's engines.

Would the Romulans have sent a pilot on such a mission? Perhaps they'd been planning to use the kidnapped Aenar to remotely launch more such attacks against other worlds, using ever faster and harder-to-intercept ships. His stomach lurched at the thought.

Trip noticed belatedly that Ehrehin was standing beside his seat and leaning toward him, apparently trying to listen in via his own suit's com system. "Tell me, Trip. What's just happened?"

I wasn't fast enough. That's *what's just happened.*

"The Romulans already launched their attack against

Coridan Prime," Trip said aloud, his throat suddenly feeling as dry as Vulcan's Forge. "And it sounds like it turned out pretty much the way you'd expect. The Coridanites probably never stood a chance."

I couldn't protect them from the Romulans. Just like I couldn't protect my sister Lizzie from the Xindi.

Trip felt Ehrehin's gloved hand gently pressing against the padded shoulder of his environmental suit, in what Trip took to be a fatherly gesture of solace. He reached up and placed his own hand on the scientist's arm.

It was only then that he noticed the length of cable that coiled away from his shoulder, leading down to the floor near Ehrehin's seat to the not-quite-closed floor-level compartment that housed the cockpit's power relays.

"What the hell?" Trip tried to stand, but failed because of the unexpectedly hard downward shove the frail old man administered. Trip plopped awkwardly back down into his seat as Ehrehin scrambled away from him, retreating awkwardly toward the aft compartment. Trip struggled out of his chair again, laboriously regaining his feet as he tried to get hold of the cable that he only now realized was attached to the back of his own suit, rather than to Ehrehin's.

But before his glove-clumsy hands could get a solid grip on the cable, a brief flash of light sent blinding golden spots swimming before his eyes, and his muscles suddenly went rigid. Trip's paralyzed body swayed, tipped, and finally crashed all the way down to the deck. He fell with a bone-jarring impact onto his side, his body wedged ungracefully between the pilot's and co-pilot's seats.

The power relays, Trip thought woozily. *He used the power relays to stun me.*

Trip supposed it would have been worse for him had the old man opted to simply immolate him with some hidden disruptor pistol he easily could have picked up during the confusion of their hasty escape.

On the other hand, all he could do was look up helplessly through his faceplate as Ehrehin moved with evident caution back into view and began entering commands Trip couldn't quite see into the pilot's console. From the change in the vibrations in the deck beneath him, Trip could tell that the old man had dropped them out of warp.

Trip's soul deflated as he struggled vainly to move a body that had essentially turned to stone. Soon Valdore's ships would catch up to them, making his failure complete. *Looks like somebody really oversold Spymaster Harris on how well I play with aliens.*

Trip knew that his fate would soon be subject to the tender mercies of the Romulan military. And if Ehrehin could still be taken at face value on at least *one* subject, Admiral Valdore wouldn't be interested in taking him back to Romulus in irons. He fleetingly wished that Ehrehin *had* just burned him down with one of the *Ejhoi Ormiin*'s incendiary guns.

No. There's no way I'm gonna let this happen.

Trip fought harder than ever to move his body. He was rewarded by a loud tapping sound that he quickly realized was one of his boots coming into sharp contact with the bottom of one of the cockpit chairs. He was elated to have achieved movement, albeit uncontrolled.

But Ehrehin must have noticed, because a second brief but crippling surge of current shot through the cable and into Trip's body, penetrating his insulated suit as though it weren't even there. As consciousness began to flee behind another salvo of bright, vision-obscuring spots, his final coherent thoughts were of T'Pol, with whom he still shared an intimate if tenuous mind-link.

And whom he would never again see, nor bring any succor from the grief to which he had already subjected her.

He tumbled over the edge of oblivion wondering whether she would sense the distant echoes of his death.

FORTY-SEVEN

Monday, March 3, 2155
The Presidio, San Francisco

"I REGRET TO INFORM YOU ALL that my government cannot participate in the Coalition under the present circumstances."

I've finally said it, Ambassador Lekev of Coridan thought as the chamber was engulfed by the surprised, collective hush of the assembled delegates and representatives from the four other prospective Coalition worlds. *For good or ill, the deed has at last been done.*

Suddenly it was Lekev's turn to exhibit mute surprise when Ambassador Avaranthi sh'Rothress of Andoria—rather than the more senior Andorian Ambassador Thoris, or the ever-argumentative Gral of Tellar—rose to disperse the shocked, murmur-laced silence. Lekev expected that silence to devolve very quickly into a cacophonous gabble of raised and argumentative voices.

"Why would your government choose to withdraw *now,* of all times?" sh'Rothress said, her voice high-pitched but resonant. "Your home planet has never been more sorely in need of the assistance and support of its allies than it is right now."

A sudden outbreak of perspiration made Lekev's simple, formfitting coverall bind and chafe against his skin, and he released a weary, resigned sigh behind his traditional Coridanite diplomatic mask. Lekev himself had made sh'Rothress's present argument to Chancellor Kalev, as well as to the most influential members of her cabinet, but to no avail. Since he had failed to persuade his government's intransigent senior leadership to alter their course, he'd been faced with a difficult choice: he had to resign, or else meekly fall into line. Even if doing the latter risked so escalating Coridan Prime's ongoing civil strife that the seemingly inevitable collapse of Kalev's government came sooner rather than later.

His furrowed brow concealed behind his mask, Lekev panned his gaze across the rest of the diplomatic assemblage, all of whose constituents seemed tensely anxious to hear his response. Minister T'Pau and Ambassadors Solkar, L'Nel, and Soval of Vulcan looked on in grim silence, while the Tellarite and Andorian contingents seemed almost to be vibrating with barely suppressed alarm. Even the human representatives—Prime Minister Nathan Samuels and Interior Minister Haroun al-Rashid, both of whom were usually far less excitable than either the Tellarites or the Andorians—looked toward Lekev with pleading apprehension in their oddly Coridanite-like eyes.

If only I had the courage to remove this mask, here and now, Lekev thought, wondering whether the humans would find his true face more familiar and less forbidding than the mask that duty and Coridanite tradition dictated that he never remove in the presence of non-Coridanites. But he knew that such a blasphemous act of defiance would not only earn him dismissal and imprisonment on his homeworld—if not outright execution—it would also certainly fail to persuade his government's headstrong chancellor to alter her decision to abandon the new interstellar alliance. Still, doffing the ritual mask that doubtless made Lekev appear so very alien in the eyes of once-valued diplomatic partners might serve to remind at least *some* in Coridan Prime's leadership hierarchy that these Terrans, Vulcans, Tellarites, and

Andorians were far more like the Coridanite people than they were different.

Lekev's eyes caught a hint of motion at the edge of the chamber, and he turned his gaze toward it. On the stairs that connected the edge of the council chamber to the gallery level above it, a group of blue-uniformed figures was making a silent entrance, coming to a quiet halt at the railing that overlooked the tense proceedings. No one else in the room appeared to have noticed their arrival.

The hard, chiseled features and determined look of the foremost of the blue-clad humans drew Lekev's attention most keenly. *Now* there's *a man who probably has sufficient courage to remove whatever masks might stand in his way*, he thought, recalling the words of inspiration that Captain Jonathan Archer had spoken here only a few Earth weeks ago—words that had kept this nascent, fragile Coalition of Planets from completely fracturing during the immediate aftermath of the Terra Prime crisis.

But circumstances had changed greatly since then, particularly for those who still clung to life on the infernal ruin that Coridan Prime had become. And Lekev knew he had no choice other than to face that grim reality squarely.

Turning his gaze back upon sh'Rothress, Lekev took a deep breath, gathered his scattered thoughts, and finally addressed the Andorian junior ambassador's well-taken question. "Coridan cannot presently afford to concern itself with external matters, Ambassador. More than half a billion Coridanites died as a direct result of the attack, and more than that have perished as a consequence of the hugely destructive dilithium fires that resulted from the collision—which our best energy and environmental experts estimate to have consumed at least half of our planetary dilithium reserves. Our science minister believes that Coridan Prime's ecosystems will take at least a century to begin to recover, should a recovery actually prove to be possible."

"You have just enumerated several excellent reasons for allowing the Coalition to stand with you at this time," said T'Pau of Vulcan. She exuded concern, but also a steadfast, rock-solid calm that Lekev could only envy.

Lekev shook his head. "Chancellor Kalev does not see matters that way, nor do the partisans in her government who comprise a majority within the Ruling Assembly."

"But surely the people of your world will see the wisdom of accepting outside help during this crisis," said Prime Minister Samuels of Earth. "Your chancellor can only put her leadership in jeopardy by failing to recognize that."

For the sake of everyone who yet remained alive on his homeworld, Lekev could only hope that the Terran was right. But he knew all too well that the truth was far more complex than Samuels knew, perhaps even defying Lekev's own understanding.

"That is certainly a possibility, Mister Prime Minister," Lekev said, making no attempt to conceal the sadness underlying his words. "Though it is probably a good deal less likely than you believe. We are a proud people, Minister. Most of us would probably not be sanguine about accepting interstellar charity. In the eyes of many, such assistance would be indistinguishable from a military occupation—and if Coridanites feel that their world has been taken by outworlders, they will behave accordingly, driving out the perceived invaders by whatever means they deem necessary. I am certain that none of the remaining Coalition worlds would relish that prospect in the least."

Lekev could only hope that such a scenario might

motivate Coridan Prime's many squabbling political factions to set aside their differences, at least temporarily. But he also felt certain that any pause in the steadily escalating civil war back home would endure only so long as the perception of an outside threat persisted, and not a day longer.

Lapsing into silence, Lekev once again raked his gaze across the faces of each of his diplomatic colleagues, eager to see and hear their reactions, while at the same time dreading them. After a seeming eternity of deceptive stillness, most of the diplomats present—with the exception of the characteristically stoic Vulcans—began airing those reactions, loudly and simultaneously. Nathan Samuels, the nominal chairman of today's proceedings, banged his gavel impotently and all but inaudibly as the room descended further into high-decibel rhetorical chaos.

His grim duty finally discharged, Lekev bowed respectfully toward the chairman's podium, then turned and exited the chamber. Outraged shouts and cries for order echoed and competed behind him.

Archer paused beside the spiral railing, and his senior officers stood quietly behind him on the stairs overlooking the small amphitheater where the delegates to the prospective Coalition of Planets were debating nothing less than the future political alignments of five solar systems.

The discussion—if the tumultuous gabble of indistinguishable shouts and cries that filled the chamber really qualified as such—was going every bit as badly as Archer had feared. *We can't afford to lose Coridan*, he thought glumly. *Especially not while the Romulans are so hell-bent on smashing the Coalition.* A sense of utter helplessness descended upon him as he watched Ambassador Lekev turn and exit the room through one of the lower-level doors.

"It appears you've arrived in the proverbial nick of time once again, Captain," said Doctor Phlox, who was standing slightly behind Archer. He was leaning toward the captain's ear, almost shouting to be heard over the raised voices of the diplomats.

Archer bristled reflexively at the Denobulan's remark. "Phlox, are you expecting me to just leap in there and make everything right?"

Phlox appeared unfazed by Archer's surly tone. "You *have* done it before, Captain."

"I'm an explorer, Phlox, and sometimes a soldier. But I'm no diplomat." He couldn't help but wonder, however, whether he could do a worse job than the alleged diplomats who were trying to shout each other down while the meeting's chairman looked on impotently.

"Frankly, I think Admiral Gardner expects you to contribute something substantive to this meeting," Phlox said, apparently undeterred.

Archer scowled. "How do you mean? He ordered me to be present for the Coalition Compact signing. That's not until Wednesday."

"Well, of course he didn't order you to be here *today*, Captain," Phlox said, his avuncular smile widening until it took on vaguely disconcerting proportions. "He knew it wasn't necessary. He'd have had to lock you up to keep you away."

Archer couldn't help but wonder if Phlox was on to something there; after all, the moment *Enterprise* arrived in Earth orbit, he'd expected Gardner to call him on the carpet because of his unauthorized attempt to reach Coridan Prime ahead of the disaster that had since struck there.

Or maybe Gardner hasn't gone after me because he regrets ordering Enterprise *to head for Earth instead of Coridan.* Archer knew that he would always wonder if he might somehow have intercepted the vessel responsible for the assault against Coridan, if only he'd had a little more time. It was easy to imagine that the admiral, whose sphere of responsibility was much larger than Archer's, was now second-guessing himself in the very same manner.

He imagined that Trip, who'd risked more than anyone else to try to prevent what happened on Coridan, must also be tying himself into knots of misplaced guilt and self-recrimination at this very moment. *That is, if he's even still alive.*

The only consolation Archer could find for any of them—Gardner, Trip, or himself—was his own bedrock certainty that the enormity of the Coridan catastrophe, as terrible as it was, would have been far worse had Trip not gotten his warning through, and had Archer failed to relay that warning to the Coridanites as quickly as he did.

"I can't believe that Chancellor Kalev really thinks that withdrawing from the Coalition is a good idea," said Malcolm Reed, who stood beside Hoshi Sato and Travis Mayweather on the steps immediately behind and above Phlox.

"Kalev has more to face than a planetary disaster," Travis said. "His people have also been in a low-grade civil war for years."

"Maybe the disaster they're dealing with will help them pull together," Hoshi said. "Unite them politically, as one people. Maybe then they'll be ready to enter long-term alliances with other worlds."

Watching the ongoing and still quite loud squabble on the debate floor, Archer wondered what that "readiness" really consisted of—and if it was really possible to maintain it. Even Soval seemed downright furious, and T'Pau appeared to be considering breaking someone's neck with her bare hands. Right now, none of the usually dignified, patrician Vulcans appeared particularly ready for—or deserving of—interstellar goodwill, even though they had achieved domestic political unity centuries ago.

And on that score, what are we *compared to* them? Archer thought, dispirited. Earth's political unity was only around fifteen years old, dating from the time that Earth's last holdout, the Independent Republic of Australia, grudgingly and belatedly followed the rest of the planet's nation-states in joining Earth's global federated government.

"Let's just hope that the Coridanites eventually decide that cooperation means strength and not weakness," Reed said. "Maybe then they'll finally join us. If they don't get co-opted in the meantime by the Klingons, or the Romulans."

Reed's last comment sent a slow shiver down Archer's spine. He hated to think about it, but he knew that Coridan's conquest by either the Klingons or the Romulans—who would end up controlling what still had to be the largest known dilithium reserves in several sectors of space—would mean certain disaster for every planet represented here today, including Earth. And the effect of that disaster would be multiplied by orders of magnitude should the representatives of the remaining worlds of the still-unformed Coalition of Planets—which now seemed to be fracturing before his eyes like an overstressed dilithium crystal—were to succumb to the fear engendered by Coridan's abrupt withdrawal by failing to sign the official Coalition Compact document.

And that signing was scheduled for a mere two days from today. *If this thing falls apart now, the Klingons and the Romulans will find us* all *pretty easy pickings*, Archer thought.

He realized then that Phlox had been absolutely right. He couldn't simply stand by and watch this happen. He had to do *something*, regardless of what he thought of his own diplomatic skills. Even if he were to fall flat on his face, no one could possibly be any worse off for his efforts.

Archer turned to face his crew. "Wait here," he said, raising his voice so he could be heard above the shouts reverberating across the chamber and beyond.

Then he turned again and strode purposefully down the stairs and straight into the center of the bedlam that reigned below.

Nathan Samuels was happy about only one thing: that he wasn't carrying a phase pistol at the moment. With the Coalition literally falling apart before his very eyes, he was certain that he wouldn't have hesitated to use the weapon on himself, and at its most lethal setting.

Once again, he vainly banged his gavel on his lectern. But no one was listening, or could even hear above the tumult.

Then he heard a high-pitched whistle that pierced the wall of noise, startling every raised voice in the room into silence. The Vulcans, whose hearing was no doubt more acute than that of anyone else present, all appeared to be in some real physical pain as a result of the sound.

Samuels was only slightly surprised to note that it was an extremely grim and resolute-looking Jonathan Archer who had stepped into the wide breach that his whistle had torn in the curtain of dismay and raised voices.

"The chair recognizes Captain Jonathan Archer," Samuels said with a slowly spreading smile. He hadn't forgotten the words of encouragement Archer had delivered the last time the Coalition of Planets' debating practices had nearly become lethally contentious, in the wake of John Frederick Paxton's recent acts of terrorism.

Archer took several more steps into the chamber,

stopping when he reached the center, around which were arranged the long, semicircular tables occupied by the delegates.

"Thank you, Minister," he said, nodding respectfully toward Samuels before returning his steely gaze to the assembled delegates, who had nigh miraculously remained quiet but for a few murmurs. Everyone present evidently had respect for this man—even the argumentative Tellarites, apparently—and seemed genuinely curious about what he intended to say.

"In spite of what's happened here today, I still believe this Coalition is going to work," Archer said, addressing the room in a strong, resounding voice.

Respect or no, the senior Tellarite delegate Gral rose to his feet, clearly unable to contain his reaction. "Hah! How can you be so certain of that, human?"

Archer displayed his even, white teeth. Following Tellarite etiquette to the letter, he said, "Because, Ambassador Gral, not even one so socially maladapted as yourself is stupid enough to allow this Coalition to fail."

The Vulcans raised surprised eyebrows while Minister Haroun al-Rashid grinned and Ambassador Thoris glowered. Gral folded his arms before him and nodded, but hurled no invective in the captain's direction. Samuels breathed a quiet sigh of relief when Gral quietly took his seat again, evidently having taken Archer's Tellarite-style harangue as amicable, and not ironic or hostile.

"All of you are probably far better equipped than I am to imagine the consequences to all of us should this Coalition fail," Archer continued. "And nothing illustrates that better than what has just happened on Coridan Prime."

Archer began pacing slowly across the room's center, gesturing broadly with his hands as he spoke. "When I first took command of *Enterprise*, I expected to be surprised by whatever we might find out there. I also expected that we would make some new friends. I knew that we probably wouldn't be able to avoid making a few new adversaries as well. So far, we've encountered more than our share of the latter. The Suliban. The Klingons. The Tandarans. The Xindi.

"Now we face the Romulans, who have already done more damage than all of the others combined. And we don't even know what they *look* like yet. Like the Klingons, they can bring each of our worlds to its knees if they manage to prevent us from trading with the Coridanites for what's left of their energy reserves. Of course, that trade will be damned tough to manage without the common purpose of a broad interstellar alliance.

"And what happens next, with no Coalition for any of us to lean on? I'll tell you what." Archer pointed toward Gral as he continued to pace. "You Tellarites will start squabbling again with the Coridanites over trade issues, and that'll mean war. It won't be long before the Andorians get dragged into it." He glowered at Thoris, then faced Soval and T'Pau with a very hard stare. "Maybe the Vulcans will have to send ships and troops at that point, too, since the Andorians have been your main competitors for dilithium for a long time, and since neither of you has ever had much reason to trust the other."

Still pacing, Archer turned to face both Samuels and al-Rashid, the latter having taken a seat near the chairman's podium at one of the curved tables. "Earth will probably get swept into it by then, too."

Archer paused as he made his way back to the exact geographical center of the room, from which he addressed everyone present. Samuels heard not a murmur from any of the delegates nor from their aides. The captain commanded everyone's full attention in a way that Samuels couldn't help but envy.

"But I don't think you need any of this explained to you by an explorer—or by the soldier I'll be forced to become if you lose your nerve and make the wrong decision here today. All of you know there's only one way the Romulans can succeed. Each one of our worlds has had to learn the painful lesson that united we stand, divided we fall. Let us all stand together." Archer walked back toward the spiral stairs at the chamber's edge.

Gral slowly rose again from his seat and began applauding, establishing a slow, steady rhythm that echoed across the chamber. The echo intensified, and it took Samuels a moment to realize that Soval and T'Pau had joined him, followed by al-Rashid and Thoris, a few moments later. Samuels himself added to the rising wall of noise, a sense of relief flooding him as he realized that the cause might not be entirely lost after all.

Samuels banged his gavel on his lectern and declared a brief recess.

"How do you *do* that, sir?" Travis asked as he prepped Shuttlepod One for launch from the landing pad on the council building's roof.

"I was just thinking the very same thing," said Malcolm, who had just finished strapping into one of the seats positioned slightly aft of the cockpit, near those occupied by Hoshi and Phlox. "I have to assume that the Academy offers special command-track speech courses."

Archer grinned over his shoulder at Malcolm from the copilot's seat beside Travis. "What exactly are you talking about, Malcolm?"

"I'm referring to that rousing little gem of extemporaneous persuasive oratory you just delivered to the delegates, sir," Malcolm said, returning Archer's grin.

"You don't need to push so hard to get that promotion, Malcolm," Archer said in a bantering tone. "What's important is that everybody has agreed to go ahead and sign the Coalition Compact on Wednesday, just as originally scheduled."

Everybody except the Coridanites, that is, Archer thought sadly, though he still hoped that Coridan's chancellor would reconsider her decision sooner or later; Kalev would have to realize at some point that the Romulan Star Empire probably wasn't finished taking shots at her homeworld.

"I'm sure T'Pol is going to be sorry she missed your speech when we get back aboard *Enterprise* and tell her all about it," Malcolm said.

Archer snorted dismissively. "You know how much T'Pol hates listening to speeches. She's probably thanking her lucky stars that she drew bridge duty instead. Besides, all I did was say what I'm sure Samuels and al-Rashid were both already thinking. If I hadn't said it then, one or the other of them probably would have eventually."

"You needn't be so coy, sir," said Malcolm, his words dripping with a degree of admiration that went way past Archer's threshold of tolerance. "You were bloody brilliant."

Archer tried to summon a stern frown, but found that it wouldn't quite fit over his smile. "All right, Malcolm. Belay that, or you can forget about promotions altogether. One more word of hero-worship and I might even consider busting you down to bilge cleaner."

"If you ask me, the delegates were way overdue to have somebody read them the riot act," Hoshi said. "None of the Coalition worlds can afford to have them squabbling. Not with the Romulans on the move."

Archer nodded silently in Hoshi's direction. *They know they'd better hang together. Unless they want to hang separately.*

"What *about* the Romulans, Captain?" Travis said as he brought the antigrav thrusters on line and gently raised the shuttlepod into the cloud-scudded, late-afternoon sky. A heavy fog appeared to be rolling in from the bay.

Archer wasn't quite sure what to make of the question. "They're still out there, Travis. And if we're not extremely careful, they'll be *here* sooner or later."

"That's exactly my point, sir. All the delegates are well aware of what the Romulans did to Coridan Prime—so why haven't they discussed making a formal declaration of war against the Romulans?"

Archer sighed wearily. During the short recess in the proceedings just before he had returned to the shuttlepod with his officers, he had privately posed that very question directly to Prime Minister Samuels.

"They can't," Archer said, shaking his head in frustration. "Their hands are tied by the language of the Coalition Compact itself."

"But I thought the Compact contained a clause that says an attack against *one* Coalition member is the same as an attack against *all* the Coalition members," Malcolm said in unconcealed bemusement. "Just like the old NATO agreements from a couple of hundred years ago."

"The Compact *does* say that, Malcolm," Archer said. "But Coridan won't be signing the Compact on Wednesday, remember? They've dropped out. Therefore, the Coalition Council won't be able to invoke that clause on their behalf."

"There must be *something* they can do, Captain," Travis said, sounding as frustrated as Archer felt. "After all, we all know that the Romulans represent a clear threat."

"Knowing something and proving it aren't quite the same thing, Travis," Archer said as he stared through the front windows, beyond which the cobalt sky had already given way to a deep purple, which in turn was quickly yielding to the blackness of space. "As far as we can tell, the projectile ship that wiped out half of Coridan didn't leave a trace of itself behind. And even if it did, the Coridanites aren't likely to let us turn what's left of their home planet upside down searching for it. Besides, several parties other than the Romulans are claiming 'credit' for what happened on Coridan. And the Romulans themselves, of course, aren't talking."

A bright pinpoint of light hung over the Earth's nightward terminator. Archer watched as it grew swiftly in brightness until it became recognizable as something far closer to Earth than any of the distant, fixed stars behind it. Its familiar saucer-and-twin-nacelle shape continued growing steadily in the window.

Enterprise. Home.

While Travis continued making his characteristically graceful approach to the ship, Hoshi spoke in incredulous tones. "So without hard evidence that the Romulans were actually behind the Coridan Prime attack . . ."

Archer completed the thought for her, though he realized that everyone present had probably already done the geopolitical math. "The Coalition Council would be debating a *preemptive* war declaration."

Preemptive war, of course, was strictly forbidden by the Compact. Given the terrible consequences such wars had wrought upon Earth during the previous century—particularly during the Eugenics Wars—Archer saw this prohibition as a wise policy, at least in the abstract. He disagreed vehemently, however, with its present application to the Romulans, whose responsibility for the Coridan attack was really beyond doubt, at least so far as Archer was concerned.

On the one hand, he could certainly understand why the Coalition delegations from both Earth and Vulcan would be loath even to *appear* to be in violation of the charter before its ink was dry. On the other, he hoped he could count on the Andorians and the Tellarites to have the great good sense to stand on ceremony less than the rest of the Coalition would.

Like Section 31? Archer asked himself, not liking the answer in the least. But he had to face the sad truth of the matter, which was that another Coridan-like disaster might strike anywhere within the Coalition, and at any time. Perhaps even right here on Earth, whose wounds from the horrendous Xindi attack of not quite two years earlier still had yet to fully heal.

As Mayweather adroitly maneuvered Shuttlepod One back into its launch bay, Archer thought, *If the Romulans ever hit Earth as hard as they did Coridan, at least we'll have the support of the other Coalition worlds.*

FORTY-EIGHT

Tuesday, March 4, 2155
San Francisco

DRAWING THE HOOD of his dark traveler's robe up so that it covered most of his head, Charles Tucker rounded the damp and deserted street corner, hugging the shadows of two of Grant Avenue's most venerable brick buildings as he entered an even darker alley. Since this particular crevice between ancient pre-Third World War structures was located just off Greenwich Street, Trip had expected to catch at least a glimpse of historic Coit Tower looming overhead; however, the evening fog's omnipresence and the Moon's utter absence conspired to render the familiar landmark effectively invisible.

A perfect night for a spy to be out and about, Trip thought, suppressing an absurd urge to giggle.

The all but impenetrable gloom all around made Trip distinctly uncomfortable, to say nothing of the ripe-garbage smell that must have originated inside one of the local restaurants' large, back-alley trash bins. He smiled as he reminded himself that he had survived encounters with any number of far more dangerous things, particularly over the course of the past couple of weeks. Still, he couldn't avoid considering how ironic it would be if he were to get killed by a street criminal—or maybe even by some nut-job Terra Prime-loyal Vulcan basher—in some dark and stinking alley on his own home planet, fresh from having survived a harrowing sojourn deep inside Romulan territory.

"Good evening, Commander," intoned a quiet, even voice shrouded in darkness. The voice, which sounded uncomfortably close, made Trip jump involuntarily, though he recognized it immediately.

"Let's meet in your office next time," Trip said. "I'm not a big fan of these film noir locations. I want a bigger ship. And a pony."

Harris stepped closer, chuckling as Trip finally glimpsed his silhouette. The other man's unassuming shape seemed to devour whatever scant illumination was present; Trip decided this was because he was clad in the same dark, leatherlike garment he'd been wearing the last time they had communicated. According to Malcolm, it was almost a required uniform for bureau insiders.

"Sorry to have startled you, Commander," Harris said.

Trip shook his head. "Nothing much really startles me these days."

"I suppose not." Harris chuckled again. "I'm eager to read your report. Coridan notwithstanding, I trust congratulations are in order for a job well done?"

"You tell me, Harris," Trip said as he handed Harris a small cylindrical object. "For starters, here's the data rod Phuong was carrying."

Trip's eyes had adjusted well enough to the darkness to see the wariness taking shape on Harris's face. "*Was* carrying?" the spymaster said.

"When the Romulans killed him," Trip said, nodding. "I'm sorry to have to bring you such bad news."

"I trust you also have some better news, Commander. Please tell me you made Phuong's sacrifice mean something." The wariness in Harris's expression had given way to unmistakable grief, making Trip regret having broken the news of Phuong's death so bluntly.

Trip felt that grief quite keenly as well, having come

to regard Phuong as a comrade-in-arms—and now one that had fallen in a battle that he, Trip, had survived, at no small cost in terms of self-recrimination. Trip supposed he would never stop asking himself if he could have done more to save Phuong.

"I owe him at least that much," Trip said at length. "I have good reason to believe that the Romulans won't succeed in perfecting Doctor Ehrehin's warp-seven drive anytime soon. Here are the details." He handed Harris a second data rod.

"Were you able to bring Ehrehin to Earth?" Harris wanted to know. "Or did you have to kill him?"

Trip shook his head. "Neither."

Harris's scowl pierced the darkness. "Then how can you have 'good reason' to believe *anything*, Commander?"

Trip responded with a wry smile. "I guess you had to have been there, Harris. You see, we discovered a huge gap in our intelligence about the Romulans. Starting with this." He lowered the hood of his robe, turning his head so that Harris could get a good look at his elegantly pointed ears and gracefully upswept eyebrows.

Harris gasped, though he was clearly trying to contain his astonishment. "My God. The Adigeon surgeons made you look like a Vulcan."

Trip nodded. "But only because Romulans and Vulcans are 'kissing cousins,' so to speak. I know, it surprised hell out of me and Phuong, too. Of course, we're going to have to keep this under our hats."

"Of course, Commander. This will have to become one of the bureau's most closely guarded secrets. If this were to become public knowledge, it would probably shred the Coalition Compact." Harris paused, sighing, evidently still reeling from what he'd just learned. Then he fixed Trip with a hard gaze, like a pair of searchlights lancing through the gloom. "We are both going to have to work harder than ever to manage the Romulan problem now."

"We," Trip thought. *As if my staying on this Romulan thing has already been decided.*

Trip found it impossible to avoid making an accusation. "You never expected my 'death' to be temporary, did you, Harris?"

The spymaster paused, sighed again, then answered with surprising candor. "No, Commander, you're wrong. I expected your demise to be *entirely* temporary—unless, of course, you had gotten yourself killed by the Romulans, which you have to admit wasn't all that unlikely a prospect, especially on one's first covert assignment. What I *didn't* expect was that, of the two of you, Tinh Hoc Phuong would be the one to die."

To hell with this, Trip thought, and very nearly began walking away. "Thanks for that ringing vote of confidence in my abilities, Harris."

"You've just *proven* your abilities, Commander—by surviving, just the way you always did when you kept *Enterprise* up and running out on the galactic frontier. And if you've really managed to short-circuit the Romulans' warp-seven drive the way you say you have, then you've accomplished in just a couple of weeks what would probably have taken Phuong's covert ops at least as many months to pull off. On top of that, the Coalition wouldn't even have known about the suicide attack against Coridan Prime if not for your warnings, which we received as well. With Phuong dead, the bureau—and Earth—will need your abilities more than ever if we're to keep the Romulans from pulling ahead of us technologically."

"I agree," Trip said. "But I think I ought to start by getting my ears bobbed and heading out to Coridan Prime to see about getting one of *their* warp-seven ships to Earth. Beat the Romulans to the punch, just in case I turn out to be wrong about Ehrehin."

Harris shook his head. "We already have a number of disguised covert operatives working on just that, Commander, all of them well versed in the intricacies of Coridanite culture, politics, and technology. To be frank, in spite of all their expertise, I'm not all that hopeful for their chances of success, given the very thorough job the Romulans did when they wrecked Coridan's shipyards."

Trip didn't particularly like the drift of the conversation. "You're saying you want to send me back to where I just came from—where I damned near *died*—because I'm the only one who's already dressed for the part?"

Harris seemed not to notice Trip's unhappy tone. "There's no better candidate, now that Phuong is dead. We need *you* back inside the Romulan sphere of influence, Commander, cultivating more permanent sources of humanoid intel for us there. However successful you might have been in monkey-wrenching Doctor Ehrehin's warp-seven program—and regardless of the outcome of our Coridan ops—the Romulan Star Empire isn't going to stop trying to outdo us in the race for better tactical technology or faster engines. And whether the Coalition members want to believe it or not, the Coridan disaster *was* the first step toward war."

He paused, letting the words sink in a bit before continuing. "So can we count on you for just one more mission among the Romulans, Commander? And more importantly: Can Earth and the rest of the Coalition count on you?"

"You need me to stay dead," Trip stated. The idea was very nearly unbearable.

"Only for a while, Commander. A year or two, perhaps. Our most pessimistic experts foresee perhaps five years of Romulan conflict at the very outside."

Five years of my life, if my life lasts that long, Trip thought grimly. *Against the safety of my planet, and everyone I love.*

Trip wanted nothing more than to go back to his family. To T'Pol. To his old life aboard *Enterprise.* To reassure everyone he cared about that he was all right. And to remain for the rest of his days out of the shadows where he now dwelled.

But he also knew that he couldn't escape his duty to his home planet. His duty to his dead sister, and to the millions of others who had been summarily slain because nobody had seen an alien threat coming out of the clear blue sky until after it was too late.

His duty to all the teeming billions of innocents on Vulcan, on Tellar, on Andoria—and on Earth—who could die just as those slain by the Xindi had died. Just as innumerable Coridanites had been murdered by the Romulans.

If he were to fail to act.

"All right," Trip said at length.

The spymaster smiled and shook his hand, then placed another data rod squarely in Trip's palm. "Outstanding, Commander. Here are the mission details, biometrically coded so that only you can read the data. You will, of course, have access to all of the bureau's resources while you are in our sphere of influence. But you will also, of course, be entirely on your own if you should be captured while operating within Romulan space."

Trip nodded, feeling as though he had just signed a pact with the devil himself. Maybe he had. But what was his alternative?

"I know the drill, Harris."

"You'll be leaving on a civilian transport bound for Vulcan on Thursday morning. Once on Vulcan, you'll catch a Rigelian freighter for the next leg of your voyage. The details, along with the documents and background you'll need to support your new undercover identities, are all provided on the data rod."

Before melting back into the shadows, Harris added, "Make the most of the time between now and your departure date, Commander."

As he exited the alley and began retracing his steps along Grant Avenue's fog-slicked sidewalks back toward his hotel, Trip decided that he would do precisely what Harris had suggested. Though maybe not quite in the way he anticipated.

FORTY-NINE

Wednesday, March 5, 2155
Candlestick Park, San Francisco

ARCHER DIDN'T MUCH LIKE the small dressing room that Nathan Samuels' people had issued him. Located near the open-air center of the ancient public auditorium, the little chamber had walls constructed of what appeared to be old cinder blocks that had been repainted countless times over the centuries, and the room felt paradoxically cold and drafty in spite of the alleged presence of one of the finest environmental control systems currently available. According to local legend, the entire stadium had *always* been cold and drafty, even in the dog days of summer nearly two centuries ago when one of the facility's main uses had been for the exhibition of the now sadly defunct sport of baseball.

The cursor on the padd he'd set down on the dressing room table blinked at him mockingly, as though the device were aware that he was having an extraordinarily difficult time making the final revisions to his speech. He knew, of course, that he should have *ceased* tinkering with it at least a day or two ago, but he felt insecure enough as a public speaker—in spite of Malcolm's having sung the praises of his extemporaneous speechifying—to feel a continuous need to edit and revise the words he'd already written and rewritten.

Those words were, after all, going to be delivered live before an audience of nearly one hundred thousand humans and assorted other sentients from across the sector and beyond, to say nothing of the billions who would view the day's ceremonies remotely from their various homeworlds. All of them expected to see history made when the Coalition Compact was finally signed later this afternoon by the assembled representatives of four diverse worlds.

Archer started when he heard a sharp knock against the dressing room door, then forced his jangled nerves back under control. Rising from his seat once he felt reasonably composed, he turned to face the door.

"Come."

The old-fashioned door, doubtless centuries old, swung open on its steel hinges and admitted a characteristically stoic T'Pol. Archer glanced down at her right hand, from which dangled a small suitcase; he knew it contained a small cache of personal effects that was bound for Trip's parents. Like T'Pol, they had been given no alternative to believing the lie to which Archer had been a party. Once again, guilt clutched at his heart, though he knew he had no choice other than to endure it in silence. He noted that T'Pol was holding the case's handle gingerly rather than squeezing it in a death grip that might have shattered it. Not for the first time, he envied her Vulcan composure, though he couldn't help but wonder how much the effort was costing her.

T'Pol quickly looked him up and down, then raised a critical eyebrow. "I'm gratified to see that you are already wearing your dress uniform, Captain. However, I would have recommended that you don it while the room's lights were activated."

Archer sighed and tugged at the buttons that fastened the uniform's somewhat constricting white collar. "Very funny, T'Pol." He turned toward the mirror, from which a very tired and nervous-looking man stared back. "It's not like I wear one of these every day, you know."

"Indeed."

"Does it *really* look that bad?" He turned back toward her.

She set the suitcase down and approached him. "Stand still," she said as he silently endured the indignity of allowing her to finish straightening his slightly skewed collar. Just as she finished, her communicator beeped, and she backed up a few paces to take the incoming message.

Archer retrieved his padd and returned his attention to its display while fervently wishing that he'd stayed in his quarters aboard *Enterprise* to finish preparing his speech. The comforting presence of Porthos, as well as the absence of a multitude of hero-worshipers just outside his door, would have gone a long way toward calming his frayed nerves. And the ever-loyal beagle wouldn't have even *considered* offering him any unsolicited sartorial critiques.

He doubly regretted having left the ship after he heard T'Pol's next utterance: "Captain, Commander Tucker's parents have just arrived."

Charles Anthony Tucker, Jr., had always been tall and broad in the shoulders, not at all given to putting on excess weight. But after Lizzie's unexpected death nearly two years earlier, his frame had become much sparer, almost gaunt. Since he hadn't wanted to look as though his apparel had come from a tent and awning company, he'd had to buy all new clothes a few months after the Xindi attack.

Today he felt certain that he'd soon have to replace his entire wardrobe yet again.

During their nearly four decades of marriage, Charles's wife, Elaine, frequently told him that he had the face of a man who loved to laugh. He wished he could still be that man, if only for her. If he could, then perhaps he might be able to do something about the deep lines of pain and stress that stood out in sharp relief across Elaine's once smooth and porcelain-like features.

But Charles had never felt less like laughing than he did today. He and Elaine had come to Candlestick Auditorium, after all, essentially to bury the younger of their two sons—even though there was, of course, no actual body to bury, thanks to the "burial in space" clause Trip had written into his will.

Just as there had been nothing to bury after Trip's sister Lizzie had been at the wrong place at the wrong time when those damned Xindi had come calling, dealing death from a calm blue springtime sky. . . .

Charles vainly forced himself to consider that much younger version of himself who so loved to laugh. But instead, all he could really focus on was how much that man had lost during the past couple of years. *Thank goodness we still have Albert,* he told himself, though the thought did little to assuage his grief. Albert had declined Archer's invitation to meet with him today, explaining that he preferred to stay away from the day's ceremonies. He'd said he preferred to grieve in his own way, with his husband, Miguel, and their own small nucleus of friends and loved ones. Charles looked forward to seeing their only surviving child again soon, but wished with all his heart that the circumstances could have been different.

He entered the narrow but brightly illuminated conference room alongside Elaine, who gripped her small handbag so hard that her knuckles whitened until they made a perfect contrast with her somber black dress. They both continued standing as they faced the man who had guided them through the auditorium's vast backstage labyrinth, the sympathetic-looking male Denobulan who had identified himself as Phlox, the chief medical officer on *Enterprise*—and as one of Trip's closest friends. The Denobulan's startlingly blue eyes gleamed with unshed tears, making him appear so distraught that Charles's heart went out to *him*.

"I'm sure you did everything you could to save him, Doctor," Elaine said, just as Charles was about to say something very similar. He hoped that the doctor would at least take whatever comfort he could from their absolution.

"Thank you, Mrs. Tucker," said Phlox, though he suddenly looked even more distraught than he had before. "But when you've treated, saved, and lost as many patients as I have . . ." He interrupted himself briefly, as though trying to gather his thoughts, or perhaps reining himself in for fear of saying too much. After taking a deep breath that he let out almost as a sigh, he resumed: "Well, let's just say that no physician can ever be completely above second-guessing himself—particularly if the patient is someone to whom the doctor feels close."

The room's single door opened again, admitting a man and a woman, both of them displaying somber expressions. The latter was a tall, attractive Vulcan dressed unexpectedly in a Starfleet uniform; a neatly aligned trio of rectangular rank bars on her collar identified her as a commander. The Vulcan woman clutched a small suitcase at her side.

Commander T'Pol, Charles thought, recalling her image from numerous news vids, as well as the many times Trip had mentioned her during his correspondences home. Although there were many things, of course, that his son had left unsaid, Charles always had the impression that Trip had been rather sweet on T'Pol, or perhaps vice versa. When the news services reported that the terrorist John Frederick Paxton had created a human-Vulcan hybrid infant using DNA from both Trip and T'Pol, Charles had found his dashed dreams of grandfatherhood suddenly rekindled, which surprised him after the terrible blow Lizzie's death had dealt the whole family. Of course, fate had quashed those hopes with finality when it decided to take Trip from them as well as Lizzie.

Charles immediately recognized the grim-faced, somewhat taller human standing beside T'Pol as Jonny Archer, to whom Trip had first introduced both him and Elaine some twenty years earlier, though neither Charles nor Elaine had seen him very much at all during most of the last decade or so. Though he was smartly turned out in a formal blue-and-white Starfleet dress uniform, the captain seemed to have aged quite a bit since he'd last seen his face on the compic, about two weeks ago. Charles supposed that between the Xindi crisis he had already endured, the recent Coridan tragedy, and the large role the media had credited him with in the formation of the Coalition of Planets, this man must almost literally be carrying the weight of entire worlds upon his wide shoulders.

Archer extended his right hand, and Charles shook it numbly as Phlox began making introductions all around. Then Charles tried to make the Vulcan hand sign for T'Pol in lieu of a handshake—he was proud that he understood at least that much about Vulcan culture—but gave up when he realized that the gesture was slightly beyond his ability.

"Thank you for your letter, Captain," Elaine said, shaking the captain's hand and offering an almost courtly nod to T'Pol. "I guess I really wasn't expecting something so uplifting after you called us with . . . the news about Trip."

A distraught expression very much like the one he'd seen Phlox display crossed Archer's face like a bank of dark storm clouds. "I'm so sorry about this, Gracie. It's not the kind of letter a captain ever wants to have to write. But I felt I owed it to you both, as Trip's commanding officer. And as his friend. You both deserve to know how heroically your son died."

A sudden upwelling of tears rose, poised on the edge of Charles's lower lids, like a dam about to break. Archer's face looked distorted, viewed through a prism of grief. Charles closed his eyes so that all he could see was Trip's smile. Trip as an infant, an eight-year-old, a teen, a young man. All he could hear was Trip's laugh. All he could think was that it was good to know that his son had made so many wonderful, loyal friends during his far too brief life.

Realizing that he was no longer in any condition to speak, Charles felt enormous gratitude toward both Archer and T'Pol when they seemed to wish to do the bulk of the talking.

"Within a few minutes, you both will be conducted to seats in the VIP section," T'Pol said.

Archer nodded. "I wanted to be sure both of you got to see and hear as much of today's ceremonies and speeches as you wanted. I know that Trip . . ." He paused for a moment to compose himself. "He would have wanted you to see the future that his sacrifice will help the rest of us build."

The Vulcan woman raised the small suitcase she carried, then set it down almost reverently on a nearby conference table.

"I have gathered Commander Tucker's personal effects," she said.

Charles walked to the table. Like a man dreaming, and therefore not entirely in control of events, he laid the case flat and thumbed the simple latch mechanism, popping the lid open.

Atop a neat blue pile of folded Starfleet uniforms sat a small articulated toy replica of Doctor Frankenstein's monster, patterned after Boris Karloff from the ancient flatscreen movies. Karloff had been a favorite of Trip's from about the age of seven, even though those grainy old black-and-white movies sometimes gave him nightmares. Charles smiled as he picked up the figure and held it up to see it more closely. For nearly four years, this little prop had accompanied his son across countless light-years. What had it represented to Trip? His ability to face without flinching the things that scared him the most? Charles looked to Elaine, saw the tears streaming down her face while his own remained poised at the brink.

Placing the action figure to one side of the case, he saw that directly atop the uniforms lay a framed photograph of a triumphantly grinning Trip. Trip was holding one of Charles's own heavy-duty, duranium-reinforced fishing rods, along with a glistening marlin that had to have weighed nearly as much as a man. Elaine had taken that photo when they'd gone deep-sea fishing off the Gulf Coast not long before Trip had accepted his assignment to *Enterprise*. That entire day came back to him in a flash: the smell of spray and sunblock as they'd fished, the taste of the hush puppies and fried catfish and beer they'd had for dinner that night.

The sight of Trip's wide smile.

Charles felt Elaine take his hand and squeeze it tightly, as though she were gripping a lifeline. He recalled how hard he'd always tried to surround Trip with laughter rather than tears. Despite that, more tears rose, threatening to displace the ones that had already taken up residence in the corners of his eyes. *Simple hydraulic engineering,* he thought. *Liquids can't be compressed. Trip would appreciate that.*

Still hand in hand with his wife, Charles turned away from the open case so that he faced Archer and T'Pol. "Thank you," he said, after he'd finally found his voice. "I think we're ready to find our seats now."

Let's hope the future Archer invited us to witness is worth it, he thought.

And then the tears spilled over the brink, and kept coming in torrents.

Mom and Dad must have arrived by now, Trip thought, standing in a small vestibule adjacent to the auditorium's broad corridors and seats. Dressed again in a simple, dark Vulcan traveler's robe, he felt reasonably unobtrusive as he swept his gaze across the crowds that were quickly accumulating everywhere in the old stadium, from the field-level seats to the bleachers, and all the way up to the skyboxes. Anyone who saw him would assume he was just another of the hundreds of Vulcans currently living on Earth, or perhaps one of the hundreds more that had arrived just this week specifically to observe today's formal signing of the Coalition Compact, and the forging of galactic history.

Trip had to admit to himself that he was half-hoping to see his parents, or perhaps his brother Bert, somewhere in the crowd. He felt certain that Captain Archer would have moved entire worlds to make certain that everyone in his family was given seats in one of the auditorium's best VIP boxes. And while he ached to see his folks and his brother again, and wanted nothing more than to reassure them, part of him was glad that he *hadn't* encountered them, and actually hoped that he wouldn't; he simply didn't trust himself not to reveal his presence to them, and with the Romulan threat still gathering on the horizon, he knew he didn't dare risk doing anything that might compromise his usefulness on that front.

Although his parents' faces, thankfully, didn't pop out of the crowd as he scanned it, he did unexpectedly recognize a different pair of faces. Though they wore civilian clothes rather than the MACO uniforms that had become so ubiquitous aboard *Enterprise* during the darkest days of the Xindi crisis, Trip immediately recognized the luxuriant long black hair of Corporal Selma Guitierrez and the strong cleft chin of Sergeant Nelson Kemper. Guitierrez wore a denim baby-carrier that contained an infant, blissfully sleeping despite the noise and tumult of the still-settling crowd.

That must be their little girl, Trip thought, working hard to suppress an extremely un-Vulcan smile as the young couple and their child walked directly past him without taking any apparent notice, evidently on their way to their seats. Trip recalled that Guitierrez's pregnancy, which had occurred during *Enterprise's* Xindi hunt in '53, had been the reason both she and Kemper had subsequently left the service. Their little girl—he wasn't certain, but he thought he recalled hearing that they'd named her either Ellen or Elena—had to be close to a year old by now.

Although the Kemper family quickly passed out of his view and into the milling crowd, the child had remained in Trip's sight long enough to churn up the painful memory of standing with T'Pol in the parched, red Vulcan desert to bury little Elizabeth. At that instant, all the tragic might-have-beens he'd either faced or turned his back on throughout his life returned to him at once, threatening to bury him in an emotional rockslide. Not wanting to allow anyone to see a weeping Vulcan, he stuffed his rising agony back down as best he could.

He started walking toward one of the STAFF ONLY entrances, grateful that the skill set of a competent spy overlapped considerably with that of a decorated Starfleet chief engineer. His path took him directly past one of the VIP skybox seating areas, where he saw some other familiar faces, the sight of which filled him with still more wistful thoughts. T'Pol wasn't among them, making him both glad and disappointed. But there was

Malcolm, who knew the truth about his "death," seated next to Hoshi and Travis, who didn't. Whatever grief his absence had caused them appeared for the moment to have been subsumed by their eagerness to hear Captain Archer's upcoming speech.

None of them had looked in his direction, and if they had, all they would have seen was yet another Vulcan observer. *Just another alien face, in a sea of alien faces.*

Trip moved on, more determined than ever to do what he'd come here to do. His parents might not have been sufficiently trained in the art of keeping secrets to allow him to risk revealing himself to them today. But T'Pol was a different matter.

Of all the people he cared about—and had been forced to deceive so cruelly, thanks both to the Romulans and Section 31—*she* was certainly capable of handling the plain truth.

"There they are," said Albert Edward Tucker, stabbing his left index finger into the general direction of the VIP boxes adjacent to the one in which he sat.

"What?" said Miguel Cristiano Salazar, who was seated beside Albert. He strained to see whatever or whoever it was that his partner was trying to call to his attention.

It was obvious to him that Bert's grief over the loss of his younger brother was still eating him alive. Over the past week or so, as the date of the Coalition Compact ceremonies had drawn close, that grief seemed to have begun to metamorphose into an almost incandescent rage.

"Enterprise officers, I'm pretty sure," Tucker said, pointing again for emphasis.

"Where?"

"There." Bert sounded impatient, exasperated, but Miguel knew it was only the pain talking. Still, it could

get tiresome. "There, in the box that Vulcan guy in the robes just passed."

"Oh," Miguel said, finally picking the three dark blue uniforms out of the still settling crowd. "I see them now. And stop *pointing*, Bert. This isn't a World Cup match."

Bert stopped pointing, but his mood didn't become any more pleasant. "If they're sitting in one of the VIP boxes, then they must have known Trip pretty well."

"Wouldn't *Enterprise* officers have been able to get better seats than that?" Miguel said.

Bert answered in an unintelligible mumble and continued staring daggers at the trio of Starfleet officers who might or might not have been Trip's shipmates.

Miguel wished that Bert had made his decision to attend today's event when some of the better VIP boxes—like the one near the stage, where Bert's parents had been seated—had still been available. That way, Bert might never have even caught sight of Trip's alleged colleagues.

Of course, better seats would have put Bert that much closer to Captain Archer. Miguel felt grateful, at least, that Bert had declined the captain's invitation to meet with him today backstage, to receive Archer's personal condolences. He certainly didn't want to have to manage *that* confrontation.

Finally tiring of watching Bert glare sullenly in the direction of the Starfleet people, Miguel said, "It's not their fault, you know."

Bert turned that harsh glare upon Miguel. "*Isn't* it, Mike? Any one of them could have been the one to die. Why did it have to be Trip instead?"

Miguel had tried to be patient, but Bert was pushing him to his limit. "That's not fair. The galaxy is a dangerous place."

"You're goddamned right it is. And Trip might still be

alive if Starfleet wasn't out there sticking its head into the lion's mouth. Lizzie, too."

Folding his arms across his chest, Miguel said, "Why don't you just start up your own Terra Prime cell, then? I hear they're looking for a new leader now that Paxton is in jail."

Bert reacted with speechless incredulity, as though he'd just been slapped across the face. "My God, Mike. Is that what you think of me? That I'm some sort of racist isolationist?"

Miguel regretted his words the instant they'd left this lips. After all, hadn't Terra Prime wounded Bert as well? The death of the half-Vulcan child that Paxton's terrorists had created, in part, from Trip's flesh, was no doubt also still an open wound.

"You tell me, Bert," he said, trying to shift to a more conciliatory tone. "Look, I know you're in pain. But here we are, among thousands of people who've come from all over the planet—a lot of them are even from *other* planets—to celebrate the arrival of the future."

A future that just might make your family's sacrifices worthwhile, he thought. He knew he couldn't utter the thought aloud—at least, not yet.

Bert merely fixed him with another hard stare that seemed to last for hours.

Finally, Bert's expression softened. "I'm sorry, Mike. I know you're just trying to help. I guess I'm just not in the mood to celebrate. At least . . . not yet."

Miguel nodded, and gave Bert a gentle hug. He knew that the grieving process always took time, just as it had for Bert after Elizabeth Tucker died in the Xindi attack. And he understood that some wounds could tear the scabs right off all the older ones.

But he also knew that there were only two directions in which one could look: forward and backward. As he tried to focus his attention forward, onto the distant stage from which the future was to be summoned today, he noted that Bert had turned in his seat, to resume staring in the direction of the three Starfleet officers.

Backward, at least for now.

Miguel sighed. It was likely to be a very long afternoon.

The box in which Malcolm Reed found himself seated was so high that he half expected to succumb to explosive decompression at any moment. Or at least a real gully-washer of a nosebleed.

With Hoshi Sato and Travis Mayweather seated to his right, he looked below and saw a carpet of seats and boxes, occupied by both ordinary civilians and official delegates from worlds across the sector and beyond, spreading downward and away into apparent infinity.

And just beyond lay the stage, which supported the raised, brightly spotlighted dais where galactic history was to be made beneath an impossibly distant backdrop of blue-globe-and-laurel-leaf Earth flags, complemented by the multicolored banners and symbols of three other worlds. Unlike the stadium's multitude of seats, boxes, and viewing stands, the dais remained empty as yet. The air seemed charged with anticipation.

But not quite enough to ameliorate Reed's annoyance at the all but cosmic distance that separated him and his colleagues from the dais from which their captain was to give his address.

"Are you certain these are the right seats?" Reed asked no one in particular.

"Yep," Mayweather said, speaking just loudly enough to be heard above the murmurs of the not-quite-settled crowd.

Reed harrumphed under his breath. "They don't seem very 'VIP' to me."

"I'm sure the admiral wanted us to have a view that took in the *scope* of the occasion," Hoshi said with what might have been the merest ghost of a smirk.

Reed wasn't quite certain whether or not she was being ironic, although he had assumed that Admiral Gardner had put them up here as a passive-aggressive way of punishing both Captain Archer and his command staff for having attempted to intervene in the Coridan Prime disaster rather than proceeding immediately home to Earth, per Gardner's initial orders.

"From this distance you can't tell an Andorian from a Tellarite," he grumped.

After Phlox conducted Trip's grieving parents toward one of the VIP boxes, Archer returned to his ancient, crumbling dressing room to finish making the final preparations for his speech, for better or worse.

When he opened the door, he found a black-robed male Vulcan waiting for him.

"Can I help you?" he asked, wondering how his visitor had gotten past the security personnel who had been hovering nearly invisibly nearby ever since Archer and his crew had arrived at Candlestick.

Archer's jaw dropped like an anchor when the Vulcan responded with an incongruous ear-to-ear grin—and spoke with a voice that he had half expected never to hear again.

"Cap'n, it's *me*. It's Trip."

Archer's bemusement quickly gave way to a broad smile of his own. He walked over to his old friend and grabbed him in an unself-conscious bear hug.

"Easy, Captain. In spite of how I look these days, my ribs are still only human."

Archer released him and took a step back, studying his old friend's surgically altered features, his dark hair, prominent brow, and upswept eyebrows. Most striking of all were Trip's elegantly tapered pointed ears. He doubted that Trip's own parents would have recognized him, but he also had the grace not to utter that particular thought aloud.

"So you're a Vulcan now," Archer said with a wry smile. "Not that I'm not happy to see you, Trip . . . but why are you here?"

"I figured you'd be nervous about delivering your speech, so I won't stay long. Written it yet, by the way?" Trip's grin broadened.

Archer made a mock frown as he picked up the padd that contained the text of his speech, along with an intimidatingly vast amount of source material drawn from the historical records of four planets. The device now displayed the surprisingly profound words, first uttered centuries ago, of Shallash, the second Liberator of Tellar; Archer was determined to find a way to work them into his own presentation somehow.

"Still working on it," he finally said noncommittally.

"I came to wish you luck, Jonathan," Trip said. Archer couldn't remember the last time Trip had addressed him by his first name, but he knew that his old friend had more than earned the right. Besides, Trip was no longer his subordinate. He was simply a friend, and an ally.

Trip reached into his black robe and withdrew a single folded sheet of paper, which he placed carefully in Archer's hands. "I also came to ask you to deliver this to T'Pol before you give your speech," he said. "I'd tell you to knock 'em dead, by the way, but that would probably be in poor taste. So how about 'break a leg' instead? I'll be watching."

With that, Trip turned and exited through the same door Archer had used to enter. Still carrying his padd, Archer tucked the note into his jacket, then followed Trip's footsteps back out into the corridor.

He wasn't a bit surprised to find no trace of his friend.

Raising his padd to resume his eleventh-hour revision of his speech, Archer walked down the corridor and entered a backstage anteroom adjacent to a staircase that led upward to the raised speaker's dais on the auditorium's wide stage.

Looking up briefly from the padd, he saw that T'Pol and Phlox were already awaiting him there, the latter offering a broad smile, the former bearing a disapproving scowl. Once again, T'Pol strode up to him and began adjusting his collar, making him feel like a little kid who'd just been caught sneaking away to the playground while still dressed up in his Sunday best.

"Please stand still," she said sternly. With an involuntary roll of his eyes, Archer complied while still trying to see the text on his padd.

But T'Pol evidently wasn't quite finished upbraiding him. "If you hadn't waited until the last minute, you would have had time to memorize your speech."

His gaze still on the scrolling text, he murmured, "You sound like my ninth-grade teacher."

Archer glanced away from his display and saw that Phlox was examining a padd of his own. The doctor seemed quite impressed by whatever he was reading.

"There are dignitaries here from *eighteen* different worlds," Phlox said in his customarily punctilious but upbeat tones. "It's a good sign. I wouldn't be surprised if this alliance begins to expand before we know it." He paused to fix his azure-eyed gaze firmly upon Archer. "You should be very proud of yourself, Captain."

Archer waved his padd in the air, then returned to studying his speech. "I'll be proud of myself if I get this speech out in one piece."

Phlox shook his head in gentle reprimand. "That's *not* what I meant."

Archer allowed the hand that held the padd to drop to his side momentarily, and met Phlox's mild gaze. "I know what you meant, Phlox. And I appreciate it. But this is not about me."

T'Pol looked annoyed, at least for a Vulcan. "Why do so many humans refuse to take credit where credit is due? There are times when modesty and humility are quite illogical."

Archer noticed some movement in his peripheral vision. He turned toward the stairs that led up to the dais, and saw a young, shaved-headed male Starfleet ensign walking resolutely down the steps toward him.

"Whenever you're ready, sir," the ensign said after coming to attention before him.

Archer nodded to the ensign, dismissing him, and the young man immediately disappeared back up the steps, no doubt to join the detachment charged with guarding the various dignitaries and speakers who would be using it throughout the day as the formal Coalition Compact signing ceremony neared. Beyond the anteroom, Archer could hear the murmur of the crowd receding as his date with destiny approached. They were waiting for him.

"Well, I've got three wives waiting," Phlox said, walking toward Archer. "I'd better go and join them." He paused beside Archer for a moment and placed a fatherly hand on his shoulder. "I'd wish you good luck, Captain, but you've always had an ample supply." Phlox's warm smile stretched until it became impossibly broad.

"Thank you, Doctor," Archer said, then watched the doctor's back as it retreated from the antechamber. Turning toward T'Pol, the captain favored the Vulcan with a wry grin. "You'd better get out there. You don't want to miss me screwing this thing up."

T'Pol looked uncharacteristically uncomfortable. "I'm going to remain down here, if you don't mind."

"You never liked crowds, did you?" Archer said, smiling. Padd still in hand, he turned toward the stairs and began ascending them while trying to construct an emotional levee to contain the rising tide of nervousness he was feeling. *They're waiting for me out there!*

T'Pol spoke behind him. "You look very . . . heroic."

Archer paused on the staircase in mid-step, allowing this rare compliment from the usually stoic Vulcan to wash over him. He turned back toward her and stepped back down into the antechamber.

He stood face-to-face with T'Pol, not wishing to trivialize the moment by smiling or joking about it. Although he knew it went against everything he understood about Vulcan propriety, he gathered her into a warm but platonic embrace. He wasn't certain, but it seemed to him that she was trying to return the hug, at least insofar as a Vulcan could consent to making such an apparent display of emotion.

The embrace lingered for a measureless interval until Archer heard the ocean-tide noise of the crowd rising again. They were still waiting for the day's first speaker, perhaps checking their chronometers and wondering what had become of him.

As he gently separated from her, he remembered the note that Trip had entrusted to him—a note that Archer hadn't looked at and whose contents Trip hadn't explained. He reached into his coat and extracted the single folded sheet, wondering whether it contained a final farewell—and if he'd see his oldest friend ever again.

Archer wordlessly handed her the note, then withdrew a few paces as she unfolded the paper and read its contents, her unlined face betraying not the slightest reaction as her dark eyes absorbed Trip's message.

Then something unidentifiable, and perhaps even worrisome, passed behind T'Pol's dark eyes.

"Are you sure you don't want to come up and watch the speeches?" Archer asked.

She nodded. "Thank you, Captain. I am quite certain."

Archer nodded silently, then walked back to the steps that led up to the dais.

It's finally showtime, he thought, his heart racing as he ascended the steps yet again. He mounted the stage and strode onto the dais, clutching his padd nearly hard enough to shatter it.

And as he tried vainly to take in the impossible hugeness of the audience, Archer decided he'd much rather face a dozen bloodthirsty, *d'k tahg*-wielding Klingons.

FIFTY

Wednesday, March 5, 2155
Candlestick Park, San Francisco

As T'POL OPENED THE DOOR to Archer's dressing room, apprehension and eagerness struggled within her even more vehemently than the debates between Sessinek, T'Karik, and Surak that her mother T'Les had told her about so often during her childhood.

She was greeted by a young-looking male Vulcan who sat in the small room's single chair as if he had been waiting for her to arrive. The first peculiarity she noticed about him was his rather prominent brow ridge.

The second was his voice.

"Hello, T'Pol," he said. Although his face was unfamiliar—unless, she thought, she had glimpsed it once before in a dream—his voice, though altered, was unmistakable. After all, very few Vulcans had ever picked up an Alabama-Florida accent.

"Trip?" In spite of what had been written on the extremely surprising note the captain had delivered to her—an apparently genuine handwritten message from Trip Tucker that purported to have been written *today*—she could scarcely contain her surprise at seeing him.

A sheepish grin spread itself across the man's face, confirming his identity as conclusively as had the sound of his voice. "Maybe I dreamed it, but I'm *pretty* sure I told you we weren't going to lose touch," he said. "By the way, that Starfleet uniform looks really good on you."

He approached her and gently took the folded white

sheet of paper she still carried between her suddenly nerveless fingers. "Mind if I take this back? I have to keep the fact that I'm still alive a secret. From *most* people, that is." He folded the sheet again and tucked it into a pocket inside his black traveler's robe.

It occurred to her then that the instinct she had experienced immediately after Trip's "death" now stood vindicated. Her early, and apparently illogical, conviction that Trip—along with the mind-link she'd shared with him before their romantic entanglement had dissolved—had indeed somehow survived had been borne out. She was dumbstruck for a seeming eternity, until she found the one word that best expressed her bewildered state of mind:

"Why?"

His smile faded, and a look of intense regret colored his now uncannily Vulcanoid features. "The Romulans were about to perfect a new warp seven–capable spacedrive. Somebody had to infiltrate the project and stop them. Somebody who already had some close-up familiarity with their technology."

"And did you succeed in stopping this project?"

He chuckled, shaking his head. "You know, I'm still not completely sure about that. I guess we'll all find out soon enough. I can only hope I did a better job on that front than I did in preventing their attack on Coridan."

"The devastation on Coridan Prime would have been far worse had we not warned them. I assume you had something to do with enabling us to do that." She paused, then added, "*You* were Lazarus."

Trip nodded. "I warned Captain Archer about what the Romulans were planning for Coridan as quickly as I could. I wasn't quite quick enough, though. But I keep telling myself my warning made *some* sort of difference anyway, just so I can get to sleep at night. Sometimes it even works."

"So out of all the possible candidates in Starfleet, Starfleet Command selected *you* to infiltrate the Romulan Star Empire."

"Yes. But it wasn't exactly Starfleet Command. It's a covert ops bureau buried deep inside Starfleet Intelligence. In fact, Starfleet Command would probably deny even knowing about it."

"Deceit," she said, her voice edged more sharply than she had intended. "How very human."

"Oh, come on, T'Pol," he said, his brow furrowing. "Humans sure as hell don't have a monopoly on deceit."

"Vulcans do not make a habit of lying, or of concealing the truth."

"Then you folks must be quite a bit better at it than *we* are. But even Vulcans get caught sometimes in the middle of a whopper. Do I have to remind you about the Vulcan operatives who were secretly spying on the Andorians on P'Jem? Or how your former fearless leader V'Las set up those terrorist attacks last year, then tried to pin 'em on T'Pau and the other Syrrannites?"

Including T'Les, my mother, she thought. T'Les had died during that terrible time.

Though Trip's words stung her, T'Pol carefully schooled her mien to maintain its best display of Vulcan equanimity. There was no point in continuing to argue the point; she knew that he was right. Nevertheless, she still felt incensed—illogically, she had to admit—that he had deigned, whether under orders or not, to keep concealed from her something as important as the faking of his own death. She stared at him in silence, not trusting herself to speak again until she succeeded in calming her roiling emotions, or at least in centering herself somewhat.

"You should have taken me into your confidence," she said at length, finally breaking the silence that had begun to stretch awkwardly between them.

"You're probably right, T'Pol. And I'm sorry." His eyes glistened with regret, and she was startled when she realized that her own eyes were waging a struggle of their own against a rush of unshed tears. *Probably*?

"Who else knows?" she said aloud.

Tears finally began running freely down his cheeks. "Malcolm. Phlox. The captain."

Only those with an operational need to know, she thought, understanding but still somewhat resentful. And angry. And hurt.

"I'm so sorry, T'Pol."

Still battling her own emotions, she said, "I am . . . gratified that you survived."

"Gratified, but also damned pissed off," Trip said, smiling through his tears.

"Vulcans do not experience such base emotions."

"Horse apples they don't."

"I certainly hope no one else sees you in this emotional state," she said, though in truth she wasn't eager to let anybody see *her* anytime soon either.

"What, are you afraid I'll give Vulcans a bad name?" Trip said, chuckling at his own comment as he wiped at his still-flowing tears with the heels of both hands.

T'Pol stood watching him, feeling awkward and inadequate to do anything to comfort him, or herself for that matter. Her arms felt like useless vestigial appendages, so she clasped her hands behind her back to keep them out of her way. She wondered how he would react if she were to initiate the same sort of affectionate human embrace to which Captain Archer had spontaneously resorted only a few minutes ago.

Then, as she studied his overwrought face, a fundamental realization struck her: He had said he had been sent into the Romulan Star Empire as an infiltrator. Therefore Charles Tucker now wore the face of a Romulan.

And the face of a Romulan was all but indistinguishable from that of a Vulcan.

"Your . . . appearance suggests that Romulans and Vulcans are kindred species," T'Pol said once she'd found her voice again.

"Looks that way."

Oddly, her emotions began to calm now that she had an external problem of some importance with which to occupy her mind. "Does Captain Archer know?"

"I'm sure he'll figure it out once he's a little bit less preoccupied."

"Of course," she said, nodding, training her attention back upon the core of Trip's surprising revelation. "If the Romulans truly are a throwback to the warlike, colonizing period of our ancient ancestors, then all the Coalition worlds are in grave danger. The Romulans will never stop attacking us voluntarily."

"I know," Trip said.

At that moment T'Pol understood with immediate, heart-breaking certainty that he intended to go back among them, and probably quite soon. She could sense from the resolve in his voice that it would not only be useless to try to talk him out of it, but also that it would be dangerous to the Coalition should his mission be interrupted or delayed.

And there was another grave danger as well, one that could not only disproportionately affect her homeworld, but might also shatter the entire alliance if it wasn't addressed properly.

"The Coalition will be fragile for a long time, Trip, even after the delegates sign the Compact," she said.

"I figured that kind of goes without saying," he said, regarding her with evident curiosity. "What exactly are you getting at?"

"I speak of Vulcan's . . . evident kinship with the Romulans. Should this secret ever get out, the other

Coalition members—even Earth—will distrust us. The Andorians would almost certainly demand our withdrawal from the alliance, or else abandon it themselves. Even if the Andorian-Vulcan war that would almost inevitably result didn't directly involve Earth and Tellar, it would render the entire Coalition more vulnerable than ever to Romulan conquest."

Trip seemed to be listening with what T'Pol regarded as an appropriately Vulcan degree of sobriety—so long as one overlooked his tear-streaked cheeks, and his greenish bloodshot eyes.

"Looks like we've both done the political math the same way," he said after she'd finished making her case. "Don't worry, T'Pol. Your people's secret is safe with me. And I'm just as sure it'll be safe with my . . . associates here on Earth. And with Captain Archer, too. As far as I know, that's everyone else who's seen the dirty family linen. I'm sure it's going to be kept strictly off the record."

She gathered Trip's meaning clearly, despite his often perplexing human metaphors. Relief swept through her, like the cooling winter nightwinds that blew so infrequently across the desiccated sands of Gol.

"And *your* secret is safe with *me*." She felt certain that there was no way she would voluntarily reveal to anyone what had actually become of him. Being officially dead was his best protection, considering the dangers inherent in interstellar espionage, and the consequences, should his true fate and activities be revealed, were too grave to be contemplated.

He grinned again. "I know, T'Pol. And I think I finally came to understand that when I was in Romulan space and thought I was going to die there. . . .

"I only wish I'd realized it sooner."

He approached her closely then, put his arms around her, and gathered her in for a kiss. Though surprised, she did not resist, and even found herself reciprocating.

Nearly as soon as it had begun, the kiss was over. "So long, T'Pol. I'll see you again after this Romulan business is finished. I promise."

Then he turned, headed for the door, and was gone.

T'Pol stood in the tiny dressing room for several minutes, stunned and silent, alone with her thoughts and her regrets. So much still remained unsaid between them, though she supposed that neither of them had any real need to hear any of it spoken aloud by the other. After all, the vestige of their mind-link still remained.

She knew that the only constructive—and logical—thing she could do was to look forward, hoping, if not entirely believing, that their paths would indeed cross again someday.

But she was also logical enough to know that no one could entirely avoid taking at least an occasional backward glance.

Reaching into the small hip pocket on her uniform, she extracted a tiny gleaming metal bracelet and raised it nearly to eye level. The dressing room's bright lights immediately brought out its finely etched inscription:

Elizabeth T'Les Tucker.

Her dead infant daughter, and Trip's, named for Trip's dead sister and T'Pol's dead mother. Created with test tubes and incubators by a craven Terran criminal, the child's remains now lay buried on Vulcan, though she wasn't born there, nor anywhere else, strictly speaking. T'Les was buried under those very same sands as well.

Whatever else she could have been or might have become, little Elizabeth now represented the vanishingly small chance that T'Pol and Trip might have had for a future together.

Silently, T'Pol put the bracelet away.

Then she allowed herself to weep once again, this time for everything that might have been.

* * *

Archer found the air in the open-dome stadium damned cold, despite the relative thickness of his dress-uniform jacket. Standing under an overcast sky, his heart was lodged firmly in his throat as he stood at the podium, facing countless thousands of people hailing from no less than nineteen planets, including Earth. Addressing them, as well as the cameras that would carry his words to billions more, was a daunting prospect, to say the least.

And a lot of these people consider me a hero, dammit! he thought, cursing himself for his continued nervousness. He looked up from the lectern that concealed his padd, imagining all the faces that he couldn't see clearly in the enormous, faceless crowd, while focusing his gaze on the nearest rows. These were filled with luminaries of numerous species, and many of them would affix their signatures to the historic Coalition Compact later today.

He felt buffeted by the intense pressure of their eyes and their expectations: Admirals Black and Gardner from Starfleet Command; Captain Erika Hernandez, Archer's one-time lover and current counterpart aboard the *Starship Columbia* NX-02; Prime Minister Nathan Samuels and Interior Minister Haroun al-Rashid of Earth; Ambassadors Soval, Solkar, and L'Nel, and Minister T'Pau of Vulcan; Ambassadors Thoris and sh'Rothress of Andoria, as well as Shran and his new bondmates, Shenar, Vishri, and Jhamel; Ambassador Gral of Tellar; and various members of the press, most of whom were equipped with head-mounted imaging equipment.

All of it trained squarely upon *him*, like some mass-media firing squad.

Archer scowled involuntarily when he noticed Travis's old flame, the covert Starfleet Intelligence operative Gannet Brooks, sitting among the ranks of the journalists. The press—including the estimable Ms. Brooks—had picked up and run with certain unauthorized remarks made off the record by someone in Nathan Samuels' office concerning Archer's Monday conversation with the prime minister about the Coalition delegates' reluctance to take military action against the Romulans, despite their having attacked Coridan Prime. Although both Archer and Samuels had been ducking interview requests ever since the story had broken—Archer had offered only a neutral but calculatedly surly "no comment" in response to every question the press had hurled his way in public—many among the press seemed convinced that Archer intended to bang the drums of war from the lectern today.

He remained just as convinced as ever that the Romulan threat simply wasn't going to go away, at least not without a great deal of military "encouragement." But a declaration of war was the last thing he wanted this day to be about.

Though he couldn't see any members of his crew, Archer tried to draw strength from the knowledge that Malcolm, Travis, Hoshi, and Phlox were here somewhere pulling for him, probably along with anyone else from *Enterprise* for whom Lieutenant O'Neill had authorized shore leave.

Of course, his crew would expect eloquence from him, too. *It's too damned bad Starfleet Academy doesn't really offer elocution classes for captains*, he thought, recalling the observation Malcolm had made a couple of days earlier.

His gaze swept over the nearby Vulcan contingent, settling quickly on Soval, who was watching him with his usual reserved expression, though Archer thought he spied a fair amount of curiosity on the diplomat's face as well. How could he flounder on the dais right in front of Soval? For years, the Vulcan ambassador had considered Archer an unworthy failure, until he'd finally won Soval over following the Terra Prime crisis.

Archer closed his eyes and took a deep breath, reaching more deeply into his inner resources than he could ever remember having done before. He recalled having briefly carried the disembodied *katra* of the long-dead Vulcan philosopher Surak around in his head when he had helped T'Pau gain control of Vulcan's government last year. Some of Surak's knowledge seemed to have stayed with him for a short while afterward, such as the ability to use the paralyzing Vulcan nerve-pinch that T'Pol had never succeeded in teaching him.

Surak, old friend, if there's any trace of you still left in my brain, I hope you'll let me use it to calm myself the hell down.

Archer opened his eyes, offered the crowd a gentle smile, and began to speak.

FIFTY-ONE

**Day Eight, Month of Havreen
Dartha City, Romulus**

CENTURION TERIX, once again charged with conducting Admiral Valdore's briefing, finally appeared to be winding down his presentation. "Coridan Prime has suffered what can only be described as a mortal wound, Admiral."

Ah, to be so young and optimistic, Valdore thought. He allowed the barest trace of a smile to cross his broad lips as he recalled his own stint as a callow young centurion.

Valdore sat behind the heavy sherawood desk in his office in the Romulan Hall of State, scowling up at the semitransparent holographic image that hovered in the air between himself and Terix.

"There are wounds," Valdore said, "and there are *wounds*. I myself have recovered from many injuries that others had declared mortal. In a century or so, the Coridanites could well experience just such a healing themselves."

The centurion seemed taken aback by Valdore's reaction. "They lost more than half a billion people in the initial attack alone, Admiral. Along with fully half of their planetary dilithium reserves."

"Which leaves them with a remaining population of upwards of two billion. As well as around half of their planetary dilithium reserves."

"May I point out, Admiral, that Coridan Prime has withdrawn from the Earth alliance?" Terix said. "The so-called Coalition of Planets has been more than correspondingly weakened, not only by Coridan's departure, but also by the sudden and precipitous diminishment of locally available dilithium."

Valdore nodded. "Indeed. But our incomplete destruction of Coridan seems to have made the worlds that have opted to *remain* within that alliance more steadfast about maintaining it."

The centurion's face was flushing a florid, coppery green. "Permission to speak freely, sir?" he said.

"I fear no man's perception of the truth, Centurion. Speak."

"Forgive me, Admiral, but if I didn't know better, I'd say you were determined to wrest defeat from the *bhath* of victory."

Valdore chuckled at that. "I am merely attempting to see the likely consequences of the Coridan attack through the same lens through which First Consul T'Leikha is likely to view them. And likewise, the Praetor. You may do well to think of such exercises as a survival skill." As he made this last comment, he bared his even, white teeth in a manner that could never be confused with a smile. And while his teeth bore scant resemblance to the curved, serrated *bhath* of the mountain-dwelling, fiercely predatory *hnoiyikar* to which the centurion had referred, Valdore could see that the younger man had taken his meaning instantly.

Terix swallowed hard as he offered the traditional elbow-against-the-heart military salute. "Of course, Admiral. I beg forgiveness."

"Dismissed."

After the young officer had turned on his heel and exited, Valdore remained alone in his office, staring silently at the image of a devastated Coridan that the centurion had neglected to deactivate.

Despite its superficial resemblance to a military victory, the sight brought him no joy. Indeed, the suicide mission had been planned by First Consul T'Leikha and the interim military commanders who had been in charge of the Romulan Star Empire's defense and war making during the time of Valdore's recent imprisonment following the unfortunate drone-ship affair.

In fact, Valdore's direct involvement in Coridan's devastation had extended only to giving the plan's final "execute" order, lest he balk and face the wrath of both T'Leikha and the Praetor, and end up either executed himself, or find himself dwelling again in a dim, dank cell like the one the former Senator Vrax now occupied. Valdore had seen no alternative to authorizing the attack, though he felt confident that he never would have conceived such a plan had all the decisions been left up to him.

But these facts did little to expiate the guilt Valdore felt as he watched the image of Coridan's wreckage continue in its slow, stately rotation through the glare of its virtual sun. *Was this really a mission for a military man?* he thought. *Or was it simply the slaughter of innocent women and children and elders in their beds?*

Though he was far too loyal a soldier to speak his misgivings aloud, the part of him that had decades earlier served as a senator alongside Vrax couldn't help but wonder if the Coridan attack was truly worthy of the unsheathing of even a single fighter's Honor Blade.

And the guilt he carried was exacerbated by the realization that the destruction he'd sanctioned had failed to achieve its intended political effect: the abortion of the signing of the official Earth alliance agreement, which was to have crippled the so-called Coalition's ability to defend itself.

But the official papers *had* been signed, according to the Coalition worlds' own public newsnets, which the Empire's intelligence services had long made a habit of monitoring as closely as possible. Now the four remaining Coalition of Planets partners were apparently cleaving together more closely than ever before, and their civilian media were loudly asking when their governments intended to do something about "the Romulan threat." Therefore Valdore's hopes for a campaign of relatively resistance-free—and therefore largely bloodless—conquest now lay dashed at his feet.

There would be war, *real* war rather than the mere subjugation of demoralized and therefore already half-conquered worlds. And it would certainly come soon, despite the Coalition's relative paucity of dilithium to power its ships.

But that wasn't the worst of it. Thanks to a recent extremely poor run of luck, Valdore lacked access to the new Aenar telepaths he'd need if the fleet's newest telepresence-piloted warships were to fly effectively and on schedule. He was also beginning to lose faith that the recently recovered and bizarrely incoherent Ehrehin was really capable of delivering a working singularity-powered stardrive prototype any time in the foreseeable future. What had those dissidents done to him before he'd been picked up by the fleet, alone and nearly catatonic in a small escape pod? Of course, the hope always remained that Ehrehin would one day become lucid enough again to carry the project to fruition, but Valdore had long made it a practice never to rely overmuch upon hope as a tactical weapon. If Ehrehin's revolutionary new stardrive remained an unrealized dream, then the destruction of all that Coridan dilithium—and the carnage associated with it—would all have been for naught.

With a weary sigh, Valdore reached across his desk and thumbed a control toggle, which caused the battered and charred remains of Coridan to vanish abruptly. Touching a button beside the toggle, he said, "Valdore to Nijil."

"Nijil here, Admiral." The chief technologist's voice sounded logy and rough-edged. Since Valdore knew that the abstemious scientist had never acquired the habit of drinking to excess, he chose to regard that as a good sign: Nijil also understood that war loomed near, and was therefore pushing himself as close to exhaustion as he dared in order to steer the inevitable conflict toward its most favorable possible outcome.

"Nijil, how is development progressing on the new generation of weaponry?" Valdore asked.

"So far, Admiral, all the development and testing have progressed exactly according to the Senate-approved schedules."

"Very good, Nijil. But it's not quite good enough. I need you to expedite the project. . . ."

After dismissing the harried engineer, Valdore considered the practicalities yet again. All previous attempts to create a practical invisibility cloak for the concealment of large, manned vessels had always resulted in the test ship's destruction after a few brief *siure*. Despite the many failed trials he had authorized over the years, Valdore remained convinced that such a device could be the key to Romulan military supremacy.

They cannot fight what they cannot see, he thought, smiling a predator's smile.

FIFTY-TWO

Friday, March 21, 2155
Deep space

CHARLES TUCKER LEANED AGAINST the thick transparent aluminum observation port, watching as the ship's warp field distorted the shapes and colors of the stars beyond far more slowly than seemed right. The private Rigelian passenger transport was by no means new, but Trip could at least be thankful that it wasn't so ancient that it had to stay below warp three to keep from blowing itself up. Still, he found it difficult to get used to traveling across so many light-years at such a leisurely pace.

He also found it hard to prevent that impatience from showing, though he knew that he needed to keep that emotion reined in—along with all the rest of his emotions, for that matter—for however many weeks or months remained in this voyage. He still appeared to be a Vulcan, and would pose as a kevas and trillium merchant from that world for the duration of his passage out to the galactic hinterlands, from which he planned to take a prearranged yet discreet ride on an Adigeon freighter back into Romulan space.

Once there, he would begin his next assignment on behalf of Section 31, the Coalition of Planets, and the people of the planet Earth.

And the great state of Florida, he thought, trying to picture the faces of his parents and his brother. He was dismayed at how difficult it was for him to imagine those faces smiling, rather than contorted with grief.

Tired of viewing the gently shifting starfield, and just as tired of the distinctly unfriendly stink-eye he was receiving from the towering, fanged purser who apparently didn't much like passengers getting handprints on his tidy observation ports, Trip began walking through one of the narrow guest corridors toward his modest stateroom.

Once the door was securely shut behind him, he kicked off his boots, then carried them to a small closet, where he stowed them neatly. He would have preferred either canvas deck shoes—which would have been conspicuously out of place on a Vulcan, even way out in the middle of nowhere—or at least something that felt more like real leather than his boots did. Unfortunately, he had to content himself with footwear made from vegetable fiber in order to continue passing himself off as a Vulcan, who were all essentially against the killing of animals, either for food or for apparel.

Trip stepped back to the stateroom's desk, where he had left a small data padd beside the sample case that contained the gemstones that were part of his merchant cover-identity. Raising the padd, he inserted the encryption-protected data rod. He'd been carrying the rod since shortly after he'd recovered consciousness in a stolen *Ejhoi Ormiin* scout ship moving at high warp through Coalition space, very close to regions claimed by the Romulan Star Empire. He had already lost count of the number of times he'd played the rod's message— a message that had clearly been recorded in haste while Trip had been lying insensate on the cockpit's deck plates.

He keyed the start command, and the lined and surprisingly kindly-looking face of Doctor Ehrehin—partially obscured by the environmental suit helmet he'd been wearing at the time—appeared yet again on the padd's small display.

"I hope you will have the opportunity to view this message in safety, Cunaehr." The old man closed his eyes, pausing momentarily as though about to correct his small name gaffe. Then he went on, perhaps in deference to Trip's undercover anonymity.

"I truly regret the necessity of having to render you unconscious, my young friend. However, I needed to drop this vessel out of warp—but only long enough to exit in an escape pod that I will aim toward the four Romulan military vessels that still pursue us. I've programmed the helm to return the engines automatically to maximum warp once my pod has departed. My hope is that Valdore's ships will fail to catch up with you, or perhaps even give up the pursuit once their crews realize that they've recovered me, which was their primary objective anyway."

As on each previous occasion when Trip had listened to Ehrehin's unexpectedly candid words, he marveled at the old man's courage, which actually bordered on the foolhardy. After all, Valdore's forces might well have caught up to the fleeing scout ship without destroying it, even after Ehrehin had returned to them. Had that happened, they probably would have found the scientist's recorded message, which surely would have damned him as a traitor. Ehrehin couldn't have believed himself so indispensable to his Empire's war machine that he could have avoided imprisonment—or even outright execution—as a consequence. Trip could only wonder if the scientist had embedded programming inside the message designed to erase it should the wrong parties try to view it, perhaps by using the scout vessel's internal sensors to warn the shipboard computer of the presence of other Romulan personnel.

Trip continued staring at the padd as old man continued: "As you've no doubt guessed already, I must decline your invitation to live among your people. I *am* a

Romulan, after all, and I am loyal to the traditions that have always made our civilization great, going back to the time of the Sundering. But because I am an **eth**ical student of science, I also deplore the reflexive militarism that has lately corrupted the Empire to the point that it would allow a Praetor to attempt planetary genocide. So while I will return to my people, I cannot in good conscience complete my work on the *avaihh lli vastam* engine, which I now know our Praetor would put to the meanest, basest imaginable use. Your words, as much as the disaster I visualize befalling Coridan, have opened my eyes.

"Good fortune, my young friend, in all your . . . future endeavors." The old man paused and smiled ironically, having just declared his patriotism while wishing Trip "happy spying" almost in the same breath. "Though we are creatures of very different worlds, I believe we both work for the same end. Perhaps our efforts will eventually help to bring about peace—or at least make a war that now appears inevitable somewhat less destructive than it would have been otherwise, had neither of us acted.

"Let that be our mutual legacy, whatever good two men can do. And I hope that whatever good we both do in the years to come will live on after us, long past the time when we are both dust.

"Farewell."

Ehrehin's image vanished from the padd, and Trip dropped it onto the desktop.

Stretching out on the stateroom's narrow bed, Trip looked up at the simple duranium grillwork of the cabin's ceiling, behind which he could hear the worn air-circulation fans of the ship's life-support system chugging away tirelessly.

He considered the mission, another voyage deep into Romulan space, that lay ahead. With a little luck, the files and contacts he'd copied from the memory rod he'd recovered from the slain Tinh Hoc Phuong, along with the new information he'd just received from Harris, would help him alter the trajectory of Romulan society, at least incrementally.

" 'Just one more mission,' " Trip said to the empty cabin, as he recalled his most recent meeting with Harris back on Earth.

And thought wistfully once more about home, and everyone he'd yet again left behind.

EPILOGUE

The early twenty-fifth century
Terrebonne Parish, Louisiana

"Wow. It still seems pretty damned unbelievable, Nog."
Jake moved his wineglass to the table beside his antique
chair. The low fire crackled occasionally in the background, though the sound of rain pattering against the
roof and the windows mostly drowned it out.

Nog drained his own glass, then set it down on the
hearth beside his chair, next to the now-empty bottle.
"So, are you saying you *don't* believe it?"

"I didn't exactly say *that*, Nog. The document claiming to be Commander Tucker's own sworn testimony—
verified by a scan of his retina-pattern taken in the
middle of the twenty-third century, no less—makes this
stuff pretty hard to dismiss."

"That one pretty much clinched it for me, too," Nog
said. "So why is it still unbelievable to you?"

"It's not," Jake said with a thoughtful frown. "I'm just
saying it still comes as a huge surprise to discover all
this new information about somebody whose life and
death were as well documented as Tucker's."

Nog nodded. "Too bad he didn't find a way to head off
the whole Earth-Romulan War."

Jake shook his head. "I think having grown up as the
son of Ben Sisko gives me a little bit of perspective on
this sort of thing, Nog. At the end of the day, Commander Tucker wasn't a superhero; he was just a chief
engineer with a knack for spying. Besides, as nasty as that

war was, the Federation we know today rose out of its ashes. The Federation might never have come about at all without the six-year gestation period that began with the signing of the Coalition Compact."

"And I might be chasing latinum slips and dabo tokens somewhere in the Ferengi Alliance to keep myself in fine wine and tube grubs. Good point."

Jake shook his head in bemusement. "I still have to wonder why the standard history places Trip's supposed 'death' six years after the date when it *actually*, uh . . . didn't happen. If you know what I mean."

"Misdirection," Nog said. "Maybe somebody—Section 31, most likely—figured that the big brushstrokes of Commander Tucker's life would be easier to hide if they were left out in plain sight and attached to a date in Federation history that everybody knows. That way, anybody who tries to find out the real truth behind Tucker's life and non-death is liable to start digging in the wrong place entirely."

Jake nodded. "Everybody knows a lot more about the early Federation than they do about the Coalition of Planets that came before it."

"Exactly. That's the grave you bury the treasure in— the one you know nobody is interested in digging up."

"It's all so damned strange," Jake said, drawn inexorably back into the mystery of Commander Tucker's life and death and life. "Charles Tucker living on under various aliases, for decades and decades after his 'death.'" He knew, of course, that they still had to go through a lot of material concerning Tucker's surprisingly lengthy latter period to discover the details of what he'd been up to during the entire span of those times. "It's like finding out that Abraham Lincoln was still alive during World War I, fighting against Kaiser Wilhelm."

"Do you think the evidence might have been faked somehow?" Nog asked.

"Maybe it's just wishful thinking on both our parts," Jake said as he slowly shook his head. "Or maybe it's just the wine. But I really think this all holds together a bit too well for it to be fake, with the possible exception of the stuff that claims to be told from the Romulan viewpoint. And I'm willing to chalk *that* up to artistic license on the part of the historian, who would have needed to fill in the occasional gap here or there with some educated guesswork of his own. But so far I really can't see a fatal flaw in any of the rest of it. It's almost as though we've been reading Commander Tucker's private diary."

"That's my thought, too, especially after experiencing the, um, racy parts," Nog said. "*And* after examining all the corroborating documentation. Anyway, this new take on Archer-era history holds together for me a lot better than the standard version does—you know, with Captain Archer's whole command crew not receiving a single promotion, even after having served together aboard the NX-01 for *ten years*. Or Archer's dog somehow not having aged a day during that entire time. Or Archer's famous Big Speech at the 'Stick, which makes a lot more sense now in the context of the post-Coridan disaster era than it does in the post–Earth-Romulan War time-frame where most of the histories place it. Or the pirate ship that could barely manage warp two somehow catching up to *Enterprise*, which had to be traveling at nearly warp five when—"

"You're preaching to the choir, Nog," Jake said, holding up a hand as he interrupted. He rose from his chair, ignoring the pain that stippled his lower back as he moved toward the hearth to stir the fire with one of the iron pokers he kept there. The rejuvenated flames sparked and immediately began to spread their renewed warmth through his entire body.

"But there *is* one thing that still really bugs me about

this whole business," he said as he returned to his chair. "I find it very weird that we've apparently had Tucker's official death date completely wrong all these years. I know that history is littered with a lot of small errors that everyone eventually accepts as fact after enough time goes by. But I have to wonder if this *particular* discrepancy was really that type of innocent mistake—or if it happened because of somebody's deliberate plan."

"Who knows?" Nog said, shrugging. "Maybe somebody recorded the date wrong deliberately, just to make it that much harder to uncover the *real* story of Charles Tucker."

"Or maybe it was done purposely by someone who hoped that someday, a pair of old codgers with nothing but time on their hands would notice that one inconsistency—and then follow it all the way down to the bottom of this mystery." Jake grinned.

Nog returned the grin, displaying rows of uneven, sharpened teeth. "No wonder you've fallen so in love with writing whodunits these last few years." But the Ferengi's smile collapsed a moment later into a far more thoughtful expression. "Seriously, Jake, we may have a problem on our hands, now that we know what we know. We have a serious decision to make."

Jake nodded, understanding. "Do we go public with this stuff? Or do we keep it to ourselves?"

"You were a news writer before you became a novelist," Nog said. "I think I can guess which way you'd decide."

Jake nodded. "And you'd be right." Every one of his journalistic and writerly impulses screamed for the need to publish this discovery, regardless of whether or not he got any share of the credit.

At least he wanted to see it published, if all the supporting documentation really would bear up under close scrutiny. *And the bright light of sobriety tomorrow morn-*

ing, he thought, contemplating the empty wine bottle on the hearth ruefully.

"I'm not so sure that's a good idea, Jake. At least, not yet."

"Why?" Jake asked, perplexed. "Nothing here is classified, otherwise you couldn't have shared it with me."

"Do you like westerns, Jake?" Nog asked, the question seeming to have come out of what Benjamin Sisko probably would have described as 'left field.'

"Westerns? As in novels? Like Louis L'Amour, or Larry McMurtry?"

"No, westerns, as in *movies*," Nog said, his features suddenly animated by a renewed burst of youthful energy. The sight made Jake pine momentarily for those carefree days they had spent together causing innocent trouble on Deep Space 9's bustling Promenade, under Constable Odo's ever-watchful eye.

"Westerns," Nog continued, "as in John Ford, the twentieth-century hew-mon flatvid director. I got interested in his work during the war, when I was convalescing at Vic's apartment."

Jake remembered those days very well indeed. The high points, like the Allies' retaking of DS9, or the final victory at Cardassia Prime, had been stratospheric; the lows, like the murder of Jadzia Dax, or the incident at AR-558 that had cost Nog his leg, had been abysmal.

But Nog had been discussing flatvid cinema rather than reality, and Jake wasn't sure that he could recall the particular films Nog was referencing. "I'm waiting patiently for what you're saying to start making some sense to me, Nog."

Nog shook his head in mock despair. "Jake, don't you remember the ending of *The Man Who Shot Liberty Valance*?"

Understanding finally dawned upon Jake when he realized that he *did* recall that particular film—especially its ending, which he'd found a good deal more memorable than most other entries in the western genre.

"'When the legend becomes fact, print the legend,'" Jake quoted.

While he had to concede that Nog had a point, he still wasn't entirely convinced that the newly unearthed Tucker files ought to be hidden away indefinitely. Or just which of the many legends associated with the Earth-Romulan War and the subsequent founding of the Federation needed protecting the most. After all, there was still so much more they both had to find out, particularly regarding Commander Tucker's specific activities during those times, and across the many subsequent decades through which he'd apparently lived.

After a lengthy pause, Jake finally came to a decision. "All right, Nog. I'll agree to decide *not* to decide anything. At least until we both learn a lot more about the fact and the legend both. That okay by you?"

"That's okay by me," Nog said, grinning.

The rain outside continued its irregular tapping against the windows. Dawn was several hours away.

Nog reached into his pack. Jake half expected him to extract a second ancient bottle of wine, along with a corkscrew as old as Commander Tucker himself.

Instead, the Ferengi pulled out another data chip and handed it to him.

"So," Jake said, turning the translucent plastic cylinder over and over between his fingers. "What exactly happens next?"

A grinning Nog once again activated the holo-imagers built into his padd, so that both of them could find out for themselves.

ACKNOWLEDGMENTS

While any errors and fubars contained herein are the sole responsibility of the authors, we cannot neglect mentioning our debt of gratitude to the many others whose contributions either to the *Star Trek* universe or to our personal lives have greatly enriched the contents of this volume and others: Rick Berman and Brannon Braga, whose original teleplay for the *Star Trek: Enterprise* series finale "These Are the Voyages . . ." provided our initial jumping-off place; Pocket's own Margaret Clark and CBS's Paula Block for their long-suffering patience; Mike's wife, Jenny, and their sons, James and William, for both long-suffering patience and inspiration; the online linguistic scholar(s) who assembled the vast Rihannsu language database found at http://atrek.org/Dhivael/rihan/engtorihan.html, for furnishing various Romulan time and distance units, Romulan numerals, and word roots that helped us create several Romulan proper names; Dr. Lawrence M. Schoen, whose assistance in the construction of idiomatic Klingon phrases was invaluable during the writing of our 2005 *Star Trek: Titan* novel *The Red King*, and whom we also somehow neglected to mention on that volume's acknowledgments page; Dayton Ward and Kevin Dilmore, for originating yet another Romulan unit of time for our current tome, as well as for unwittingly furnishing us with an obscure Vulcan diplomat, whom we stole from their 2006 *Star Trek: Vanguard* novel *Summon the Thunder*; Judith and Garfield Reeves-Stevens, for supplying the original Old Romulan name for the capital city of Romulus, and for shaping the canonical story arc that immediately precedes the time-frame of this book ("Terra

Prime"), along with Manny Coto ("Demons"); S. D. Perry, whose novel *Star Trek Section 31: Cloak* anticipated Judith and Garfield Reeves-Stevens' canonical revelations about Section 31's distant past; Heather Jarman, for doing the bulk of biocultural spadework on the details of the four Andorian (and by extension Aenar) genders, as well as for establishing some nifty Andorian mythology (in *Paradigm*, her *Star Trek: Worlds of Deep Space 9* novel) that we just plain stole (sorry, Heather, but I swear it wasn't nailed down); David Mack, for the inspiring image of the Burning Sea of Coridan he provided in his recent *Star Trek: Deep Space 9* novel *Warpath*; Geoffrey Mandel, for his *Star Trek Star Charts*, which supplied a few handy place names which we left scattered between here and Romulus; Keith R. A. DeCandido, Susan Shwartz and Josepha Sherman, whose novels *Articles of the Federation* and *Vulcan's Heart* enabled us to hide a historical Easter egg or three within these pages; Franz Joseph and the team of Rick Sternbach and Michael Okuda, whose respective reference manuals *Star Fleet Technical Manual* (1975) and *Star Trek: The Next Generation Technical Manual* (1991) provided Trip with some very serviceable technobabble at precisely the right moment; the gifted astronomical software mavens at SPACE.com Canada, Inc., whose *Starry Night Backyard* program enabled us to portray authentic lunar phases in all night scenes set on Earth, both in this volume and in its predecessor, *Last Full Measure*; Connor Trinneer, for breathing life into Charles "Trip" Tucker in the first place; and the legions of Trip fans out there who were happy to see us reinterpret canon, spit in the Grim Reaper's eye, and seek out and exploit every available loophole on Trip's behalf.

ABOUT THE AUTHORS

ANDY MANGELS is the *USA Today* bestselling author and coauthor of over a dozen novels—including *Star Trek* and *Roswell* books—all cowritten with Michael A. Martin. Flying solo, he is the bestselling author of several nonfiction books, including *Star Wars: The Essential Guide to Characters* and *Animation on DVD: The Ultimate Guide*, as well as a significant number of entries for *The Superhero Book: The Ultimate Encyclopedia of Comic-Book Icons and Hollywood Heroes* and for its companion volume, *The Supervillain Book: The Evil Side of Comics and Hollywood*.

In addition to cowriting several more upcoming novels and contributing to anthologies, Andy has produced, directed, and scripted a series of over thirty half-hour DVD documentries—and provided other special features—for BCI Eclipse's Ink & Paint brand, for inclusion in DVD box sets ranging from animated fare such as *He-Man*, *She-Ra*, *Flash Gordon*, and *Ghostbusters* to live-action favorites such as *Ark II*, *Space Academy*, and *Isis*.

Andy has written hundreds of articles for entertainment and lifestyle magazines and newspapers in the United States, England, and Italy. He has also written licensed material based on properties from numerous film studios and Microsoft, and over the past two decades his comic-book work has been published by DC Comics, Marvel Comics, Dark Horse, Image, Innovation, and many others. He was the editor of the award-winning Gay Comics anthology for eight years.

Andy is a national award-winning activist in the Gay community, and has raised thousands of dollars for charities over the years. He lives in Portland, Oregon, with his long-term partner, Don Hood, their dog Bela, and their chosen son, Paul Smalley. Visit his website at www.andymangels.com.

MICHAEL A. MARTIN's solo short fiction has appeared in *The Magazine of Fantasy & Science Fiction*. He has also coauthored (with Andy Mangels) several *Star Trek* comics for Marvel and Wildstorm and numerous *Star Trek* novels and eBooks, including the *USA Today* bestseller *Titan: Taking Wing; Titan: The Red King;* the Sy Fy Genre Award-winning *Star Trek: Worlds of Deep Space 9 Volume Two: Trill—Unjoined; Star Trek: Enterprise—Last Full Measure; Star Trek: The Lost Era 2298—The Sundered; Star Trek: Deep Space 9 Mission: Gamma Book Three—Cathedral; Star Trek: The Next Generation: Section 31—Rogue;* stories in the *Prophecy and Change, Tales of the Dominion War* and *Tales from the Captain's Table* anthologies; and three novels based on the *Roswell* television series. His work has also been published by Atlas Editions (in their *Star Trek Universe* subscription card series), *Star Trek Monthly,* Grolier Books, Visible Ink Press, *The Oregonian,* and Gareth Stevens, Inc., for whom he has penned several *World Almanac Library of the States* nonfiction books for young readers. He lives with his wife, Jenny, and their sons James and William in Portland, Oregon.